THE SCARRED MAGE OF ROSEWARD

BOOK THREE: WRAITH

SYLVIA MERCEDES

© 2021 by Sylvia Mercedes

Published by FireWyrm Books

www.SylviaMercedesBooks.com

Cover design by Jesh Art Studio

*Dedicated with many, many, many thanks
to our beloved Miss Chaylee*

CHAPTER 1

A CHILLING SENSATION STIRRED ACROSS THE DEEPER reaches of her unconscious. At first it was hardly noticeable—the barest whisper, a shiver—and she was so deeply asleep that she could easily dismiss it. But the sensation intensified by the moment, drawing her unwillingly toward wakefulness.

Boggarts blast it! She wasn't ready to wake up yet.

Turning inward, she pulled drowsiness over her mind like a thick down quilt. Maybe it was just a dream. A dream was all right if it didn't turn too vivid. If it didn't transform into nightmares . . .

A sudden gust howled across her spirit, rattling her to the core. She couldn't ignore it. She couldn't pretend. Not anymore.

Nelle opened her eyes.

The cold world around her was as dark as a tomb. She blinked hard, trying to draw her mind back into full wakefulness, to remember where she was exactly. *Noxaur?* she thought. A sliver of dread wedged in her heart. Was she still held captive in the Kingdom of Night?

But wait. Dull reddish light gleamed on familiar stones just overhead. With a groan, Nelle rolled onto her side, peering from her alcove bed into the chamber dimly lighted by coals on the hearth. A whole host of pains flared through her body, some minor, others more significant. Her side throbbed where she'd been stabbed by a tree branch, and her skin smarted from multiple shallow cuts, healing but not yet fully healed. She winced and sat up slowly, drawing the thin blanket up over her trembling shoulders. That sensation, that chill in her soul, was still there. She closed her eyes and shook her head, trying to drive it away. But it wouldn't be driven.

"Something's not right," she whispered.

When she took another look around the room, everything was where it ought to be. There were the table and chairs where she'd spent many long hours, quill in hand, poring over parchments and strange texts. And the fireplace with its banked coals was surrounded by an assortment of battered kettles and cooking pans and a rusty set of fire irons. One door of the armoire sagged open to reveal the many books and scrolls stuffed chaotically into its various niches. Nothing looked amiss.

But the air felt . . . *wrong.*

A soft whine tickled Nelle's ear. Frowning, she looked down at the warm spot on her little bed where she expected to see a gangly, gimpy-winged wyvern curled up and snoring softly. The spot was empty, though she could see the indentation where her scaly companion had rested not long ago.

"Worm?" she whispered. Her voice sounded strange in that petrified air.

The whine sounded again, soft but unmistakable. She leaned out of the alcove, using the blanket like a cloak, clutching the fabric against one shoulder. Her gaze quested up into the rafters. The hearth light couldn't reach that high, but she thought she made out a little bundled form clinging to one of the support beams near the ceiling. "Worm?" she said again. "Is that you?"

Two glowing eyes blinked down at her. She saw a flash of sharp white teeth, heard a little burbling bray.

Then she gasped and almost doubled over as a gust howled across her soul. Several moments passed before she realized it wasn't a physical sensation. She'd felt it without actually feeling . . . yet with a profoundness that made it *real.*

"What the blazes is that?" she choked. The gust abated, then blew even harder. Only a firm conviction that it *shouldn't* affect her physical body kept her upright.

Dropping the blanket, Nelle scrabbled out of the bed and

stepped barefoot onto the cold stone floor, startled to see her body clothed in overlarge trousers and a billowing, blood-stained man's shirt. Oh, right. Kyriakos's wives had taken her gown, and she'd been obliged to borrow garments from Mage Silveri. She was pulling the gaping shirt's laces tighter when a third gust threatened to knock her from her feet.

The wyvern in the rafters turned Nelle's squeal of fright into a duet.

Nelle spun in place, searching the room. Had some invisible monster penetrated the lighthouse's protections? But this tension in the air didn't feel like a monster. It was more like . . . more like . . .

Staggering under the spirit gale's assault, Nelle crossed the room to the lighthouse door, gripped the latch . . . and hesitated. It wasn't safe to open the door at night—the Thorn Maiden prowled Roseward Island from dusk to dawn. But whatever caused this terrifying sensation didn't feel like a Noswraith. It was even bigger and much wilder.

Nelle drew a long breath. Should she back away? Return to her alcove? Cover her head with blankets and cower, hoping the mage would descend from his tower chamber and do something?

"No bullspitting chance," she growled and turned the latch.

Immediately, the door blew out of her hand and crashed against the wall. Nelle staggered back several paces, squeezed her eyes shut, and turned her face away, flinging up her hands against the wind that billowed into her face and snarled her hair. A brilliant glare seared through her eyelids, and for a fear-throbbing heartbeat she thought she'd been struck blind.

The next instant, she realized again that this experience wasn't physical. Her eyes were still whole and fine and fully under her control. With an effort of will, she pried open her eyelids.

"Seven gods preserve us!" she gasped.

Usually, the view from this doorway extended from the lighthouse perched on the cliff shores of Roseward Isle to sweep across the wide and ever-changing Hinter Sea. Under ordinary circumstances, the sight was overwhelming enough to make Nelle's heart stutter.

This was far, far worse.

A weirdly roiling storm careened across the sky, reflected on the waves below. Although it moved in somewhat the same manner as clouds, it looked more like light somehow made solid. Or fire that didn't rise in tongues of flame but instead spread out in churning, ever-growing, never-extinguishing masses. Its colors shifted from red to green to violet to colors for which Nelle had neither name nor a place within her mortal reason to compre-hend.

She'd glimpsed something like this before—last night, when she'd worked the Rose Book spell to complete the binding of the Thorn Maiden and let her mind partly stray into the *quinsatra,* the dimension of magic.

She stared, eyes rounding, mouth gaping, as though fully opening herself to the horror bearing down upon her. The *quinsatra* didn't belong in this world. And yet . . . and yet . . .

With a whimpering cry, she grabbed the door and tried to slam it shut. The blasts of energy nearly ripped it from her hands again, threatened to fling her off her feet. "No! *No!*" she screamed. "It's not *real!*"

Of course, it was real. Terribly real.

But it wasn't fully physical. Not yet. And as long as she remembered this, she stood a fighting chance.

By sheer force of will she dragged the door shut and collapsed against it, feeling it rattle in its frame. What a frail, flimsy, foolish barrier it was against that coming onslaught. But it was all she had.

She turned and faced into the room. After that ferocious glare of magic, it seemed darker than before. Panic churned in her gut. It was all she could do to keep from doubling over and being sick on the floor rushes.

Up in the rafters, the wyvern brayed pathetically. She tossed it a quick glance. "You ain't kidding!"

A clatter of footsteps sounded overhead. Nelle's gaze shot to the open stairway leading through the high ceiling of the chamber to wind up the lighthouse tower. Mage Silveri was coming.

Her hand almost unconsciously flew to her bosom, feeling the cold contours of a little gold locket resting beneath the thin folds of shirt. She'd fully intended to make use of the poison hidden inside that locket, to smear the last dose of the Sweet Dreams on her lips and take the mage by surprise the moment she saw him. It was, after all, high time she did what she'd come to Roseward to do. The Sweet Dreams would knock Silveri unconscious for many hours, allowing her plenty of time to creep up to his chamber at the top of the tower, find the Rose Book he kept hidden up there, and make her getaway.

But there was no bullspitting way she was going to venture out onto the Hinter Sea now. Not with the whole *quinsatra* breaking loose overhead.

She lowered her hand and simply leaned against the door. The mage appeared a moment later, rushing headlong down the stairs, clad in tight trousers and a loose, open shirt, his hair wild and white around his shoulders. His eyes watched his feet as he descended the stair a little too fast for safety; only after he leaped over the last three steps and stood on the ground floor did he look up.

He saw her.

His face, already pale other than the recent raw cuts just beginning to heal into puckered scars, drained of color. His eyes widened, and he staggered back, nearly tripping over the bottom step.

"Miss Beck!"

"Mage Silveri." Nelle pulled herself upright. His gaze swiftly traveled over her, taking in his own garments hanging loose from her scrawny limbs. She jerked a thumb over her shoulder. "There's an awful lot of magic out there. It don't look good."

His mouth opened, closed, opened again. Then he shook his head and passed a hand over his face as it darkened into a terrible glare. "I told you to leave! I told you to go, to get away from here!"

"Yeah, well." Nelle folded her arms across her chest. "I didn't. It's my choice, and I didn't. Don't you remember?"

She watched realization spread across his face, shock mounding on horror as he recalled their encounter the day before, when she, wearing nothing but the scanty garment given her by Kyriakos's wives, had put her arms around him. Had told him she wouldn't leave him. Had raised her face to his and kissed him . . .

He'd pushed her away, convinced she was no more than a Noswraith illusion. After all, the Thorn Maiden's favorite game was to torment with false seductions and dangerous promises. And Soran Silveri, after fifteen years' imprisonment on Roseward, had learned to be wary of her wiles.

But their encounter hadn't been a dream.

Heat rushed to Nelle's cheeks as she stood facing him. What would he think now of that delicate, tentative kiss she had offered him? Now that he knew it was real?

But the mage swiftly recovered from his surprise and shook his head, scowling furiously. "You should have listened to me," he snarled and marched across the room, brushing past her on his way to the door. He reached for the latch.

Nelle leaped to his side and grabbed his cold wrist. "It's bad out there, sir!"

"I know." He tossed her hand off and threw the door open.

Nelle yelped and flung up both hands to shield her eyes again from the glare of brilliant magic. Squinting painfully, she peered through her fingers at Soran in the doorway, his hair tossed wildly back from his shoulders, his eyes wide as he stared directly into that tortured sky.

"*Ruvyn-satra*," he said, his unnaturally calm voice carrying clearly to Nelle's ears despite the thunderous gusts. "A magic storm."

"Is this kind of thing *normal?*" Nelle cried.

Soran shook his head slowly, dashing her hope. The line of his jaw tightened, and one nilarium-crusted hand flashed in the strange light as it caught the doorpost, gripping hard. "I have seen only one other since my imprisonment began, and that from a great distance and nowhere near so massive as this."

"Well, boggarts then." Fighting against the gale, Nelle moved to stand at the mage's side. The storm bore down faster now, eating up the small patch of blue sky that still hung above

Roseward. "What . . . what do we do?"

"Do?" He looked down at her, his eyes flashing with weird light. "It's a *ruvyn-satra*. We shut the doors and windows and hope the protections on this lighthouse are enough to weather the storm. Other than that . . ." Leaving the sentence unfinished, he stepped suddenly through the doorway.

"Where are you going?" Nelle darted out a hand to catch his arm. "Didn't you just say we had to wait it out?"

He pried her hand away, but she only caught him more firmly with her other hand. "My wyverns," he said, meeting her gaze hard. "They are beings of pure magic. If they are left exposed to that front, their essences will be reabsorbed into the *quinsatra*. I must get them."

Nelle's eyes swiveled, taking in that oncoming rush of frantically churning light and power and energy and utter chaos. "Are you insane?"

One of his eyebrows quirked. "Probably."

With that, he wrenched free of her hold and strode swiftly to the top of the path leading down to the beach far below the cliff on which the lighthouse stood. Moments later the top of his head disappeared below the edge, and Nelle stood alone on the threshold, her hands empty, her mouth ajar, her eyes straining to see against the glare of the magic storm.

"Bullspit!" she growled and, turning to look back over her shoulder, glared up at the wyvern cringing in the rafters overhead. "You stay here. At least one of us should try to survive this thing."

Without waiting to hear the wyvern's answering squawk, she hauled the door shut. When the raging gale sought to tear it from her hands, she merely wrenched harder, refusing to be cowed. A whimper trembled on her lips as the latch clicked into place, but she wasn't about to let Soran face that storm alone.

Biting out curses, she bowed her head and fought her way to the cliff edge. The path down seemed narrower, more treacherous than ever before. She feared with every step that the magic force billowing across the white-capped waves would snatch her feet out from under her and send her crashing to the rocks below.

"It's not real!" she shouted. "It's not real, it's not real, it's not real!" With an effort, she forced her mind to accept that the wind she felt stinging her skin was nothing more than the salty breeze carried across the ocean waters, not the tremendous, burning force it tried to make itself in her head. It was a battle of balance, a mental game that took up so much of her concentration and energy, she nearly missed her step several times and was obliged to flatten her back against the cliff wall, clinging to rocks until she caught her breath.

The farther she went, however, the more her brain strengthened on the ideas she fed it. By the time she reached the end of the path and gained the rocky beach below, she was able to split her perceptions almost evenly between the magical whirl shocking her senses and the calmer physical reality.

"All right," she muttered, steadying her balance. "Wyverns." Her bare feet objected to the sharp landscape, but that was the least of her immediate concerns. A quick glance up and down the beach revealed Soran not many yards away.

He stood at the base of the cliff with his arms upraised, calling in a strange language. Above him, the wyverns peered out of their little cave-like nooks in the stone, rattled their tongues, and flared their crests. At first it looked as though the entire flock would refuse to answer their master's summons.

Then one bold green creature shot out from its hiding place and, flapping wildly, descended swiftly to its master's arm. Soran did something Nelle couldn't quite perceive. It looked as though he performed a swift folding motion . . . and the next moment, the wyvern had vanished, and the mage tucked a piece of parchment safely into the front of his shirt.

"I see," Nelle muttered. The wyverns were, after all, spell-beasts. Their lives and existence were made up entirely of magic, but that magic was tethered to the physical world by words written down on paper. Which meant they were, in a sense, paper beings as well. Soran called again, and more wyverns descended, one after another, into his waiting hands. Perhaps the mage would be able to catch them all.

And what good was she doing, standing here? Nelle gasped

and staggered as another blast of magic assaulted her mind. Her senses throbbed painfully: her skin scorched by what felt like burning embers, her ears assaulted by an endless roll of thunder, and her eyes ablaze with refulgent light in myriad unnatural colors. She fought to drag her awareness back to a proper level of reality.

When a sad, mewling cry caught her ear, she squinted up at the cliffside behind her.

A tiny orange wyvern, smaller than the others, clung to the rocks approximately twenty feet above her. The gale was too strong for its little wings, and it dared not let go of the rocks for fear of being ripped from its perch and hurtled headlong into uncontrollable currents of magic. It craned its long neck, blinking large, pleading eyes down at her, and uttered a despairing *meep.*

Nelle cast a glance Soran's way. But he was hard at work catching and folding his wyverns as they descended on him in a mass of terrified brays and flapping wings. He hadn't seen her yet, much less the poor little wyvern trapped above. She looked back over her shoulder at the storm rolling in, the wild bursts of magic and energy lighting up both sky and sea.

It would strike Roseward's shores in another ten minutes. Maybe less.

"Boggarts and brags!" she growled, then hurled herself at the cliff. Her hands found holds; her toes found crannies and crevices. Mother's training flooded through her limbs, and she climbed swiftly, glad in that moment to be barefoot, glad to be wearing trousers rather than a gown that would catch the wind like a sail. She concentrated on the climb, refusing to think of what lurked at her back.

As she approached, the wyvern turned to face her, hissing and snarling between more pathetic *meeps*. "Don't even think about biting!" Nelle growled as she reached to catch it.

It snapped and almost snagged her finger. Nelle recoiled, adjusted her grip on the wall, then darted out her hand and caught the little creature by the back of its long neck. It brayed and thrashed, terror driving it to panic. The wind caught in its wings and dragged it away from the wall, pulling Nelle's arm with it. She held on but swung out over empty space, her fingers gripping the stone, all her weight suspended from one hand and one foot.

Shouting a wild stream of curses, she yanked the wyvern back against the wall so hard it went limp. For a moment she feared she'd killed it. But the next moment it shook itself and wrapped the long coils of its tail down her wrist, folding its wings tight against its body.

"Good wormling," Nelle said encouragingly. She gave it a try, but the trick to folding the little creature into paper form was beyond her skill, so she popped the scaly body inside her shirt, wincing at the scrape of hind claws along her skin. Thankfully, it didn't struggle but curled into a small knot against her stomach.

"Right," Nelle muttered. "Hold on then."

She began the descent. Going backwards was trickier, for she had to work by feel rather than sight. The gale had picked up, and more and more of her body wanted to believe the illusion of burning, melting. She saw blisters break out on her hands, and though she knew they weren't real, they might not remain an illusion much longer.

"Miss Beck!"

She tipped her head, peering under her arm at the stony ground still a good fifteen feet below. Soran stood looking up at her, his hair a wild storm about his deathly pale face. His eyes were huge disks shining with fear. Fear for her?

"It's all right!" she shouted back, hoping he could hear her above the increased pulse of the magic storm. "I've got the—"

A blast of magic knocked her flat against the wall. Only instinct developed through years of Mother's hard training made her fingers clamp around the stones, made her body brace and hold steady. She was half convinced her hair burned away one strand at a time, and she shut her eyes, striving to block out the sensations.

When the blast subsided enough for Nelle to peer down at Soran again, the surge had knocked him to his knees, and he struggled to regain his footing. Lifting her gaze from him, she dared to look out across the beach and gauge the distance between the storm front and the shore.

Something floated on the waves.

She shook her head, attempting to shake strands of hair from her eyes. Was she seeing things? Was it an illusion? An illusion of bits of driftwood lashed together in haphazard fashion, buffeted by churning waves?

And sprawled in the center of that makeshift raft, in the center of that illusion . . . was a child.

CHAPTER 2

SORAN LANDED HEAVILY ON HIS HANDS AND KNEES, HIS back hunched against the *ruvyn* wind's force. Closing his eyes, he clenched his teeth and willed his body to obey him, to reject the reality of the storm, to exist only in the physical realm. It wasn't a fight he could win, and for the moment his mind was over-whelmed.

But the blast moved on. He blew out a long breath, a wordless prayer, and wrenched his head up.

Somehow, miraculously, Nelle had managed to hold on to the cliff wall. What in the seven holy names possessed her to climb up there under these conditions? The girl was certainly mad! She fought to reclaim her grip, her brilliant red hair blowing around her face, reflecting the light of the coming storm like so many strands of fiery magic.

Soran struggled to his feet, looking back over his shoulder. The storm closed in fast. They must return to the lighthouse before it was too late. Should he try to climb up to reach Nelle? Urge her to hurry and risk startling her into losing her grip? Could he—

"Soran!"

Her voice reached him through the pulse of magic in the churning sky. She peered at him under her arm, her eyes wide and round and bright. "Soran, look!" She tossed her head, jerking her chin to the left, down along the beach.

Frowning, he turned to look where she indicated, where the sand and pebbles of the beach strand gave way to larger rocks. Sharp boulders jutted from the white foaming waves. Had she seen a wyvern caught among those stones? Soran narrowed his eyes.

Then he sucked in a sharp breath.

Something approached the rocks, dragged by the waves. At first glance it looked like nothing more than ocean flotsam and jetsam jumbled together. But a second glance revealed a little figure clinging to battered bits of rotten wood, all that remained of a raft.

Soran took five paces in that direction without pausing to

think. Before he could take a sixth step, another gust of *ruvyn* wind knocked his feet out from under him. He landed hard, his head narrowly missing a sharp rock. Once more he could do nothing but close his eyes, close his mind, and wait for the blast to let up.

Nelle's scream shocked him back to his senses. He bolted upright to see her struggling to hold on as loose stones pulled away from the cliff wall. With a wordless cry he sprang to his feet and lurched toward her. The stones gave way, and she tumbled fifteen feet to crash into him, knocking him flat on the beach. His arms folded around her even as his head spun and he struggled to catch his breath.

He opened his eyes to find her face close to his, her pale features partially veiled in wisps of hair. "Are you all right?" Her voice was breathless.

He grunted. When she started to pull away, his arms unconsciously tightened. She pushed harder, however, and he let her scramble awkwardly off him. Something bulbous writhed inside her shirt, and she hastily untucked the fabric from her rope belt and pulled a small, terrified wyvern free. So that's why she'd risked her neck climbing the cliff.

"Here," she said, shoving the wyvern into Soran's hands. "Do your trick." Immediately, she whipped about and, with the baggy shirt billowing behind her, set off at a run across the beach.

"Where are you going?" Soran cried, yanking at the wyvern,

which was trying to climb onto his face in its frenzied terror.

The words she tossed back at him were almost lost in the wind: "I'm going to get that child!"

She was mad. No doubt about it. Absolutely out of her mind.

Soran wrenched the wyvern's flailing claws out of his shirt, heedless of the long rip it made, and hastily folded it back into paper form. He tucked it in with the other wyverns and sprang to his feet. He had to catch Nelle before she did something disastrously foolish. She was already nearing the first of the jagged boulders. Did she really think she could climb out across them and reach that driftwood raft?

Cursing by every one of the seven gods, Soran sped after her, all too aware of the savage, light-bursting, magic-churning force descending upon them. He reached Nelle as she climbed a jagged boulder, heedless of how the sharp edges cut into her hands and feet. Catching her by the back of her shirt, he yanked hard, forcing her to turn and face him. "There's nothing you can do!" he cried, shouting to be heard. "No one can survive prolonged exposure to a *ruvyn-satra*. Whoever is out there is already dead."

"You don't know that," Nelle snarled and wrenched free of his grip. He reached for her again, determined to overpower her if necessary, but another blast of magic sent him reeling.

Nelle, better protected from the blast by the boulder, recovered more swiftly than he did. By the time he reached for her again, she was already on top of the boulder and springing lightly from stone to stone out over the churning waves. From his angle, Soran couldn't see the raft anymore, but he guessed she was making her way toward the point where it was bound to crash.

Curse the day he first set eyes on that girl! She would be the ruin of him, the ruin of everything he'd fought for throughout these long years of solitude. He really ought to leave her to the consequences of her madness and suicidal heroism.

With these thoughts careening inside his head, Soran climbed the boulder, caught his balance, and set out across the rocky outcroppings, less swift and sure on his feet than she was. One more great gust would fling him into the foam, never to surface again! He tucked his chin, ignoring the sting of saltwater spray against his skin, the burn of magic whipping against his soul, and focused his awareness on Nelle.

Suddenly she crouched and slid down the side of the boulder until only the top of her head was still visible. Soran, shifting for a better angle, saw the driftwood raft heading straight toward her. The figure lying on it half dragged in the water—so small, clad in pitiful brown rags. The child's rigid fingers clung to salt-hardened ropes, but Soran couldn't tell whether those fingers clung for life or were already frozen in death.

Nelle positioned herself to intercept the raft, but at that angle it would certainly knock her off her perch.

"Nelle!" The wind swallowed Soran's shout. He tried to reach for her, but it felt like plowing through the thick fog of a dream. His hands were too slow, too clumsy, his feet glued to the rocks beneath him. Hopeless, he shouted again: "Don't do it!"

She adjusted her grip on the rock, then stretched out one hand, snatched the back of a ragged shirt, and yanked the child off the raft. Those little frozen fingers refused to let go, and the craft smashed into the stones, narrowly missing Nelle. Waves swept the child underwater, and the force wrenched Nelle from her perch. Soran glimpsed a swirl of red hair against white foam. Then, nothing.

"*No!*" He flung himself down the side of the boulder, his nilarium-crusted hands digging into the stone itself, punching out grips. Water swept up to his chest, dragged at his lower body, and he dangled by one arm, struggling to hold on. His other hand reached out into the waves, seeking . . . seeking . . .

Something brushed along his arm. Fabric?

His fingers closed tight, and he hauled, every muscle in his body straining to its limit. Oh, if ever the gods were to endow him with supernatural strength, let it be now, let this be the moment! He heaved. An arm shot up out the water, flailing. He heaved again, and Nelle's head emerged, her mouth wide as she gasped for air.

Soran turned, pushing her toward the rock. Her one hand caught hold, but the other still dragged in the water. She turned desperate eyes up to Soran. "Help me!" she cried. He shifted position, reaching for her again, but she shook her head. "The child!"

She still held onto the little one under the water.

Grinding his teeth, Soran let go his hold on her shirt and angled out into the churning foam. He saw something indistinct, a pale form beneath the waves. He reached, caught hold of a bony arm, and pulled the child up to the boulder beside him. The small limbs hung lifeless, the body a dead weight. If he were wise, he'd let it drop, give it up to the sea and the *ruvyn-satra*.

But Nelle, moving with surprising nimbleness despite her dunking, scrambled to the top of the boulder and stretched her arms down. "Give him to me!" she cried.

Grimacing, Soran hefted the child partway out of the waves, high enough for her to catch one skinny forearm. She wasn't strong enough to lift even such a small weight, not at that angle while contesting the sea's prior claim. With a grunt of effort, Soran used his free arm to hoist the child upward until Nelle was able to wrap both arms around its chest.

"I've got him!" she cried. Soran's arm sagged, relieved of the child's weight. Digging both hands into the rock, he climbed up beside Nelle, water pouring from his clothes in streams. Nelle bent over the child, pressing her ear to its chest.

Soran looked back over his shoulder. The storm was almost on top of them. He grabbed Nelle's arm and hauled her upright. "No time," he said, when she turned wild eyes up to him. "Give him to me."

Defiance flashed across her face. But then she saw the churning power looming over his head. Nodding, she let him scoop the little one over his shoulder. With scrawny arms dangling down his back and scrawny legs held tight across his chest, Soran followed Nelle back over the rocks toward the shore.

By some miracle, they made it to the beach. Nelle sprang down, and Soran handed her the child just before the next *ruvyn* wind howled into them. They collapsed to their knees, Nelle bent over the child, Soran wrapped protectively around Nelle. It was a harsher gale than the last one, harsh enough to strip flesh from bone. The boulder behind them offered some protection, but not much. Soran's mouth opened, and he felt his throat constricting in a scream he couldn't hear as wave after wave of burning crashed over his spirit.

It wasn't real . . . It wasn't real . . . But it was so terribly real!

When it passed, however, he was still whole. His body shook with pains it hadn't truly experienced, and in places his skin flared as though burned. But he was whole.

Nelle shuddered in his arms. He pulled back, looked down at her. She too was unscathed. So far.

"Can you move?" he asked.

She turned her pale eyes up to him, her expression horror stricken. But the next instant, it hardened into grim determination, and she nodded.

Soran again took up the child and, after a few staggering paces, set out at a run for the cliff path. Part of him didn't believe they would make it. The storm would hit, would blast them to nothingness long before they reached the lighthouse. The sheer uninhibited magic would tear through every particle of their bodies, melting and fusing and melting again until they were nothing but unrecognizable lumps of flesh-turned-stone on Roseward's beach. Part of him knew he couldn't fight it.

But the rest of him forged onward without thought, without fear, without concern for reality. Nelle hastened at his side, sometimes gripping his arm for support, driven by her own stubborn survival instinct. Soran led her up the path, his face turned firmly away from the sea, though he felt each wave of shock and heat as the storm closed in.

At the top of the cliff, he paused to wait for Nelle to step up beside him, then drove her ahead of him to the lighthouse, his back to the storm. She all but fell against the door and fumbled with the latch. The magicked barricade wouldn't respond to her, but when he touched the door, it swung open.

Then they were all three inside. Soran let the child drop from his shoulders in a heap of lifeless limbs on the floor. Turning, he grabbed the door and, using all his remaining strength, closed it against a final furious blast of magic. He felt the instant the magic struck and thought it would break through and end them.

But the door snapped shut. The protections of the lighthouse flared to life.

And suddenly it was as though the storm existed in another realm entirely, far beyond this dark, insulated world.

CHAPTER 3

FOR A LONG, BREATHLESS WHILE, NELLE COULD DO nothing but lie where she'd first sprawled on the floor rushes. One prickly rush tickled her cheek and nose. She lacked the energy to move away or scratch the itch. Her mind burst with echoes of thunderous magic, and her body flared with random patches of pain, trying to make her believe those harsh winds had blasted her beyond all recovery.

But eventually her breathing normalized. Her skin, though still raw in places, no longer felt blistered and peeling. Her bones no longer flared like hot irons melting her from the inside out. She took long, steadying breaths, releasing them slowly.

She would survive. The realization brought a small, stubborn smile to her lips. She would survive. This time.

With a groan, she pushed up onto her elbows and looked around the dim chamber. The fire on the hearth had died to almost nothing, but her night vision had always been keen—a hereditary gift from her half-fae mother.

She brushed hair from her face, turning toward the only movement in the shadows to see Soran pace slowly along the walls. Running his silvery hands up and down the stones and mortar, he called to the spells implanted in those stones, whispering strange words, incantations.

Nelle frowned as she watched the mage at his work. If she didn't know better, she'd think he was working fae magic. She'd seen similar spells implanted in the walls of Ninthalor, Lord Kyriakos's citadel. Mortals didn't work magic in such a way. The ward stones set around the perimeter of Roseward Isle were all carved with spell words—written magic. But the fae could not write, so they had to find other ways to drive their magic into whatever physical objects they wished to influence or manipulate.

But Soran had never demonstrated skill for this type of magic. Were the protection spells implanted in the lighthouse stones not of his creation? Was he merely working the magic left behind by another? If so, whose magic was it?

Nelle's head drooped. Her brain felt . . . *heavy*, somehow. Full of too many questions piled on top of too much fear. She closed her eyes and felt pressure mounting just beyond the walls of the lighthouse. The pressure of magic—storming, unleashed, wild magic. It was too much to bear, so she quickly opened her eyes again.

The child lay close beside her, flopped on his side, his back to her, his face turned away. Was he breathing? With energy borne of panic, Nelle sat up and reached for that still form, gently turning him onto his back to gaze into his slack gray face.

A boy child, she decided. Almost certainly. But exquisitely beautiful! Perhaps not human? Yet he *felt* human. Mortal. She couldn't explain why, but she couldn't deny the feeling either. There was blood on his face, and though she couldn't be certain in that low light, she thought it might be red. She searched for the wound and found a small gash along his temple. Fresh blood. That meant he lived, right?

She bent over and pressed her ear to his chest. The faint thrum of a heartbeat sounded like sweet music. "Thank the gods!" she breathed.

She couldn't leave the poor cold waif on the floor, but for the moment she lacked the strength to move him. Instead, she fetched her blanket and one of the fur rugs from her alcove bed and brought them back to the boy, making a little nest around him where he lay. Soran was still occupied with the spells, so she didn't bother asking permission before turning to the armoire and rummaging inside. She found a bottle of *qeiese*, a fae liquor she deemed revolting, but . . .

With a shrug she returned to the child and knelt beside him. The bottle was already unsealed, so she opened it, lifted the child's head slightly, and tipped a small amount toward his parted lips. It poured uselessly along the corners of his mouth and down his chin. "Boggarts," Nelle muttered.

"Don't waste it."

Soran knelt on the other side of the child, his white hair luminous in the darkness. He took the bottle from her un-resisting hands, then beckoned for the cap. She watched resentfully as he stoppered the bottle and set it aside. Anger churned in her gut, and the moment the mage looked up at her, she let it out in a burst.

"You were gonna leave him. You were gonna let him die."

Soran sat back slightly as though she'd taken a swipe at his face. "No one can survive prolonged exposure to a *ruvyn-satra*," he said. His low voice held no defensiveness, only cold facts. "Not unless . . ."

He let the words trail into silence, looking thoughtfully down at the boy. His brow tightened into a knot.

Nelle waited several moments, but he didn't seem likely to continue. "Well," she said, "he *did* survive. Looks like he's an *unless*. Whatever that means."

"Yes." Soran gave her a level look. "But you couldn't have

known. It was unwise of you to risk your life so rashly."

She tucked her hands under her arms, her stomach burning uncomfortably. She knew he was right. And she'd risked not only her own life, but Soran's as well. And, by extension, many, many other lives.

Nelle shuddered, loath to let her imagination venture down these dark avenues. Shame burning in her gut, she hung her head. But then she looked again at the little boy's face. So young, so innocent. How long had he been lost out on the Hinter Sea? Alone. Helpless against all the wilds of the worlds and the dangerous spaces between.

"He'll catch a chill lying here," Soran said after a long silence. He glanced at Nelle from under his eyebrows. "Shall I move him to the bed?"

Was he asking her permission? Nelle looked back blankly, uncertain how to respond. Well, perhaps in a way the boy was her responsibility now. She nodded.

The mage lifted the child as though he weighed nothing at all. Nelle plucked up the blanket and rug and followed him to the alcove. When Soran laid the boy down, she tucked the blanket around him again. Did a flush of life stain those gray cheeks? Or was it merely a trick of the hearth fire's low light?

While Nelle settled the child into what she hoped would be a comfortable position, Soran moved to the fire and added a log or two. When it flared up, Nelle glanced uneasily at their supply of

35

kindling and fuel. There wasn't much. Ordinarily, Soran re-stocked every few days, but . . . well, the last few days had been nothing short of chaotic. Regular household tasks had fallen by the wayside.

They hadn't prepared for a storm like this.

A chill that had nothing to do with cold ran down Nelle's spine and along her limbs to the tips of her fingers and toes. Eager to shake it off, she rose and moved across the room to the tables and shelves where she kept her stock of supplies from Dornrise, the palatial manor house at the other end of the island. Could its vine-choked walls possibly survive the blasts of magic now bearing down on Roseward?

"If nothing else, let the larder survive," Nelle muttered as she pulled a tin off the shelf and lifted the lid. Maybe three days' supply of tea leaves remained if they were frugal. A small blessing, but she offered up a swift prayer of thanks nonetheless, tracing a circle in the air with two fingers.

Setting the tin aside, she fetched the copper teakettle and filled it from the clean-water barrel, taking care not to waste a single drop. Since Soran had a fire blazing, she might as well make use of it. Besides, she suddenly felt a desperate need to throw her mind and body into some ordinary work.

Choosing not to look toward the mage—and ignoring the way his eyes followed her every move—she hung the kettle on its hook over the fire. Then she raked some hot coals out onto the hearth stones and set the flat pan down to heat. Flapcakes were in order. After the ordeal they'd just survived, they certainly deserved some sugary, cinnamon-spiced flapcakes.

Not many minutes later, the blue wyvern scuttled down from its hiding place among the rafters. Its fears temporarily banished, it made a nuisance of itself, twining around Nelle's knees and rubbing against her arms while she poured batter, flipped cakes, and added them to a growing stack on a plate. Every now and then it made a swipe for the topmost cake, but she had grown used to its wiles and nimbly smacked its nose each time. It hissed and flared its crest, but eventually it gave up and slunk across the room to sulk under the table with its head on Soran's foot.

The mage sat at the table, leaning on one elbow. Watching her.

A thick layer of silence underscored the sizzle and pop of each flapcake as it cooked and the murmur of the kettle as it boiled. Now and then, Nelle thought she heard a rumble like thunder. But that may well have been her imagination.

Having finished her work, she chose not to break the silence while placing a plate of cakes and a cup of dark tea before the mage. Rather than take her accustomed place across from him, she moved to the alcove and knelt beside the child. A long strand of inky black hair lay across his forehead. She brushed it back softly and frowned at how warm his skin was to the touch. Too warm. Feverish.

Leaning closer, she gently inspected the wound at his temple. It was already closed over, the fresh blood hardened into a dark scab. The air of Roseward hadn't lost its strange healing properties despite the storm overhead. Another small blessing.

"Hey there," Nelle murmured, stroking the boy's face and giving his bony shoulder a gentle shake. "Are you hungry, fella? I got flapcakes."

His shallow breathing seemed to hitch. Had he heard her? He let out a long gust of air and returned to a steady rhythm of light, quick breaths.

"Best let the Hinter air do its work," Soran's voice rumbled in the shadows behind her.

Nelle stiffened. She didn't particularly want to face the mage. Not just now.

But it wouldn't do to sit there and let her flapcakes go cold.

Sighing softly, she rose and returned to the table. Avoiding Soran's gaze, she sat at her place, reached across the table, and dragged the plate toward her, snatching the topmost cake with her fingers. She took a bite, but the burst of cinnamon sweetness seemed to turn to ash on her tongue.

Breathing another sigh, she slumped back in her chair, rolled the cake into a tube, and offered it to the wyvern, which swallowed it whole with a delighted snap, nearly taking a chunk of her finger with it.

Soran sat across from her, equally silent. He hadn't touched the cakes.

"What's the matter?" Nelle asked at last, flashing a glare his way. "Don't you like 'em?"

"I was wrong."

The words hung between them like strange silver threads of magic in the air. Nelle waited, holding her breath, forcing herself to meet the mage's eyes.

"I . . ." Soran swallowed, lowered his lashes, then looked up at her again. "I should not have tried to stop you from saving the child. It was wrong of me. Your impulse, though rash, was also right." He drew a long breath and rubbed a hand down his face, pulling at the ugly scars under his eyes and around his mouth. "Self-preservation has become my way of life. Not from any strong desire to live. Certainly not that. Merely from the desire to . . . to keep my sins contained."

The Thorn Maiden. He was talking about the Thorn Maiden.

If he were to die, she would escape her bonds and make her way to the mortal world. The havoc she would wreak there was beyond all imagining.

Nelle shuddered, swallowed, and looked down at her hands. "You know, I'm . . ." She hesitated, pressing her lips into a hard line. But she'd started now, so she might as well continue. "I'm sorry too. For putting you in that position. I know you ain't selfish. Your whole life is spent protecting folks who don't even know you exist. So, I'm sorry, but also . . ."

What more could she say? *I'm sorry, but I'm not, and I would do the same thing all over again.*

She glanced sideways at the boy sleeping in the alcove. He would have died, dashed to pieces on those rocks.

"I understand." Soran's voice reached out to her, warm and strangely gentle. She met his gaze for a moment, then stared down at her hands again. They sat in silence while the flapcakes went cold.

Finally, Nelle tossed another one to the wyvern and forced herself to take a bite of a third. "Go on, eat up," she urged the mage around her mouthful. "We don't know how long we're stuck here. Can't be wasting good food."

His silvery eyes flashed to her face. She almost thought she saw a hint of a smile pull at the scarred corners of his mouth. He obediently took a flapcake, rolled, and ate it, chewing slowly.

Nelle waited until he'd finished and reached for another before she asked, "So what's the *unless?*"

"I beg your pardon?" He lifted an eyebrow, his fingers hovering over the plate.

"You said no one can survive long exposure to that storm outside unless . . ." She tilted her head, waiting for him to fill in the gap.

"Ah." He withdrew his hand and rested it on his knee instead. "Well, you must understand: A *ruvyn-satra* is a rent in . . . in *realities,* as it were. A tear between this realm and the *quinsatra,* the realm of magic, caused by a powerful explosion of un-controlled magic. A dragon's death, for instance, might be enough to rip open the realities. But a less powerful source, such as the sundering and violent collapse of a Great Spell, has been known to cause a *ruvyn-satra*, given the correct circumstances." He looked at Nelle. "Are you following me?"

"I . . . think so," Nelle glanced again at the sleeping child. "What about him, then? How does he fit into all this?"

"It is possible," Soran said slowly, his own gaze following hers to study the little form lying under the thin blanket, "that he is the source of this *ruvyn-satra*."

"What? *Him?*" Nelle gaped at him, then shook her head and looked at the boy again. Her perceptions had developed tremendously over these last two weeks she'd spent on Roseward, enabling her to detect magic in ways she'd previously never believed possible. But she'd sensed no magic in the child. "I thought he was mortal. He bleeds red blood, and he ain't . . . he . . ."

"I believe he may be an *ibrildian*."

If she hadn't heard the strange word before, Nelle wouldn't have understood Soran, so low and grim was his voice. As it was, that one word stood out like a needle pressed against her eardrum.

She recoiled, tucking her arms around her body.

"An *ibrildian*," Soran began after a long pause, "is a hybrid

41

child born of mortal and—"

"And fae. I know."

His head turned sharply. She felt his gaze on the side of her face. "You do?"

She nodded grimly. "Yeah. It's what I am too. Ain't that right?" She lifted her eyelashes slowly, turned her head, and met Soran's stare. "It's why I can work magic like I do. Why I picked it up so quickly."

He swallowed hard. His mouth opened, closed. He looked down at his hand, which slowly closed into a fist. "When did you learn this?"

"Kyriakos." Nelle spoke the fae lord's name bitterly. Her lip curled. "He told me what I am. Explained why he was so keen on . . . on having me."

A shudder ran down her spine as the too recent memories filled her head. That red room. Those subtle perfumes. Heady seductions that had driven her half wild with desire, all but banishing her reason.

Heat flamed in her gut, and she hastily shook her head and pushed on, determined not to dwell on such things. "You told me that he'd once had many mortal wives and hybrid children. He explained a little more. About how powerful *ibrildian* children can be."

She let her voice trail off. In the silence that followed, she heard Soran breathing hard and, when she looked up, saw his nostrils flaring. He was angry. At her? Or—

"Damn my soul," Soran growled, suddenly burying his face in both silvery hands. "Damn my sordid, twisted soul, I should never have put you in this position! I should never have let you stay. I should never have—"

Nelle stood, leaned across the table, and yanked at Soran's hands, pulling them away so that she could look into his eyes. "What you *shouldn't* have done was keep it from me. My being an *ibrildian*, I mean. The rest of it . . . Boggarts, how many times do we have to go over this? I *chose* to stay. *I* chose. Not you. You don't get to choose what I do with my life. Got that? So, no more of this 'I shouldn't have' nonsense! I'm sick to death of it."

He stared at her, and though in that moment he looked much older than his years, his face riddled with scars and framed by still-damp strands of white hair, his eyes were those of a small boy, duly chastened. He blinked slowly, lowering his lashes to brush against his pale cheeks. Then he nodded.

Nelle sat down with a thump and folded her arms. Her shirt was damp from her plunge into the Hinter Sea, and her hair had gone all springy and fuzzy. She tossed it back from her face. "So," she said at last, "why didn't you tell me? Seems like I had a right to know."

"Yes," Soran agreed slowly. "You did. Of course, you did. But . . ." He shook his head. "I thought perhaps to protect you. The very existence of *ibrildians* is outlawed according to the

Pledge, the peace agreement settled between mortals and the fae after the Great War. If, once you return to Wimborne, the Miphates were to get word of your powers, they would hunt you down. And they might kill you. If you're lucky."

Her mouth went dry. "And if I'm not?"

"They'd take you. Use you. Try to keep you hidden from Eledria while they explore into your blood, dig into your soul." His eyes met hers, hard. "I was one of them, remember. I know how they think. I know how I would have thought and behaved once upon a time if given access to an *ibrildian*. All that power, all that potential . . . right at my fingertips . . ."

Nelle tucked her chin, disliking the tone of his voice. He sounded too much like Mage Gaspard. That same longing, that same craving.

Was this the true Soran Silveri? The brilliant Miphato, pride of the Evenspire University. Always willing to push the boundaries of reason and morality in his quest for more power, having no regard for those he hurt in the process.

The man who, in his hubris, had created a Noswraith. The very nightmare he had, just the day before, turned loose on Ninthalor, instigating the slaughter of hundreds . . .

What a fool you are, Peronelle Beck.

Nelle winced at her own voice, sharp in her head. She tried to shake it away, but it continued, insistent: *Do you honestly believe you can tame such a monster? Are you that much of a simpleton?*

She closed her eyes, squeezing her arms tight around her body. But was it really as straightforward as all that? Was this man seated across from her truly a monster? Yes, he'd unleashed the Noswraith. But what else could he have done against those dreadful Noxaurian forces? Kyriakos would have enslaved her, used her, draining her power to satisfy his ambition while simultaneously abusing her body to satisfy his lusts.

But what of the others? The innocent folk within that palace? The sister-wife who had helped Nelle escape? She did not deserve the crushing embrace of the Thorn Maiden.

He stopped it. When you told him to, he stopped it. And he nearly died as a result.

He's not a monster . . . not entirely . . .

Nelle let out a breath she hadn't realized she held, blowing softly between tense lips. "Well," she said at last, breaking the long silence. "Next time you think you've got to keep something from me to . . . to *protect* me . . . don't. Just don't." She lifted her head, met his gaze across the table. "I can't protect myself if I don't know what I'm up against."

"You are right, Miss Beck." Soran dipped his head solemnly and placed a hand over his heart. "I give you my word—I will withhold from you no information to which you have a natural right."

She started to smile, but it hurt somehow. Here she was, sitting bold as brass and demanding promises from this man, while she herself kept so many secrets. Dangerous secrets. Plans to betray the trust he had so reluctantly begun to place in her.

Who is the real monster here?

Perhaps the time was come for truth. The whole truth, not the partial truths she'd spun into convincing stories as she wormed her way into the mage's good graces. Perhaps the time was come to confess everything—her reasons for coming to Roseward, her mission to find and snatch the Rose Book for Mage Gaspard. If she revealed all to Soran, perhaps they could work out a solution.

He might even agree with her that it was better to hand the Rose Book over. After all, Mage Gaspard was a Miphato, trained right alongside Soran back in the day, his friend and cohort in the exploration of forbidden magic. Soran was cursed, crippled by the fae king Lodírhal. He would never be the mage he had once been, never command the magic which had once burned at his fingertips. While Gaspard had certainly grown in his powers over the last fifteen years. Maybe he could do what Soran could not. Maybe he could create a new spellbook to bind the Thorn Maiden before she burst free.

It made sense . . . so long as Nelle didn't think too closely about Gaspard himself: the man who had kidnapped and manipulated her, threatened her, threatened her father, and forced her to do his dirty work. Could such a man truly be trusted with a Noswraith spell?

Did she have any choice?

A sudden longing to unburden her spirit filled her heart. Nelle looked across at Soran and found him studying her again, reading the distress in her face. "Miss Beck?" he began, leaning toward her slightly.

"Mage Silveri." Her voice cracked, and she licked her dry lips. "Mage Silveri, while we're on the subject of truthfulness and all that, I think maybe—"

A sharp, high-pitched wail broke the shadows in the corner of the chamber.

Nelle spun toward the alcove. The little boy sat up suddenly, flinging back the blanket. His eyes were huge, staring, but didn't seem to see anything of the world around him. His jaw sagged wide in a prolonged scream of terror.

"Oi!" Nelle leapt from her seat and sprang across the room, wrapping her arms around the child. He was like a wooden block in her arms, and his screaming did not cease. "Oi, fella!" she said, trying to pull him toward her. "It's all right! It's all right, you're safe now. Do you hear me? Do you—"

"Nelle, get back!" Soran stood before her, reaching out to her. "It's not safe!" He caught her arm, started to pull her away.

In that moment, Nelle felt the mounting pressure of magic inside the child. It was going to burst in a moment, like one of those explosions she'd seen in the sky over the Hinter Sea. And where could they go to escape? Back out into the storm?

"No, wait!" Nelle cried, shaking off Soran's hand. She put her arms around the boy again. He couldn't hear her, she was sure. Whatever terrors filled his head drowned out her voice, blocked her presence. But maybe . . . maybe . . .

She pulled his head down to her heart and sang into the hair atop his head:

> *"Hush-a-bye, don't you cry*
> *Sleepy now, my little love*
> *When you wake, I'll give to you*
> *A sparrow and a soft gray dove*
> *A lark, a linnet, and a jay*
> *To sing for you throughout the day."*

She sang through verse after verse, recalling all the promised gifts—birds and butterflies and lambs and flowers. She sang as her father had once sung to her when she used to wake from night terrors screaming in her bed. It wasn't much of a song. The tune was simple, just a few notes skipping back and forth across her tongue. But with every repetition, she felt again the same soothing calmness that had once poured from Papa's comforting presence into her heart. She channeled that feeling, a kind of magic, straight from her heart into the boy's.

His screaming stopped abruptly, and he sagged against her, his cheek pressed to her shoulder. The mounting power extinguished inside him like a snuffed candle, and for a moment

Nelle feared he'd died in her arms. Frightened, she peered down into his little face, then looked up desperately at Soran.

The mage knelt and laid his silver hand on the boy's head, closing his eyes. "He lives," he said at last, looking up at Nelle. "He's asleep. Peacefully, I believe."

"Seven gods!" Nelle breathed and rolled her eyes heavenward. "I didn't imagine that, did I? All that magic building up inside him?"

Soran shook his head slowly. Fear shimmered in his cold gray eyes. "That was more magic than I've ever seen in any one person. I wonder . . ." He shook his head and sat back on his heels, studying the child. The lines of his face seemed to deepen in the fire's glow, and the puckered scars stood out ugly and raw. "I wonder who he is?"

CHAPTER 4

NELLE REMAINED IN THE ALCOVE FOR SOME WHILE, holding the child and rocking him gently. He seemed unaware of her presence, yet she couldn't quite bring herself to lay him down again.

What kind of life had he lived? What terrors had he endured, both out on the Hinter Sea and before? That scream—and the pent-up power it had revealed—spoke volumes, hinting at things Nelle suspected she'd rather not know in detail.

While she held the boy, she watched Soran as he cleared up the few dishes and tended the fire. The wyvern had taken the opportunity to help itself to the last of the flapcakes when their backs were turned. Soran chased it back up into the rafters, where it sat, fat and happy, noisily chewing its hind toes.

Once the table was clear, Soran reached into his shirt and withdrew the many folded spellpapers, the wyvern spells. His plunge into the water had soaked most of them through, so he unfolded them now with great care and strung them up near the fire, but not so near that they risked singeing. Nelle frowned as she watched him, worried for the fate of the creatures contained within those pages, those written words. Hoping they wouldn't emerge damaged from their ordeal.

Once the pages were dry and Soran began to collect them again, Nelle eased away from the child and laid him down on the stack of furs. He uttered one pitiful murmur but otherwise simply curled into a ball as she tucked the blankets around him. Soon she would try to get him to drink something. But not yet.

She moved to Soran's side and helped him collect the spellpapers. The spells remained intact as far as she could discern. When she tilted one page, peering at the inked words by the flickering firelight, she could feel a shimmering life down inside.

"Should we read them out?" she asked, looking around at Soran, who stood at the table.

He shook his head, carefully stacking the parchments. "We'd be swarming in wyverns. Hungry wyverns," he added with a significant look at the blue creature above. It burbled at him sleepily, showing its teeth. "They'd eat through our supplies in half a morning."

"Good point." Nelle handed over the three pages she'd collected. "How long do you expect we'll be stuck in here? With the storm, I mean?"

Soran didn't meet her gaze. "There is no way to know. It depends on . . ." He flicked a glance at the sleeping child. "It depends on many things. Not least of which is whether or not the protections on the lighthouse hold."

Nelle looked around at the walls. If she concentrated, she could feel the spells within them hard at work, those strange spells so unlike Soran's own magic. If she concentrated harder, she could just sense the power of the storm beyond them. But she could hardly believe they were in danger, it seemed so distant.

"Is there anything I can do?" she asked quietly. "To help with the spells, I mean?"

He looked directly at her then, and his expression was so strange, she didn't know how to read it. Was it surprise? Confusion? Wonder? It couldn't be tenderness. Not from him. Not from Soran Silveri, of all people.

"I thank for your offer, Miss Beck," he said, his voice quiet. "It is . . . It has been a long while since I had anyone to whom I might turn for help, and I don't know . . . I can hardly imagine . . ."

He bent his head, letting a hank of white hair cover the side of his face. Then he collected the stack of dried parchment and, turning away from her, strode across the room to the armoire. He stored the spellpapers on a shelf inside, shutting the door with a firm click. Only then did he turn to face her, and that odd expression was gone, replaced by the usual stern lines.

"For the present, there is nothing any of us can do," he said, his voice crisp and businesslike. "I would suggest you get some rest. I must see to the binding spell. Though the Thorn Maiden is unlikely to attempt a breakthrough during a *ruvyn-satra*, I won't take that risk."

With those words, he made for the stair.

"Wait!" Nelle cried, then quickly looked the child's way, afraid she may have disturbed his sleep. He didn't stir, but she stepped away from the table anyway, crossing the room to close the distance between herself and the mage so she could lower her voice. "Will you be safe up there? In the tower, I mean, with the storm blowing and all. There ain't much glass left on those windows, and—"

"Don't worry about me." Soran rested one hand on the wall, his right foot already placed on the first step. He turned to her, and once more she believed she saw something in his eye, but it was there and gone so quickly, she couldn't quite grasp it. "If we survive this storm, we'll survive it together. I swear. And then . . ."

She waited. When he didn't continue, she reached a tentative hand to his arm. "And then, Soran?"

The instant her fingers touched his sleeve, a jolt went through him. He pulled back with a sharp intake of breath, then began swiftly ascending the stair. "Good evening, Miss Beck," he growled over his shoulder, leaving her to watch the back of his head and the slump of his broad, powerful shoulders as he disappeared through the hole in the high ceiling.

Nelle listened to his steps until she could hear them no more. Part of her wanted to climb the stairs after him, to see for herself that the tower was safe. "Bullspit," she sighed at last and turned away from the stair, pacing back to the table. She took a seat, crossed her arms, and studied the play of firelight on the hearthstones. Frustration simmered in her breast.

Gaspard had allowed her three weeks to retrieve the Rose Book and return to Wimborne . . . but though only two weeks had passed since her arrival on Roseward, she knew much more time had escaped back in her own world. How many days, months, or years would she lose waiting out this storm? How much longer would Gaspard wait before he took his vengeance on her poor, defenseless Papa?

Or had he done so already?

Nelle shook her head fiercely. No good in thinking that way. Sam had brought her word only two days ago, telling her that Gaspard was still willing to honor his part of their bargain if she fulfilled hers.

Nelle hugged herself tightly. She saw strange, horrible shapes dancing in the firelight, playing among the flames, and creeping in the shadows. Images and half images of her own formless fears.

"You've got to do what you set out to do," she whispered. "It's the only way."

The only way for Papa.

The only way for Soran.

The only way . . .

She jerked her head up with a start, her body bracing just in time to keep from falling off her chair. Boggarts, had she nodded off? The fire had burned low; only a few flames remained among the shimmering red coals. She blinked blearily and pressed the heel of her hand into each eye, one after the other. Something had woken her. But what?

Then she heard it, the sound that had struck her awareness and drawn her back to the waking world. A small, pathetic whimpering.

"Mummy? Mummy? Mummy?"

"Oh!" Nelle gasped and turned to the alcove bed. The low firelight was enough for her keen eyes to see the child sitting upright, his little hands gripping the threadbare blanket. "Oh, is that you?"

Two bright eyes turned to her. Firelight reflected off their whites, making them shine like beacons in the shadows.

"Mummy?"

Nelle rose and crossed the room, moving cautiously to avoid frightening the poor child. He withdrew from her, pressing his back against the stone wall, and his eyes widened. They were such strange eyes! At first she thought they were black, but as she drew nearer, she saw they were instead a deep, vivid purple. Definitely not human.

"It's all right," she said quietly and crouched while still several steps from the alcove so as not to crowd him. "I ain't your Mummy. Sorry. I'm Nelle." She pressed one hand to her heart and nodded encouragingly. "Nelle, right? I'm a friend."

The boy sniffed and rubbed the back of one bony hand across his nose. He didn't speak.

"Are you hungry?" Nelle made signs of eating. He watched with mingled curiosity and distrust, but when she rubbed her belly, he seemed to catch on suddenly. He nodded, slowly at first, then with more vigor.

"All right. That's good. That's a start." Nelle stood up, looking back over her shoulder. The flapcakes were long gone, thanks to the wretched wyvern. What else did they have on hand to tempt the poor child and win his trust?

She smiled. "I know."

Before she could talk herself out of it, she crossed to the armoire, opened its doors wide, and fished inside for a certain tin box decorated with a relief of crowns and prancing deer. Queen's

SYLVIA MERCEDES

Cakes. The most perfectly delicious confections ever dreamt up by mortal minds. Surely Soran wouldn't begrudge a few in this instance. He never indulged in the sweets himself.

Carrying the box back with her, Nelle crouched, popped the lid, and breathed deep of the buttery sweetness. She held them out to the boy, smiling encouragingly. He drew back.

Then she saw his nostrils flare. A new light of interest gleamed in his eyes, momentarily driving out the fear.

"Go on," Nelle urged. She selected the topmost cake and took a bite. "See?" she said around her mouthful. "They're nice!"

She would have happily finished the whole thing, but the boy, emboldened, darted out a hand and took the rest of the cake. He stuffed it into his mouth, and his eyes brightened still more as he munched.

"Here now, go slowly," Nelle said, retracting the box when he dived for more. "Queen's Cakes are meant to be enjoyed, not inhaled." She picked out a second one and handed it to him. It suffered the same fate as its predecessor, gulped down so quickly, she doubted he even tasted it. The third cake was eaten with more obvious pleasure, however, and by the time he tucked into a fourth, he took smaller bites and chewed them thoroughly before swallowing, savoring the experience.

"That's enough," Nelle said when he held out his hand for a fifth cake. "Too much sweet on an empty stomach will make you sick. How about a drink. Some water?" She mimed drinking next.

The boy watched her, wide-eyed and unresponsive, until she started to feel silly, gave up, and simply went to fetch a cup, leaving the box of Queen's Cakes on the table as she did so. When she returned, the boy held back until she took a sip first. Only then did he reach out both trembling hands and accept the cup, taking long, slurping gulps until he'd drained it.

"Poor little bog," Nelle said, sitting cross-legged in front of him. "You've had quite the time of it. Where did you come from, I wonder? Did you make your way out here from the mortal world? Or from somewhere in Eledria?"

The boy lowered his cup and stared at her with unnerving focus. He had crumbs on his plump lower lip, and Nelle resisted the urge to wipe them away with her thumb. Soran was right; he was certainly *ibrildian*. Even pinched with fear and hunger, even streaked with blood and saltwater, his features were much too perfect to be fully human. And those unnatural eyes were a dead giveaway.

Strange, though . . . she couldn't get any sense of magic off him. She could almost believe she'd imagined that tremendous buildup of power from earlier. Almost.

Was it possible this small waif could be the source of the storm? If so, how? And why?

Shaking her head and realizing her expression had grown stern during her silent contemplation, Nelle quickly smoothed her forehead and offered the boy another smile. "Let's try again, shall we? My name is—"

The boy flung out one arm, pointing behind her, his eyes wide as two purple moons. "*Vulre! Vulre trazana! Vulre!*"

Nelle choked on a scream and fell backward, landing on her elbows. She twisted in place, half expecting to see some monster in the shadows behind her. Could the Thorn Maiden have made it through Soran's bindings?

No. It was the wyvern.

"Spitting brags and boggarts blast you!" Nelle cried and scrambled to her feet. The wyvern on the table, its snout deep in the box of Queen's Cakes, blinked bulbous eyes at her but continued stuffing cakes into its mouth as quickly as it could.

Nelle lunged, trying to catch it by the back of its sinewy neck. But it whipped around and leaped, its tail knocking the box over and spilling the remaining cakes. Nelle was just quick enough to catch it by the tail. Ignoring how the sharp scales dug into her palm, she heaved it up and swung it around. It brayed, spattering crumbs everywhere and writhing in her grasp, its one good wing flapping hard.

"Wretched worm!" Nelle roared, shaking the spell beast as hard as she could. "I ought to toss you right out that door, let you fend for yourself in the storm. And why don't I, eh? Give me one good reason!"

The wyvern hissed, squawked, then twisted its neck, craning to look around and behind her. It let out a frightened *meep* and doubled up to wrap its claw-tipped wings around her forearm, clinging and trembling.

Nelle turned in place. "Seven holy names!" she cried and jumped back a pace.

The child was standing. Both his hands were up, turning and twisting in the air before his chest. He appeared to be drawing characters in the air, and Nelle could almost see the burning after-image of each line and swirl as it formed. She felt the tension in the atmosphere, the building of magic pulled from the *quinsatra.*

"No, wait!" she said quickly. Not quite thinking before she acted, she swung her arm around behind her, hiding the wyvern from view, then flung up her other hand and shook her head. "It's all right! It's all right, fella. This beastie here, he's harmless Just a greedy toad, that's all. He can't hurt you. And there's plenty more food, I promise. See?" She darted to the table, picked up a half-eaten Queen's Cake, and held it out to the boy. "There you go. It's nice. It's nice, right?" The stream of blather poured from her tongue, her voice too bright to be convincingly relaxed.

But it seemed to work on the child. His fingers stilled, and the accumulation of magic dissipated, leaving behind not even the faintest impression of power. He blinked up at her, innocent and deadly and terrifying and sweet.

He accepted the Queen's Cake and stuffed it into his mouth. When he'd chewed and swallowed, he wiped his mouth with the back of his hand and pointed at the wyvern still clinging to her arm. "*Vulre*," he said. After a moment he added, "Dragon?"

"What? This thing?" Nelle swung her arm out front again and lifted the creature to eye level. It let go of her forearm and sagged upside-down, suspended by her grip on its tail. "He ain't a dragon. He's just a wyvern. A spell. Can't you see? He's magic, that's all."

"Magic?" The boy's voice quivered gently. He reached one finger toward the wyvern's nose. The wyvern twisted its neck and sniffed the extended finger, then flicked a long pink tongue between its teeth and licked it.

The boy giggled.

Within minutes, the child was back on his bed with the wyvern curled in his lap. Nelle watched in amazement as the spell beast turned onto its back, inviting belly rubs, which the boy offered with great enthusiasm as though enjoying a soft round puppy as opposed to a scaly lizard-thing.

"Well, as long as you ain't about to blast anyone to oblivion," Nelle muttered as she cleaned the mess of cake crumbs and ruefully inspected the insides of the empty box. She stuck a finger inside, fished out a last chunk of uneaten cake, and surreptitiously popped it in her mouth before either the boy or the wyvern noticed.

By the time she'd finished sweeping up the mess, all was quiet in the alcove. The boy and the wyvern curled up together, the boy's arm wrapped around the wyvern, the wyvern's head resting on the boy's neck. Both were fast asleep, the boy breathing softly, the wyvern snoring like an avalanche.

"It's a miracle anyone can sleep through that," Nelle muttered. She angled her chair in front of the fire to warm her feet while keeping an eye on the alcove. For several minutes she simply sat there, listening to the slumbering duet.

Then a rueful smile tugged at the corner of her mouth.

It was wrong. So wrong, and she shouldn't dare to admit it. But she couldn't help it: She was grateful for the delay. Glad she wasn't already on her way back to Wimborne, leaving Roseward behind forever. Leaving this strange new life, a life of magic and adventure such as she'd never imagined. A life of purpose.

A life that included Soran Silveri.

"I'll never see him again," she whispered, studying the dance of flames across the glowing coals. "When I go, that'll be it. The end."

Her smile vanished. Her heart turned to a solid, painful lump in her breast. She quickly lifted a hand to dash away the stray tear trailing down her cheek.

The Thorn Maiden was quiet that night.

Soran bowed over the Rose Book and concentrated on calling to life the magic contained within those battered, water-stained pages. In places, the ink was almost worn through, and he struggled to discern the words. He remembered what they were meant to be, of course—he'd read this spell so often, he recalled it perfectly. But the magic only came alive via the meeting of the material and immaterial, the mind and the mind's thoughts captured in written form. Without both ingredients, there simply was no magic.

He pressed on, turning each page carefully. The spellbook was as frail as some ancient document unearthed from a tomb. It was hard to believe that fifteen years ago he himself had tooled and ornamented the leather cover, pressed and stitched these pages, and written each precise line. Only fifteen years.

It felt like so much longer.

If not for the *ruvyn-satra*, the Thorn Maiden would no doubt take advantage of the book's ruinous state. Soran grimaced as he read, trying not to let his thoughts wander from the spell itself, the binding patterns he wove of words and power to keep the Noswraith contained within her own dark world.

But what about a few nights from now? When the magic storm had run its course, rolled by overhead, and dispersed at last across the vastness of the Hinter Sea? Would he be able to stop her?

He knew the answer. All too well.

Tonight, however, he reached the final pages of the spell without incident. It was surprisingly easy without the flagellations of the Thorn Maiden assaulting his sanity. He closed the book at last, gently bound the straps that held it shut, and leaned back in his chair.

His gaze rested for a long while on the spell, his mind fully aware of the magic contained within. Dark magic he should never have called from the *quinsatra*. Forbidden words he should never have dared to pen.

He closed his eyes, groaned, and twisted his tense neck. Letting his head rest against the back of his chair, he lifted his gaze from the desk and turned slightly to stare out through the open windows of his lighthouse tower, out across the sea. Terrible lights and still more terrible shadows played across the sky, twisting in unnatural undulations. He heard the rumble and roar of tremendous explosions, but the sounds reached him as though through several thick panes of glass, and he viewed the sights as though from a great distance.

He didn't fully comprehend how the protective spells set within the lighthouse walls worked—it was mortal magic on a level of expertise he had never seen even among the most senior Miphates of the Evenspire. As he understood it, though the lighthouse remained physically rooted in the soil of Roseward Isle, it was not, as it were, physically *bound*. Thus, the storm passed on by without touching the magicked stones.

Queen Dasyra had known what she was doing when she planted those spells.

Soran rose from his chair and walked around the basin of oil in the tower's center to his narrow bed beneath one of the tall windows. A gray robe lay draped in folds over the foot of the bed. He slipped it on, then turned back to the windows, looking down to the cliffs and the beach far below, where magic-churned waves lashed in a foaming frenzy against the rocks. He found his gaze moving to the very rocks Nelle had raced across in her bid to rescue the child.

In his mind's eye he saw her again, so small against the enormity of power bearing down upon her. So small and yet so fearless. Always so fearless . . .

She'd chosen to stay.

Cursing softly, Soran closed his eyes, bowed his head. After every mistake he'd made, every peril she'd faced—after seeing the worst of who he was revealed so baldly when he unleashed the Thorn Maiden in the fullness of her wrath—after everything, Nelle had chosen to stay. With him.

She couldn't, of course. Not with the spellbook compromised and the Noswraith on the verge of breaking through. She must leave before that happened, whether she liked it or not.

But she hadn't run off with . . . with . . . that handsome young man. Sam. Her friend whose name she'd spoken in half-waking confusion when responding to Soran's kiss. Sam, who'd come in search of her, braved the crossing between Wimborne and Roseward, the perils of the Hinter Sea. He was the right sort of man for a woman like Nelle. Courageous. True-hearted. Young. His face unscarred, his soul untarnished. She should have gone with him.

And yet . . .

He saw her again—that image he'd believed was a dream. Clad in that little bit of flimsy black nothing Kyriakos had dressed her in, her pale shoulders and bosom exposed, her strong, slender limbs displayed to full advantage, making him ache with need.

Had he misunderstood what she offered in that moment? That heady, heat-filled, almost unreal moment when she'd touched his face, drawn his body close to hers, and kissed his scarred, misshapen lips without a trace of fear. Was it an invitation? Did she ask him to respond, to give as she gave? To cast himself, heart, body, and soul, into the world of sweet vulnerability and delight that opened only to lovers?

And he'd refused her. Pushed her roughly away and retreated.

As he always did.

He pounded his fist against the stone. "You did what you had to do!" His words were as sharp and rough as broken rocks, grating on his ears, tearing at his heart. But they were true. Dream or otherwise, he couldn't give in to temptation. Life and love were not for the likes of him—disgraced, cursed, a bane upon every world by his very existence. He had a sentence to fulfill, and then a death to die.

While Nelle had her whole life ahead of her.

Standing upright, he straightened his long robe and smoothed back the straggling locks of his hair. The storm danced tumultuously before his vision, but his soul no longer writhed in rhythm with that torment. He composed himself, ordered his thoughts, shoved his feelings down as deep as they would go, and locked them behind iron-clad doors.

He would get her through this storm. He would protect her from the Thorn Maiden's intrusions a few days more. Then, when the ocean cleared and while the bridge connecting Roseward to the mortal world remained intact, he would convince her to go. If that required harshness, even cruelty on his part, so be it.

With this purpose firmly fixed, Soran turned to his bed, planning to lie down and catch a little sleep. But though his body was almost numb with exhaustion, attempting to close his eyes and sleep just now would be futile. He would simply lie there thinking of her.

Besides, he was painfully hungry.

After a last look over his shoulder at the Rose Book lying so harmlessly on his desk, he made his way slowly down the stair. Telling time was impossible during a *ruvyn-satra*, but he guessed it must be an hour or two before dawn. All was quiet below. Nelle and the *ibrildian* child must both be sound asleep.

Sure enough, as he emerged through the hole in the high ceiling and glanced around the shadow-strewn space, Soran spied two lumps in the alcove bed. One was the child, the other the blue wyvern, tangled together and sleeping soundly.

Nelle lay beside the stone hearth with no blanket, no cushion for her head except the crook of her own arm. Her hair fanned out around her face, catching light from the dying coals, vivid in that shimmering warmth. She still wore his garments, his loose white shirt not quite disguising the softness of her womanly frame. The wide neckline had pulled to one side, exposing her shoulder, and his baggy trousers somehow emphasized the curve of her hips. She'd rolled up the cuffs, revealing the well-toned muscles of her calves, a pair of dainty ankles, and two bony white feet, much battered from running barefoot on the beach.

Soran stopped short on the stair. His resolve faltered. For the moment, he wasn't a living dead man, cursed and crushed under the weight of numerous sins. He was just a man. Full of fire, full of longing.

His jaw hardened. Shrugging, he slipped the heavy robe from his shoulders and draped it over his arm as he descended the last few steps. He took care to make no noise as he crossed the room to the hearth, where he crouched and gently draped the garment over the young woman's sleeping body, covering her from her bare feet up to her shoulder.

Then he stood, turned his back, and stared unseeing into the shadows, drawing long, even breaths.

Once he was certain he was master of himself, he moved to

the stash of supplies Nelle kept on the shelves along one wall. Over the years he had grown used to eating little, subsisting almost entirely on seagull eggs and the sustaining air of the Hinter Sea itself, which prolonged the natural span of mortal life despite the harshest privations. But in the last two weeks, Nelle had brought real food back into his life. Humble but flavorful meals, which had unexpectedly awakened his appetite.

He found a loaf of crusty bread in a basket under a cloth. Nelle had discovered it in the larders at Dornrise—larders which, no matter how often she pillaged them, never seemed to diminish in bounty. Another of Dasyra's unasked-for blessings, no doubt.

Taking a chunk from the loaf, Soran moved to sit at the table. While he ate, he told himself not to look at Nelle, yet his eye wandered to the now rather shapeless lump hidden beneath his mounded robes. Only the brilliant tangle of her hair was still visible. It was beautiful, soft and vibrant like the girl herself—

"Hungry."

Soran nearly jolted out of his chair, turning sharply to the shadows beside him. A little figure stood at his elbow, and a pair of strangely glittering purple eyes gazed up at him, blinking slowly. Momentarily confused, Soran shifted his gaze from those eyes to the alcove and back again. How could the boy have moved so quickly, so silently?

The child tilted his head and blinked again. His face was

inhumanly beautiful, but its expression was unmistakably mortal. "Hungry," he said again and pointed from his mouth to the bread in Soran's hand.

"Oh. Ah." Awkward in his surprise, Soran held up the partially eaten crust, offering it to the child. "Here, take it. There's . . . there's more."

The boy snatched the proffered food eagerly and stuffed most of it into his mouth. His eyes widened, flashing to Soran's face. He nearly choked as he tried to chew and swallow and speak all at once, and Soran half wondered if he ought to try to pry the bread from the boy's mouth. "Easy, easy!" he said, patting the boy's back. "Take your time. There's plenty more food where that came from."

The boy choked again but managed to force the mouthful down his throat. Shaking his head, he looked up at Soran, and his entire face burst into a startling, almost terrifying smile.

"Mummy!" he exclaimed.

Soran stared.

Then his eyes widened as realization hit. In a burst of horror mingled with agonized hope, he knew exactly who this child was.

CHAPTER 5

NELLE WOKE FEELING BOTH STIFF AND UNCOMFORTABLY warm. At first she didn't have the energy to move. She simply lay there, scowling, and slowly let her senses come back into focus. There was flickering heat at her back, but beneath her, no soft rugs piled into a makeshift bed. Just hard stone and prickly floor rushes, and her own numb arm pillowing her head.

She drew a breath . . . and inhaled the mingled scent of parchment, ink, and brine. A pleasant combination that smoothed out some of her frown. Soran. This was Soran's smell. Then her frown returned, tightening her brow. Why was she smelling Soran so strongly?

Slowly she cracked open one eye and found a fold of coarse fabric draped over her shoulder. Soran's robe. Thickly woven, intended for warmth and durability rather than comfort. No wonder she was so overheated. Had she pulled the robe over herself when she lay down on the hearth? She didn't remember.

A bright, trilling sound startled her. Nelle blinked her other eye open, then shifted a hand to rub at both eyes. The sound lilted again, and she recognized it this time: laughter. A child's laughter.

Tossing hair out of her eyes, Nelle pushed up onto one elbow. Immediately her arm prickled with pain as blood flow renewed. "Bullspit."

"Good morning, Miss Beck."

Twisting her torso uncomfortably, Nelle looked over her shoulder. Soran crouched behind her. His nilarium-coated hand grasped the copper kettle's piping-hot handle and, impervious to burn, slid it off the suspending bar. "I've boiled water," he said without looking her way. "Would you care for tea?"

"Um." Nelle shook her head blearily, then, grimacing again at the sparks of pain in her arm, pushed into a seated position. The thick robe fell in a puddle around her, and she realized that her shirt had pulled far to one side, exposing her shoulder. What else might it expose? She thought of the gold chain and locket she kept hidden against her skin. The last thing she needed was for Soran to see it, to recognize it, to ask how she'd come by it.

Hastily she yanked her shirt back into place, eyeing the mage closely.

But without turning her way, he carried the kettle to the table and poured its steaming contents into the clay teapot. A pleasant aroma of brewing tea leaves filled the air.

Another peal of laughter drew her attention to the alcove where the boy sat cross-legged on the pile of furs. He held half a loaf of bread in his lap and was breaking off and tossing chunks to the wyvern. The wyvern stood on its hind legs, its one good wing spread wide, and performed a series of spinning dances, chortling and waddling and making quite the fool of itself in exchange for each bite.

The boy giggled. The wound on his head had healed over and, at least from this angle, Nelle could discern no trace of a scar. His color was better, a fresh flush of pink underlying his ivory cheeks. His hair hung black and straight well below his shoulders, looking thicker and healthier than before.

"Someone's recovering nicely." Nelle stiffly rose from the hearthstones, groaning at every ache and pain. At least her arm felt mostly normal again. She gave it a shake from shoulder to wrist, then padded to the table and slumped down in her usual chair across from the mage.

Soran set a battered cup in front of her, lifted the clay teapot, gave it a little swirl, and poured out a stream of steaming liquid. He did not think to strain the tea leaves before pouring, and

Nelle's lips quirked to one side as she watched little dark specks twirling in the brew. She didn't mention it, however. No point in embarrassing the man. She picked up her cup, took a sip, and refused to grimace when tea leaves slid down her throat.

"We survived last night," she observed, lowering the cup and spinning it slowly in her fingers. "How's the storm looking?"

Soran took a sip from his own cup and winced. His eyes flicked her way, questioning, perhaps, whether she'd noticed the unstrained leaves. She offered a blank expression back, so he took another sip. Then he shrugged. "The storm is as strong as ever. But the protections hold. We are, for the time being, safe."

Nelle grunted. Another burst of laughter drew her gaze, and she watched the wyvern try to balance on its own twining tail. It failed, toppling over in a heap of scales and limbs, but the boy tossed it a large chunk of bread even so.

"How's he look to you?" Nelle asked. "Seems all right, don't he?"

"Indeed. I believe he will make a full recovery." Soran leaned forward, forearms resting on the table, and lowered his voice to ask, "Do you see anything odd about . . . about what he is doing, Miss Beck?"

"Odd?" Nelle frowned. "You mean other than giving up good bread to that greedy worm?"

"Look at the bread," Soran said.

Nelle cast him a short glance. What an odd thing to say! But his expression was earnest. Intense, even. She raised one eyebrow and turned back to the little tableau. The bread was, of course, the enchanted loaf she'd taken from Dornrise. No matter how many times she pillaged from the breadbasket in the great-house larders, the same loaf always reappeared the next time she looked. It had a hard round crust with a simple cross scoring, and the inside was soft and deliciously flavorful with just a hint of herbs and honey. One of the many magical conveniences she'd begun taking for granted since coming to Roseward.

"It don't look odd to me," she said after several moments' contemplation.

"Watch when he tears off the next piece," Soran said.

Nelle did as he said. At first, she saw nothing. Then she uttered a little, "Oh!" and sat up straighter.

When the boy tore off a chunk, the half loaf itself did not diminish. It remained exactly the same size and shape as before. Piece after piece the boy tossed to the wyvern without the bread altering in the least.

"I ain't never seen it do that before!" Nelle said. She narrowed her eyes, trying to see more clearly what took place, trying to get a sense of the magic. But the boy remained stubbornly unmagical to her perceptions.

She turned to Soran. "How's he doing that?"

"He recognized the magic." The mage leaned in a little closer, his shoulders hunched, as though he feared to be overheard;

though who he thought might hear them, Nelle couldn't begin to guess. "He recognized the magic because it is his mother's."

"Huh?"

Soran's eyes took on a haunted look, a little too bright, a little too intense beneath his furrowed brow. "You remember," he said, "what I told you about my imprisonment. How the fae king Lodírhal of Aurelis cursed me and sentenced me to a lifetime here on Roseward."

Nelle nodded. It was a tale she was unlikely to forget.

"After Lodírhal left, I was in a bad way. Newly cursed, unable to create spells for my own protection, I was at the mercy of anything the Hinter Sea might throw at me. I was unprepared for the horrors Eledria offers unwitting mortals, and my energies were entirely consumed with trying to keep the Thorn Maiden from bursting her bonds, slaughtering me in a heartbeat, and finding her way to Wimborne. In those first few days, I quite despaired.

"But on the third day, Dasyra turned up. Mage Dasyra as she was once known in our world. *Queen* Dasyra here in Eledria. King Lodírhal's mortal wife."

"But I thought—" Nelle clamped her teeth and lips shut to stop the series of questions. Better to let Soran tell his tale in full.

"Mage Dasyra was the greatest wielder of mortal magic during the Torinian Age, some four hundred years ago. I knew her name, of course. She is well known, even revered among the

Miphates, for it was she who first wrested the Evenspire from fae control and, in a great battle, drove them out of what is now Wimborne City, breaking their hold over Seryth.

"Not long afterward, she fell in with Lodírhal of Aurelis and, through a series of unknown circumstances, became his bride. She has lived ageless among the folk of Eledria ever since and ultimately claimed them as her people while simultaneously serving as a protection between them and her own kind."

That series of unknown circumstances must have been unusual indeed, Nelle thought. What could possibly persuade a mage who'd adamantly fought against the fae to become the bride of a fae? She wished she might learn that story.

But Soran resumed his own side of the tale: "As I said, Dasyra arrived unheralded at Roseward and set to work, establishing protections and provisions for my care and keeping. I do not know what all she did during that time—my attention was still mostly focused on the Rose Book and the Thorn Maiden. The ward stones were her work, however. And all the protections planted into the lighthouse walls. And, as I'm sure you've guessed, the ever-replenishing larder at Dornrise."

Nelle nodded slowly. She had often wondered about that.

Turning in her seat, she studied the child. He and the wyvern were curled up together on the bed once more, the boy asleep, the wyvern gnawing away at the half loaf. The magic continued to work, replenishing and replenishing, until at last the wyvern gave up, heaved a huge, glutted sigh, and draped itself over the boy like a scaly blanket.

"What about him?" Nelle asked. "I thought you said all *ibrildian* children were outlawed at the time of the Pledge. And . . . and Kyriakos." She shuddered, not liking to speak the name. "You said he was made to give up his mortal wives and children. By force."

"I remember some of the story, though not all," Soran said. He cast a sideways glance at the sleeping child and kept his voice low. "As I understand it, two hundred years ago, at the time of the Pledge, Lodírhal refused to give up his mortal wife. It nearly destroyed the fragile peace negotiations. But neither side could move forward without the King of Aurelis, so eventually the mortal mages and rulers were convinced to allow Dasyra to remain with her husband, but under the condition they have no more children. And their son—Prince Castien—was to be turned over to the Miphates."

Nelle's heart went cold. "To be killed?"

Soran shook his head. "Neither Lodírhal nor his queen would have agreed to such a plan. No, he was merely to be kept, contained. Ultimately to have his magic suppressed, rendering him as normal and unthreatening as possible. In his mother's world, his mortality would soon gain dominance, and he would live only a normal span of years. Perhaps he'd always be a little more beautiful, a little stronger, a little more vibrant than his peers. But he would live, age, and die like a mortal, thus ridding the world of his power before it ever fully manifested."

"So . . . is that where he's been all this time? With the Miphates?" Nelle licked her dry lips and pushed hair out of her face. "But that don't make sense. The Pledge was signed three hundred years ago. He should have died of old age long before now."

Soran bowed his head slightly. "Before the young prince could be turned over to mortal custody, he was kidnapped."

Nelle's eyes widened. "Lodírhal?"

"So it was at first believed. Lodírhal had been so adamant about keeping his mortal wife, even to the point of letting the bloody war continue, that many thought he wouldn't hesitate to spirit away his own son rather than give him up to the Miphates he hated so vehemently. The ensuing scandal nearly destroyed the Pledge before it could be ratified." Soran sat back in his chair, one nilarium fist still resting on the tabletop. "In the end, however, after much investigation and deliberation, it was determined that the child had been murdered. Queen Dasyra was certainly convincing in her despair. So, the Pledge was signed, and the child was given up for lost."

Until now.

Those words hung unspoken in the air as both Nelle and Soran turned to observe their sleeping guest. How innocent he looked by the dull firelight, his arm wrapped around the wyvern, his face slack with sleep. Could he truly be the center of such world-defining political intrigues? Perhaps it was all a mistake. Perhaps it was merely wild speculation on Soran's part.

But the boy had recognized Queen Dasyra's magic. And, without demonstrating any magic of his own, had manipulated it in ways Nelle hadn't thought possible.

"The mingling of Lodírhal's blood with that of his mage wife would have produced a child of truly rare abilities," Soran said. "A hybrid such as the worlds have never seen. The Miphates of centuries past would have been hard-pressed to contain him all these years. No . . ." Soran pressed his lips into a tight line, shaking his head slowly. "No, I do not believe he's been in the mortal world all this time. He has been kept somewhere in Eledria. Under powerful lock and key where not even Lodírhal and all the forces of Aurelis could find him."

"And you think he's the cause of this magic storm?" Nelle asked quietly. "You think it's possible?"

"I think it highly likely. If the spells used to contain him were as powerful as I believe they must have been, their untimely breaking would have been enough to rend the realities between this realm and the *quinsatra*."

"Untimely breaking?"

Soran met her gaze across the table. "For instance . . . if the fae lord who worked the containment spells were killed un-expectedly. Violently. The force might be great enough to shatter even his most powerful spells."

Nelle opened her mouth but couldn't bear to ask the questions springing to her lips. She didn't need to. She knew what he
was thinking.

When Soran unleashed the Thorn Maiden on Ninthalor, how
many of Kyriakos's people had she slaughtered? Could Kyriakos
himself have fallen under her onslaught?

Kyriakos, who had rebelled against the Pledge, against the
kings and queens of Eledria.

Kyriakos, who was known to collect *ibrildians*.

Nelle heaved a great sigh, leaning back in her seat. It was all
speculation, of course. They had no proof. But if the child truly
was Prince Castien . . .

"What do we do?" she asked, her brow knotting as she
watched the boy roll slightly in his sleep, the wyvern nuzzling
into his neck. "Do we try to get a message to King Lodírhal?"

She stopped. Realization struck like a gut punch, and she
couldn't make herself turn and meet Soran's gaze. This was the
leverage he needed. If the child truly was who Soran believed, he
could be a bargaining chip: the young prince's life in exchange for
Soran's.

Nelle's stomach twisted. It was an ugly thought. But so clear
and undeniable. She knew without looking at the mage that he
was thinking the same thing. After all these years, all these
hopeless, tormented years, might he now possess the tool he

needed to free himself?

Would he use it?

"*We* will not do anything," Soran said, breaking the silence. "Not yet. We will care for the boy until the storm passes. Then you, Miss Beck, will return to Wimborne while the bridge still holds. *If* the bridge still holds. When I am certain you are safe, I will decide what is best from there."

Nelle flashed a quick glance his way, heat flooding her face. After all this, he could still speak so casually of her going?

Then again, what was the point of arguing? She had to go. She knew she must. Whatever became of Soran or the child was not her business. Her business was to protect Papa. Nothing more. Nothing less. To allow added complications would be pure stupidity.

She folded her arms and turned to the boy. One hand crept up to feel through the thin fabric of her borrowed shirt the outline of the locket on its chain.

Her choices were simple, her next moves clear.

But she couldn't deny the shadowy dread that hovered over her soul like a bird of prey ready to tear and devour.

The day dragged, one hour trailing slowly after the next.

Since Nelle let the fire burn low, trying to spare their supply of wood, the chamber was gloomy. She almost lit a few candles, but really, what was the need? They may as well sit in darkness. Occasionally a flash of unnatural light broke through the high windows, followed by a rumble of tumultuous magic. Though it sounded distant, Nelle sensed that the storm even now churned in the sky directly overhead.

When the noise passed, a strange, otherworldly calm settled in.

Nelle tried to keep herself busy with small tasks—polishing the pots and pans, arranging and rearranging their supplies. All the while, she kept an eye on the boy, who slept on with no trace of discomfort. His face was oddly peaceful, pillowed on the wyvern's lumpy side. Whatever torments he'd experienced out on the Hinter Sea seemed washed away. For the moment at least.

Soran had ascended the tower stairs shortly after gulping down the last of his tea. He remained up there as the day crept on, doing gods knew what. Probably filling the time with small, unnecessary tasks like she was. And avoiding her company.

Nelle cast a resentful glare up the empty stairway, then turned that same glare around at the hearth, the shelves, and the collection of battered cooking utensils. She'd done all she could with them and swept the hearth besides. Now what?

"I don't plan to sit here and go slowly mad." Even as she set her broom in the corner and dusted her hands on her borrowed trousers, an idea popped into her head.

After a determined search, she located her snatcher's satchel in the armoire atop a stack of spellbooks and shoved her hand inside to feel the binding of her own blank spellbook and the rough bristles of a quill pen. A smile tugged at her lips.

Moments later, she lit a single candle, slid the book and quill onto the tabletop, and pondered them thoughtfully.

Her smile faltered, then vanished.

When she returned to Wimborne, she would have to give up all magic. Gods knew, her life there was precarious enough already! The last thing she needed was to draw the attention of the Miphates by dabbling in forbidden magic. By revealing her true nature.

She sat for some while, telling herself to be wise, telling herself to be practical. It was time to steel her mind to the realities facing her, to stop living in the foolish daydreams she'd foolishly allowed to creep in during the last two weeks.

Then, her lips pressed into a thin line, she shoved away from the table and returned to the armoire in search of the parchment spells Soran had stashed there the day before. She selected the topmost spell and brought it back to the table with her, smoothing out the parchment to study Soran's careful handwriting. The characters were familiar—the same Serythian alphabet she'd grown up learning.

But the words were Old Araneli, an ancient fae tongue—a language never intended to be captured in written form. As a result, characters had been added to the regular alphabet, strange swirls and dashes and jots to indicate both sounds and whole phrases that couldn't otherwise be expressed. It would require years and years of training to begin to unlock the secrets of the language, many more years to be able to write it with any clarity or purity.

But Nelle knew from recent experience that she didn't need a perfect grasp of Old Araneli to successfully capture a spell. None of the spells she'd managed to create had been written in the fae tongue, though bits and pieces and a few odd characters had worked their way in. Perhaps her *ibrildian* nature instinctively knew where and when to bend the rules of mortal magic. Perhaps if she trusted to that nature more fully, she would see greater success. Perhaps . . .

Perhaps she was crazy.

Nelle picked up the quill and opened her blank spellbook. Soran had magicked her quill to write without need to dip it in an inkwell. He had also performed a ceremony of quill-binding, which was, at least according to tradition, intended to aid the process of channeling her mind and magic from the immaterial realm of thought and imagination into the material realm of ink and page. Nelle couldn't tell if it actually worked that way or not, but she liked to think the binding had given her a little boost of confidence if nothing else.

She began to copy Soran's careful script. Simply copying his work would not produce the proper magic, but it was a place to start. She could feel it working almost at once—the shimmer of power that meant her mind was connecting to the *quinsatra*. Perhaps the magic storm's proximity helped.

Slowly but surely her concentration absorbed into the work. She copied Soran's words, adding her own flair here and there, a little more slapdash energy and urgency, and finally . . .

A flutter. Faint but recognizable.

A sensation like a wing unfurling in her mind.

Nelle gasped. Her concentration broke, and her quill slid awkwardly to one side with a broad slash of ink. The simmering magic seemed to boil up, burst, and seep away from the page, returning to the realm of its origin. The spell, whatever it might have become, was broken.

"Bullspit," Nelle growled and tossed the quill down. She looked back over the work, noting how her painstaking lettering of the first few lines gave way by the middle of the page to the awkward, rushed scrawl that was her natural hand.

"A right mess that is," Nelle said, rubbing her temples with the tips of her fingers, her elbows leaning heavily on the tabletop. Had she imagined the momentary flash of life that had seemed to take shape beneath her pen? Probably. In her sleep-deprived state, her brain could conjure all sorts of nonsense.

"I try?"

With a start, Nelle turned in her chair, gripping the edge of the table with one hand. "Seven gods! I didn't know you was there."

The boy stood at her elbow, his purple eyes fixed with intense interest on the spellbook. He blinked slowly, then swiveled those odd eyes up to meet her gaze and gabbled something in a language she didn't know. One small, slender, long-fingered hand extended.

"I try?" he said again.

Nelle frowned. "You . . . want to try to make a wyvern?"

He nodded solemnly and wiggled the tips of his fingers.

Was it safe to let him attempt spell-making? Then again, he was so young. If he had truly been imprisoned all these years—all these *centuries*, by mortal count of time—it was unlikely anyone had taught him to write. What harm could he do?

"All right," Nelle said slowly and slid from the chair, giving him her place. Soran probably wouldn't like it. But Soran didn't like much of anything these days. And he wasn't here.

She turned her spattered page over, presenting the child with a fresh new page, then handed him her quill. He took it, twirling it slowly in his fingers, watching how it moved. Nelle drew the parchment containing Soran's wyvern spell a little closer. "So, you just try to copy what's here. Understand?"

The boy looked up at her, his brow knotting. Then he sucked in his plump lips and chewed them thoughtfully. With a shrug, he bowed over the book and . . .

It didn't look like writing, not proper writing. It was,

somehow, more like painting. No small characters lined up with orderly procession from left to right or even right to left. Instead, he drew a long diagonal stroke and then, without breaking the line, purposefully looped back with large, rounding curves. He dragged the quill up and down the page with slight variations three times before finally lifting the nib. Then he began to apply small strokes and dashes in various turns and corners of the main image. At first Nelle thought he was trying to draw something, perhaps a wyvern. But the image was far too abstract.

He's just a little boy, she reminded herself. When she was his age, she had loved to scribble the odd assortment of lines and blots on any available surface when given the opportunity. As long as he was entertained, it couldn't hurt any—

Her heart jumped to her throat. "What the boggarts!"

Something had moved. There on the page.

She blinked . . . shook her head . . . looked again. Told herself she was mistaken.

But it moved again with a ripple like an undulating spine rising out of the parchment in a languid stretch. It vanished again, then returned clearer than before, and this time a tail lashed over the edge of the page.

"What is going on down here?"

Nelle whipped her head around to the tower stair. Soran peered into the room through the hole in the ceiling, his gaze fixed on the two of them bent over the table. "What is he doing?"

"Magic!" Nelle gasped, though she knew it was unnecessary. "He's doing magic!"

Soran leapt down the steps, growling as he came, "And you're *letting* him? Don't you understand—"

"No! Wait!" Nelle jumped between the mage and the boy, nearly ramming her upraised hand into Soran's chest to keep him from rushing at the table and grabbing her quill out of the child's hands. "Look what he's doing! Look *how* he's doing it!"

Soran glared down at her, then turned his attention over her shoulder, looking at the boy and the book. The boy hadn't so much as flinched at the interruption. He continued to work with intense concentration, adding fine details to his already complex assortment of strange shapes and non-patterns.

A wyvern half sat up from the page—a living, shimmering, magic-made wyvern, still bright and fresh with the lights of the *quinsatra*, somewhat transparent but swiftly solidifying. It was much smaller than any of Soran's creations and far more delicate. Its proportions were different as well. Whereas the wyverns Nelle had grown used to had batlike wings, this wyvern was more birdlike. Its feathered wings folded neatly across its back. Its head, though distinctly draconian, was also far more delicate than the blunt-nosed, crested wyverns of Roseward. Its eyes were black and liquid yet pulsing with inner light.

The boy added a last jot, then sat back and let the quill drop from his fingertips. The new wyvern sat up and curled a long, feathery tail around its dainty haunches. It chirruped at the boy, tipping its head to one side, the motion sharp and birdlike. The boy held out his hand, and the wyvern lifted its chin, allowing him to run a finger down the length of its long neck and across the prominent breastbone.

"It's so beautiful!" Nelle whispered. She held onto Soran's arm as though to restrain him, but he had gone quite still. When she dared to glance up at his face, she saw that he was as entranced as she.

The boy chirped back at the wyvern and shifted his arm slightly. The little creature, accepting the invitation, stepped onto his wrist and there unfurled its wings—four wings arranged almost like those of a butterfly but adorned with translucent white feathers.

An ugly bray broke the rapt stillness. The blue wyvern, which had been dozing on the alcove bed, sat up suddenly, flared its crest, and roared at the intruder. The dainty new wyvern started and, in a flash of magical light so bright it made Nelle flinch and look away, dived from the boy's wrist down into the spellbook. It disappeared in an instant, becoming nothing but the arrangement of lines and swashes and dots caught on paper.

The boy sighed and turned a glare upon the blue wyvern. "Bad," he said. "You bad."

The wyvern brayed again and waddled across the room, crest still flared, muttering its disapproval. When it reached the boy, it laid its head on his lap. The boy shrugged and stroked its crest until it lay flat.

Nelle and Soran watched without speaking. Nelle, realizing suddenly how her fingers dug into the mage's arm, let go and stood back a pace. "Have you ever seen anything like it?" she asked.

"No." Soran, moving as though in a fog, reached over the boy and picked up the spellbook. He lifted it, turned it, angled it toward the candlelight, turned it again. "This is like no language I've ever seen."

He lowered the book slowly, peering down at the boy, who sat stroking the blue wyvern's head, his soulful eyes blinking innocently up at the mage, entirely unaware of the confusion he'd just caused.

"How did you do this?" Soran asked, indicating the spell with a nod. "How did you . . . how did you call that beast to life?"

The boy blinked again. Then he spoke a series of strange, fluid words. Nelle watched Soran's face and saw from his expression that he understood. "What did he say?" she asked.

"He said . . ." Soran pursed his lips and shook his head. After drawing a deep breath, he tried again. "He said that he *told the story*. That is all. He told the story of the wyvern, and it became true."

CHAPTER 6

"IT MUST BE HIS *IBRILDIAN* MAGIC," SORAN SAID SOME while later.

Nelle and the mage sat in their usual places at the table, watching the boy, who had coaxed the shimmering wyvern out from its spell again and was entertaining himself playing with it on the hearth. The blue wyvern, bitterly jealous, had retreated into the rafters, where it growled and muttered and occasionally let out an unpleasant bray. On these occasions, the boy would look up and call out foreign words that sounded comforting and scolding by turns. Otherwise, he continued to play with his new creation. In short order, he'd taught it a series of tricks—little dances and twirls, which it performed with heavenly grace.

"This is what the Miphates feared," Soran said, resting his elbows heavily on the tabletop and studying the boy closely. "That perfect blend of fae and mortal magic which is forever beyond their grasp."

"Well, I'm *ibrildian*." Nelle blew softly through her lips. "I can't do nothing like that!"

Soran waved a dismissive hand. "Your blood blend is more diluted. Unless I'm much mistaken, your mother was half fae, which means you are more mortal than fae. Thus, your approach to magic will lean more toward mortal understanding. Even so, the magic I've seen you perform is similar."

"How can you say that? I ain't managed to make anything living, that's for sure!"

"No." Soran met her gaze, both eyebrows climbing his scarred forehead. "But, like the boy, your powers do not seem limited to the laws and regulations that govern my own abilities. You have successfully called objects into being, using what I can only describe as a *bizarre* blend of your own Serythian language and garbled, half-recognizable Araneli. If I were to attempt as much, I would never come close to succeeding even with the simplest of spells. But you make it look easy."

Nelle grunted. "I just . . . I do it as I see it."

"Indeed." Soran indicated the child with a jut of his chin. "And so does he, apparently. He sees magic in a different way than either you or I do. Perhaps his vision is clearer than ours."

Nelle watched the boy raise both hands, holding his index fingers and thumbs to create a small circle. The dainty wyvern rose on its four luminous wings, performed a quicksilver loop, and darted through that circle, vanishing. The boy cupped his hands together and unfolded them slowly, revealing the wyvern crouched in his palms.

Were Soran's suspicions confirmed then? Was this child indeed the long-lost prince of Aurelis? And if so, what did that mean for . . . for everything?

"We can't let him make any more spells," Soran said, his voice heavy but firm. "Power like his can't help but draw attention. For the moment, no one will detect him through the *ruvyn-satra,* but once it passes, he will be in extreme danger."

Nelle nodded. But how Soran expected to keep the child's abilities suppressed, she couldn't begin to imagine. She knew how it felt to suddenly feel and recognize the abilities right at her fingertips, the new worlds opening before her. Denying that part of her soul, her essence, would be . . . agony.

She shook her head and buried her face in both hands, her elbows leaning heavily on the tabletop. "I don't like it. Children ain't meant to be *contained.* They're supposed to be nurtured, right? Helped to grow into what they're meant to be."

"In an ideal world, perhaps." Soran's chair creaked as he shifted position, leaning back. "But in this world, Miss Beck, we have to—"

He broke off suddenly, his voice choking on a gasp that brought Nelle's head up sharply. She saw Soran turned in his chair, saw his eyes widening. She whipped her head around, looking where he looked.

The child was at the door, his shimmering wyvern perched on his shoulder. His hand gripped the latch.

"No!" Soran cried, bolting up from his seat. "Don't open that!"

The child looked back at him, his face a solemn mask, his eyes white-ringed and blazing with a strange light. "I must go," he said, his words like the strokes of a clear, bright bell.

"The storm!" Soran lunged two paces. "You open that door, and—"

He was already too late. Nelle knew it with a hazy, distant, disembodied sort of certainty. She couldn't even quite feel afraid. Sure, her body experienced the surge of reactions one would expect when faced with certain destruction—the rush of blood to the head, the burst of fear in the back of the brain, the juddering halt of the heart. But it seemed to happen to someone else, some other Nelle, while she herself watched helplessly from a distant vantage.

The child turned the latch.

The door blasted open, ripped from his grasp.

A rushing wind made of pure light, pure sound, pure . . . something for which no mortal language had a name, knocked

Soran from his feet, knocked Nelle from her chair, and inundated every thought, every feeling, every sense. It was a kind of oblivion, like death, and Nelle fell into it without hope.

Then she opened her eyes. She wasn't dead. Through the onslaught of magic, she could just discern the physical world around her. She lifted a hand, trying to shield her face, and glimpsed the silhouette of the child still standing there in the doorway, apparently untouched by the gale. He took the wyvern from his shoulder, cupped it in his hands, and held it up to his mouth. He seemed to whisper something close to its dainty, tilted head.

The wyvern, in response, spread wide its four wings. Suddenly it wasn't a delicate butterfly-like thing but grew and swelled into a being of magnificent power, larger than an eagle. It crouched just outside the door, its long neck stretched up to the magic-riven sky, and opened its mouth to sing out, in an otherworldly voice, a song of challenge or triumph.

The boy climbed onto the wyvern's back and wrapped his thin arms around its neck.

"Wait!" Nelle cried, surging up from the floor. She couldn't tell whether her physical body was doing what she told it to do or if she moved only in spirit. Either way, she sprang across the room, reaching for the boy and the wyvern. "Don't go! You can't survive in that!"

The boy glanced back at her over his shoulder, his expression

SYLVIA MERCEDES

mildly confused. Then he looked upward and shouted something in a language Nelle didn't know.

The wyvern's muscles gathered and uncoiled in a powerful motion, the great wings slapping at the magic currents. It rose into the air and vanished into the blinding dizziness of the magic storm within moments.

Nelle, staggering over the threshold of the door, fell in a heap of soul and bones. The *ruvyn-satra* overwhelmed her like a tidal wave.

The first wave rolled over him, obliterating thought and feeling. The force of the blast through the door had knocked him on his back, cracking his head against the floor, but that pain was nothing compared to the tremendous force of magic bursting on his soul.

But he couldn't stay down.

Some urge for survival pulsed through him. He lifted his head and raised one arm, trying vainly to protect his face from that pulsing glow of unchecked power. He saw a shadow move and fixed his gaze upon it as a small relief from the blinding flashes. Blinking hard, he looked again and realized what the shadow was.

"Nelle!" he cried.

The force of the *ruvyn-satra* wind swallowed his voice, but he thought he heard her call from a great distance: "*Wait! Don't go!*"

Her slender silhouette stumbled to the doorway, gripped the posts.

And fell through.

Out into the light.

Out into the storm.

A wordless roar tore from Soran's throat. All reason abandoned his mind, giving place to pure instinct. Against every protest of pain or fear, he surged upright. Arms out in front of him, he strove against that driving blast. He couldn't back down, he wouldn't. Step by step, inch by inch, he fought his way to the door.

There, he poised in the doorway and felt Queen Dasyra's protections, her powerful spells, still striving to keep the worst of the storm from tearing through into the lighthouse. Like a thin veil of silk protecting him from a furnace. To step through that veil would mean certain death.

He didn't hesitate.

One step over the threshold, and he fell. His body simply collapsed, unable to bear the heat, the weight, the glory of the storm. As he fell, he felt something beneath him. Nelle. She too had collapsed the moment she stepped outside Dasyra's shield. She was probably dead already.

He didn't care. If she was dead, so was he. But at least he'd found her. He managed to wrap his arms around her slim frame.

She might be dead, but he would offer her what protection he could, nonetheless. Let it be his last act. One act of selflessness to finish off a long, wretched life of self-absorption.

His heart beat—once, twice, three times.

Then it went on beating—ten, twelve, twenty.

Soran's brow tightened. He wasn't dead yet. Miraculously.

And the *ruvyn-satra?* Was he wrong to believe its power had receded somewhat? If he tried now, might he be able to sit up, to rise?

He tightened his hold on Nelle, grinding his teeth, refusing to believe, refusing to hope. This was the end. It had to be.

But his heart went on beating, and his lungs went on expanding and contracting with each ragged breath. And the terrible pulses of light and shadow faded from his mind.

Finally, he shook his head and opened his eyes.

He saw grass. Long blades of grass blown flat by a powerful wind. And above the grass . . . was that blue sky? Crystal-clear, heavenly blue?

"Seven gods!" Soran breathed and lifted his head a little higher, gaping like a child at the world around him. It all seemed new. New and frightening and wonderful all at once. The lighthouse loomed above him, battered but still whole. White, wispy clouds trailed across the sky, and golden sunlight beamed down, gentle and warm.

The storm had passed more suddenly than it had arrived,

leaving behind a filmy shimmer in the air, a gleam not quite visible to physical sight but unmistakable to those trained in magic. Like a final coat of gloss added to a painting, deepening the color and the shine. It would fade eventually.

Meanwhile, if he stayed where he was, he risked letting that gleam seep into his skin. There the surplus of magic would react with his mortal blood, causing agonizing seizures and violent death.

This was no time to sit around marveling.

Though every muscle protested, Soran heaved his body up, forcing his arms to loosen their hold around Nelle. He looked down at her pale profile, desperate for some sign of life. Trying to be gentle, he rolled her over, pulled her against his chest, and contrived to get to his feet while supporting her weight. He half carried, half dragged her over the threshold into the lighthouse, breathing a huge sigh of relief as Queen Dasyra's protections closed around them again. Then he slammed the door, plunging the chamber into deep gloom.

The blue wyvern, chortling maniacally, performed figure-eight patterns around Soran's feet as he staggered across the shadowy chamber. When his foot came down hard on the creature's tail, it spat, hissed, and scuttled up into the rafters, there to glower down at them, its goggly eyes bright and accusing.

Ignoring the spell beast, Soran carried Nelle to the alcove, laid her down on the pile of furs, and arranged her arms and limbs carefully. He couldn't see her face, couldn't tell if she still lived. Cursing softly, he moved to the fireplace. The gale of the *ruvynsatra* had blown the flames out, leaving only smoldering coals, but he found a stub of candle and hastily lit it before returning to Nelle's side.

Holding the candle over her, he studied her face by its glow. The small flickering flame infused neither warmth nor life into her skin. Soran's throat closed with dread.

"Nelle?" he whispered hoarsely, bending over her, touching her face with his fingertips. Curse his lifeless, useless hands! They felt nothing through the nilarium coating. He set aside his candle and gently pressed his head to her chest, searching for a heartbeat.

A murmuring pulse sounded against his ear.

He closed his eyes and let out a great sigh. She lived. Yet again she'd thrown herself heedlessly into danger and lived.

"I don't know whether you're blessed or cursed," he muttered, starting to lift his head. "But one way or another—"

He stopped. A hand gripped the back of his head, holding him in place, pressing him against the soft fabric of her shirt. He lifted his gaze, trying to see her face, but could discern nothing in the shadows.

"Nelle?" he whispered.

A wordless murmur answered, followed by a long pause. The

hand on his head tightened its hold, then relaxed enough to let him sit upright and bend over her, bringing his face close to hers. The candlelight gleamed in her half-open eyes.

"I'm here," Soran whispered. Her hand fluttered, and he caught and held it in his cold, hard fingers. "I'm here, Nelle. You're safe."

"The . . . the . . ." She drew a long, ragged breath, then tried again. "The boy?"

"He's gone." Soran shook his head. He hadn't seen exactly what took place when the child threw open the door. Had that first blast of the *ruvyn-satra* destroyed him? No, probably not. But where he had gone and whether he would survive, Soran couldn't begin to guess.

Regardless, there would be no messages sent to King Lodírhal to reveal the apparent return of his long-lost child. There would be no hoped-for gratitude or possible leverage. But that didn't matter, not really.

All that mattered was keeping Nelle alive.

"I saw the Evenspire," Soran whispered. Could she hear him? Her eyes were closed again, her face turned toward the wall. He'd have thought she slept but for the tightening across her brow. "The connection between Roseward and Wimborne isn't broken. Not yet, anyway."

How long it would hold? Hours maybe. Days at best. It was a miracle the *ruvyn-satra* hadn't shattered it to pieces.

"You've got to leave," he said, speaking to the curve of her tensed cheek. "You've got to. I can't . . . I couldn't bear it if you were to be trapped here when the Thorn Maiden . . ."

She turned suddenly to him, her eyes flaring open. How blue they were by the candlelight, shimmering with a glassy, feverish glow. Was she awake? He couldn't tell, not even with her gaze fixed intently on him. She might be dreaming, hallucinating. The magic may have seeped too deep into her head.

"Nelle?" he said tentatively, leaning toward her. "Nelle, can you—"

She caught hold of the front of his shirt, her grip surprisingly strong. "Stay with me," she gasped. She struggled to maintain focus, but her eyes began to roll back in her head. "Soran, stay with . . . me . . ."

Her head lolled to one side. But her breathing was slow and steady. She slept. A deep, hard, exhausted sleep.

Soran rested his hand on top of hers. Even in sleep, she clutched his shirt. He couldn't very well send her back to Wimborne in this state. She needed time to recover, a few hours at least.

He attempted to pull back, but her fingers tightened. So, he sat in uncertainty, scarcely daring to breathe as he gazed down at her helpless face and limp body. Warring needs raged within him, urging him in ways he did not like to acknowledge. He should break away, put distance between them. Climb the stairs to his tower chamber. Shut doors. Hide.

Instead, he gave up.

He slid onto the pile of furs beside Nelle and slowly, gently, drew her into his arms. The ties of his shirt were loose, and when she rested her head on his chest, he felt the warmth of her cheek against his bare skin. He shivered, closed his eyes, and pressed his face into her hair. The scent of her was almost overwhelming. He breathed her in like sweet perfume.

"I'm here," he whispered. His lips moved unconsciously, kissing the top of her head once, twice. Then he turned his face away, grimacing at the desire churning inside him. He'd given in up to a point, but here his resolve held.

He would hold her. Comfort her.

But nothing more.

"Sleep," he said. "I've got you. Sleep now, Nelle. Sleep now, dear, wild, foolish girl."

CHAPTER 7

MAGIC BURNED INSIDE HER VEINS, BOILING BENEATH HER skin.

There was a strange kind of delight in the sensation, a beauty in the pain. A sense that if she could only shrug off the heavy mortal frame currently holding her spirit captive, she might become one with this power, and also, in the dissolution of individual identity, discover the truth and wholeness of reality.

But another part of her soul screamed: *No! Hold on! Hold on! You can't die yet!*

Some primal survival instinct drove her to lean into that small, nagging voice. The more she leaned, the sharper and deeper the pain, but with the pain came other sensations as well. Cool skin beneath her cheek, puckered with scars. The steady *boom-boom-boom* of a heartbeat. Strong arms wrapped around her, holding her close, warming and comforting.

And that smell. The unmistakable combination of dusty parchment and sea breezes that she had come to associate, even in her unconscious, with one person.

"Soran." Nelle's lips moved, their dry, blistered skin cracking with the effort. Her raw throat thickened, and she swallowed with difficulty. "Soran."

She tried to open her eyes and found it too difficult. Giving up, she let herself be lost in that enveloping scent, in that sensation of being held, cared for. How long had it been since she'd felt anything like this? It was almost like . . .

Like coming home.

"Soran," she whispered again. But her voice was lost to the oblivion of sleep.

When next she stirred, a cold emptiness had replaced that feeling of safety. She squeezed her eyes tight, trying to retreat into dreamlessness. But it was too late now. She was awake.

At least the pain was gone. Her limbs felt hollow and her chest was sore, but otherwise she seemed to be whole.

Slowly she drew and released a long breath, opening her eyes. The brick arch of the low alcove ceiling met her gaze. She turned her head to one side and saw the lighthouse door standing wide open, daylight pouring through.

The storm. It was gone.

They'd survived.

Nelle sat up. A mistake, she realized almost at once. She buried her face in her hands and nearly flopped back down on the fur rugs as the darkness swimming at the edge of her vision rushed back in. She leaned against the bricks at her back until the dizziness passed and the whirling in her stomach subsided. In her mind's eye she saw flashes of memory. The boy opening the door. His wyvern spreading its four wings and growing. The horror of unchecked magic assaulting every sense—

Something burbled and nudged at her elbow.

Nelle lowered her hands and looked down into the wyvern's blunt-nosed face. It raised its crest inquiringly and tilted its head to one side. "I'm all right, worm," Nelle said, stroking the crest down flat. Heaving a sigh, she turned her gaze again to the open door. For a moment she simply sat there, her brain sluggish.

Then, slowly, she realized: She was alone in the lighthouse.

Soran had stepped outside. He must have. She could almost *feel* the emptiness in the tower above her, like the light of life gone out from a corpse.

How long would he be gone? A few moments? A few hours?

Long enough for . . .?

Nelle grimaced, not liking to finish the thought. But what else was she supposed to think? What else was she supposed to do?

The storm had passed. She must fulfill her mission.

This might be the last opportunity she would ever get.

"Bullspit," she muttered, and pushed the wyvern away as she crawled out of the alcove. Her body ached from the inside, her very bones throbbing with painful tremors left by that assault of magic. She staggered for the tower stair and paused at its base, tipping her head back to examine the hole in the ceiling.

The Rose Book was up there. It had to be. All she had to do was take it. And then somehow slip past Soran, retrieve Sam's boat, and make all speed away from Roseward.

Simple, really.

Yet her feet were like lead.

"Come on, girl," she whispered. "You know what's going to happen. As soon as he returns, he's going to send you away. And you'll have to go this time."

She'd managed to put him off until now. She'd argued and deflected and avoided for two weeks. But her time was up.

"Get moving," she said, setting her jaw. She lifted a foot, planted it on the first step. "Get moving, or else . . . or else . . ."

Before she could take a second step, a sound caught her ear. Footsteps. Just outside.

Soran.

For an instant she froze, her breath caught in her throat. But she didn't have more than an instant. She must make a choice. Now.

Stepping away from the stair and putting her back to the door, Nelle reached inside her shirt, yanked out the locket. It flicked open all too easily, and a familiar burning aroma filled her nostrils. *Rishva*. That's what Kyriakos had called it. Fae poison.

And her last dose.

Nelle dipped her fingertip into the smear of ointment remaining in the locket and hastily rubbed it over her chapped and tender lips. It stung as it worked its way in but left behind a subtle sheen. She'd seen the effect before on Mother's mouth. The enchantment made the lips plumper, more alluring.

"Miss Beck?"

Nelle snapped the locket shut and turned to face the doorway. Soran stood silhouetted, backlit so that she could not see his face. Did he realize what she was doing? Did he smell the trace of poison in the air?

"I hope you are quite recovered, Miss Beck." The mage stepped into the room, ducking to fit under the lintel. A strange tension underscored his voice, belying the rigid formality of his tone.

Standing there with her back against the cold wall, Nelle could almost feel again that sensation of warm arms wrapped around her, holding her through the pain of the magic as it ripped through her body. Had those moments of comfort, of closeness, of safety, been nothing more than a dream?

She shook her head, trying to drive such thoughts away, and

managed to curve her mouth into a wan smile. "I am much better, Mage Silveri. Thank you." She swallowed, cleared her throat, and continued, "Any sign of the boy?"

"I'm afraid not." Leaving the door open behind him, Soran crossed the room to the armoire and took out what looked like a water flask. He moved to the table where her snatcher's satchel lay, picked it up without ceremony, crossed to the supply shelves along the wall, and pulled out the magicked half loaf of bread. "I've been down to the shore," he said, stuffing the bread into her satchel. He proceeded to fill the empty flask from their supply of drinking water. "The bridge to Wimborne holds, but only by a thread. It will dissolve by nightfall, I fear."

"Nightfall," Nelle echoed, watching him. She realized suddenly that he was gathering supplies for her journey. No arguments. No commands. The bridge was breaking. She had to go. If she stayed one more night on Roseward Isle, she would surely die.

Right along with him.

Soran turned to face her at last. "Here are supplies enough to last you three days," he said, holding out the satchel. "The flask will refill at least three times before the magic gives out. The loaf, I believe, will last longer still. I know you said you have enemies in Wimborne, so . . . so I hope this will be enough to get you farther down the coast, away from the city. You can make a new life for yourself." He hesitated a moment, then turned away from her, returning to the armoire. "I have some gold," he said, muttering the words as though he didn't care if she heard him or not. "Somewhere in here, I think. It might help . . ."

Nelle straightened her shoulders and stepped lightly across the room, the aches in her limbs momentarily forgotten in a sudden surge of adrenaline. She moved silently so that he wouldn't hear her, and when she reached out and touched his shoulder, she felt the startled thrill shoot from him through her arm, bursting like sparks in her own thudding heart.

"Soran," she said.

He did not turn.

Should she try to pull him around? To catch his head in her hands and drag his face down to hers for a kiss? Her fingers tightened.

"Miss Beck." His voice rumbled in a growl so low that she struggled to discern the words. "Miss Beck, remember that you cannot use magic once you return. It will be too dangerous for you. The Miphates would hunt you down. It's best if . . . if you forget everything about your time here on Roseward."

"Everything?"

Suddenly there was no plan. Suddenly there was no mission. No Papa waiting for her to rescue him. No Gaspard holding threats above her head. No Rose Book, no Thorn Maiden, no fae kings or curses.

There was only this man—this proud, humbled, broken,

powerful man.

"Everything?" Nelle said again and grimaced against the tears prickling in her eyes. "Soran, I love you."

She heard his breath catch, but otherwise he made no sound. His shoulder stiffened beneath her hand, hard as stone.

"I love you." The words came more easily the second time, and she exhaled in relief. Why had she waited until now to finally unburden her heart of this painful, beautiful truth? She could almost laugh at her own timidity. "You can't be surprised!" she continued, her voice lighter, brighter. "Not after all that's happened."

He was going to speak; she felt the tension mounting inside him. She waited, both hopeful and afraid. For the moment, the burn of the Sweet Dreams on her lips slipped to the background of her awareness.

"Miss Beck," he began, and she winced. Her fingers tightened on his shoulder. "Miss Beck, you cannot love me. You must not."

There was something in his voice, a dark timbre she did not quite understand. It set a fire burning in the pit of her stomach. "Soran—" she began.

"No!" He whirled to face her, yanking out of her grasp. "I won't let you."

He loomed over her, the light from the doorway etching his face in harsh clarity, emphasizing every disfiguring scar. But she did not see the scars. Her gaze fixed instead on his brilliant gray

116

eyes shining with a fervor that almost frightened her. But she wouldn't look away and she wouldn't back down.

"You don't get to tell me what to do," she said. Her hand moved, hovering a moment near his cheek before gently coming to rest. He closed his eyes, and she felt the muscles of his face tighten under her palm. "You don't get to tell me what to think. What to feel. My heart is my own, and I will spittin' well give it where I choose. Where *I* choose, Soran. Not you."

He shook his head. Suddenly his arms reached out, his hands gripped her upper arms. His mouth twisted, the scars pulling at his lips, his teeth flashing in a grimace of pain. "Nelle. Don't."

"Tell me," she said, breathless but determined, "that you don't love me. Say it."

"I . . . I can't."

"Can't tell me? Or can't love me?" She tilted her head to one side, trying to catch his eye as he looked away from her. "Which is it, Soran? Tell me, or I'll—"

Before she was ready, before she could brace herself, before she realized quite what was happening, he pulled her to him. Pulled her into a kiss that sent a shockwave rippling straight to her core.

She responded at once. Her arms wrapped around his neck and pressed him closer, her mouth parting to the force of his kiss. He was hungry, desperate, and she answered in kind. For a moment she forgot about the poison on her lips. For a moment she let herself feel only the foundation-shaking collision of their bodies and souls.

One of his hands moved to her hair, pulling her head back. The other hand, cold and hard, slid the wide neckline of her shirt down over her shoulder, nilarium fingers brushing her skin. She shivered at the chill, and he growled, frustrated. Quickly he changed the course of his kisses, moving to her cheek, her jaw, down her neck to the soft curve of her shoulder and collarbone. The warmth and softness of his mouth chased away the icy touch of nilarium. She tangled her fingers in his hair, her back arching in response to his lips, her mind and body on fire.

Then she felt the change.

A shudder raced through him. He choked, caught his breath, and drew back from her, his lips parted. His eyes struggled to focus. He choked again, his many scars standing out in ridges of pain.

"Nelle?" he gasped, his cold hand sliding from her hair down to her cheek. His fingers tensed, trying to catch hold of her.

"I'm sorry," she whispered as he sank to his knees. His eyes rolled, focused, rolled again. She reached out, touched his face, her heart twisting with pain. Tears streamed down her cheeks, unchecked. "I'm sorry. There's no other way."

He collapsed on his side, his hair splayed out on the floor.

The Sweet Dreams had done its work.

CHAPTER 8

SORAN LAY WITH ONE ARM TWISTED BENEATH HIM. HIS shoulder ached where it had hit the floor. His head ached too, but he wasn't as aware of that pain as he struggled to drag his mind into focus, to force his half-open eyes to fight against the encroaching darkness. Unconsciousness ebbed and flowed around him. Only a will of iron kept him from succumbing, from letting himself be pulled into the beckoning shadows of his mind.

Nelle.

Had she done this to him?

No, he must not be thinking clearly. It was the Thorn Maiden's work. It must be. Or some other enemy, come upon them unawares.

Nelle wouldn't . . . she wouldn't . . .

He heard the familiar creak as footsteps descended the tower stair. With an effort that sent stabs of pain shooting through his skull, Soran raised his eyelids just a little, just enough to look. Nelle. She was there. He watched her bare feet tripping lightly down the steps to the ground floor. He tried to raise his gaze, to search for her face, but couldn't. Unconsciousness claimed him again.

In the darkness inside his head, something waited. Something many-coiled and violent, surrounded in an atmosphere of sweetest perfume.

So, my love. At last, you see the truth of her nature.

A slithering sensation moved across his soul, tearing as it went. He tried to withdraw, but the walls of his mind pressed too close. He was trapped.

Too late for you. Always too late, I fear.

A long, agonizing tear ripped across his awareness. His soul bled black blood.

Why could you never learn? There is only one true and pure love in all this world. The love you created in me from the first moment of my being. The love I have longed to share with you . . .

"Soran."

Nelle. Her voice, soft but clear, spoke in his ear.

The sound drew him back into physical reality. His half-opened eyes cleared, peering through his lowered lashes. She knelt beside him. His arm no longer ached, and he realized that she must have rolled him over. He seemed to be lying on his back now, gazing up at her. Her fingers brushed strands of hair from his face.

He tried to speak. *What is happening? Are you all right? Were we attacked?* The words were there on his tongue, but he could not force them through his lips. His burning lips . . .

Nelle leaned over him. A long hank of red hair fell over her shoulder, brushing against his cheek before she tossed it back impatiently. Her freckled face filled his vision, blurring and clarifying by turns.

"I didn't have a choice," she said. "I'm sorry. I'm sorry I never told you the truth. Why I came to Roseward. Much of what I said was true, but . . . but I didn't tell you everything."

What was she talking about? Hard suspicion knotted in his heart.

Nelle . . . no. Not Nelle. Not her.

"I know you won't forgive me." Tears shimmered in her eyes but did not fall. "I want to save you. I think I can. I know you can't stop the Thorn Maiden, not on your own. But Mage Gaspard . . . maybe he can."

Gaspard.

Gaspard?

A spasm shot through Soran's soul, powerful enough to make

his limbs jolt. Not enough to drive out the paralysis holding him fast, but enough that Nelle started and withdrew a little, her eyes widening. Gaspard! What about Gaspard? What had he done? How did she know him?

Nelle sat back, and he saw something tucked under her arm—a ratty, rotted, red-leather cover.

The Rose Book.

NO!

The scream ripped through his spirit, tearing more deeply even than the Thorn Maiden's embrace. But he could not give voice to it in his physical body. He was trapped. She'd poisoned him. Nelle had poisoned him.

Betrayed him.

No, no, no! Not her! Not Nelle! Let her be true. Let all others be false, be liars. Let his own soul be damned for his sin. But let Nelle be true!

She clutched the book to her breast. He saw the awful reality in her face, the guilt shining bright in her eyes. The layers of sweet masks she had worn as she played with him, toyed with him over these excruciatingly lovely weeks, crumbled away.

He should have seen it long ago. He should have known.

She was just like Helenia.

"I hate to leave you like this." Nelle bowed her head. "The Sweet Dreams will wear off by tomorrow morning, and you'll be safe overnight. The Thorn Maiden won't hurt you ever again."

She started to rise but stopped. His vision darkened again, blurred, but he struggled to focus. He saw her jaw tighten as though she fought with herself.

Then she turned, bowed over him once more. Her eyes shimmered above his, blue as the sky on a clear summer day.

"I don't know if you can hear me," she whispered. "And I know what you'll think of me when you wake up and find what I've done. But I meant what I said. I love you, Soran Silveri. I always will."

She closed her eyes, bent her head. Was he imagining that slight pressure against his burning lips, that gentle touch? No. It couldn't be real. This was nothing but a dream. It had to be. It had to be!

Oh, please all the seven gods, let it be a dream . . .

He sank into the deep well of his mind. Darkness closed over his soul. Some part of him was vaguely aware of Nelle rising, of her footsteps crossing the floor, the firm clunk of the door being shut. But that part of him was so distant it might not exist at all. There was nothing real anymore save this darkness.

And that which moved in the darkness.

I am going now, my love. She is taking me from you. I cannot stop her. If you had let me kill her when she first arrived, we wouldn't have to part, but alas! You proved yourself the faithless lover, chasing after her pretty face and shapely form, even when you knew. You knew I was here. Waiting for you. Loving you.

Longing for you . . .

Thorny arms wrapped around him, drawing him close, tearing into his mind, deep as plunging daggers. But soon they began to fade, fade, fade.

Farewell, my darling. Farewell, my own. I go on to new worlds now to find new loves. But I will never forget you.

Her voice dropped low and sweet, one last ripping wound.

I love you, Soran Silveri. I always will.

Then she was gone. And there was only darkness.

Sam's boat was still in the cave where they had hidden it four days ago. Nelle checked it over carefully for signs of damage, but the magic storm seemed to have left it unscathed. Her snatcher's satchel dragging against the small of her back, she hauled the boat out of the cave and down the beach. It was harder to manage without Sam's help, but she was determined.

It was time to put this whole world behind her. Time to return to reality.

She looked out across the water while she hauled the boat, fixing her gaze on the Evenspire. It might vanish at any moment, and when it did, so too would vanish all chance of finding her way back to Wimborne. This thought lent strength to her tired, aching limbs. She pushed the boat at last into the foamy surf, her trouser legs soaking with freezing water up to the knee.

Scrambling aboard, Nelle assumed her position on the rowing bench and began to pull away. Away from the beach where she had first met the silent, hooded mage. Away from the cliffs wherein the wyverns made their nests. Away from the lighthouse standing battered but strong high above her.

Away from Soran.

Tears misted her eyes and slid through her lashes, but she scarcely felt them. Her cheeks were already wet and frozen from sea spray and drizzle. Though the sky had been bright and clear in the magic storm's wake, dark clouds had rolled in while she descended the cliff path and hauled the boat. A storm—not a magic storm but still dangerous—could break at any moment. If she weren't so desperate to get away, she wouldn't dare brave the open water.

But she couldn't stay. Not another day. Not another minute.

No wyverns flitted in the sky overhead; they were all still safely folded up in their little spell pages, stored away in the mage's armoire. All save the crippled wyvern, of course.

Was that him she saw on the cliff's edge, a small gangly blue figure, awkwardly running back and forth on its haunches, wings upraised?

"Poor little worm," she whispered. "You shouldn't have let yourself get attached to someone like me. You should've known better . . ."

Nelle sniffled and tried to focus her energy on the push and pull of her oars. But her gaze drifted across the wide, seemingly endless water. Would she find the Veil and pass through, back into her own world? Would Wimborne still be there? Or had Roseward drifted too far off its course and into the Hinter between worlds?

With a grunting prayer, she pulled harder. Though she did not like to look at it, she made herself focus on the lighthouse tower itself, needing something to help her keep her bearings as a rough sea battered at her small craft and the gathering clouds overhead growled dire threats.

Then the heavens opened. Rain fell in sheets, pounding her bowed shoulders, soaking through her thin shirt. Nelle hastily settled one oar so she could tuck her snatcher's satchel a little closer to her side. She could only hope the stout leather would be enough protection for the Rose Book inside. What would happen if the book disintegrated before she'd crossed through the Veil? Would the Thorn Maiden manifest beside her in the boat and tear her to pieces out here on the water?

Or she might appear beside her fallen master. She might wrap him in her innumerable arms to shred his flesh and his soul while he lay unconscious and helpless . . .

Nelle closed her eyes against the battering rain and screamed all her rage and sorrow, shrieking into the relentless, uncaring wind. But it was a futile sort of wrath. What did she or her stupid mortal feelings matter in the face of forces so far beyond her control or understanding?

Gnashing her teeth, she gripped both oars with white-knuckled fingers, pulling, pulling, pulling. The waves tore at her boat, trying to spin her out of control until she nearly vomited with dizzying fear roaring in her head.

A sensation like ice lanced through her heart. She gasped and doubled up, dropping her hold on her oars. For some moments she could only sit there holding onto herself, shuddering at the pain that vibrated through every bone of her body.

Slowly, after what felt like agonized years, dull awareness returned.

The rain had stopped.

Nelle blinked and, still shivering, pulled herself upright.

Roseward lay in clear view, calm under a sunny sky. All was still and peaceful. Lifeless.

Pushing soaked lengths of hair out of her face, Nelle turned sharply. Wimborne sprawled before her. She wasn't even half a mile from the shore. There were the docks where the river let out into the sea. There was the ruinous Tyrane Fortress where she'd spent the night as Gaspard's captive. There were the majestic palaces and manor houses built on high outcroppings to provide their lordly occupants the best, most sweeping views.

And there stood the Evenspire, straight and tall as a giant's spear, casting a long shadow out across the water.

It all looked exactly like she'd left it.

Drawing a ragged breath, Nelle faced Roseward and pulled for the shore. After the storm she'd just escaped, this stretch of water was almost too easy. Her boat flitted along briskly despite her awkward strokes. She watched the island shrink and felt her heart shrinking right along with it.

Every few strokes, she turned to check the shore again, aiming for the old fortress. Would Gaspard be there waiting for her? What if years had passed since she left this world behind? What if Gaspard had given up on her return?

What if no one she knew was still living?

Before she had a chance to parse through this sickening idea, she spotted three figures approaching along the beach, coming from the Tyrane tower. Two were broad, slouchy men in grubby tunics and heavy boots, but the third . . . she would know that tall, athletic frame anywhere. Those broad, bony shoulders, those long, rangy arms, and that unmistakable sauntering stride.

"Sam," Nelle whispered. Then she added with a snarl, "Bullspit."

These were Cloven's men. So Cloven must still be under Gaspard's thumb.

Well, perhaps she should be grateful. At least Sam was with them. But could she trust Sam?

Probably not.

Nelle turned her back to the men to row the last few yards. As soon as her boat crunched into the beach, she hopped out, soaking her damp trousers all over again, and hauled it up far enough that the waves couldn't drag it back out to open water.

The three men strode toward her along the strand. Sam walked a few paces ahead of the others, his dark hair blown loose by the sea breeze. Nelle turned to meet him and was surprised to see a dark growth of beard framing his jaw. She'd seen him only two days ago. Certainly not time enough for a full beard to grow in.

How many more days, months, or years, had passed here in the mortal world while she was trapped by the *ruvyn-satra?*

"Ginger!" Sam called out, raising a hand in greeting. "As I live and breathe. The watchman said he saw a redheaded girl in a boat coming from Roseward, but I hardly dared believe it."

Nelle gave the boat one last heave to make certain it stayed in place. Then she stood upright, sliding her snatcher's satchel around to rest on her hip, and gripped the strap with both hands. "How long has it been, Sam?" she asked.

The bright smile on his face faded, replaced by a grave expression which, when coupled with his beard, aged his face. "A year, Nelle. A full year."

Her stomach pitched. She clutched the strap like a lifeline and braced her legs, only just managing to stay on her feet. A pit of fear yawned before her, threatening to drag her down. Another year? And what of her Papa? She looked into Sam's eyes, trying to work up the courage to ask. But her mouth hung open; her lips were numb.

Sam, his eyes flicking swiftly across her face, took another step toward her. "Don't worry," he said, putting out a hand. "Everything's going to be—"

One of the two larger fellows growled and stepped up beside Sam, glowering. "Orders say no one's to talk to the snatcher. Mage Gaspard is on his way. We got to take her up."

Nelle looked the big man up and down slowly. Mother's training kicked in, and she found herself noting all the potential weak spots on his body. His bulging gut might be too cushioned with fat for her elbow to do much damage, but the way he sagged on his feet indicated a bum knee. She could use that. One swift kick, and he'd stagger, giving her opportunity to jab her fingers into his throat, then bring her elbow down on the back of his neck as he doubled over. By then the other two would be in motion, and Sam was quick, she knew from experience. But Sam's weakness was an unwillingness to hurt her, a weakness she could leverage, if only . . .

There was no point in thinking this way. She couldn't defend herself.

She had to save Papa.

"All right then. Take me up, why don't you?" she growled, lifting her gaze to meet the ruffian's squinting pale eyes.

Sam reached for her satchel. She jumped back sharply, flashing her teeth at him. "Nuh-uh. This is for Gaspard and no one but Gaspard. You hear me?"

Sam's brows drew together slightly. She saw the hurt in his eyes but didn't care. What right had he to be hurt? This was his fault as much as anyone's. If he had any honor, he'd have broken from Cloven long ago. But Sam, for all his big heart, was as keen on snatching his next big break as the next desperate soul. And Cloven's promises had always been too tempting to resist.

"All right, girlie, let's go," said the second of the two goons, a man she recognized. He'd been in her attic home that night when Cloven tied her father to a chair and threatened his life unless Nelle brought home a certain quill pen stolen from the Evenspire. She remembered seeing blood on this fellow's knuckles.

Swallowing the bile that rose in her throat, she allowed the two big fellows to flank her. Sam cast her one last entreating look, which she staunchly ignored. So he turned on his heel and led the way up the beach, making for the ruinous fortress at a quick pace. Nelle struggled to keep up, her legs still wobbly from the bouncing waves of the Hinter Sea.

A strong desire to pause, to look back over her shoulder, to seek one last glimpse of Roseward pricked in her heart. But she deliberately focused on the swaying strands of Sam's queue. No looking back. No regrets. She'd done the job.

Now she would deal with the consequences.

CHAPTER 9

"I'M SORRY. I DON'T LIKE LEAVING YOU IN THIS PLACE. IT won't be long, I swear. Word's gone to Gaspard, and he'll be here soon as he can."

Nelle stood in the dark, windowless cell, her back to Sam. So, after all this, she was right back where she'd started. Gaspard's prisoner. She tightened her grip on her snatcher's satchel and drew her shoulders back.

"It's fine, Sam," she lied, her voice leaden.

Sam, standing in the open doorway, shuffled his feet behind her. She could easily imagine how he rubbed the back of his neck and shook his head regretfully. Damn him and his regret! What good had it ever done anyone?

"Are you going to shut me in?" she asked, turning suddenly to face him. A small patch of light from a window outside the cell lit up half his face but not enough for her to read his expression.

"I don't want to," he said. "It's just the job, you know? But they're not going to hold you long. Once you've turned over whatever that is"—he waved a hand to indicate her satchel— "Gaspard will set you free. Cloven just wants to make sure you don't run off on us before the handoff, that's all. He's afraid you'll try to sell elsewhere, you see."

"Cloven thinks I'd abandon my Papa for the chance at a bigger cash-in?" Nelle shook her head, her lips twisting with the need to either spit or curse. Before she could decide which, she saw Sam duck his head, avoiding her eye. That constant gnawing worry in the pit of her stomach intensified tenfold.

"Sam," she said, "what is it? What do you know about Papa? Did you find him? After you left Roseward, you told me you'd find out what happened to him."

Sam didn't answer. He stepped back, and she feared he would shut the cell door then and there without speaking another word.

"No, Sam!" She lunged, caught hold of his wrist, latched on tight. "You've got to tell me! Did . . . did Gaspard hurt him?"

"It's going to be all right, Nelle," Sam said, pulling his arm without enough force to break free. He looked down into her eyes, his expression so strange she couldn't begin to read it. "I promise, Mr. Beck is—"

A scrape of stone and iron drowned out whatever else he might have said. A door at the end of the narrow corridor opened, and Cloven appeared in the shadows so suddenly that Nelle let go of Sam and stepped back, surprised and disgusted all at once. Though it had been only a few weeks since she'd last seen him, three years had passed for Cloven, and the time had not been kind to him. His once impressive muscular frame had sagged into fat around the gut, and his square face had turned jowly, splotched with ugly red patterns his beard couldn't quite disguise. When he grinned, the light from the window revealed empty gaps in his gums that had not been there before.

"Welcome home, pretty Peronelle." He spoke in a rumbling purr. "I knew you'd make it. Gaspard doubted, but I told him Seroline's daughter was good for the snatch. I told him, and look how you've gone and proved my word!"

"Your word is garbage," Nelle snarled. She took an aggressive step toward him, but Sam caught hold of her shoulder and hissed in her ear, "Don't be stupid, Nelle!" She strained against his hold, crying, "Where's my Papa, you son of a brag?"

Cloven's gaping smile grew. He beckoned to Sam. "Bring her. The mage is here, wants to see her right away."

"Yes, sir," Sam said. The words made Nelle sick. She cast a glare up at Sam, who didn't meet her eye. "Come on, Nelle," he said quietly and pushed her into motion, gripping her shoulders.

It wasn't as if she had a choice.

Cloven led the way from the cell and down a narrow stone stair. The sea wind howled around the tower, finding its way through chinks and cracks in the mortar, but the structure itself was surprisingly solid despite being one of the more ancient buildings in all Wimborne. Nelle didn't recall much of the history surrounding the Tyrane fortress, but she thought perhaps it had been abandoned, not for any structural compromise, but rather due to a series of curses left behind generations ago, when the fae were finally driven from Wimborne.

Not quite realizing what she did, Nelle reached out with her fae senses, trying to detect some trace of lingering magic. She felt nothing, however. Perhaps the curses were long gone. Or perhaps her powers of perception had faded now that she'd returned to the mortal world. Just as well if so. She wasn't supposed to use her magic. She wasn't supposed to know anything about magic at all.

Cloven brought them to a long hall on the ground floor of the fortress. It had once probably served as an armory but now stood empty. The tall, sea-facing windows let in light that fell in bars across the cracked stone floor. The brilliant contrasts of brightness and shadow made seeing difficult, but Nelle, squinting around Cloven's lumbering bulk, spied the figure standing at the end of the hall—tall, robed, and solemn.

Her heartbeat quickened.

"Here she is, your mageship." Cloven's loud voice echoed harshly against the stone walls and high ceiling. "I told you, didn't I? Best snatcher Wimborne has to offer, and she's made it back to us at last."

Mage Gaspard didn't acknowledge Cloven with so much as a glance. His gaze fixed with the intensity of a viper's on Nelle, but he held his tongue. Sam marched her toward him until she stood a mere three feet away, directly in one of the patches of sunlight while Gaspard remained in the shadows, his eyes glittering. Even with her *ibrildian* eyesight, Nelle couldn't read his expression. She drew herself up straight and met his gaze without blinking. A painfully long silence ensued.

"Well?" Gaspard spoke at last.

No preamble. No eloquent banter. Just that slightly breathless urgency underscored by many years' worth of impatience.

Nelle hesitated. How many times had she thought about this moment, justifying the choices that would inevitably lead her here? She felt the weight of the book in her satchel press against her hip. She could try to run . . . but where? Come nightfall, the Thorn Maiden would rise. And no one could bind her back. No one except—maybe—this man.

There` could be only one choice.

"Where is my father?" she demanded, clutching the strap of her satchel tight. Her voice quavered when she spoke, and she hated herself for showing weakness.

Gaspard laughed, a strange, almost lunatic sound. He took a step, moving out of the shadows and into the sunlight. She looked up into that handsome, predatory face and nearly recoiled. But Sam stood at her back, and she had nowhere to go.

"Poor sweet child," the mage said, shaking his head. "All this time, did you really think I would bother scouring Draggs Street after one useless old man? Just to have his hands chopped off?" He reached out and, before she could think to duck away, chucked her under the chin. "As far as I'm aware, Mr. Beck is alive and still possessed of all necessary appendages. Not that I've bothered to inquire as to his health of late. I'm sure our friend here would know," he added, tossing a glance to where Cloven stood by the wall. "You may ask him at your leisure, if . . ."

All traces of mirth vanished from Gaspard's face. His eyes grew hard and poisonous. "Did you get it, girl?"

Nelle's head whirled, and her knees threatened to buckle.

She'd betrayed Soran for . . . for a lie? Or was this another lie as well?

She wanted to scream, wanted to fight. She wanted to hurl herself at Gaspard and tear his eyes out with her own curled fingers.

Two figures closed in on either side of her, the same two thugs who'd met her along with Sam on the beach. She saw their fists curl, ready to do violence at a nod from the mage. She looked up into Gaspard's eyes and hoped he sensed the hatred she felt for him burning through her gaze.

Drawing a deep breath, she slipped the Rose Book out of the satchel.

He reacted like a child suddenly offered a favorite sweet. His face lit up with greedy excitement, and he sprang at her, snatching the book from her hands. He turned his embroidered back to her, and she heard the delicate sounds of pages being turned, heard him gasp and whisper to himself.

Nelle exchanged sideways glances with the two thugs. One of them blinked impassively while the other offered a suggestive leer and mimed kisses at her. She answered with a rude gesture and crossed her arms.

"I'd be careful if I was you," she said, speaking to Gaspard's bowed shoulders. "That spell won't hold much longer. If you know what's good for you, you'll make a new one right away."

Gaspard looked over his shoulder, his dark eyes shining with a strange, frightening joy. "And you've learned so much about magic over these last three years, snatcher girl?"

"I may've picked up a thing or two."

The mage's smile grew. His face was still very handsome, just as she remembered it. But that smile of his was ugly enough to make her flesh creep. "I'm sure Soran was pleased to have such a willing, um . . . *student* at his disposal."

Her stomach clenched. "Are we done here, Gaspard?"

This was the moment when she fully expected him to give a

139

swift order to his men. The moment when she expected them to draw their blades and turn on her. The moment when she would fight for her life. And most likely lose. Sam wouldn't help her. Though he stood strong and solid at her back, he would never cross Cloven. He would stand by and let them plunge their knives into her body while he looked on with so much useless regret.

Her pulse raced. She shifted her stance slightly, preparing for whatever came next.

She wasn't prepared, however, for Gaspard to step forward abruptly, his face still blazing with exultant triumph, to catch her by the back of the head and kiss her. It was a hard, possessive, ugly sort of kiss, and Nelle screeched and gnashed her teeth and would have bitten him if she could. He pulled back and deftly blocked the blow she swung at his face, catching her wrist.

"Enough of that, my venomous little beauty," he said, his fingers gripping painfully. He wrenched her arm, and she gasped and went down to her knees. She started to rise again, but he pushed her onto the hard stone floor. "You owed me a kiss after that poison you dealt me when first we met."

"I don't owe you nothing, pig!" she snarled and tried to rise. But he maintained his grip on her arm and applied more pressure, making her cry out. She distantly heard Sam's voice sputter protests, but it made no difference. If only she'd not used the last of the Sweet Dreams! If only a trace remained on her lips, enough to make Gaspard double up with sickness!

The mage bent over her, his mouth close to her ear, breath tickling her neck. "You owe me *everything*. Never forget it." With a last push that sent her face down into the floor, he let go. "But you've done well. Against all hope, beyond my wildest dreams. Yes, you made me wait rather longer than I liked, but still . . ." He held up the red volume and drummed his fingers along the gold rose on the cover. "In light of your success, I won't bear a grudge. Go now. Scramble back to the rat hole from whence you crawled. I'll send a message if I have further need of your services."

She threw back her tangle of hair and glared at him, baring her teeth. Gaspard only laughed again and beckoned to the two men beside him as he turned, stepped back into the shadows at the end of the long hall, and vanished through a doorway, leaving Nelle crumpled on the floor.

Sam knelt beside her, placing a hand on her back. Nelle lacked the strength in that moment to shrug him off. What had she done? Oh, what had she done? Giving the Rose Book to that monster . . .

"There, Nelle," Sam murmured, his hand moving in soothing circles along her spine. "There, it's all over now."

"Get her up, boy," Cloven growled. His large, booted feet shifted into Nelle's line of view. "Send her on her way. And you, girl, no more of that sniffling. You're lucky Gaspard sees use for you in the future. I thought sure he'd spill your guts right here on the spot."

Nelle pulled up onto her knees, her arms wrapped around her middle. The last thing she wanted was to let either of these men see her broken. She glared up at Cloven and hissed, "Bastard!" with all the venom she could muster. But it came out weak and foolish, and she wished at once she could take it back. Too late now, so she continued, "Mother would *hate* you for what you've done."

One dark brow rose up Cloven's blotchy forehead. "Eh, well. I dealt with enough of Seroline's hatred while she lived; I'm sure I can deal with a bit more from beyond the grave." He motioned to Sam again, who obeyed, taking Nelle by the elbow and pulling her to her feet. "See you around, pretty Peronelle," Cloven said, waving them off.

Nelle bit her tongue, refusing to answer, and let Sam guide her back down the stone hall. Her head was spinning, and she scarcely paid attention to where they went, vaguely aware of a series of doors, a courtyard, and a portcullis and bridge, until they emerged at last under the open sky. Sam then guided her up a sandy road away from the ruins and back toward the city proper. She realized she was sagging heavily against him, realized that he had slipped an arm around her waist. That was too much.

With a wordless growl, she pushed him away so viciously, he staggered and nearly fell. "Oi, Nelle!" he cried, his eyes flashing hurt. "Careful, or you'll knock yourself over next. I'm only trying to help, you know."

"*Help?*" Nelle spat. "Is that what you call this? Do me a favor, Samton Rallenford—*don't* try to help me. Do you hear?"

"Oh, come on now," he said, stepping toward her, his hands outstretched. "You don't mean—"

She was too fast for him: Her arm made a short arc, and her hand smacked across his face with a sharp crack. He yelped and doubled over, clutching his cheek. Her fingers stung, but she didn't care. Shaking her hand out, she gnashed her teeth. "I never want to see you again. Got that? We ain't friends anymore. I ain't sure we ever were."

Still bent over, Sam looked up at her. To her horror, she saw tears shining in his eyes. Real tears.

"Nelle," he said so quietly she had to read her name on his lips. "I'm sorry."

"Yeah." Nelle sniffed and roughly rubbed the back of her hand across her nose. "Yeah, I just bet you are."

With that, she marched on up the winding beach road, leaving Sam behind. Wimborne loomed ahead, huge and smoky and fetid and familiar. The life she had left behind, now beckoning her home.

She'd never escape. She'd never stop being the snatcher girl from Dragg's Street. Anything else, any hope, any dream of what she might have been, of who she might have become . . . it was all for nothing.

CHAPTER 10

SHE WAS EVEN MORE BEAUTIFUL IN DREAMS THAN SHE was in his memory. In dreams, even the slightest of imperfections in the symmetry of her face or the desirability of her figure melted away, leaving behind an image of pure sensual perfection.

He saw her now. In the empty spaces of his mind left behind by the Thorn Maiden, dreams crept in as they hadn't for many long years. No thorns tore at his unconscious. Instead, hazy snatches of imagery filled his head, random visions of his youth caught in a sickening yet beautiful aura.

He saw her in her wedding gown, poised on the staircase above the foyer, one hand resting lightly on the banister, her head held high as she received the gasps of praise from onlookers below.

He saw her as a long-limbed child, her figure only just beginning to soften into a womanly shape, running wildly across the lawn, her dark hair flowing behind her as she tossed him a teasing grin.

He saw her opening the door of his room, her face highlighted by the low fire on his hearth, her body loosely clad in a silken robe that strained across her full bosom, ready to fall away.

He saw her again and again . . . all those sweet, excruciating moments which, no matter how he tried to suppress them, would never truly leave his heart.

Helenia. His first love. His first heartbreak. The torment of his soul.

Soran groaned, desperate to retreat from those images. He must remember who he was; he must remember where he belonged. Not here, not in this world of idealized memories. He had a job to do, didn't he? He must . . . he must . . . but he couldn't remember . . .

Helenia, wrapping her arms around his neck. Whispering soft and low: "*You know you're the only one I ever loved. He can go hang himself for all I care.*"

Her soft flesh pressed against his body.

"*Why did you marry him? Why didn't you wait? You promised you'd wait!*"

Her lips toying with his earlobe. *"Why do you waste your breath? Give me what I need. Give me what I crave. Give me—"*

Then she fell. Crumpling in his arms. Blood poured from her mouth, dripped down her chin, her bosom, and spread in a stain across the beaded bodice of her gown. He stared into her face, frantically searching for the spark of life already fled. Only . . . only . . .

Only it wasn't Helenia he held in his arms.

"Nelle?"

With a choking gasp, Soran's body spasmed and his eyes flared open. For an instant he wasn't dreaming. He saw the ceiling rafters overhead, felt the tickle of floor rushes under his body, the hard stone floor.

His lungs constricted, unable to draw more air. And he fell again, sinking into darkness. But this time the darkness didn't fade into dreams. His mind remained present just behind his eyelids. After what felt like an age of concentration, he dragged his awareness back up from the depths, becoming aware of the world around him.

The lighthouse. He was in the lighthouse. Lying on the floor. Poisoned. Paralyzed? He grimaced and, with an effort, managed to twitch his right hand. Not paralyzed then.

Nelle.

His heart thudding against his ribcage, Soran gasped with pain and managed to wrench his eyes open. He stared at the rafters overhead. They seemed to rotate slowly. He refused to close his eyes again, waiting until the rotation ceased and the world settled.

She came for the Rose Book.

All along that was her plan. To find and take the Noswraith spell. But . . . but why?

Gaspard.

Soran grimaced, his jaw clenching painfully. Gaspard. The fool! All these years, and he still hadn't lost his thirst for power, his need to find and claim and possess the secret, the forbidden.

He'd sent Nelle. Nelle, of all people.

Why her?

Shame flooded Soran's being in a hot rush. Of course. Gaspard *knew* him. Knew his vices, knew his weaknesses. Gaspard had known it would only be a matter of time before his old friend proved himself an idiot yet again, falling for the pretty girl and her pretty face and her appearance of innocence. Back in his student days, he'd never been one to deny himself any easy pleasure, all the while telling himself it didn't matter because his heart was true to Helenia.

Gaspard knew. And Gaspard had schemed a brilliant scheme.

So. Nelle was just a tool. A trap baited with sweetest honey.

Soran clenched his fists, fingers curling slowly. What, by the names of all the seven gods, was that drug she'd used on him? Some fae enchantment, no doubt—activated by a kiss.

Something Kyriakos had given her? No, she must have brought it herself. So, all her apparent ignorance of her powers, of her heritage, must have been a lie as well.

He should have seen through her from the start.

Slowly, painfully, Soran pushed up onto his elbows. Rolling onto his side, he heaved again and managed to get into a seated position. The fire was dead on the hearth, the coals long since turned gray and lifeless. Morning light poured in through the windows. How long had he lain unconscious? Overnight, apparently.

Which meant the Thorn Maiden was gone. Otherwise, she would have torn him apart while he slept.

"Damn," Soran growled. He got to his feet, nearly fell again, but managed to fling a hand out to catch hold of the armoire. He waited until the room stopped spinning, then staggered for the door.

A faint scratching, whining noise met his ear. When he wrenched the door open, the wyvern, sitting upright on the doorstep, gazed bug-eyed up at him. It *meeped* and raised its crest.

"I know," Soran said. "She's gone." He leaned heavily on the door frame, struggling to catch his breath. The drug, whatever it was, had left him terribly lightheaded. But he had no time to waste.

Pushing past the whimpering wyvern, he made his way

through the door to the edge of the cliff. Through the distant clouds he could just see the Evenspire. It was farther away than it had been the last time he looked. But he could still see it. That was something, at least.

Maybe . . . maybe . . .

Lodírhal would come to Roseward. Sooner rather than later now that the *ruvyn-satra* was past. Word must have reached him already of a Noswraith attacking Noxaur, and he would come to investigate.

How would he react when he discovered the Thorn Maiden had been taken to the mortal world?

Soran frowned grimly. Lodírhal would be delighted by this turn of events. He'd say let the mortals have a taste—a very small taste—of what the fae experienced under Noswraith assault. He would leave the monster to ravage Wimborne.

And he would kill Soran without a second thought.

"Let him," Soran muttered. "Let him come. Let him stab me through the heart."

But he didn't mean it. Not yet, anyway. The Thorn Maiden was his creation. His mistake. He could not leave her unbound and loose in the mortal world.

Somehow, he must get her back to Roseward. Before it was too late.

CHAPTER 11

THE FAMILIARITY OF DRAGGS STREET CLOSED AROUND HER IN A stranglehold.

Nelle walked with her head down, her hair a ragged veil shielding her face. She was painfully aware of her bedraggled state—the trousers tied at her waist with a bit of rope, the loose, stained, wrinkled shirt meant for a man twice her breadth, and her cold bare feet. She looked weak, vulnerable, a prime target.

But it was still early in the morning. The worst rats of Draggs society were still deep in their holes, sleeping off vices of the night before. A few vicious-eyed children darted up to pinch her and try to trip her up. Nelle whirled on them, snarling and swearing, swatting at their ears, and they scampered out of reach to watch her more warily from alleys and doorways.

The weight on her heart threatened to bend her in half as she stumbled on down the street. At least she was back where she belonged. Back among the rotten alleys and squalor and desperation and savagery that made up this world. Her world. And she was as rotten, squalid, desperate, and savage as anyone here.

She made her way at last to the listing row houses above the muck-clogged banks of the River Wim and drew within sight of her old—for want of a better word—*home.* Lifting her gaze to the attic window, she searched for some sign that Papa might still be there. She'd paid old lady Dirgin through to the end of the month. But if it really was three years since she'd left . . .

A bubble of fear swelled in her throat. Nelle surged up the crumbling front steps to the door of the third house from the left and pounded hard until her fist stung. "Mistress Dirgin! Mistress Dirgin!" she cried. The door rattled in its frame, and she might have knocked it in if she'd kept pounding long enough.

It felt like years but was probably less than a minute before stumping footsteps sounded from inside. "What in the scatting hell?" a harsh voice bellowed. "Some scat-brained wench a hollerin' at my door like she's gone and—"

The door opened. Mistress Dirgin's grim face appeared, red with rage. Immediately, all the blood drained from her sagging cheeks. "Seven gods above and below!" she gasped. "Is that really you, girl?"

"Where's Papa?" Nelle gasped. She almost fell through the door but grabbed the doorpost and held on hard. She wouldn't cross this threshold again unless she had to. "Where is he, Mistress Dirgin?"

"Why he's . . . he's in the kitchen." The old woman pointed over her shoulder with one jutting thumb. "He's havin' his breakfast jus' now an'—"

"What?" Nelle shook her head. That made no sense. She and Papa were never permitted down to the kitchens, and Mistress Dirgin certainly never fed them breakfast. "What's he . . .?"

She took another look at Mistress Dirgin's haggard old face, and suspicion dropped in her belly like a stone.

Without bothering to finish the question, she pushed past the landlady, ignoring a stream of protesting expletives, and hastened down the narrow passage, dodging tenement children along the way. She burst through the low door into the kitchen, startling the man seated at the table.

The man in a faded waistcoat that had once boasted bright silver buttons, all of which were sold and replaced with wooden ones, years ago. The man whose broken nose would never look quite right on his fine-boned face. The man with a dreamer's glint in his eye, who never knew what to make of the ugly realities of his own existence.

SYLVIA MERCEDES

The man who had fallen in love with a wild, dangerous, madcap beauty, giving up all his worldly prospects to be with her . . . and lost everything as a result.

"Papa," Nelle whispered.

Mixael Beck sat with a wooden spoon partway to his open mouth and stared at her, his face devoid of recognition. Then, slowly, the haze in his eyes cleared, replaced by a sudden light.

"Nellie?"

He dropped the spoon and sprang to his feet, overturning the bowl of watery oatmeal. He darted around the table, wrapped her in his arms, and pressed her face into the scratchy fabric of his shoulder. She breathed in the musty, moth-eaten smell of him, hardly believing he was real. The weight of years bore down on her, and she realized, truly *realized* how long it had been since she'd seen her father.

"Nellie, Nellie, Nellie-girl!" he whispered into her hair, rocking her gently, as if she were a child. "Where have you been? Where have you been, my little wildling? I thought Cloven had done for you! I thought you were at the bottom of the river! I thought . . . I thought . . ."

His voice choked with sobs, and his whole body quivered like a leaf. Poor Papa wasn't strong. Nelle braced herself, steeling her spine and swallowing back tears. She had to be strong for him.

"I'm sorry, Papa. I'm sorry," she said, her voice rough with the effort not to cry. "I got caught up in bad business, couldn't get

154

away. But I'm here now."

"Are you real?" He stood back, cupping her face in his trembling hands. "I've dreamed so many times, and it's never been true."

She placed her hands over his, blinking hard against the mist in her eyes. "I'm real, Papa. I'm home. And I won't leave again, I promise. I'll take care of you."

A strange expression crossed his face. For a moment, his beautiful features looked their proper age—the lines around his mouth deepened, and the skin beneath his eyes and along his jaw sagged. "Oh, Nellie," he said. "Nellie, I was in such a bad way when you left. I had to make my own way, you know, and . . ."

Nelle grimaced and gently pulled her father's hands away from her face, holding them tight between her fingers. "What did you do, Papa? Is it Cloven again? I'll skin the man; I swear I will! I'll flay his bullspittin' hide!"

But Papa shook his head, dropping his gaze. "Well, no. Actually, I . . ."

"He got married."

Mistress Dirgin's harsh voice sent daggers through the back of Nelle's head. She closed her eyes, shuddering, but turned and faced her former landlady. The skinny rail of a woman stood with her arms crossed over her chest, sucking unpleasantly on one of her few remaining teeth, and eyed Nelle like she would eye a half-dead mouse.

Nelle eyed her right back, her lip curling. She didn't want to believe it. She knew she had to, but she simply didn't *want* to. Surely her beautiful, gentle, foolish Papa couldn't tie himself to . . .

"Ahem. Nellie?" Her father's hand rested on her elbow, and she looked up to see him offer a weak sort of smile. "You know my wife, of course. Mistress Dirgin—Mistress *Beck*, that is—was always so kind to us as her tenants—"

"No, she wasn't," Nelle growled.

Papa went on speaking as though he hadn't heard her. "—and after you disappeared, we discovered our mutual loneliness. The world, as you know, can be a cold, cruel place, especially if one is alone. So, Mistress Dirgin—"

"Mahilda," the old lady snarled.

"Yes. Mahilda and I decided to unite ourselves in the bonds of marital—"

"We got hitched." Mistress Dirgin stepped into the kitchen and pointed at the bowl of oatmeal left spilled and forgotten on the table. "'Ere, d'you think I'm made of money that you can go wasting good fodder?" She snatched a rag and tossed it in Nelle's face. "Clean it up. I ain't got time nor patience for a lazy slattern about the place. You're a grown-up gel, and you can work for your keep, or else you can—"

"My love!" Papa sprang forward and dropped a kiss on the old lady's hollow cheek. "If you would be so kind as to allow Nelle and me a moment in your front parlor? We have much we must discuss."

Mistress Dirgin scowled up at him, sucking on her tooth again. "If you think I'm going to fetch and carry for her ladyship, you can scatting think again!"

"No, no, certainly not." Papa laughed merrily, pinched her chin, then quickly slipped an arm around Nelle's waist and guided her up the kitchen stair and back into the close, musty hall. "Never fear, sweet Mahilda! I will settle all of this in a trice."

Nelle scarcely had a chance to glance back over her shoulder at the sour face of her new stepmother—*Stepmother! Spitting dragons!*—before the kitchen door shut. "This way, quickly," her father said, stepping around a wet-faced child and a growling skeleton of a dog. He led her to the front room, opened the door, and spoke sharply, "Out now! Out, I say! The room is ours for the morning!"

A cluster of shadowy figures shifted and rose from various articles of what passed for furniture. They shambled past Papa, who led Nelle into the now empty room and shut the door behind him. It smelled of mold and rot and other things Nelle didn't like to consider, but the furniture had once been fine. Probably stolen goods.

"Here, Nellie, have a seat," Papa said. Nelle obeyed in a numb stupor, perching on the edge of a hard chair and folding her hands tightly in her lap. He settled across from her on a rickety stool, bracing his feet so as not to overbalance and tumble to the floor, and regarded her with wide and watery eyes.

"Papa . . ." Nelle began.

He grimaced and held up a hand. "I didn't really have a choice. It was marry her or be forcibly removed from the premises. My leg was broken. You were gone. I . . . I couldn't face slow starvation on the streets. I'm sorry, my dear."

Nelle stared down at her hands. But did she really need her father to apologize for doing what he could to survive? Wasn't that what they all did in Draggs?

"I understand," she whispered. And shuddered. "I . . . I hope you're happy?"

"Ah! Well." He shrugged and rubbed his long-fingered, delicate hands together. "Happy is as happy chooses. Is that not so? But enough about me. Where have *you* been?" He reached across the space between them, capturing her fingers in his. "I've been out of my mind with grief. I thought you dead or worse! You can't possibly know the torments I suffered."

Nelle smiled weakly and rubbed a thumb across the top of her father's hand. "I'm . . . not sure I can explain it," she said, her voice suddenly thick.

"Do try, my dear." Papa leaned toward her, his eyes bright with concern. "Were you imprisoned somewhere? Enslaved? Were you mistreated?" His gaze traveled briefly over the ragged garments she wore. Men's garments. He frowned suddenly, and she watched his expression shifting as his mind played through a series of distasteful possibilities. "You look well," he said at last.

Nelle snorted. "I am well. I . . . I was not imprisoned or mistreated. I was . . ."

She'd been happy. Happier than ever before. Happier than she'd ever known she *could* be. Only she hadn't realized it at the time. She'd eaten far better these last few weeks—years—than she had in a long time. She'd had plenty of fresh air, exercise, and stimulation for her brain and body.

And she'd enjoyed the society of a man who'd given her leave and opportunity to be completely herself. A man who gave more than he received. A man who looked upon her as . . . as an *equal*. Not in knowledge or experience or education, of course. She wasn't fool enough to imagine herself his equal in any of those. But in personhood. In value.

Yes. She'd been happy on Roseward.

She pulled her hands from Papa's grasp and placed them over her face, breathing deeply. "I'm so tired, Papa! I can't hardly think straight. Is there . . . Do you think Mistress Dirgin would let me rest a while?"

She looked up in time to catch the expression crossing her father's face before he tried to hide it. She knew what it meant: There was no chance his new wife would let his daughter stay.

But Papa quickly shook his head, forcing his tight-pressed mouth into a weak smile. "There's no one up in the old attic

159

space just now," he said. "You might lie down on your old bed for a few hours at least. After that . . . uh . . ."

"I understand." Nelle rose, wrapping her arms around her cold body. "A little rest. That's all I ask."

Papa stood and took her hand again. "Don't fret, my dear. I've got a plan, you know. Cloven and I have been talking again, and—"

"*What?*" Nelle yanked her hand free. "Why the spitting hells are you talking to that man? Didn't you *just* say you thought Cloven had killed me?"

"Well, yes, but he *didn't*." Papa waved a hand, indicating her obviously living self. "You know, Nelle, you can be terribly judgmental at times. I've always said so. I know you don't like the man, but one of these days, Cloven will make us all rich. You'll see."

He nattered on in this way even as he led her out of the front room and around to the back stair. By the time they reached the low door of their former attic home, Nelle had stopped hearing him. The roaring blood in her ears was too loud. Papa opened the door for her, bowing her into the close attic space, and she entered on silent feet. She felt like a ghost—as if her spirit were meant to be long gone but some sordid thread kept her tethered to this place where she no longer belonged.

She couldn't react when Papa planted a kiss on her cheek. "Rest well, child," he said. "We'll speak again when you wake.

And we'll figure out a place for you to go."

"Thank you, Papa." She pushed him from the room, gently but firmly. "Thank you," she murmured again and shut the door.

She stood a moment, listening, until she heard his footsteps retreat slowly back down the stair. Back down to the kitchen and his cold breakfast and his awful wife. Her stepmother.

A painful knot forming in her throat, Nelle turned to face the little room again. Only dim light eked through the one grimy window, but she could see that it was all very much as she'd left it. Apparently Mistress Dirgin hadn't been able to find other tenants desperate enough to live up here among the rats and the bugs and the bats. Even the little stub of candle remained in the wooden bowl on the windowsill, sunken into its own drippings.

Nelle moved to the window. Its glass was too warped and dirty to see through, but she found the latch and, with a little push, managed to get it open. She gazed out across Draggs Street, across the rooftops and chimneys, then lifted her eyes to the Evenspire, always within sight no matter where one went in the city.

Was Gaspard up in his quillary even now, poring over the Rose Book? Soaking in the knowledge and the magic of Soran Silveri, which had always been beyond his grasp? Would he realize what needed doing and bind the Noswraith afresh? Or would he attempt to recreate the spell, to call his own nightmare into flesh?

"I just hope he tries," Nelle whispered bitterly. "I hope he tries . . . and I hope the fae king comes and takes his hands and curses him and see how he likes it!"

Each beat of her heart felt like a stab. She pressed a hand to her chest. She was lost. And suddenly so empty inside. She needed to think. She needed to figure out what to do next, where she would go. How she would save Papa from this newest self-destructive predicament. But her brain was sluggish, and no thoughts would form.

Nelle sank down on her old pallet bed, curled up on her side, wrapped her arms over her head, and closed her eyes. How long was it since she kissed Soran and left him in an unconscious heap on the floor? Was it really only a few hours? Or had weeks, months, *years* flown by?

How had he reacted upon waking, upon realizing what she'd done? Had he cursed her name, sworn vengeance? Did he hate her?

Would he ever forgive her?

She squeezed her eyes shut, hugging her knees to her chest. Her mouth moved almost against her will, whispering, "I'm sorry. I'm sorry. I'm so sorry . . ."

CHAPTER 12

SOMEHOW, HE'D ALWAYS KNOWN THIS DAY WOULD come.

Soran knelt on the floor beside his desk in the topmost chamber of the lighthouse. He pulled a crate of books toward him and swiftly removed the first few volumes, setting them to one side. These were his greater spells. What remained of them. Spells he had crafted in the years after completing his university training, after donning the robes of a full-fledged Miphato.

Most of the books were empty shells now, the spells they'd once contained long since depleted in his ongoing battle to bind and hold the Thorn Maiden. Two of the most powerful remaining spells he'd expended only five days ago, when battling Kyriakos and his minions.

But there was one . . .

One he had hoped he would never need to use.

Soran lifted out the last of the books, uncovering the parchment lying folded beneath. It was sealed with black wax and marked with the signet ring of the Myrdin Supreme, the highest ranking Miphato in all Seryth. It was Soran's own work, but he had been obliged to present it before the seat of the Myrdin, requesting authorization to keep it. It was the most powerful spell in his collection . . . or it had been until he wrote the Rose Book.

If only the Myrdin had refused to give his seal. If only he'd commanded Soran to destroy this spell page all those years ago.

But if he had, there would now be no hope for Wimborne City.

"Not that there's much hope as it is," Soran murmured, lifting the sealed parchment from the crate and turning it over in his fingers. He could feel the potential power burning inside. Long had he wondered if he would someday be driven to this moment.

Now the moment was come, and a strange leaden sense of resignation filled his soul. He couldn't even truly fear.

Soran tucked the spell into the front of his robes, then paused long enough to go through the books, searching for any remaining spells that might be useful. They were terribly picked over, but five that might serve were still whole, still strong. After all, he didn't know exactly what manner of opposition he would face when he reached Wimborne. Something told him Gaspard wouldn't give up the Rose Book without a fight.

If Gaspard was still alive by the time Soran got there.

Leaving the emptied spellbook bindings strewn across the floor, Soran swiftly descended the tower stair. The wyvern waited for him in the room below, burbling and chirruping unhappily to itself. When it saw Soran, it rushed him, twining around his feet as he gathered a few supplies and made for the door.

"I'm sorry, little friend," Soran said, pausing just long enough to bend down and stroke the wyvern's head. "I hate to abandon you like this. You and all your brethren. If I make it back, I swear I will liberate all of you before . . . before the end. Just now, however . . ."

Just now there was no time. He had to cross the island to the harbor village a mile away, where he knew a few boats yet remained hidden in boathouses near the shore. Then, if he were lucky, if he were gods-touched lucky, he would row for the mortal world and reach Wimborne City before it was too late.

For everyone.

CHAPTER 13

Eight Months Later

"NELLE! *NELLE!* YOU GOT A VISTOR, GEL!"

Nelle looked up from a suds-filled basin, pausing while running a not-quite-white petticoat down the ridges of a washing board. Her red, blistered hands were like claws, unable to uncurl even as she lifted one to wipe a strand of hair from her eyes. Turning, she gazed across the crowded wash yard to see Mistress Ainsely in the shop doorway.

Ainsley was a tall, spare, chinless woman with a glint in her eye that hinted at some deep-seated, long ago but never forgotten sorrow. She ran her team of washerwomen with a hard yet fair hand, demanding efficiency and punctuality above all else. So long as her girls gave the hours and labor, she gave back in coin. Sometimes she even let the delivery girls take home the pennies they picked up in tips. A Draggs girl down on her luck couldn't ask for a better mistress.

She did not like interruptions during business hours, however. And she definitely did not like visitors.

Nelle blinked in surprise. The two girls sharing her washtub and other girls at other tubs around the courtyard paused as well, tossing Nelle questioning looks, eyebrows upraised and mouths stern.

"'Ere!" Mistress Ainsley snapped, drawing all eyes back to herself. "I didn't say none other of your names, did I? Get back to it. And Nelle, hurry your hide over here quick, girl. I ain't got all day."

This couldn't be good. Nelle draped the petticoat over the washboard, hoping she'd be allowed to return to her station after seeing whoever this mysterious visitor might be. She wiped her hands on her already damp apron and scurried between washstands, avoiding the sidelong glances cast her way by her fellow washerwomen.

Ainsley stood, arms folded, at the door leading from the yard into the shop, her thin lips sucked into a grim line. Nelle bobbed a curtsey and murmured, "Sorry, Missus. Here, Missus."

"I told him to wait on the street," Ainsley said, tossing her head and shrugging one bony shoulder. "Told him to come back after sundown, but he's a persistent spitter. Something about him seemed . . . not quite right. I don't like a scene, girl; I hope you realize this."

Nelle nodded, wide-eyed. She couldn't begin to guess who it might be. Papa, perhaps? Had his wife finally had enough of him and booted him out her door? But Papa didn't know where Nelle worked; at least, she didn't think he did. She visited him faithfully on her off day, every other week, but had never told him exactly where she took lodgings or how she cared for herself.

"You want I should send him away?" she asked meekly.

Ainsley grunted. "See him about whatever his business is and make sure he don't come back. When you're done, I got an errand for you up in Elmythe Lane, so don't be long about it."

Nelle nodded hastily, bobbed another curtsey, and ducked through the door into the dark, gloomy building, making her way swiftly through the presses and bundles of carefully folded laundry to the front of the shop. This was the nicest part of the building, freshly painted and always smelling furiously of lavender. A business had to give potential customers a good impression when they first walked in off the street, after all.

Nelle stepped around the receiving counter to the door, pausing to peer through cracks in its panels, trying get an impression of whoever waited outside. She saw only the movement of various people, carts, and horses passing on the street. Perhaps the visitor had grown tired of waiting and gone on his way. Just as well. She wasn't feeling particularly friendly.

Opening the door, Nelle peered out and called a tentative, "Hullo?"

A foot slid into the opening between door and doorpost, and a face appeared right in front of hers. "Ginger! It *is* you!"

Nelle let out a gasp and tried to slam the door. The boot didn't budge, though its owner winced in pain. She glared up into that familiar face.

"Samton Rallenford!" she snarled. "I know I made myself clear. I never want to see you again. Get out of here, now. Get!"

His fingers curled around the door. He wrenched it out of her grasp and shoved it open, then reached in and caught hold of her wrist, dragging her outside. She twisted to get free, but his grip was too strong, and she didn't want to cause a stir. Ainsley would not appreciate a brawl breaking out on her doorstep.

So, Nelle let Sam draw her out of the building and around to the side alley. There, with a ferocious growl, she twisted again, and this time managed to get free. "If you've got a message from Cloven, tell him I ain't taking no more jobs from him. I don't care what he does to me; I don't care if he skins me alive! I won't work for that man ever again, you hear me?"

Sam looked down at her. How terribly pale he was! Eight months had passed since last she'd seen him—eight months since she'd struck his face and left him behind on the beach. It was a long time, sure, but she wouldn't have expected to see such a profound change in a healthy young fellow like Sam. He was hollow-eyed and strangely unkempt. His beard had grown in thicker, a mass of tangles. His hair, no longer in its neat queue, hung shaggy around his shoulders.

"Ginger." He sagged suddenly against the alley wall. "I've looked everywhere for you. We've got to get out of here. Now."

"What?" Despite herself, Nelle's heart twisted with concern. "What's Cloven got you into now?"

Sam quickly shook his head. "I've broken from Cloven. Permanently. Two months ago. And I've been on the run ever since. I should've left Wimborne, but he had all the gates watched and all the bridges, and I couldn't. Besides, I . . . I didn't like to leave you."

Nelle blinked up at him, her mind whirling to catch up. On the run from Cloven? It must be a bad business then. Did it have anything to do with . . . with . . .

But she didn't want to think about *that*. She never wanted to think about *that* again.

"Well, you needn't worry about me," she said, crossing her arms and hardening her face. "I don't care what mess you've got yourself into. I stand by what I said. You had no call to come searching me out, either. You might've led them right to me. Now I'll have to watch my back."

Sam quickly shook his head. "No, I wouldn't put you at risk. I made certain I wasn't followed. I threw them off a couple of weeks ago, and I laid low to make certain of it before I hunted you out. I wouldn't do nothing to hurt you—"

She couldn't stop the grunting laugh that burst from her throat. "Wouldn't do nothing to . . .? You just don't get it, do you?" With that, she turned to leave the alley. "I got work to do and no time for you. I hope for your sake you make it out of Wimborne, but—"

His hand closed on her shoulder, pulling her back, turning her to face him. She lashed out at once, to strike his face, to drive her elbow deep into his gut, to bring her knee up sharply between his legs. But he was prepared for each of these maneuvers and, despite his pale and wan appearance, hadn't lost much of his strength. A few quick deflections, and he had her pinned against the wall, his body weight pressed against her to hold her in place. She snarled and tried to bite his ear, but he jerked back in time.

"Please, hear me out!" he whispered, his voice oddly trembling. He was so close, she could feel the wild beat of his heart. His breath came in short gasps against her hair. "I know I can't change what I done to you, but I want to do right by you now. You've got to leave Wimborne. Tonight. And I want you to go with me. I've got a way out at last—scraped together enough to pay Horald down at the old East Bridge, and he's going to sneak us out at midnight tonight, just when the watch changes."

Nelle growled and wriggled, but he wouldn't let up the

pressure holding her in place. "Your troubles with Cloven are your troubles, Sam. I ain't getting mixed up in any of this. I've got a job. I've got a roof over my head. I'm done with that life, and I'm done with *you*."

Sam drew back just enough to look into her eyes. There was something in his expression, something she couldn't quite understand. Fear, for sure, but other emotions as well. He opened his mouth, and she heard several words start to take shape before he bit them back. Whatever he wanted to tell her, he couldn't find the will to speak it out loud.

"Please," he said at last, dropping his chin so that his ragged hair fell over his forehead and hid his desperate eyes. "I'll wait down by old East Bridge tonight. Meet me there. Once we're out of Wimborne, once we're far away, I'll tell you everything, I swear. And you don't have to stick with me then if you don't want to. I'll understand. Just come with me tonight. Please."

Nelle drew a long breath through her nostrils. "Fine," she said at last. "Fine, but let me go. I've got a job to do, and I don't get paid if I don't do it."

"You'll come?"

"Sure. Sure, Sam. Old East Bridge. Midnight."

He stepped back then, letting go of her. His chest heaved, and his fingers curled and uncurled. "Don't stand me up," he said at last. "It's important."

Nelle shook her head. She had absolutely no intention of

making that rendezvous, but at this point, what did one lie, more or less, matter? "I'll be there," she said.

Then, pushing past Sam, she stepped out of the alley back into the street's gray light. She heard a slight scrambling sound and knew that if she looked back, Sam wouldn't be there anymore. He was still a snatcher, preferring to make his way across rooftops rather than in plain sight.

Straightening her threadbare skirts and pushing loose strands of hair back into the bun at the base of her neck, Nelle returned to the shop. Ainsley waited inside behind the counter, quill in hand, going over a ledger. A large basket of washed, pressed, folded, and wrapped laundry sat beside her. She looked at Nelle from under her thin brows as the shop door opened and shut. "Well?"

"I got rid of him." Nelle approached the counter and checked the address label pinned to the sack. She recognized it at once—a nice townhouse in Estward from which Ainsley took regular business. Nelle had personally washed many of the lovely, lacey, *intimate* items contained therein. "This my load?"

Ainsley grunted. "You know I don't stand for my girls to take callers," she said, her attention seemingly focused on her ledger, but her voice sharp. "You going to stay in your room upstairs, you can't have more of his like nosing around here."

"I won't. I sent him packing straight enough."

"He's a nice-looking lad."

Nelle eyed her mistress. Was this some sort of trap? "I've known him since I was a kid, but I'm done with him now. Told him so months ago. Thought he took the hint."

Another grunt, then Ainsley waved the hand holding the ratty quill, lucky not to splash ink from the nib. "Off with you. They're expecting the wash this afternoon. Don't lollygag along the way."

Nelle raised an eyebrow but said nothing as she heaved the basket off the counter and onto her hip. She shouldered her way back out the door and into the street, looking both ways and even quickly scanning the rooftops. No sign of Sam, so she set out, chin tucked, arms straining to support the heavy weight of the wash load.

Mistress Ainsely's business was located on the edge of Draggs, but none of her clientele came from that part of town. The denizens of Draggs had no extra coin to spend on soap and lavender scent for their holey shirts and trousers or their festering undergarments. Most of the business came from the surrounding, slightly better neighborhoods. But some of those living in nicer neighborhoods had history with Draggs and never fully forgot former connections.

Lady Ryvelle of Elmythe Lane was no true lady, at least not in the classic sense of the word. Nelle had gathered from whispers among the girls around the washbasins that young Ryvelle had started out life as a humble flower-seller down in Draggs, but due to a bounty of golden hair, a good figure, and a quick mind, had soon left that business behind for more lucrative endeavors. She'd been savvy in how and where she spent her hard-earned coin, and over the years had built up a certain type of business that served a certain type of customer . . . and serve them well, by all accounts.

Now she lived in fine style in one of the nicest houses in Estward, where she entertained guests three times a week. She spent the rest of her time frequenting all the most elegant gatherings Wimborne had to offer, and some said she even dined with Mayor Quindove and his wife on a monthly basis.

Nelle made her way swiftly up through the various streets, taking short cuts as she could, but always sticking to the more trafficked areas. Eight months after her return to Wimborne, she still hadn't gotten over the habit of watching for Cloven and his men in the shadows. She'd never glimpsed anything to cause her uneasiness, but that in and of itself made her uneasy at times.

Still. Eight months. And the city hadn't come crashing to ruin. Which meant perhaps taking the Rose Book to Gaspard had been the right choice. He had apparently managed to contain the Noswraith spell, written a new binding.

And Soran lived.

Surely he lived.

Nelle heaved a sigh and shifted the heavy basket. Her time at Roseward was long past and would soon fade from memory. It had lasted only two weeks. Just a bright spark in her life, there and gone again. Already it seemed more like a dream than anything else.

But sometimes . . .

Even amid the bustle and busyness of Wimborne . . .

Even with her arms elbow-deep in hot suds . . .

Sometimes, when she lay on her little narrow bed in the room Mistress Ainsley rented to her above the wash shop . . .

It was too easy to let her mind wander into places it shouldn't go.

A squeal of wheels and a horse's angry snorting brought Nelle abruptly back to herself. She jumped to one side and turned to protect the basket from a spray of mud flung up from the street. It struck her skirts instead, damp and cold. "Bullspit!" she shouted and scowled after the cart and driver. "Spittin' boggart-brain!"

Aware of eyes upon her, Nelle quickly glared around. She was now in Estward, nearing her destination, and the folk in this part of town didn't use such strong language even in the privacy of their thoughts. A woman in a neat straw cap shuffled a small child to her other side, putting distance between it and the uncouth washer-girl. A gentleman in a sweeping cloak curled his lip her way. Others averted their eyes, unwilling to look at a mud-spattered Draggs wench any more than they must.

Nelle lifted her chin and marched on, her arms aching and her pride stinging. But really, what right had she to any pride at all? She knew what she was. More importantly, she knew what she wasn't. She knew what her future held.

Eventually, those dreams of Roseward would fade.

She went around to the back door of Lady Ryvelle's grand, gray-stone townhouse, set the basket down and knocked. She stood a little while, leaning her shoulder against the wall and idly looking around the tiny back garden with its iron-rail fence strung with a few yellowing vines. After a few minutes she knocked again, then a third time, louder. Finally, she pressed her ear to the door and, convinced she heard movement and voices inside, tried the latch. It gave way to gentle pressure, and she eased the door open a crack.

"Hullo?" she called.

"Seven gods, who is that?" Cook's voice, usually a bright, hearty trill, sounded fragile. "Go on, girl, send whoever it is away at once. We can't have anyone about the house at this time!"

The next moment, a housemaid appeared, her pretty face framed by a white-lace cap. Usually she met Nelle at the door with an expression of supercilious superiority, but today she was pale, round-eyed, her mouth pinched into a tight, fearful line.

"Oh! It's only you!" she exclaimed when she spotted Nelle in the doorway.

"I come with the washing." Nelle nudged the heavy basket over the threshold. "Is everything all right?"

"All right?" The maid peered back over her shoulder as

though expecting some grim ghoul to jump out at any moment. "We are *far* from all right! But just you get going, and never mind how—"

"Nelle, girl, is that you?" Cook put her head around the corner. She, too, was strangely pale and harrowed-looking, her gray hair frizzing out around her head like a wooly halo. "Oh, Nelle!" She lunged past the housemaid and caught Nelle in a strong-armed embrace. Nelle gasped, surprised and uncertain how to react. Cook, though friendly, was not given to such demonstrations. A loud sniff in her ear, and Nelle's shock redoubled. Was the old woman crying?

"What's going on?" Nelle cried, grabbing hold of Cook's plump shoulders and pushing her back a pace or two. "Has something happened to Lady Ryvelle?"

"Oh, not to her ladyship, thank the gods!" Cook replied, grabbing hold of her apron and mopping her tearstained face. "Not directly, anyway, though the poor woman is in a state, *such* a state!"

"It isn't the laundry-lass's business what state our lady's in," the housemaid said, turning a strict eye on Nelle. "Be off with you now, and—"

"What happened?" Nelle demanded, firming her stance and addressing her question to Cook.

"A horror, a true and ghastly horror!" Cook said. "The lady had one of her gentlemen over last night, as is her business and

179

no one else's. And he stayed over, naturally. But this morning . . . Oh, this morning . . ."

As Cook sank into convulsive sobs, Nelle turned to the housemaid and raised one eyebrow. The girl, who despite every protest and effort appeared on the verge of collapse, immediately spilled the rest.

"He was found dead in the bed. Right next to our lady," she said, her trembling voice nearly inaudible through the noise Cook made. "Cut to ribbons. Blood everywhere! But he never made a sound, not even to wake our lady. Lidda went in to help her dress in the morning and found him, and Lady Ryvelle sleeping like an angel beside him. She woke her up, and our lady fell to hysterics, and we've been all in an uproar since! Got the Green Caps over right away, but they can't make sense of it. Imagine, a man being torn apart in his sleep like that!"

CHAPTER 14

NELLE STOOD OUT IN THE STREET, THE COLD WIND blowing sharp against her wet skirt, slapping the fabric against her legs. She didn't feel the cold, however, or the damp. She didn't feel anything.

In her mind's eye she saw the sleepers, the pirates, sprawled around the Dornrise banquet table. Their bodies slashed to pieces while they lay in peaceful slumber.

It can't be.

It can't be!

After all this time, surely the Thorn Maiden couldn't be at large in Wimborne. Surely Gaspard had bound her, held her.

Surely she wouldn't be out rampaging in the night, preying on the sleeping, the helpless. Surely . . .

Nelle turned and looked up at the townhouse, her eyes scanning the various windows and the moldings decorating the stone walls. If it weren't broad daylight, she might clamber up to one of those upper floors and make her way inside. As it was, she turned and scanned the rooftops.

Yes. That might work.

Leaving the empty wash basket beside the front steps, she darted around to the alley at the end of the row of townhouses. There weren't as many decorative moldings on the side hidden from view of the street, but there was a very long drainage pipe. When Nelle tried her weight on it, it seemed sturdy enough.

She kicked off her shoes and climbed the pipe hand over hand, her bare toes finding cracks and protruding stones in the wall. At any moment she expected someone to shout at her from below, but no one did. She reached the roof, grabbed hold of the edge, and shimmied along until she was level with a round attic window.

She gave a sharp kick. The glass cracked. Another kick, and it broke.

A few precarious moments, and she managed to maneuver herself through the opening into the dusty attic space. Lack of light didn't matter—her *ibrildian* eyes adjusted swiftly to the gloom. She made her way between support beams and a few random oddments someone below had put up for storage.

The far wall was, at first glance, solid. But Nelle had explored enough of these townhouse attics to know better. The builders hadn't bothered to brick between the attics along the row, choosing instead to put up flimsy plaster. It didn't require much effort to break through into the attic of the next house over.

Lady Ryvelle's house was the fourth in this row. Nelle moved quietly from one attic to the next. Hopefully, any folk down below would ascribe any telltale sounds to nothing more than a rather large rat overhead. So long as they didn't send servants scurrying up with clubs or knives, she should be safe.

Dirty, cobwebby, and choking on dust, Nelle reached the fourth attic. There she swiftly located a trapdoor in the floor, oh! so gently lifted it, and peered down into the hall below. These were the servants' quarters, but at this time of day all the servants should be up and about their business.

Easing herself through the opening, Nelle landed on the floor in a crouch, paused, and listened. All was still. She stood and padded on silent feet to the stair. A frisson of quiet confusion vibrated through the air of the house as she made her way quietly down to the lower levels. The air *tasted* of panic.

Creeping down a passage to the third floor, Nelle paused at the sound of two rumbling voices speaking low and tense to one another.

"It's the lady herself, right? Got to be her what did it. No one else had opportunity."

"Steady on," the second voice, older and harsher than the first, answered. "Why would a lady of her profession, as it were, go and slash up one of her best-payin' customers?"

"Maybe he, uh, you know. Maybe he—"

"*Maybe*, rot. This ain't the first case like this to crop up, you know. I heard from Sergeant Maldren just last week, another one of those Miphato fellows was found in similar state. In his own rooms up in the university, no less. Lady Ryvelle was seen at the Chamber Revels that same night, so unless she was able to be two places at once, it couldn't ha' been her . . ."

Nelle withdrew from the corner, pressing her back to the wall, blood pounding in her ears.

A Miphato. A *Miphato.*

And not the first, but a *second* victim.

"Gaspard?" she whispered, her veins running with ice.

The Green Caps moved on, clearing her path. With an effort, Nelle pulled herself together and continued down the passage. She knew the layout of houses like this—Mother had taken her into Estward for snatches on more than one occasion—and she guessed Lady Ryvelle's room would be on the second floor in the front of the house, facing the street. She made her way undetected down to that level, narrowly avoiding another Green Cap and a haggard-looking footman. The first door she tried opened at her touch, and she peered into a sumptuous bedchamber full of shadows but for the sliver of daylight falling through a crack in the curtains.

That small light highlighted the contours of a body lying under a sheet on the large bed in the center of the room.

Nelle slipped inside, shutting the door softly behind her. For a moment she stood with her back pressed to the door, the knob digging painfully into her spine. The stench of blood and death was almost enough to send her fleeing. When she forced her eyes to scan the room, they swiftly adjusted to the dimness, as always.

There . . . draped on the back of a chair close to the cold fireplace. Miphates robes, gorgeous with embroidery. Green and blue and purple, picked out in bright gold threads. Just like . . . just like . . .

The sheet was stained with patches of blood, still bright red and fresh. It was all Nelle could do to cross the room, to stand quietly beside that covered corpse. For several terrible moments she couldn't find the courage to twitch back the covering, to see what she needed to see. Did she need to know? Perhaps there was a simple explanation for all of this. After all, it wasn't her business. She wasn't connected to any of the sordid intrigues of the Miphates. She wasn't.

But that, of course, was a lie.

Choking back a whimper, Nelle caught hold of the sheet and pulled it aside, revealing the strangely calm, peaceful face of the dead man. She let out a gasp like a prayer.

It wasn't Gaspard. This man, whoever he was, was much older. Several decades older, unless she missed her guess, with a soft, flabby face and heavy bags under his eyes. Not Gaspard. Not Gaspard . . .

Whatever relief she felt in that first moment soon vanished. Nelle pulled the sheet back further still. Every inch of the man's flesh from his neck down appeared flagellated, torn to ribbons. The blankets beneath him were soaked through, and a large puddle stained the rug on which Nelle stood.

No man should have been able to sleep through such torture. Not under natural circumstances.

There was only one explanation. One terrible, undeniable truth.

"She's here," Nelle whispered. "She's free."

Two hours remained until sunset when Nelle ended her trek from Estward up to Northon District. The guards posted at the district gates would never let her in without proper authorization, but she knew a place where she could climb the wall with minimal risk of being seen and soon was stealthily slipping from street to street, always just out of sight of any Green Caps on patrol.

As she approached the Miphates University, however, her pace slowed, and she chewed the inside of her cheek. Getting over the wall was one thing. Infiltrating the university was a very different story. She'd done it before, of course. But that time, she'd had a chance to prepare.

Now there was no time to waste. She must get in. She must find Gaspard. She must . . .

"Bullspit," she muttered, peering up at the forbidding university gate from her hiding place in an alley. Guards patrolled the upper wall. Not particularly alert fellows, but too many of them to make scaling the wall in broad daylight a viable option.

She craned to peer over her shoulder, watching the sun in its descent. It would set all too soon. And then the Thorn Maiden would prowl freely through Wimborne again.

After backing away into the alley, Nelle made her way around to the west side gate, which was used by the servants coming and going. Surely there would be some traffic this time of evening. She found a likely vantage point in the shadow of a fine residence house within sight of the gate and waited. Every inch of her body wanted to twitch with impatience, but she forced herself to be still. Stillness was one of the most important tricks of a snatcher's trade. It didn't matter how quick the foot or nimble the hand if the snatcher lacked patience to wait for the right opportunity.

But no matter how still she kept her body, she could not still her mind enough to prevent a sliver of regret from slipping through—regret for the job she was even now throwing away with both hands. She wouldn't dare return to the wash house now, hours late. Ainsley would call the Green Caps on her. She wasn't a forgiving mistress.

Nelle withheld a sigh. It had been a good job. Not a job with a future, but what right did a Draggs girl have to worry about something as ephemeral as the future?

Not that it would matter, Nelle reminded herself bitterly, her eyes fixed on the gate. If the Thorn Maiden was free, nothing else would matter soon enough.

She had seen the Noswraith physically manifest. She had witnessed its insatiable hunger for blood firsthand. It might not be able to take physical form here in the mortal world, but . . .

"She will take root and spread, slowly but surely, from mind to mind. And eventually, Miss Beck, she will destroy everything you know and love."

As Soran's dire prediction whispered in the back of her mind, Nelle shuddered.

But just at that moment, a bright, cheerful whistling caught her ear. She slid a little deeper into her alley, craning her neck to see down the street.

It was a courier. The university employed a half dozen of them—swift, lanky lads, immediately recognizable by the garish blue-and-orange uniforms and floppy feathered caps that made up their uniforms. This boy must be returning from an errand. He walked with his hands in his trouser pockets, kicking a stone along his way, enjoying a few moments of freedom before reentering the tight-reined life within the university walls.

Nelle eyed the boy up and down, gauging his build, his strength. He couldn't be more than twelve or thirteen years old, with little muscle on his skinny frame. "You'll do," she whispered.

Then she shook her hair out from its bun, ran her fingers swiftly through the tangled strands, straightened her gown, and batted her eyelashes. She was out of practice, but Mother's training was still in there somewhere.

Pasting a winning smile on her face, she stepped out of the alley and called out, "Oi! You there, fella!"

The messenger boy started and missed a kick at the tumbling stone. He looked around, his brow puckered in a not particularly intelligent expression. His gaze landed on Nelle and immediately brightened. He might be young, but he was certainly old enough to appreciate when a young lady gave him any notice whatsoever.

"Can you come here a quick minute?" Nelle beckoned, tilting her head fetchingly. "I was just on my way back from the jewelers, and I dropped my lady's pin. I got to find it, or I'll be in the worst trouble!"

"You're a lady's maid?" the boy asked as he approached. His gaze ran over her faded and patched washer-girl dress, and his forehead puckered. "You don't look much like—"

It was already too late. Nelle caught him by the front of his shirt and yanked him into the alley, out of sight from the wall or the gate. She whirled him around, pressed him face-first against the wall, and struck him hard on the back of the head in just the right spot. The poor boy didn't even have a chance to yelp before he was sinking insensible to the ground.

Nelle, her heart pounding, cast a quick glance up and down the alley. Everything was still.

"Bullspit it all," she whispered and rolled the boy over, quickly untying the underarm laces of his fancy doublet. It was the work of a few moments to strip the boy down, remove her own dress, and clothe herself in the uniform. Doing the laces up under her own arm proved a challenge, but she managed it in the end.

She draped her discarded skirts over the boy's nearly naked body like a blanket, then plucked the feathered cap from his head. Hastily she tied her long hair in a knot and stuffed it under the cap, pulling the floppy brim low over her forehead. That was the easy part.

She returned to the end of the alley to peer out at the gate. Now things would get a bit more . . . complicated.

Sliding her hands into her new trouser pockets, Nelle sauntered out into the open, whistling. She even found the little stone and kicked it along several paces before finally approaching the gate. "Oi!" she called, rattling the bars. "Anyone there?"

The gatekeeper took his time appearing. Nelle knew him at once—Old Tankenhurt, a wizened fellow who had probably left eighty behind long ago. He'd worked this same post back when she served here as a scullery wench. Hopefully, it had been long enough—and his watery eyes had faded enough—that he wouldn't recognize her.

To her relief, Old Tankenhurt merely glanced at the bright colors of her uniform, grunted, and opened the gate. He muttered something that sounded like, "Rr alr-ys rr ad-uns rr," and spat enthusiastically.

"Couldn't ha' put it better myself," Nelle said, touched her cap, and darted through the gate before the old man could change his mind.

Avoiding the kitchens—and all those former coworkers who might recognize her—she made her way into the big square university building, ambling along at a boyish gait, all elbows and knees and swagger. The Miphates in residence kept quarters on the opposite end of the building from the students, and with a little guesswork and a few wrong turns, she soon found her way to private apartments. A footman sat at the end of the hall, idly buffing his nails between yawns. Probably nearing the end of his shift and thinking more about his supper plans than anything else.

Nelle sauntered up to him and, pitching her voice into her best imitation of male adolescent surliness, said, "Message for Mage Gaspard. Which one's his room then?"

The footman barely glanced up from his nails. "Fourth on the right," he said with a toss of his head.

"Thanks, mate." Nelle touched the brim of her hat and started down the passage, trying to convince herself with every step she took that the footman's eyes weren't watching her walk away. That he wasn't noticing how the boy's uniform clung to her hips or a certain feminine turn in her step. At every moment she half expected him to call after her. Perhaps she should have knocked him out. But that would have meant leaving a large unconscious body in the hall. She couldn't risk it.

These thoughts roiled in her head until she reached the fourth door, where she paused and dared a glance back the way she'd come. The footman was still at his post, leaning back in his chair now, his legs out before him and crossed at the ankle, his fingers laced behind his head. He took no further notice of the courier lad.

Letting out a tight breath, Nelle faced the door. Now she'd come to it, she hesitated to knock. Memory sparked of the last time she'd seen Gaspard, of that hard, cruel kiss he'd pressed on her lips. Her stomach churned.

But the image of the slashed and dead Miphato lying in Lady Ryvelle's bed was too vivid to be ignored.

Nelle set her jaw and rapped smartly on the panel.

"Yes? Who's there?" the voice inside barked as though startled. It didn't sound like Gaspard. Gaspard was always smooth, always controlled. Was this the right room?

Well, she'd knocked now. She couldn't very well scurry away

without trying.

"Message for Mage Gaspard." There was no answer right away, so she added, "Supposed to be important."

Another long silence. Nelle stood her ground, refusing to let her gaze turn sideways to see if the footman watched her. She started to count slowly, as Mother had taught her: *One . . . two . . . three . . .*

She'd reached fifteen before the voice on the other side of the door spoke again. "All right, come in and be quick about it."

The latch turned when she tried it. Nelle gently pushed the door open. The room within was darker than the passage without. Heavy curtains were drawn fast across tall windows, and the fireplace was cold and dead. She got an impression of . . . *stacks.* Stacks of books. Piles of clothes. Mounds of bedding. Even heaps of furniture turned on end.

Her *ibrildian* eyesight passed over these quickly, however, her attention drawn to the desk at the far end of the room where a single candle burned. A figure sat at the desk, his back to her. More books mounded all around him, and papers were strewn across the floor at his feet. Was it Gaspard?

Entering the room, Nelle drew the door shut quietly behind her. After a moment's pause, she dropped the bolt. It clunked into place, loud in that still chamber. The figure at the desk started at the sound and sat upright, turning to look over his shoulder. The dim candlelight partially illuminated the haggard

193

features of Mage Gaspard.

A long, ragged scar carved from his forehead, across the bridge of his nose, and down one cheek.

His eyes rested unfocused on Nelle, his brow puckering slightly as he took in her bright uniform. "Well, boy," he said in that same growling bark. "You have a message for me? Deliver it at once."

Nelle lifted her chin slightly. Then, with a sweep of one arm, she pulled the broad-brimmed hat off her head and let her red hair come tumbling down.

Gaspard's eyes widened. He sprang from his chair, knocking it over. "You!"

CHAPTER 15

THEY STOOD ACROSS FROM EACH OTHER, CAUGHT IN A moment of perfect tension as the mage's exclamation echoed in the corners of the room.

Nelle took a step forward. "Hullo, Gaspard."

The mage uttered a strangled cry and fumbled on the desk behind him. His hand came up, and the sharp edge of a penknife flashed in the candlelight just as he lunged. But he gasped and doubled over before he'd taken two steps; his free hand pressed into his side, his eyes wide with pain.

Nelle didn't stop to wonder. She sprang nimbly across the space between them, dodging nebulous stacks, caught the mage's upraised wrist, and twisted. He snapped a curse and tried to swing at her with his other arm, but she already had his own momentum working against him. The penknife fell into her outstretched hand. The next instant, she swung him around and slammed him face-first into the wall. Gods, how weak he was! The man who had towered so threateningly over her just eight months ago was now withered and frail in her grasp.

He cursed viciously. She caught him by his shoulder, pulled him around, and pressed him up against the wall again, holding the penknife under his chin. He stared down at her, shock and rage mingled in his face. The flickering candle cast a harsh red glow across the many scars crisscrossing his face. Some were fresh, the cuts still bloodied and raw.

Nelle's heart sank. It was too late. It was already too late.

Or maybe not . . . She clenched her jaw, trying to suppress the fear rising in her throat. After all, if the Thorn Maiden were fully unleashed, Gaspard would be dead, wouldn't he? She must be at least partially bound.

"Where is it, Gaspard?"

"Where's what?" he choked. A vein pulsed in his forehead.

"You know what," she growled. "Where is the Rose Book?"

"What is it to you? You are no mage, no witch. You're nothing but a snatcher! What I do with my spellbooks is none of your concern."

"You made it my concern when you sent me to snatch it for

you." Nelle angled her penknife slightly, drawing a bead of blood. Gaspard tried to pull back, but his head hit the wall with a dull thump. "So, tell me, where is it?"

His eyes flicked to the door, then back to her face. "Not here. It's illegal magic. I dared not bring it here where it might so easily be detected."

"That's right." Nelle grimaced unpleasantly. "If it got about that you was playing with Noswraith magic, your fellow mages would come down on you like thunder, wouldn't they. Would they get Master Shard to cut off your hands so you can't work magic no more? Or would they execute you outright, do you think?"

Gaspard spat something incoherent, a slur by the sound of it. But her knife moved, drawing a delicate line of blood just under his jaw, and he held very still.

Nelle shrugged slightly. "Mind, I don't really care what happens to you. But I saw something this morning. Something that made me uneasy. Something that made me think someone ought to be told what you've been up to. So I'll ask again, Mage Gaspard, and I expect an answer this time: Where is the Rose Book?"

"It's hidden."

A shiver crept up Nelle's spine, tickling in the back of her brain. "So it . . . it didn't break apart? You didn't re-bind the Noswraith, make a new spellbook to contain it?"

Gaspard's eyes narrowed. "How do you know so much about it?"

She pressed the penknife a little deeper. "Answer the question!"

His nostrils flared with a swiftly indrawn breath. "It's . . . it's under control."

"Is it? Because just today I saw one of your fellows. A Miphato. Dead."

The mage's body tensed as though every muscle were suddenly wound tight. She could almost hear his heartbeat pounding through the layered fabric of his robes. "Orisys?" he said. "Orisys is dead?

Nelle hadn't heard the name of the man in Lady Ryvelle's chambers. She nodded anyway. "Yeah. He's dead all right. Torn to pieces in his sleep."

Gaspard swallowed, the tendons in his throat standing out sharply. Another bead of blood rolled down and soaked into his collar. "I . . . I didn't know. I didn't mean for . . . for . . ."

"Didn't mean to kill him? What are you saying, Gaspard? Is the Thorn Maiden getting out on her own? Is she targeting Miphates? 'Cause I heard this fellow ain't the only one. I heard there was another one, died right here in his own rooms."

With a sudden heave, Gaspard pushed Nelle away. She braced herself, ready for a fight, but he simply staggered to his desk chair, set it back upright, and sagged down into it. Nelle didn't relax her stance. If she'd learned anything about this man, it was not to trust him, not for a moment. He sat in profile to her, and she noted again the patchwork of scars on his face. Most of them were thin little cuts, hardly noticeable. But that most recent one . . . it was ugly. And he hadn't bothered to get it stitched up.

"She's got you," Nelle said quietly, almost pityingly. "She's got into your head. You thought you could control her, but you can't. You ain't got Soran's know-how."

Gaspard didn't answer. He pressed a hand to his side, grimacing as though at a stabbing pain.

Nelle drew a long breath. Real fear hadn't set in yet. It would, she knew. Soon it would come roaring down on her like a beast, and she'd be lucky if she didn't end up a quivering ball of terror. But for now, it was all dullness in her head.

"Tell me, Gaspard," she said, taking a step toward the mage. "Where is the Rose Book?"

He lifted his head to peer up at her with glassy eyes. "And what will you do if I tell you? Are you going to steal it back from me, snatcher girl? Then what? What is your plan exactly?"

"I don't know. But I sure as nine hells can't leave it with you, can I? Today was just one Miphato, and you know, what do I care? What's one Miphato to me? But tomorrow it'll be someone else. Then someone else. Then someone else, and eventually . . ."

"*Eventually, Miss Beck, she will destroy everything you know and love.*"

Nelle shivered and brandished the pen knife a little higher. "Eventually it'll matter."

Gaspard leaned his head heavily into his hand, elbow propped on the desk. He opened his mouth, seemed to think better of what he was going to say, and closed it again. Then, sighing and leaning back in his chair, he crossed his arms across his breast. "It's not safe for us to discuss these matters here. I don't know who might be listening. But meet me tonight at the old Tyrane fortress. You know the place."

"Yeah. I know it." Nelle's lip curled. "Is that where you're keeping it?"

"No. But we may speak more freely there." Gaspard shook his head, his face suddenly sagging. He looked old. Much older than his thirty-odd years. Fear shimmered in the depths of his eyes. "Perhaps you are right, snatcher girl. Perhaps my reach has exceeded my grasp. Perhaps together we can find a solution to this little problem."

He was lying. She could feel the deceit in his soul, beneath the fear, beneath the exhaustion. He had no intention of working with her, no intention of giving up the power she'd so foolishly handed over to him.

But a known lie was a lie she could work with.

"All right," she said, stepping back slowly, the penknife still upraised. She paused to pick up the courier's hat she'd dropped on the floor. "I'll meet you there. Two hours from now."

"Two hours," Gaspard agreed, then added with a hint of a manic smile in the corners of his mouth, "Don't be late."

"Yeah." Nelle snorted and set the hat firmly down on her head. "Right."

She unbolted the latch, pulled the door open, and slipped from the mage's chamber back out into the swiftly darkening passage. She breathed a sigh of relief as she shut the door, blocking her view of Gaspard's tortured face. With a quick turn, she darted down the passage. The footman dozed in his chair—didn't so much as lift a glance up—and she hastened back down the stairways, taking care to meet no one along the way.

What are you doing? Her own voice pounded inside her head, accusing and derogatory by turns. *Stupid girl, what do you imagine you're going to accomplish?*

She didn't know. She had no plan, not anymore.

She only knew she couldn't leave the Rose Book in Gaspard's hands, not even for one more night.

The path leading along the beach to the old fortress afforded few good hiding places. But at night, a clever snatcher, skilled in the fine art of holding still, might lie belly-down among the dunes and remain unseen unless searching eyes knew exactly where to look.

Nelle lay in the sand now, peering between whispering

strands of grass up to the path a few yards above. She'd made her way here directly after leaving Northon District behind and assumed this position to watch for Gaspard. He would have to come this way to the fortress, and she fully intended to confront him before he got there. After all, what sense lay in walking straight into a trap she knew perfectly well to be a trap? Better to take the upper hand as soon as possible.

She felt for the penknife tucked into the waistband of her stolen trousers. It was a flimsy weapon but better than nothing. She'd been tempted to find a bit of paper and a quill, to call a spell-sword or at least a dagger into existence. But her *ibrildian* magic might attract unwanted attention. She couldn't take that risk.

A cold wind blew across the water, across the beach, whispering against her skin. Nelle shivered. She'd disposed of the hat, removed the ornate outer layers of the courier's uniform, and now wore only the undershirt and trousers. They fit her frame better than Soran's garments had, and they were easier to move about in than her dress. They provide inadequate protection against the elements, however.

Gods blight him, where was Gaspard? He'd said two hours, and surely—

A slithering passed through her mind.

Nelle tensed. Her hands, lying on either side of her face, slowly curled, digging into the sand. Had she imagined that sensation? Was the night playing tricks on her brain?

Something moved on the edge of her vision, sinuous as a snake.

Nelle turned, staring hard. But there was nothing. Only sand and tall grasses. The ocean murmured its rhythmic song behind her. Otherwise, all was still.

Or not all. A sound of footsteps reached her ear. Nelle focused her attention back to the path above. A figure approached, robes flapping with each long stride he took. Gaspard. It must be he. She adjusted the set of her shoulders, and dug her toes into the sand, ready to jump out when he drew near.

Something hissed in her ear, just to her right.

Nelle started, drawing a quick gasp, and breathed in a sweet perfume. A scent of roses?

"There!"

A thrill raced down her spine as the hard voice rang out in the night. She twisted, staring along the beach toward the ruins. Three figures hurtled toward her, kicking up sand as they came. For a moment she couldn't move. How did they know she was here? Gaspard must have gotten word to them, but . . . how?

She sprang to her feet, prepared to run. As she turned, she saw four more figures approaching from the opposite way. Had they been lying in wait for her? Still more tall, faceless forms appeared on the path overhead.

There was only one way left to go.

Nelle whirled on her heel and raced for the sea. Her slippers were too tight and threatened to trip her up, so she kicked them off and ran barefoot across the strand. She wasn't much of a swimmer, and the tide was coming in, but better to risk drowning than let herself be caught.

They flanked her, closing in fast. She splashed into the foam, crying out as sharp coldness lanced straight to her bones. She made it out to waist height, where the undertow pulled at her legs, before the first of the men reached her. He caught at her arm just as she dived, yanking her back upright. Water streamed through her hair, plastered her shirt to her body. She writhed in the man's grasp, managing to catch him off balance and send him splashing into the water. He pulled her down with him before he lost his grip.

Nelle kicked free and surfaced again. Three more men were on her already, and one grabbed her from behind, wrapping his arms around her. He lifted her right out of the water, but she used the momentum to kick another man in the face. He fell hard, and the other man toppled over backwards, dragging her back underwater again. His grip loosened, and Nelle struggled free.

She came up out of the water closer to the shore. Spying a clear patch, she pulled her legs under her and sprang upright, surging out of the water as she rushed headlong back to the beach. Splashing filled her ears as the men followed. They were preternaturally silent. No grunts, no gasps for air. Nothing but the sound of their heavy bodies scrambling out of the water.

She took only ten paces before one of them caught her from behind, grabbing a fistful of hair. He yanked, and she went down hard on her back, screaming with rage and pain. Too many hands filled her vision, too many shadowy figures loomed overhead. She kicked, scratched, tried to roll away. Hard hands latched hold of her upper arms and dragged her upright. A fist planted in her gut, driving the air out of her body in a painful gasp.

Nelle sagged, her lungs heaving, her body shuddering with cold and dread. Peering up through strands of wet hair, she used her *ibrildian* sight to study the faces surrounding her. She knew these faces, most of them at least. They were Cloven's men.

A swarm of curses churned in her throat. She wanted to spit and scream. It was no use; she lacked the breath for it.

At a silent gesture from one stooped fellow with a lazy eye, the others hauled Nelle between them along the beach, their strides so long that she couldn't keep up. They dragged her when she staggered, and her bare feet were soon battered against rocks and shells.

They half carried her along the path above the beach, across the old bridge, and into the fortress keep. She recognized the same long hall where she'd last encountered Gaspard, only this time no sunlight fell through the tall windows to illuminate the darkness. If not for her Hybrid vision, she would be totally blind.

At the far end of the hall stood a man with his back to her. She didn't need to see his face to recognize Cloven's great bulk. Though no one called out to him, he turned as they drew near, his arms at his sides. His face was stern, hard, but his eyes seemed to stare off into some faraway space.

"Cloven!" Nelle called out, her voice sharp through her chattering teeth. "You still doing Gaspard's dirty work for him? Ain't you found other mud holes to root your ugly snout around in?"

Cloven made no answer. His eyes flicked over to her briefly, and his jaw moved as if . . . as if he *wanted* to say something. But he maintained that firm silence and refocused his gaze on the empty shadows over her head.

Footsteps echoed against the stone. Nelle strained her neck, trying to look over her shoulder. She saw a flutter of long robes.

"Gaspard," she snarled. "You bullspitting boggart! Tell your goons to let me go, or are you too spitting scared of one snatcher girl to risk it?"

The Miphato passed the silent men and circled to stand facing Nelle. A new cut sliced across his left cheek, and even in the darkness, Nelle could see dark blood welling and rolling down to his jaw. But his face was calmer than it had been two hours earlier, almost serene. He motioned silently to the two men holding Nelle. They let go and back away.

Nelle rubbed her arms, scowling at the men surrounding her,

her gaze traveling until it returned to Gaspard. All was eerily silent and almost perfectly dark. "Strike a light, why don't you," she growled. "It's black as death in here!"

"But we need no light to see each other clearly, do we, Peronelle Beck?"

The voice was Gaspard's, but also . . . not. There was a hollowness to it. An echo. And in the last ring of that echo was a second, fainter voice.

One Nelle recognized.

"You," she gasped and shrank back two paces.

"Yes. Me." Gaspard's teeth flashed in a smile that belonged to another face. One Nelle had seen before, made of twisted branches and thorns. *"Did you really think we were done with one another? No, no. Fate has bound us fast. You are destined to complete my liberation."*

Horror tolled like a bell in Nelle's breast, in time with the beat of her heart. The Thorn Maiden. She was here. Right here.

But she wasn't physically manifest. That had to count for something. She couldn't manifest in this world, couldn't become that horrible storm of thorns Nelle had watched pull down the walls of Ninthalor. She could only exist within people's minds. Which meant she could be stopped.

Nelle swallowed hard. "So," she said, struggling to keep her voice steady, calm. "You did it. You broke free of the spellbook."

"No, indeed. There was no need to break free, for this creature

you see before you invited me in. He thought to bind me to himself while he learned my secrets and mastered my powers. But in the end, he hadn't the strength." Gaspard raised one hand and stroked his own face as though petting a cat. It was the strangest, most incongruous sight. His fingers passed right over the fresh wound, spreading blood in a smear. *"He still fights me as he can. But he'll succumb in the end. They all will."*

Nelle couldn't seem to stop herself from taking a step back. "And the murders?" she asked. "You've been killing Miphates. I saw one of them this morning, and I know it was you. Why? What did they do to you?"

Gaspard shrugged and tossed his head in a slight, dismissive gesture. *"They sensed my presence. They didn't know what I was, but they sensed unusual magic inside this flesh vessel. They confronted him about it, and he put them off, but I knew they were close to discovering the truth, so I got into their minds. I would have taken them as my own, but they fought me. It was easier to simply kill them."*

The mage smiled then and slowly licked his lips. *"Once the Rose Book is gone, I'll be stronger. For as long as it continues to exist, my bonds are not wholly broken. When I have found it and torn it apart, I'll be much stronger. No mind will be able to resist me. So . . . where is it?"*

Nelle blinked. "I don't know. I'm here to ask *him* the same question."

Gaspard took a step closer, then another. His skin prickled across his brow and cheeks like goose pimples. Each little bump grew, however, and Nelle watched in horror as tiny thorns pierced through. His eyes widened with pain even as the Thorn Maiden continued to smile with his mouth.

"I'm not a fool, Peronelle Beck. I know this creature gave the spellbook to you. I know he told you to hide it. As long as it exists, I cannot be free. So tell me, where is it?"

Nelle glanced from Gaspard to the men standing along the walls and back again. Her mind spun frantically, trying to understand. Gaspard must be keeping some portion of his mind free of the Thorn Maiden's grasp, otherwise she would know Nelle did not have the spellbook. She stared into the mage's eyes, trying to catch some glimpse of the human soul trapped inside. But deep down in the black pits of his pupils, she saw only twining vines, tearing thorns.

She looked around at the men again, so still and so silent. Had the Thorn Maiden taken hold of their minds as well? Was this how they communicated without speaking, acting almost as a single being?

Was this what she would do to all of Wimborne?

No. There was still hope, there had to be! The Thorn Maiden was a nightmare—she only had power at night. When the sun rose, she would fade again. And for as long as the Rose Book existed, it was possible—*possible*—to bind her. To pull her back out of these minds and trap her once more in those pages.

But would the book, so battered and nearly broken when Nelle last saw it, be strong enough to the hold the spell? And who could manage to work the binding? Certainly not Gaspard.

"You try my patience." Gaspard flicked a hand.

The men peeled away from the walls, closing in on Nelle. At the edges of her vision, she almost thought she saw them as figures made of roiling vines and thorns, their faces overlaid in rose petals, but when she looked at them directly, they were the same ugly faces she knew too well.

"There's no point in fighting," the Thorn Maiden hissed, her voice echoing just beneath Gaspard's deep timbre. *"You cannot escape. You might as well tell me where the book is hidden. Once I get into your head, I'll find the answer anyway."*

"No, you won't," Nelle snarled, trying to angle herself to view the men and Gaspard all at once. "I'm telling you, I don't have it."

"Liar!"

"Call me whatever you like. But I ain't seen the book since I handed it over to . . . to this fellow." She waved a hand at Gaspard even while meeting the Thorn Maiden's gaze in his eyes. "Ask him if you don't believe me."

"He told me you have it."

"Well then, he's the liar, not me."

"We shall soon find out." Gaspard's teeth bared in a wicked grimace. *"Get her!"*

The men swarmed in. But this time Nelle was prepared. She noted how awkward their movements were, fractionally slower while controlled by an outside source than they would be on their own. She could use that.

One man swung at her head, and she dropped low, avoiding the blow. Planting her hands in front of her, she kicked out, hooking another man behind the heel. He fell into the man behind him, and in the confusion, Nelle sprang up and jabbed her fingers straight into the eyes of another man in front of her. He flung up his hands, his mouth open in a silent scream of pain, and turned away.

Cloven was there. He filled the empty space in front of her, a huge barrier of living flesh. Nelle stared into his eyes, and for a moment she thought she saw Cloven himself, the real Cloven, fighting the influence in his head.

He lunged at her. Whether by his own will or by the will of the monster who drove him, it hardly mattered. His great fist caught Nelle in the shoulder, a glancing blow, but enough to send her reeling into the wall. She caught herself, standing for the space of two gasping breaths, her arms out, her fingers splayed, braced against the stone.

Then she ran for it.

The men followed close at her heels. They'd made certain to block the way to the door leading out to the courtyard, but they'd neglected to watch the smaller door in the wall at this end of the hall. Where it would lead, Nelle could only guess. It was the only possible route of escape, so she ducked through the gaping doorway into a winding stairwell and climbed. Below her, she heard the impact of bodies as several men tried to fit through the opening simultaneously. She was already three turns up the winding stair and getting faster. Her bare feet slapped on the stone steps, but if they were in pain, she had no time to feel it.

All around her in the darkness—movement. Slithering. Hissing. The scrape of thorns on stone.

She stopped up her ears, stopped up her senses, and climbed faster, taking the steps two at a time. The stairs ended at an opening, and Nelle emerged into open air atop the battlements overlooking the ocean. Wind slapped at her face and body, blowing straight through her damp clothing. She gasped at its bite.

Footsteps echoed in the stairwell beneath her. Nelle looked back. For half an instant she saw vines crawling up through the door.

Smothering a scream, she rushed along the wall walk, pausing at a crenel in the parapet to stare out between the merlons. The tide was in. Waves lashed at the wall below.

Could she survive a plunge from this height? Was the water deep enough? Would she have the strength to swim to shore?

"It's over, Peronelle Beck!"

She whirled in place. Cloven appeared in the doorway. He

stepped out onto the walk, his huge fists upraised like two great mallets. He opened his mouth, and the Thorn Maiden echoed behind his voice. *"You cannot run from me. No one can. Come to my arms, pretty betrayer, and let me show you—"*

Nelle sprang into the crenel and launched herself out from the parapet. Arms wheeling, she fell, plunging toward the frigid sea.

CHAPTER 16

BY *RIGHTS, YOU SHOULD BE DEAD, FOOL GIRL.*

Nelle cracked open a weary eye. But it took too much effort.

With a groan, she let her eyelid drop again, shivered, and burrowed her head into wet sand. Water lapped at her bare feet, tugging gently.

You've got a snatcher's instinct though, don't you? I always knew you had.

A frown puckered Nelle's brow. That voice . . . it wasn't hers. At first she'd thought it was her familiar, critical inner self. But this was different. It was brighter, merrier. And a little bit mad.

Choking on salt and sand, Nelle spat, dragged her eyes open, and lifted her head.

Someone crouched beside her. An outline of shadow, a shimmer of moonlight gleaming. Long strands of hair billowed in the breeze, glinting red even in the pitch darkness, like threads of pure magic.

"M-Mother?" Nelle whispered.

You gauge a leap. Can you survive it? Can you not? And you know without knowing you know. That's a snatcher gift. Nothing to do with the fae blood in your veins.

Pride swelled in that voice. Nelle's frozen blood warmed at the sound. She stirred again, trying to get her hands under her, to push her upper body up from the sand. She was too weak. Better to lie still, better not to fight the cold.

The figure bent over Nelle, and for a moment she could have sworn she felt breath on her cheek. *I was wrong, you know.*

Nelle flinched, closed her eyes tight, and shook her head slightly. "Wh-what? What are you saying, Mother?"

I was wrong to demand such a promise from you: to watch over your Papa if I could not. I should never have placed that burden on your shoulders.

"No!" Nelle whimpered. "No, don't say that!" A storm of emotions stirred in her chest, battling the cold and numbness that stiffened her limbs. One by one they intensified, heating her from the inside out—resentment, frustration, shame, sorrow. Tears burned her eyes, falling through her lashes and trailing cold lines down her cheeks. "It's not a burden. I can take care of Papa, I swear."

I know, my darling. I know. Nevertheless . . .

Lips pressed against her forehead, soft and gentle. The shadowy figure pulled back, and Nelle opened her eyes again, turned her face, and looked up. For a moment she stared into two bright-gold eyes, familiar and full of fae light.

I release you from your promise.

"No! Mother!"

Nelle surged upright, her hands slapping the shallow water. Waves foamed against her legs, pushing and pulling at her wet trousers. She shivered, looking around, up and down the night-darkened beach. To her left loomed the massive shadows of the old fortress. To her right, some quarter-mile distant, were the long quays where tall ships moored.

But this stretch of beach was abandoned, silent. She was alone.

"M-Mother?" Nelle whispered. She wrapped her arms around her shivering body. It was a dream. It must have been. Mother was long dead, after all. Nelle had seen her die, had watched her fall, had crept up to her mangled body and looked into her still, lifeless face just moments before the Green Caps caught up. She was dead. Gone.

Slowly, every muscle and limb protesting, Nelle got to her feet, staggered to catch her balance. Her gaze turned to the fortress again, searching the darkness for some sign of pursuit. Apparently she'd been right to gamble her life with that jump. Not only had she survived, but none of Cloven's men had followed her off the wall.

Perhaps the Thorn Maiden's aversion to moving water affected her even through the bodies of those she possessed.

However it was, Nelle had a head start and couldn't afford to waste it. She should run. Now. Run and run and run, and never look back.

But what about . . .

She bowed her head, shivering. Was this why she'd dreamed of her mother releasing her from her promise? Was she trying to make excuses, trying to justify her own cowardice?

No. She would stay. Papa still needed her. She wouldn't abandon him or Wimborne to the Thorn Maiden. Besides, who could outrun a nightmare?

Outrun a nightmare . . . outrun . . .

"Sam!"

Nelle's eyes widened. Memory flashed through her mind of that meeting in the alley, of the strange urgency in Sam's face, the desperation in his voice as he pleaded with her to run away with him. He knew something. And he'd broken with Cloven. Did that mean he hadn't been overtaken by the Thorn Maiden yet?

Did he know where the Rose Book was hidden?

Somewhere far away, as though carried on winds blown from a distant world, the cathedral bells tolled eleven times. Sam had told her to meet him at the East Gate at midnight. Could she make it in time?

Nelle shivered but set her jaw and looked up at the waiting city. She would make it. She had to.

The roads of Wimborne City seemed longer and more winding than ever. Down every dark alley and around every turn, Nelle fancied she saw snarling thorns. In each passing stranger's face, she thought she glimpsed the Thorn Maiden's evil eyes looking back at her, and every time she brushed past someone, she expected a hand to reach out and grab her.

She must have seemed like a madwoman, jumpy and wide-eyed, not to mention half-drowned, barefoot, and dressed in boy's clothes that clung damply to her body. But her strength revived. Her clothes dried, her arms and legs limbered up, her blood warmed. Soon she was running up the streets, her hair flying out behind her, outpacing both her fear and the chill in her bones.

The cathedral bells began to toll again, twelve resounding strokes that echoed across the city rooftops. Just as the final stroke sounded, Nelle came in sight of the East Gate, the waterway through which this branch of the River Wim channeled. She picked up her pace and ran for it, calling, "Sam! Sam, are you there?"

A figure peeled out from the wall not far from the gate arch. Nelle's heart lurched even as she recognized Sam's rangy frame. Had she made a mistake in coming here? What if he was claimed by the Thorn Maiden after all? What if this was a trap?

But then he called out to her in the darkness: "Ginger? Is that really you?"

There was no trace of an echo beneath his voice. It was Sam. Just Sam.

A wave of relief rushed through Nelle's body. She hadn't realized just how fearful she was until that moment when the worst of the fear passed. Her knees buckled, and she staggered, almost fell to her knees.

Sam leaped forward and caught her in his arms. Hauling her upright, he held her close, and she leaned into his warmth and strength, closing her eyes.

"I didn't think you'd come," he said. His lips pressed against the top of her head. "Oh, seven gods, I thought sure you'd stand me up!"

For a moment she lingered, grateful for the warmth, for the support. But it couldn't last.

She pulled back, and he reluctantly loosened his hold. One hand gripped her upper arm while he lifted his other hand to cup her face, studying her by the glow of the nearby streetlamp.

"What's wrong?" he demanded, his brow constricting in a worried frown.

Nelle shook her head and pushed his hand away. "Where's the spellbook, Sam?" she said. "You've got to tell me."

The relief in his eyes gave way to a guarded look. The hand still holding her arm tightened. "What are you talking about?"

"You know." Nelle stared up at him earnestly. "You know where it is, don't you? Gaspard gave it to you. When he realized what was happening, when he realized he wouldn't be able to keep control. He gave you the book, told you to hide it, then told Cloven to kill you so the secret would die with you. That's why you broke with Cloven. That's why you've been on the run."

Sam started to pull away, paused, and took her hand. "It doesn't matter. You're here now. We can get out. Horald is as good as his word. There's a barge coming that'll carry us miles out of Wimborne by dawn. We'll be free."

"We can't just abandon the whole city!" With a vicious tug, Nelle wrenched her hand out of his grasp. "You've seen what *she's* done to Cloven and the others, haven't you? They were your crew! And now what are they? Mindless monsters serving at the will of something far more monstrous. Do you understand, Sam? She's a Noswraith, a living nightmare. She exists for no purpose but to spread fear and destruction wherever she goes. She'll take over the city, and when she's done, she'll set her sights on the next city, and the next. We can't run away from that! We've got to stop it."

He looked so haunted in the lamplight. Poor Sam. He might know little about magic, but he'd gotten an eyeful of it recently. What kind of life had he lived these last few months? Hiding during the day, never daring to sleep at night. Stalked in both body and spirit.

But he'd stayed in Wimborne. When he could have run away, put miles and months between himself and the impending disaster he saw coming for the city, he had stayed. For her.

"Please, Sam," she said in a gentler tone. "You don't have to be part of this. You can walk onto that barge and get out of here. Only tell me where you hid the Rose Book first."

"And what will you do when I tell you?"

"I don't know." She dropped her gaze to the ground. "But I can't leave it for *her* to find. If she gets it, that'll be the end. No one will ever bind her again."

"The Miphates . . ." Sam began, but his voice trailed off when Nelle shook her head.

"The Miphates can't handle a Noswraith. Not anymore. This is magic beyond the skill of all the mages in Wimborne. There's only one mage who knows this spell, and he . . . he . . ." She swallowed painfully, her hands curling into fists. "He ain't here. There's only me."

"And what can you do?"

Until he asked, Nelle hadn't been sure. Only a vague certainty that she must do *something* had driven her. She'd figured to come up with specifics along the way.

But now, with the question stated so bluntly, she had to answer. And, to her surprise, the answer was right there on the tip of her tongue.

"I'm going to read the spell. I'm going to bind the Thorn Maiden. At least, I'm going to try."

Sam stared down at her, his eyes widening. "Can you *do* that?"

"I don't know." She pressed her lips together and shrugged, drawing a long breath through her nostrils. "I've studied a bit of magic, and I managed part of the spell once before. I got an idea how it works."

Sam might not know anything about magic, but from the way he looked at her, he'd guessed that what she proposed was dangerous. Too dangerous.

"You're not going to back down, are you," he said, sounding like a man whose sentence is about to be passed, who knows his date with the hangman is certain, even if it hasn't been pronounced yet.

Nelle shook her head. "I've got to try, Sam. I've got to. It's my fault she's here to begin with."

"It's not your fault."

"I'm the one who—"

"Gaspard's the one who made you do it. And Cloven's the one who recommended you to Gaspard. And I'm the one who helped

Cloven track you down. Plenty of others bear the blame here, Nelle. Not you."

She could argue. But what would be the point? She knew her own guilt as clearly as Sam knew his. They were none of them innocent. This whole gods-blighted city teemed with guilt. Perhaps the gods themselves had allowed the Thorn Maiden to be unleashed upon it as a judgment.

It didn't matter. Guilty or not, judgment or not—she would do what she could to stop this monster.

"Please, Sam," she said quietly. "Tell me where it is. Tell me where you hid it."

Sam hung his head, resignation weighing down his bowed shoulders. He took her hand again, his fingers cold, and she did not try to pull away. "Gaspard told me to put it somewhere it would be safe, somewhere it wouldn't fall to pieces. Somewhere no one would think to look for it. But I thought . . . well, at the time, I thought maybe I should put it somewhere *you* could find it. Just in case something happened to me."

A cold stone dropped in Nelle's stomach. She knew what he would say next.

"What have you done, Sam?" she whispered. "Where is it? Where is the Rose Book?"

His eyes flashed in the lamplight, meeting her gaze. "It's in the attic. At Mistress Dirgin's place."

All the breath whooshed from Nelle's lungs.

"Papa," she whispered.

How many times in his life had he watched Roseward shrink in the distance as he traveled across the channel to Wimborne City? Soran had lost count. Once upon a time, the sight had been a regular part of his life, the journey made at least once every quarter when he returned from his brief excursions to visit his family. To see Helenia.

Never had the journey felt so long, so perilous.

Lodírhal would kill him for daring to leave his place of exile. Not that it made much difference now. He'd already broken the terms of his imprisonment by venturing to Noxaur's shore. What did one more infraction matter?

Besides, he would be dead long before Lodírhal arrived to kill him.

He could barely see the lighthouse by the light of the moon overhead. It seemed more ruinous than he'd realized. The whole island looked smaller when seen from a little distance, especially now that he'd passed through the Veil and left the Hinter air behind.

How strange it was to breathe mortal air again! He felt frailer, more vulnerable as he pulled at the oars and drove his small boat across the channel. Wimborne loomed at his back, teeming with life and death and thousands of mortal souls. He could almost feel them, like radiant heat pulsing from the heart of the city. The sensation was overwhelming after so many years of solitude; the prospect of walking those streets again made him shudder.

Yet Soran set his jaw and continued his steady course toward the strip of beach away from the quays. The tide was in his favor, at least. The waves urged his boat gently to shore until the hull crunched in soft sand. Soran sprang out into the foam and dragged the boat high enough that he was certain it wouldn't easily be caught by the rising tide and pulled out to sea.

Feeling the spells tucked inside his robes near his heart, he turned and faced the city. It was quite dark by this hour, with only a few lights flickering from various windows, like low-fallen stars in the night.

His gaze drifted to the Evenspire, and he fought the urge to march up to the university building, pound at the gates, and demand that Gaspard come forth and meet him.

But Gaspard was no fool. He wouldn't dare take the Rose Book into the Evenspire. Too many Miphates, their magic perception highly tuned, would sense the Noswraith spell the moment Gaspard dared crack the cover. No, he would have hidden it somewhere safe where he could pore over its contents at his leisure.

Perhaps his faithful snatcher would know where.

Soran's lip curled, and he set out across the beach, making for the city above. The cathedral bells tolled twelve.

CHAPTER 17

"IS THIS REALLY SUCH A GOOD IDEA?"

Nelle cast a dirty glance back at Sam before refocusing her attention on picking the lock in front of her. "We got to assume the Thorn Maiden's looking for us," she said through gritted teeth. "She ain't stupid, you know. She's got to have eyes all over the city, trying to find us. If she catches up before I've had a chance to try the spell, I won't be sitting there like a kitten without claws, waiting for her to tear me to pieces."

"Sure, Ginger." Sam leaned against the wall beside her, his pose casual even as his voice trembled with anxiety. "But exactly what weapons do you expect to find in a wash house?"

Nelle didn't bother to answer. When the gears of the lock she was picking made a satisfying click, she tucked Gaspard's penknife back into the waistband of her trousers and slowly eased the door of Mistress Ainsley's shop open, peering into the gloom. It was well past midnight by now, and the wash girls and Ainsley herself had retired long ago.

A powerful wave of lavender soap assaulted Nelle's nostrils as she slipped inside, strong enough to make her eyes water. It was very dark, but her *ibrildian* eyes saw well enough. Ignoring Sam, who followed at her heels, she slipped behind the shop counter and reached underneath. Her fingers found Mistress Ainsley's ledger along with a quill and ink.

Nelle set these items on the countertop, all the while casting nervous glances at the stair behind her. Ainsley slept in the first room at the top of the stair. Nelle moved with a snatcher's studied stealth, and Sam's footsteps were catlike and careful, but the laundry mistress was a notoriously light sleeper. Nelle didn't dare light a candle.

Could she write clearly enough in this gloom? She'd better.

Opening the ledger to a fresh page, she unstoppered the ink, dipped the quill, poised it over the page . . . and hesitated. Since returning from Roseward eight months ago, she hadn't attempted any magic whatsoever. It had been almost too easy to ignore the humming power in her veins, to forget those hours of lessons and practice. Had the magic dried up for lack of use? Had she forgotten everything?

She might just as easily forget how to breathe.

Planting the nib on the page, she began to write. The first few letters were neat enough, even written in the dark, but as she wrote on, the energy mounted inside her and came pouring out in a gush, faster than she could pen. The feather fluttered wildly as she hastened to shape the words, pausing only long enough to dip the quill in the inkwell.

The spell began to take shape. It was messy, ugly, but she didn't need it to be pretty. She just needed it to *work*. And it would work, gods willing. Power pulsed in the words she scrawled, power drawn directly from the *quinsatra* through her mind and captured in physical form. She kept writing in a slapdash, manic frenzy of creativity. Soran would surely despair at her lack of precision, but not even he could deny the magic of her words.

When she reached the end of the page, despite her fear, exhaustion, and dread of what was coming, a smile tugged at her lips. It was done. And it was good.

She tore the spell free of the ledger, folded it, and tucked it into the front of her shirt. Then, closing the ledger and dropping the quill, she faced Sam, who stood across the desk, watching her.

He gave her a quizzical look. "That's it?"

She nodded. "It'll do."

He looked as though he wanted to argue but shrugged instead. "I hope you know what you're doing, Nelle."

"Me too." She slid out from behind the desk, and together they left the shop. Nelle peered nervously up and down the street and into the dark, silent windows of the opposite building but sensed no watchful eyes spying on them as they completed their odd burglary.

Nelle used her stolen penknife to carefully lock the door. "If things go bad"—she spoke quietly as she worked—"and we get separated, let's meet back here. You said Cloven and the others didn't know I worked here, so presumably the Thorn Maiden doesn't know either. It should be safe enough for a rendezvous."

Sam grunted just as the lock clicked back into place.

They set off together at a quick pace, keeping to the shadows. Now and then they caught a glimpse of some unsavory figure. Down one alley, close to a noisome public house, haggard ladies of the night plied their trade, but no one took any interest in the two figures making their way quietly along the far side of the road. Draggs was always full of activity at night—furtive activity, the kind that spoke in whispers and gasps.

Nelle couldn't help peering into every dark corner, straining her *ibrildian* vision. She caught no glimpse of coiling vines, and when she sniffed the air, she smelled only the rank aromas one expected to encounter in Draggs. No trace of roses.

When at last they came in sight of the row houses overlooking the river, Nelle slowed to a halt. What if she was wrong? They'd been careful, sure. They'd been good snatchers, doubling back several times, taking odd and unexpected turns, always checking their backs for signs of pursuit. What if it hadn't been enough? What if the Thorn Maiden watched them even now through stolen eyes?

"Ginger?" Sam whispered beside her.

She drew a steadying breath. "Remember, meet back at the wash house," she said. "And if I tell you to go, just go. Don't wait for me. If the Thorn Maiden is there, don't try to be a hero. You don't have the weapons to fight her."

"And you do?"

Nelle touched the folded paper tucked against her breast. "Yeah. I do," she said with more confidence than she felt.

Refusing to linger any longer, she stepped out into the street, crossed over to Mistress Dirgin's house, and led the way to the backdoor. It was locked, of course, but it was the work of a few moments for Nelle to get it open. She led the way inside and up the stairs, remembering to skip over the one that squeaked.

The door at the top of the stair gave at a little pressure. Nelle stepped into the dark, empty space she'd once called home. Immediately, her senses prickled.

It was here. The spellbook.

She felt magic in the air, faint but unmistakable.

Sam followed close behind her. "It's over there," he whispered.

231

"Under the mattress."

Nelle tried to swallow, but her tongue and throat were too dry. Get in, get out, get away . . . that was the plan. But now she'd come to it, her feet were frozen in place. The Noswraith spell was too big for her, too unwieldy. All that power condensed into one small space, the pressure building to the point of explosion . . .

Did she really think she could handle it? With her little bit of training, her rough-honed skills?

But she couldn't very well leave it here. Not with Papa sleeping downstairs.

"You want me to get it?" Sam whispered.

Nelle shook her head and motioned for him to stay put. She crossed the room on silent feet, crouched, and, wincing against the radiant power stirring the air, lifted the straw mattress.

The Rose Book was there, just as Sam had said. Frail and battered, but still whole. For the moment.

Nelle carefully picked it up, holding it against her chest. Her stomach clenched with dread. Even if she had the strength to read off the spell and bind the Thorn Maiden, could the book itself withstand such a surge of power? She didn't think so. It would disintegrate before she'd read half a dozen pages.

"Ginger!"

She looked up sharply. Sam stood in the doorway, his eyes bright in the moonlight. "I hear something," he said. "Downstairs. Someone's there."

Still holding the book close, Nelle hastened lightly across the floor back to the attic stair. Sam followed, drawing the door shut behind him. Nelle began to descend, her heart beating fast against the leather book's binding.

She was nearly halfway down when a figure appeared at the bottom of the stairway, holding up a stub of candle. Flickering light illuminated haggard features and an evil, leering mouth.

Nelle's heart lurched to her throat. "Mistress Dirgin!"

The old woman's eyes widened as she held her candle a little higher. "Mixael!" she shrieked. "Mixael, it's that wench of yours! I told you! I told you she'd be back! She's come sneaking in to steal me blind, she is!"

"Mistress Dirgin, please!" Nelle held a finger to her lips. "Please, I'm on my way back out. I ain't taking nothing that's yours, I swear. I just remembered I'd left this book of mine—"

"Who's that you've got with you?" Mistress Dirgin took three aggressive steps up, angling her candle. "Are you sneaking menfolk in as well? Just to spite me with your lewd ways? *Mixael!*"

To Nelle's horror, her father's face appeared in the stairwell just behind his wife. He wore only his sleep shirt and a nightcap, his hairy legs bare beneath his shaking knees. "My dear, my dear," he said in his most soothing voice, "I'm sure there's been some misunder— Nelle?" He blinked and peered over his wife's shoulder, his brow puckering. "Nellie, love, is that really you?"

Nelle backed up a step or two and bumped into Sam. "Papa," she said. "Papa, please. I just need to go. That's all. I came for something, and now I've got it, and I don't want to cause trouble."

"What could you possibly have come to get?" Papa took hold of his wife's arm and tried to draw her down beside him, but Mistress Dirgin swore and wrenched free of his grasp, spattering hot wax from her candle. "We cleaned out that attic quite thoroughly, I'm sure."

"It's nothing, Papa," Nelle said. Her fingers tightened protectively around the book.

"Ask her what she's got there!" Mistress Dirgin pointed an accusing finger. "Ask her what she's hiding, her and her young man. They gots something! Just look at her guilty face!"

Papa peered up at her, perplexed and gentle as always. "What have you got, Nellie?"

"I can't explain. You've just got to trust me, Papa. Trust me and let me—"

The crash of a door slamming open rattled the walls. Mistress Dirgin screamed and spun in place, her candle almost flickering out. Nelle started, and Sam's hand came down hard on her shoulder, his fingers pinching painfully.

A third figure appeared below—a man Nelle knew well by sight, a slack-jawed lug with a face like a bulldog and a nose broken so many times the original shape could only be guessed at. He'd been with Cloven and the others at the old fortress.

Before Nelle could react, the man caught Papa by the shoulder and flung him into the wall with a sickening thud. Mistress Dirgin let out a piercing scream and collapsed. Her candle went out.

For a moment Nelle was blind. Then her *ibrildian* eyesight clarified. She saw the man holding her father against the wall by his throat, fat fingers squeezing slowly.

Something in her head exploded in a flare of raw, red rage.

Dropping the Rose Book, Nelle sprang down the stairwell in a single leap, slammed into the man, wrapped one arm around his neck from behind, and tore at his eyes with her other hand. The man roared, let go of Papa, and flung back both arms, trying to grab her while Papa slumped to the floor in a senseless heap. Nelle couldn't spare him more than a glance. Cloven's man rammed her into the wall. She gasped with pain, afraid his weight would break her ribs. Her hold loosened, and when the man lurched forward, she let go and fell.

She had just time enough to catch her breath before the man was on her. He grabbed the hair on top of her head and dragged her up onto her knees. His other hand caught her by the throat, lifted her off her feet and knocked her into the wall. His ugly face loomed before her fae-vision, eyes flashing with a mad yellow light. His pock-marked skin bubbled.

Thorns burst through across his cheekbones and brow; blood

flowed in tiny rivulets down his sagging jowls.

"Well done, Peronelle." The man spoke in a deep-throated growl, but the Thorn Maiden's voice whispered just behind it. *"You led me straight to the spell, just as I hoped. And now . . ."*

Thorns tore viciously through the man's cheeks, and dark vines coiled out from his face, reaching for Nelle's head. She screamed and writhed but could not escape the thorns as they pierced her flesh, ripped into her eyes. Her head exploded with pain and terror.

"That's right," the Thorn Maiden said. She no longer spoke through the man but crooned directly inside Nelle's head. *"That's right, let me in. There's room enough for me here. Let me in. Don't try to fight. I will—"*

In a flash, Nelle's hand snatched the penknife from her waistband and drove it straight into one of the man's wide eyes, as deep as it would go. Hot blood spurted out over her hand, up her arm.

He screamed—and the Thorn Maiden screamed as well. Her vines wrenched back out of Nelle's head as the man let her go and stumbled backwards, clawing at his face. Nelle landed heavily, the wind knocked out of her. Her head throbbed with the pain of thorns raked across her brain, but when she touched her face, her eyes, she found them whole. The sensation of vines piercing through her had been a nightmare, not a reality.

She looked up at the screaming man and, gritting a curse

through her teeth, lashed out with one foot. Her heel connected hard with his stomach, and he doubled up then fell heavily on his side. For a few agonized, grunting seconds, he twitched. Then he was still.

Coughing, spitting blood, Nelle pushed up onto her hands and knees. Papa! He lay at the base of the stair. She crawled over to him and grasped him by the shoulder. A cry of pain split from her mouth. She withdrew her hand and stared, horrified, at the five tiny thorns stuck into her palm.

"No!" She looked at Papa again, horror rising.

Tiny thorns pierced through his skin, and he bled from each small wound.

"No, no, no!" Nelle grabbed him again, ignoring more thorns, and rolled him over. His eyes were wide but sightless, and when she looked into them she sensed something-not-her-father looking back at her. "Papa!" she cried. "Papa, can you hear me?"

He blinked, dazed, empty. Then his gaze sharpened and fixed on her.

"Greetings again, Peronelle," the Thorn Maiden said. *"That wasn't very nice of you, was it?"*

Nelle fell back, scrambling to put distance between them. Papa rose, standing over her, and his sweet, gentle face twisted with the Thorn Maiden's smile. *"Come, my dear, that's no way to treat your father, now is it?"*

He lunged and grasped her by the neck, pinning her to the

ground. Nelle tried to scream but couldn't. She stared up into her father's eyes, and the Thorn Maiden's vines reached for her again, twining through the air between them.

"Hush now, pretty maid. It will all be over soon—"

A flash of light burst off to one side. Papa cried out, looked up in surprise, and the Thorn Maiden bared his teeth in a snarl.

Then something struck him in the chest, and he spread-eagled beside Nelle. Choking on a scream, she pulled herself upright, turned . . .

And saw Soran Silveri standing in the doorway.

CHAPTER 18

EVERYONE IN WIMBORNE KNEW THE WAY TO DRAGGS Street, even those who had never deigned to enter that most disreputable part of the city. It was like a hairy mole on the face of a beautiful lady, impossible to ignore despite the finest combination of charm and cosmetics.

His hood pulled over his head, his stride swift and purposeful, Soran entered Draggs for the first time. Immediately, the pervasive funk of despair and degradation that permeated every stone, every brick, even the very mortar of every lurching building assaulted his senses. It was enough to make him pause at the head of the street, squeezing his hands into fists, his nostrils flaring with each breath he drew. Years of living in the Hinter had sharpened his perceptions in ways he'd scarcely realized. He found he could *smell* the sorrow of this place.

And this was Nelle's home? He couldn't imagine her living here, not the bright, vivacious young woman he'd thought he knew.

But then again, she was a liar. A mistress of disguise, wearing clever masks he'd never thought to look for.

Maybe she did belong here after all.

Steeling himself, Soran surged back into motion, striding down the incline of the street into the rotten gloom of Draggs. He couldn't have said exactly what he sought. It wasn't as if he expected to bump into her on the street in the middle of the night. But some sixth sense drew him on, and he followed it. She was here. Somewhere. He would find her before the night ended.

Something prickled on the edge of his awareness.

Soran turned sharply to peer into an alley between two sagging buildings, like a fae path in the forest, waiting to lead unwary mortals astray. He narrowed his eyes. There was magic at large here tonight. He was sure of it. Powerful magic. Dark magic.

He sniffed the air, his lips pulling back from his teeth in a tense grimace. "Noswraith," he whispered.

Reaching into the front of his robes, he pulled out a slim volume and flipped it open. Once it had been full of spells, simple but well-written, ready for use. He'd used up most of them already, but in the back of the book a few thin sheets remained untouched.

He found what he sought and read the words out, his voice deep and tense: "*Ilrune petmenor. Mythanar prey sarlenna sior . . .*"

Reaching the end of the spell, he closed his eyes, breathed in, breathed out. When he looked out on the world again, it had changed. Draggs Street still lay before him in all its claustrophobic squalor. But now the veils of realities thinned, allowing Soran's magicked vision to peer through into worlds beyond. He could *feel* the Nightmare Realm around him like a coating of slime.

And in the darker shadows he glimpsed . . . movement.

Scuttling vines. Like snakes slithering swiftly out of sight.

She was here. Here in Wimborne. Right here in Draggs Street. Gaspard had failed to contain her.

How long had she been free? Who could say how much time had passed in this world since Nelle escaped with the spellbook? It felt like less than a day, but it may have been months or even years. How far had the Thorn Maiden spread in that time, creeping from mind to mind?

Soran reached for the sealed spell he'd brought with him, touching the folded parchment with trembling fingertips. But no. He wasn't ready to use it. Not yet. He must trace her to her source.

Instead, he paged through the last few remaining pages in his slim volume, found a viable spell, and read it off swiftly. Magic manifested as a ball of churning light over his extended palm. It would be good for two, maybe three uses before the spell burned away. Not ideal, but he couldn't afford to waste any of his stronger spells.

Soran continued down the street. The skittering vines grew denser on either side, less furtive in their movements. Rounding a bend in the street, he came in sight of a row of townhouses near the riverbank. His physical gaze passed over them entirely, but his magicked vision noticed something strange.

The twisting vines crawling along the ground and creeping from wall to wall between the houses along the street all made for the house standing third from the end of that row.

Soran broke into a run, raced around to the back of the house, and found an open door. It was pitch dark inside, but he could hear movement, grunting, and a whispering cry.

He leapt up the back steps into the doorway, and light from his pulsing spell-sphere illuminated the small back room, flaring over a prone body pinned to the floor, her face surrounded by mounds of brilliant red hair. Crouched over that body was a man-like form. Thorns burst from his skin like spines, and blood streamed down his body in dark ribbons. His eyes were huge and savage, staring down at his victim, whom he had by the throat.

Vines stretched out from inside him, digging into her head.

With a cry, Soran drew back his arm. Startled by the sound, the thorn-pierced man looked up, his tortured face momentarily lit by the glow of magic. He bared his teeth.

Soran let loose the spell, which sped across the small space and struck the man directly in the chest, knocking him back against the wall with a crash that rattled the whole house.

Without a word, without a cry, he fell in a heap on the floor.

The spell's light went out on impact, leaving Soran momentarily blind in the doorway. He stood there, blinking, hearing vines slither across the floor, the walls, the ceiling. When his spell-vision cleared, he saw the vines fleeing the house, pulling out of the fallen man. The thorns that retreated into his skin like a cat's claws sheathing left his body covered in hundreds of bright pinpoints of blood.

"Soran!"

He turned, looked down into her face.

Nelle.

His physical eyes could not see her, but his magicked vision could just discern her by the weird half-light of nightmarish reality. His heart lurched with sudden, unexpected pain, and for a moment he couldn't think. Not about the imminent danger of the Thorn Maiden, her vines threading through the city. Not about the sealed spell he carried, with which he intended to create his doom. Not even about her betrayal, which still burned

243

like a knife in his gut.

She was alive. For an instant, he cared about nothing else.

Then the instant passed.

He wrenched his gaze away from her, strode across the small space, and crouched over the fallen man. Rolling him over, he peered into his face, searching for signs of the Thorn Maiden still inside. She wasn't there. The man was clear.

"Is he alive?"

Nelle crouched beside Soran. Shivering, he withdrew from her and stood quickly, then watched in surprise as she caught the man's face between her hands and tenderly wiped blood from his cheeks. How did she know him?

She lifted her face, looking up at Soran. Gods, but she was beautiful! Even now, even when he knew what a traitorous monster she truly was, his heart ached at the sight.

"What was that spell?" Her voice trembled. "What did you do to him?"

"It was a stun spell," Soran replied coldly, stepping away from her. "He will live. Who is he?"

"My father."

Soran blinked. Through the Nightmare haze, he looked again at the man and recognized his features—a fineness about his cheekbones, a certain elegance, even nobility to his brow. He was not the sort of man one expected to find in a place like Draggs.

Taking another step back, Soran surveyed the scene. Another

244

man lay fallen in a bundle of limbs, something protruding from his eye. An old woman in a nightdress had collapsed on the stair, her chest rising and falling rapidly.

Nelle bent over the man—her father—again, pushing hair off his forehead and whispering, "Papa? Papa, can you hear me?"

Her voice sent a shiver down Soran's spine. He fought the sudden urge to reach out to her, to put his arms around her, to comfort her.

Instead, he folded his arms across his chest and braced himself as though for battle. "Where is it?" he said.

Nelle turned to look up at him again, tossing hair out of her wide, frightened eyes. She didn't try to pretend ignorance; she knew what he meant.

"I came here to get it," she said. "I didn't know until today that . . . that *she* was out. I was going to try to bind her again, and I . . ."

She gasped suddenly and drew away from her father, scrambling to her feet. "Sam?" She whirled, tripped over the fallen body of the other man, and lunged for the stairwell. "Sam, where are you?" she cried.

So. That handsome young man of hers was involved in all this too. Of course, he was.

Soran caught Nelle by the arm just as she started to climb around the fallen old woman. "What has happened here?" he demanded. "Where is the Rose Book?"

"It was here!" Nelle tried to yank free, but his nilarium fingers gripped too hard, so instead she tried to draw him after her up the stair. "She's gotten into Gaspard, but he had the book hidden before she could destroy it. He gave it to Sam, and Sam brought it here, and we've come to get it! I had it, I swear, I had it in my hands. But *she* followed me, using Cloven's man, and then she got into Papa, and . . ."

Soran tightened his grip on her arm, startling her into silence. He pulled her toward him, around the old woman, and lowered his face toward hers. "Where is it?" he said. His voice was a dangerous growl in the darkness.

She went very still, no longer resisting his grasp. "I don't know. I dropped it. That man—the Thorn Maiden—she had my Papa; she was hurting him. I dropped the book and tried to stop her. And Sam, he was right behind me."

"Did you see which way he went?"

She shook her head. "He didn't get past us on the stairs. He couldn't have. He's got to be—"

Soran didn't wait for her to finish. Releasing her arm and pushing her roughly to one side, he lunged up the stair. A quick duck to get through the small door at the top, and he stepped into a mean little attic space.

It was empty. But a window at the far end was broken.

Nelle's steps sounded on the stair behind him. She pushed past him into the room and stood a moment, staring around, her hands curling into fists. "He's gone," she whispered, then sprang across the room to the broken window, carefully leaned out, and craned her neck. Pulling back in, she faced Soran, her eyes wide, her face etched with fear and other emotions he couldn't name. "He got away."

So, her sweetheart had taken the book and left her behind to be throttled by the Thorn Maiden's avatars. Hardly more than she deserved.

"Where would he take it?" Soran asked, stepping toward her. "Tell me."

"We agreed to meet at a wash house not far from here."

"And you think he will honor that agreement? He left you here. Left you to the monsters."

Nelle's eyes flashed in the semi-darkness. "I told him not to try to be a hero. He's got no magic. He can't fight . . . *things* like that." Her voice was tight, her shoulders tense. But she added firmly, "He'll be there."

"Tell me where."

"I'll take you."

"No. Tell me."

She flinched. "Soran," she said softly.

He hated to hear his name on her lips, hated the softness of her voice, hated that tone of tremulous hurt underscored by fear. He hated her so strongly, it felt like love.

Turning away, Soran gripped the doorpost, unable to bear

looking at her.

"Soran," she said again, "I didn't have a choice."

"There's always a choice."

"Gaspard used me. He threatened my Papa. And I thought . . . I knew he'd been with you when you created the Noswraith, when you learned the spells. I thought he might be strong enough to bind her. I . . . I hoped . . ."

His grip on the door hardened. The wood splintered beneath his nilarium fingers. He felt Nelle draw toward him from behind, her footsteps silent.

"I ain't making excuses," she said. "I know I was wrong. But I didn't know what else to do. I'm trying to fix it now. I was going to get the Rose Book; I was going to try to bind her back."

"That's impossible." Soran shook his head heavily. "She can't be bound. Not like that. Not again."

He turned and faced Nelle, forced himself to look into her upturned face. Entreaty shimmered in her eyes, begging him to understand. And he wanted to. Every fiber of his being urged him to forgive her, to reach out to her. To take her in his arms.

But he couldn't. She'd betrayed him. And because of her betrayal, everything he'd worked so hard to prevent would come to pass unless . . . unless . . .

"Very well, Miss Beck," he said coldly. "Take me to your meeting place. At once."

Cloven's man wasn't dead. He lay in a stupor, his one eye half open, staring off into some unseen world of horror. The other eye was a mass of blood around the protruding penknife. But he was alive.

Nelle's stomach clenched as she stepped around him. She almost wished she'd killed him.

Painfully aware of Soran's presence behind her on the stair, she knelt beside her father, and her trembling fingers cradled his head. Without Hinter air, the small thorn cuts wouldn't heal so quickly. Would his handsome face end up riddled with scars? Her heart hurt at the very idea. But at least he lived.

Soran paused behind her. She felt the unspoken impatience in his stance, but he held his peace. She sniffed and wiped the back of one hand across her nose. "Will he be all right?" she asked without looking around. "That spell you used—"

"A stun spell." Soran's voice was a deep growl in the darkness. She shivered at the sound. "All traces of the Thorn Maiden have left him. He will experience some pain upon waking, but his wounds will heal."

"He'll be all right then?"

"Yes. I believe so."

Nelle pulled in both lips, biting down hard. There was no time. Even now, she ought to be out the door, halfway up the street. She couldn't linger.

But somehow she knew . . . whatever happened tonight, this was the last time she would see her father's face. She would never again glimpse his sweet, perplexed smile, she would never again feel his gentle hands take hold of hers. She would never again hear his soft voice fondly call her "Nellie girl."

"Bullspit." The expletive choked around a threatening sob. "I'm sorry, Papa. I'm sorry I couldn't protect you better."

She bent and softly kissed his forehead. "*Hush-a-bye, don't you cry*," she whispered through her tears. "*Sleepy now, my little love. When you wake, I'll . . . I'll give to you . . .*" She squeezed her eyes tight, and tears fell, landing on his face and rolling through the drying blood. "*I'll give to you a sparrow and a soft gray dove.*"

After lowering his head to the floor, she rose, swept her hand across her nose, and swallowed back her tears. Without a word or a look Soran's way, she stepped over Papa's outstretched legs and out through the open back door, out into the night. Soran followed close behind as she led the way into the darkness of Draggs.

CHAPTER 19

As she walked, nelle wrapped her arms tightly around her middle and trembled, but not with cold.

It was so strange, almost horrible, having Soran here. Here in *her* world. All these months, she had thought of her time with him in Roseward as another life entirely, disconnected from her day-to-day realities. It didn't feel as though two realities could or should exist concurrently.

But he was here. Following in her footsteps. And fully aware of who she was, of *what* she was. A duplicitous wretch, a traitor. A snatcher.

She hunched her shoulders and moved a little faster, half

wishing she dared dart into the nearest alley, scale a drainpipe to a high roof, and flee between chimneys and over ridgepoles to some place he could not follow.

But she couldn't run from the truth. He knew now. She could not hide.

"Do you know where Gaspard is?"

Nelle's steps faltered as Soran's voice broke the silence between them. She stood still, closed her eyes, and drew a breath. "I saw him just a few hours ago," she said. "At the old Tyrane ruins, down by the shore. The Thorn Maiden was there too. She thought I had the Rose Book."

Kicking her feet back into motion, she continued up the street, filling Soran in on the events of the night thus far, the arranged meeting at the fortress, the ambush, her subsequent escape. Soran listened to all silently, asking no questions.

What was he thinking? Did he believe what she told him, or did he assume every word from her mouth was a lie? How much . . . She shuddered, squeezing her eyes shut. How much time had passed for him since that kiss?

She shook her head and forged ahead faster. No time to dwell on such thoughts. The present was complicated enough. She had to get to Sam. Would he be waiting for her at Ainsley's place? Sure, he'd left her to Cloven's goon, but he'd done the right thing. He'd followed the plan. A good snatcher working with a team knew to follow the plan no matter what. It was when people started going off plan that heists fell to pieces.

He would be there. He would be waiting for her, just as they'd agreed, and he'd have the book and . . . and . . .

And then Soran would try to work the binding spell. And die.

The wash house loomed into view. It was dark and silent, no sign of waking life. Keeping to the far side of the street, Nelle strained her *ibrildian* sight, searching for some sign of Sam. She sensed nothing, but that didn't mean much. Sam was good at disappearing.

"Wait here," she whispered to Soran without looking back at him. She felt him tense as though he wanted to protest, but he held his tongue. Taking this as acquiescence, she stepped out into the street and, after a furtive look both ways, hastened across to the alley beside Ainsley's establishment. "Sam?" she called in a low whisper. "Sam, are you there?"

"Ginger!"

Like magic, Sam manifested from the shadows. Nelle's whole body shuddered with relief. He was there! And he held the book pressed tight against his chest. Light from a streetlamp glowed on his face, casting his eyes in ghoulish shadows.

"I was starting to worry!" he said, hastening toward her. "What happened? Did you—"

He stopped. His eyes widened as he stared over her head, and he took a step back. Nelle glanced swiftly over her shoulder, relieved to see only Soran, who'd moved into view across the street.

"It's all right, Sam," she said quickly. "He's here to help."

Sam withdrew another step into the alley, poised on the balls of his feet. One wrong move, and he'd scramble up the wall in a trice. She'd be hard-pressed to catch up with him on a moonlit chase over the rooftops.

Nelle motioned hard for Soran to stay put. To her relief he obeyed, taking a wide stance in the middle of the street, his arms crossed over his chest, a broad, imposing figure.

"He's the mage," Nelle said, catching Sam's eye. "The one who knows how to work the spell. He can bind the Noswraith." She held out her hand. "Give me the book."

"Are you sure?" Lamplight gleamed bright on the whites of Sam's eyes. "I . . . I've got a bad feeling."

His fae-gift. Sam had always had an uncanny ability to sense danger when no one else could. It was why Mother liked to bring him along on her snatches. He could always tell when something was about to go terribly wrong.

"Then give it over!" Nelle said, motioning urgently. "Give it to me, and you can get out of here!"

Sam shook his head and withdrew a little further. "No," he said. "I'm telling you something is wrong. Something . . ."

He turned and bolted back into the alley.

"Sam!" Nelle cried and lunged after him. She heard Soran bark something behind her but ignored him, determinedly following at Sam's heels. He had a head start on her, and she saw him leap, catch hold of something in the dark, begin to scramble up the side of a building. He'd be on the roof in seconds. "Sam! Come back!" she called in a rasping whisper. "You've got to—"

Her words broke off in a scream that echoed off the stones. Hands reached from the shadows, caught her by the shoulders, and wrapped around her neck. She breathed in a pungent breath of rotten fish and strong liquor mingled with the unmistakable perfume of crushed rose petals.

"That's right, little Peronelle," Cloven's voice rumbled in her ear. "Shout as loud as you like. Call that boy back now."

The next moment, he whirled her around and smashed her hard against the wall. Sparks seemed to flash as pain exploded in her head. Her vision narrowed to a blackened tunnel, but she fought her way back, staring up into Cloven's bearded face. His eyes flashed with a manic light.

Other figures appeared behind him, materializing out of the shadows—three large men, all scarred, their faces streaked with dried blood, lined up behind Cloven, silent and threatening.

"I've been on that fool boy's tail for months." Cloven smiled, and another blast of rose perfume made Nelle gag. "He thought he'd shaken us. But I taught him everything he knows! He can't shake me or my hounds so easily."

A sudden flare of magic, and every eye turned to the end of the alley. Nelle strained in Cloven's grasp and saw Soran holding another of his magic spheres in one hand. He raised it high, taking aim.

"Stop right there!" Cloven cried. The next moment, a knife flashed and pressed just beneath Nelle's chin. She winced, and a whimper escaped her lips. "Not another move, or she's done for!"

Soran hesitated, his eyes flaring dangerously. "What makes you think I care?" His voice was so cold, so hard.

Cloven chuckled and played the edge of his knife against her chin, drawing a line of blood. Despite herself, Nelle whimpered again.

Soran took a step back, lowering his magic light. He said nothing. His jaw clenched tight, teeth grinding.

"Ha!" Cloven barked out the laugh, sending spittle flying into Nelle's eye. "See, you can't fool me. I know this girl, just as I knew her mother before her. They've got a way about them. A way of getting their hooks in a man so deep you can never get yourself free again. Then one day you wake up and realize you don't want to be free. You'd rather be dragged along to your death by her than live any sort of life without her. I've been in your shoes, man. I know." His grip on Nelle's shoulder tightened. "I'd be doing you a favor if I slit her throat here and now. But you put down that shiny magic ball of yours, and things might just turn out different."

Soran took a step back. Then he closed his hand, and the hovering sphere extinguished, leaving that end of the alley dark.

Nelle could only just discern his shadowy silhouette. "All right," he said. "No magic. Let her go."

"Nah." Cloven looked down into Nelle's eyes. "All right, little Peronelle. Call him. Call that boy, Sam. Make him come running."

"Never!" Nelle growled the word through clenched teeth.

"Call him, or I'll make you scream." The tip of the knife tickled her neck. Nelle bit down hard, fighting the terror building up inside her. Cloven angled the blade against her shoulder, pushing back the neck of her shirt, and began to cut. Blood welled, and pain roared across her senses, sharp as fear. "Call for the boy," Cloven said again. "Bring him back."

"No need, Cloven. I'm here."

Nelle's heart plunged to her gut.

Cloven withdrew his knife slowly. Keeping Nelle pinned, he turned to look up at the roof of the opposite building. Sam was there, standing in full view, washed in moonlight.

"No, Sam!" Nelle cried. "Go! Get out of here!"

"Don't listen to her, boy," Cloven said smoothly. "Come on down. Unless you want to hear her screaming as you go."

There was movement at the end of the alley. Nelle glanced, saw Soran take a step toward her. But two of Cloven's men stepped in his way, hands up, and one of them growled, "No, you don't."

Soran paused.

Sam, as though coming to a sudden, impulsive decision, grabbed hold of the drainpipe he'd just used to escape and descended swiftly. He jumped the last several feet, landing in the alley a few steps away. He reached into his shirt and pulled out the Rose Book.

"No, Sam," Nelle whispered.

Cloven smiled. He adjusted his grip on Nelle and pulled her away from the wall, holding her in front of him, her back pressed up against his bulky body. The knife twirled just behind her ear. Blood roared in her head, a sickening hurricane of terror.

"Hand it over," Cloven said, "and I'll let her walk."

Sam's hand trembled as he held up the book. "Let her go first."

"Why should I?" Cloven jerked his head, indicating his two heavies standing between him and Soran. "I've got you outnumbered, boy. You have no power here."

"I'm still faster than you," Sam said. "Faster than any one of you. I'll be out of here in a blink if you don't—"

His voice broke off with a quiet grunt. Just a grunt. No cry, no shout, no curse to the heavens. A dull grunt.

He dropped the Rose Book. It fell at his feet, pages splayed, spine broken. His eyes widened, looked down to his side where the hilt of a long knife protruded. His hand felt for the hilt, shaking, fumbling, trying to grasp hold, to pull it free.

But another hand yanked it out in a horrible gush of blood.

Cloven's third man. He stabbed again, this time into Sam's neck. Sam didn't make a sound, not even a grunt this time. He collapsed to his knees, then fell to his side, blood pooling around him, soaking into the scattered pages of the spellbook.

Nelle realized she was screaming. That she'd been screaming. Cloven let her go, and she staggered, caught herself, lunged, and fell to her knees beside Sam. Her hands caught hold of him, and he was warm, still warm, still alive! Her fingers pressed to his side, trying to stop the flow of blood, as though she could stop the flow of death itself.

She turned his head toward her, looked down into his eyes. "Sam! Hold on, hold on. Sam, please!"

His lips moved. He tried to speak. There was so much pain in his eyes.

She bent over him, choking on sobs. Her lips pressed against his cheek, his brow. "I'm sorry. I'm so sorry." Her tears fell in his eyes, which fluttered up at her. "You should never have come back for me. You should never have . . . Oh, Sam! I'm sorry!" She kissed him again, this time on the lips. They were cold already, unresponsive to her touch. "You can let go now. You don't have to hold on anymore."

He tried to speak. She saw the muscles in his neck move, even as blood gushed from the ugly wound.

Then his breath sighed out from his lungs. The lingering light in his eye flickered out.

"Oh, Sam!" Nelle bowed her head over him, pressing her forehead to his.

Cloven was beside her. Even without looking up, she felt the hugeness of his bulk. He bent, picked up the Rose Book. It was already too late. The pages fell free from the broken binding. Nelle felt the last lingering magic of the spell leak out, just as Sam's blood leaked from his wounds. Cloven hefted the limp leather cover, the boards flapping like broken wings.

"All for a book," he said, shaking his head. With those words, he tore the binding in half and let it fall on the stones beside Sam. Nelle looked up at Cloven through a film of tears. For a terrible moment, her heart was too heavy for her to move, for her to breathe.

Then a savage cry tore from her throat. She sprang up, throwing herself at the man. Ripping the knife out of his hand, she plunged it into his chest. Cloven cried out, staggered, and fell against the alley wall.

Figures swarmed in, shadowy movement in her peripheral vision. Nelle sensed them as though from a distance, her awareness tunneled into that one terrible moment, that central horror. Someone grabbed her arm, yanked the hand holding the knife out of Cloven's body. She maintained her hold, shook off that interfering grasp, and tried to drive the knife into her enemy again.

Cloven deflected her blow. His fingers caught her wrist in an unexpectedly firm hold, drawing her toward him. "I always knew you'd be the death of me," he snarled. His legs buckled, and he sagged to the ground, dragging her with him. Somehow he managed to keep upright on his knees. His eyes swiveled in their sockets, moving over her face in a wild frenzy.

"Seroline," he whispered. Blood bubbled over his fat lip, ran into his beard. "Seroline . . ."

His flesh prickled, and thorns burst through, dark spines covering his face, his hands, piercing his garments. For an instant, Nelle saw, not Cloven, but the Thorn Maiden staring out through his eyes. Slithering vines burst out from inside him, reaching for Nelle, wrapping around her arms, her legs, her waist, drawing her closer.

A burst of magic ripped through the darkness. Nelle screamed, driven back by the impact, and landed hard on the cold ground. She pulled her head up, her vision sparking with afterglow, and saw Cloven still kneeling beside Sam's fallen body. Where his chest should be was a massive, gory hole.

With a last escaping gust of air, he slumped to his side. Thorny vines retreated into the shadows, crawling up the sides of the buildings and away into the night.

CHAPTER 20

HE SHOULDN'T FEEL THIS WAY.

Soran stood with his hand still upraised, the shock of the released spell still spasming in his arm. On the edges of his awareness, he saw the three strangers skirt around him to flee into the street away from the alley. His ears rang dully with the sound of their screams. But these sensations belonged to another world, to another man.

He stared into the alley at Nelle's limp form lying on the ground beside the two fallen men. He willed his limbs to move, but for the space of three throbbing heartbeats they would not obey him.

If she was dead . . .

She moved. Her hand spasmed, reaching out as though to catch hold of a lifeline that wasn't there.

Galvanized to sudden action, Soran sprang forward and crouched over her. His arms hardly seemed to belong to him, so violently did they tremble, yet he managed to gather her up, to cradle her head against his breast. For a moment he wasn't the beast he knew himself to be, the father of unleashed horrors. And she wasn't the traitor, the bewitcher, the irredeemable liar. He was only Soran, and she was Nelle. Just Nelle. His Nelle.

"Can you hear me?" he whispered, gazing down into her face. Her eyes were half open but dull, staring off into the darkness over his shoulder. He touched her temple, pushed hair back across her forehead. She winced at the touch of cold nilarium, and his heart lurched with hope. "Nelle?"

Her lashes closed over her dull eyes, then fluttered open again. Her vision clarified, and she looked up at him, confusion swimming in her gaze.

Then the confusion softened, replaced by an unexpected flash of joy.

"Soran?" Her hand lifted, reaching for his face.

Her fingers froze in the air. Her eyes widened, and the joy vanished. He watched as memories flooded back in, bringing with them an onslaught of horror.

She twisted in his arms, craning her neck, searching. Her gaze fixed on Sam. A strangled cry burst from her lips, and Soran didn't resist as she pushed free of him and crawled to the dead young man's side. Her shoulders bowed, and he heard her draw breath in a ragged sob.

Soran stood and took a step back, half turning away. If only he dared go to her, reach out to her, try to offer some comfort. But this was a private pain. He shouldn't be here, shouldn't be seeing this.

His gaze landed on the broken remains of the spellbook. His heart gave a little shudder in his breast. The Thorn Maiden was truly unbound now. Only one possible way remained to stop her.

He touched the sealed spell under his robes.

Nelle sat upright, sniffing loudly, and dashed tears from her face. She looked up at Soran. In the strange light of his magicked vision, she was very pale, almost phantom-like. "What now?" she asked, her voice tremulous. "What can we do?"

Soran rubbed a hand down his face, suddenly more tired than he liked to admit. "We've got to find her. At her source. When she escaped the spellbook, she would have planted herself into a mind, like a seed. Her offshoots all stem from that single source. Find the source, and she might still be uprooted."

Nelle nodded. Questions shimmered in her eyes, but instead of asking them, she said, "Gaspard. It must be Gaspard. He tried to work the spell, and she got into him. He's the source."

It made sense. Soran swallowed and drew a steadying breath.

He knew what he must do.

Turning his back on Nelle, he strode from the alley and set off up the street as swiftly as he could go. Part of him hoped she would remain where she was, hoped she would realize that the battle he now sought was far beyond her. Hoped she would let him go without a word, without a protest, let him simply walk out of her life and away to his doom.

A forlorn hope. And well he knew it.

Before he'd gone ten paces, she appeared at his side, running to match his long-legged stride. "Where are you going?" she demanded.

"The old fortress. You said you met Gaspard there tonight. He is probably there now, and if so, *she* is with him. She'll know I've come to Wimborne." The men in the alley had caught sight of his face by the light of his magic sphere, and the Thorn Maiden would certainly have seen him through their eyes. "I've got to find her. Now."

"I understand."

Soran stopped. He lowered his chin slowly, looking down into Nelle's upturned face. "You are not coming."

"Nine hells I'm not."

His jaw tightened. "I won't have you with me. Not for this fight."

She met his gaze without flinching, not even blinking.

"I don't trust you," he growled.

"I don't blame you," she replied. "But you're going to need help. She's gotten into Cloven's whole crew. I don't know how many others she's got by now. You'll need me."

"You can't help. Not with this."

Her hand moved to her breast, reached inside her thin shirt, and withdrew a piece of folded paper. "I got a spell. I can help."

One spell. Against the Thorn Maiden and all her terrible extensions. It was laughable.

But there was nothing laughable about the look in Nelle's eye. It was the look of a soldier prepared to march despite knowing full well the fight could not be won. Even now, even after everything she'd done, he couldn't help the surge of admiration in his heart. Her courage in the face of impossible odds, her determination, her strength . . . she was, by far, the most beautiful creature he'd ever seen.

He hated her.

He loved her.

"I'm going with you, Soran," she said, tucking the spell back into her shirt. "This is my fault. I've got to be there; I've got to try to undo the pain I've caused. You can't stop me from trying."

Soran bowed his head. Why fight her? She'd already won the battle, pushing her way through all of his powerful defenses. If she wished to, he would let her tear him apart.

"Very well, Miss Beck," he said.

"Very well, Mage Silveri," she replied.

This settled, they turned together and, side by side, continued up the street. He matched his pace to hers almost unconsciously. It was a long walk through Wimborne, back to the beach and the ruins.

But they had hardly started when Nelle stopped abruptly and looked back. "Wait! Wait a moment!"

Soran could only watch as she turned and raced back down the street, ducking into the dark alley they'd just left behind. He waited, uncertain, feeling the seconds pass all too quickly. Somewhere in the distance, the cathedral bells tolled twice. The night was fast progressing, and morning would soon be upon them. If they didn't get to the Thorn Maiden in the next few hours, they would have to wait for the following sunset to face her. Meanwhile, she might well strengthen her hold on Gaspard and all the other minds into which she'd crept. She might become too strong.

Just as Soran had half convinced himself to continue alone, Nelle reappeared from the alley, her hands flashing strangely in the moonlight. Soran frowned as she hastened toward him, but she held up her hands for him to see. Long claws of pure nilarium, exquisitely crafted and engraved, glinted from each of her fingertips.

"Now," she said, "let's go."

The cathedral bells tolled three times in the distance as Soran and Nelle left the city behind and ventured down to the beach. The tide was fully in by now, the water was high. A brisk wind off the sea blew through the whispering grasses and lashed at Soran's cloak as he led the way along the dirt path.

They hadn't spoken since leaving Draggs Street behind. The tension of silence had finally become too much for Nelle, so she'd drifted back to walk in the mage's wake rather than at his side. Her mind churned through all the words she didn't dare to speak, but there was too much, more than mere words could begin to express. Not now. What good were her apologies to him . . . to anyone?

Sam.

Papa.

She closed her eyes and for a moment saw both their faces before her mind's eye. Sam lying in his pooling blood, the life draining from his eyes. Papa, thorns bursting through his skin, monstrous and tortured and confused.

It was her fault. She'd done this to them, brought this horror into their lives. If not for her, Sam would still be his happy-go-lucky self, blithely avoiding all care or danger as he went about his nightly snatches.

And Papa . . . Papa would still be married to Mistress Dirgin and facing all the perplexing terrors of life in this world. But he wouldn't have suffered the Thorn Maiden's torments, wouldn't have suffered the sensation of his mind and body overrun, of being turned into the vessel of a living nightmare.

She'd wanted to spare him. And look what she'd done to him.

Nelle opened her eyes and fixed her focus on the outline of the fortress tower looming over the water. Gods, what a night it had been already! It was only a few short hours since she'd flung herself from that wall into the sea. And here she was, a stupid lamb prancing back into the slaughterhouse of her own free will.

But she wouldn't let Soran go alone.

She looked again at the back of the mage's head, his pale hair shining in the moonlight. If only there was something she could say. He would never forgive her, but might she apologize anyway? Nelle cursed softly under her breath, hunching her shoulders against the wind. She would fight by Soran's side tonight. That would have to be apology enough.

Her hands moved to her trouser pockets, feeling the weight of Mother's nilarium claws. It was good to have them back again, yet she grimaced at the memory of feeling through Cloven's pockets while his corpse slowly stiffened on the ground. Had her blow been the killing stroke? She was no trained killer and couldn't be sure the knife she'd driven into his chest penetrated anything important. Perhaps he would have lived if not for Soran's deadly blast.

No. That death was on her head. She couldn't shrug it off and lay blame anywhere else. She was a killer now.

The wind picked up suddenly, moaning sorrowfully as it tore through her loose hair and the thin fabric of her shirt. Nelle breathed in sharply.

And inhaled the perfume of roses.

She stopped, turned. Looked up and down the sandy beach, down to the water's edge where waves crashed and frothed. All was eerily quiet. Moonlight played on the water, and she could see all the way out to Roseward, to where the lighthouse stood silhouetted against the starry sky. But her skin prickled with more than cold.

Something was there. In the darkness.

"Mage Silveri." She cleared her throat and tried again a little louder. "Mage Silveri, do you feel tha—"

The sand erupted in front of her, granules stinging her skin. She leaped back, a hand over her face, and felt rather than saw the figure looming like a ghoul rising from the dead. She lowered her hand, peered through stinging eyes, and saw a man riddled with hundreds of thorns. His eyes were manic with madness and pain.

He threw himself at Nelle. Thorn vine shadows lashed the air around him.

Nelle cried out, leaping aside to avoid the attack. She landed hard, her leg buckling beneath her, and rolled from the path down the incline toward the water. When she came to a stop, she pushed herself upright, her hand reaching for the spell paper in her shirt. Why hadn't she bullspitting called the spell to life before venturing out of the city? She'd been afraid the sudden flare of magic would draw unwanted attention, but what did that matter now?

The man bore down on her. She dodged his wildly swinging arms while scrambling to her feet and ducked in where she saw opportunity to drive her elbow into his face. Something crunched. He howled and went down hard. He might be possessed, but he still felt the pain of a broken nose.

Nelle danced back out of the way and glanced around wildly. Other figures rose from the sand. She saw Soran strike one with a nilarium fist, sending the figure reeling. Then he whipped out a spellbook. Light flashed as magic poured from the *quinsatra* at his summons.

Right. She ought to be doing that herself.

Nelle dragged the spell page out of her shirt. When another figure lunged for her, she dodged and ran through the sand and dunes to avoid those swinging arms. Holding the page up, she read in gasps, a jumbled combination of Serythian and Araneli that tangled her tongue. Despite the gibberish and her slapdash writing, the magic responded to her spirit's urgency and energy.

Precision was everything . . . until it wasn't.

Magic flared in the darkness, sparking as a spell-sword grew apparently out of nothing and appeared in Nelle's hand. Its blade flamed as bright as a torch.

She whirled in place, brandishing the sword, and faced the man lurching toward her. He was a big brute of a fellow with fisted hands the size of foundation blocks. Thorns protruded from every square inch of visible skin, tearing through his clothes. He opened his mouth, roaring as he hurtled toward her. A huge red rose bloomed from his tongue.

Nelle lashed out, and the sword burned an arc through the air, cutting deep into her attacker's upraised arm. Blood spurted from the man's flesh as he screamed and fell heavily to the sand. Struggling to pull himself up again, he threw out a hand to catch Nelle by the ankle. Vines seemed to reach from inside him like snakes lunging to wrap around her, to pull her close.

Nelle swung the sword again, hacking through those vines. They fell away, and the remaining stumps shriveled and retreated. The fallen man cried out, curling into himself. But then he uncurled and started to pull himself together, his gaze fixed furiously up at her.

Nelle was not a killer. Not really. Not even Cloven's death could turn her into one. Mother had taught her how to defend herself, but not how to kill. And she didn't know this man. She didn't recognize him as one of Cloven's minions. For all she knew, he might be some totally innocent layman, snared by the Thorn Maiden and dragged into this nightmare against his will.

She stood frozen with her sword drawn back, unable to make a killing stroke. The man lunged.

A blast of brilliant magic sent him hurtling across the sand to collapse in a pile of limbs that briefly twitched, then went still. Vines lashed out from his body, retracted, then slithered through the sand toward the fortress.

Nelle whipped around to see Soran behind her, his hand still upraised from the force of the blast he'd flung. Two other bodies lay near him, sparking with magic.

His eyes met hers, his expression intent, dangerous.

Then he lowered his hands and turned, facing the fortress again. He stood a moment, his head bent, his shoulders bowed. Drawing a huge breath, he straightened again and set out, striding along the dirt path, the wind whipping in his hair into long snarls behind him.

Nelle's heart raced, and sweat dampened her skin, chilling in the brisk sea breeze. She swallowed hard, and then, still clutching her flaming sword, hastened after the mage. Gods willing, these three attackers were the last of the Thorn Maiden's captives. She wasn't sure she could stomach fighting her way through more mindless puppets.

As they approached the ruins, Nelle lifted her gaze to the one remaining fortress tower. Light flickered in its highest window. Gaspard was up there somewhere. Seated in a pool of candlelight, awaiting Soran's approach. Gaspard . . . but not really Gaspard.

What would Soran do? His every stride held purpose. He must have a plan in mind, though she couldn't begin to guess what. Without the Rose Book, how could the Thorn Maiden be bound? Had he somehow managed to create a new binding spell she didn't know about? No, with his cursed hands that was impossible. So, what then?

Water lapped at the fortress's foundation stones as she followed Soran to the dilapidated bridge leading to the upraised gate. As Soran strode boldly onto that bridge, ghostly vinelike canes seemed to crawl up the stones around him, swarming in masses. Roses bloomed and burst into flame, turning their lovely faces to follow his progress even as their petals crumbled to ash and drifted away on the wind. Not once did he so much as glance at them.

"Bullspit," Nelle muttered. Brandishing her sword, she hurried after. The thorns withdrew as she came, hiding in the darkness just beyond the glow of her flaming sword. If she dared turn to look at them directly, they vanished entirely. They were only in her mind, after all. Phantom nightmares, not of this reality. But so densely gathered! The Thorn Maiden was strong here, almost as strong as when she'd physically manifested in Noxaur.

Soran stopped. Nelle stumbled to a halt a few paces back and peered around him at an open portcullis that made her think of a monster's gaping jaw. Beyond the gate lay a small courtyard, then the main keep of the fortress, still mostly intact. She studied the shadows, searching for any sign of possessed, thorn-pierced men. Other than the shushing voice of the sea, all was still.

"What's wrong?" she asked, her voice refusing to rise above a whisper.

Soran raised one hand, which gleamed silver in the moonlight, and half turned to speak over his shoulder, not quite meeting her eye. "Stay back."

She adjusted her grip on the flame-sword. "I'm going with you."

"Let me go first."

She ground her teeth but grunted an acknowledgement, stepping back a pace. Soran continued across the bridge, his steps more cautious than before. Did she imagine the sudden rush of rose perfume filling the air, overwhelming even the briny scent of the sea?

Something was wrong here. Something she couldn't see. Something he knew and she did not.

"Soran!" she cried just as he passed beneath the arch of the gate.

Vines swarmed in a sudden rush of movement unseen to the physical eye. Nelle leaped, her sword flashing. But she was already too late.

The old portcullis dropped over the entrance with a resounding crash.

CHAPTER 21

"SORAN! SORAN, WAIT!"

His ears still ringing from the din of the closing gate, Soran spun about to see Nelle on the far side of the portcullis, her face brilliantly illuminated by her spell-sword. She rushed at the gate, grasped one of the bars in her left hand, and tugged, such a silly gesture that he almost laughed. But her expression was ferocious.

He took two steps back toward the gate. "This is it, Miss Beck," he said quietly. "This is as far as you go tonight."

"No!" She yanked at the gate again, then stepped back and swung her flaming sword at the bars. But they were made of iron. The instant her blade contacted the metal, the magic faltered, sputtered, then burst apart in a flash of blinding light. Soran flung up an arm to shield his eyes and heard Nelle cry out in shock.

Blinking hard against the afterglow, he lowered his arm. "Magic and iron do not mix," he said. "You ought to know that by now."

Nelle huddled in a crouch, her arms over her head. At the sound of his voice, she uncurled to look up at him. With a little wordless cry, she rushed the gate again, grasping the bars and pressing her face through one of the square openings. "There's got to be a way to get this spitting thing open!" She stuck an arm through, pointing. "Over there. That looks like a gatehouse. You'll find something, a lever or something. Go on! Get it open!"

Soran shook his head heavily. "Go back, Miss Beck. Return to your father. You've done enough."

"I ain't gonna let you face her by yourself!"

He looked into her eyes illuminated by the moonlight. Gods, why did he still feel this rushing flood of heat at the sight of her? It wasn't hatred, much though he would like to convince himself otherwise. Despite everything, his heart simply refused to hate her. Maybe with time he could learn to purge his heart, to feel only disdain and then, eventually, indifference.

But there wasn't time.

In a few strides he covered the distance between them. Nelle's white-knuckled hands gripped the bars, but as he approached she pried one hand free and reached for him. Almost unconsciously he responded to the gesture. His hand stretched toward hers, his cold, cursed fingers almost touching her warm slim ones. If only he dared take her hand, draw in toward her, and lower his lips to hers. If only he dared to experience that connection of bodies and souls one last time . . .

He clenched his hand into a fist and drew it back. "This is my responsibility. The Thorn Maiden is my creation. I must be the one to bring about her end."

He turned to face the empty courtyard, the ruinous keep, the tower. His gaze lifted to the window where candlelight flickered like a star in the sky above.

"Goodbye, Miss Beck," he said.

Deaf to her shouts, her curses, her pleas, he strode across the courtyard. The rose vines churned in the darkness around him, urging him on his way.

"Soran! *Soran!* Bullspitting boggarts, Soran, *come back!*"

Nelle's voice rang against the stones, echoing back a dozen times and more. She may as well have been mute for all the good it did. Soran crossed the courtyard without a pause and vanished through an open doorway.

"*Soran!*" she screamed after him, trying to shake the relentless iron bars in her rage. When she'd spent all the air in her lungs, she let go and stepped back, breathing hard.

What could she do? What could she do? She wouldn't turn back! The Thorn Maiden was in there, and she would tear Soran to shreds.

"Spitting boggarts and brags!" Nelle backed away from the gate and studied the high stone wall. She had no weapon. She'd stupidly broken her spell-sword, and she hadn't brought either ink or parchment to create another.

But maybe Soran could use something else, like a distraction. Something to draw the Thorn Maiden's attention away long enough for him to do whatever it was he had in mind.

Nelle plunged her hands into her stolen trouser pockets, pulled out Mother's claws, and slipped them onto her fingers. Approaching the wall, she crouched and sprang. The nilarium sank easily into the stones.

She began to climb.

At the base of the tower stair, Soran paused. Only one spell remained in the little volume he'd brought with him. He'd held onto it for many years now, knowing a time would come when he needed it. That time was now.

Even after so many years, it still felt too soon.

He opened the book and read out the spell, the words flaring bright as they burned in his mind. They seemed to rise from the page and turn into magic coils of light that wound round his wrists, his arms, his shoulders, and down his torso and legs until his whole body was covered in a brilliantly pulsing web. As he reached the end of the spell, the webbing light sank beneath his skin. He felt it flow into his muscles, his bones.

He drew a great breath, his eyes widening. Strength. The spell was pure strength—the might and endurance of ten men combined. It wouldn't last, of course. When the spell gave out, he would be left weak and trembling. He had a few hours, though.

And he intended to use that time wisely.

Soran began to climb, the power of the strength-spell driving his limbs. Constructed on a strong foundation, the tower still stood after years of abuse from the elements, but when the wind blew, the entire structure shifted and shook—slightly, but enough to set the nerves jumping. Step after step, vivid memories came rushing in, flooding his mind in waves. It was as though he were once more the young man who'd led Gaspard up these spiraling stairs, his heart aflame with the eager impetuosity of youth.

As lads they'd explored the tower together, soon after meeting at the university. Later they'd come many times to make use of it while pursuing their illicit studies. Miphates naturally gravitated toward towers to work their arts. The Evenspire, the lighthouse, this old ruin . . . something about the added height seemed to bring one closer to the *quinsatra*, made the flow of words to the page easier.

He and Gaspard had claimed this tower as their secret hideaway and here had delved into the dark secrets long ago forbidden to mankind. Here they'd come with eager steps, carrying illegal volumes and stolen sheets of spell-writing, to crouch in pools of candlelight in the chamber at the top of this stair, share their findings, then practice with quill and ink all they had learned.

Such fools. Such young, arrogant, hopeless fools.

Gaspard had always hated him. Soran had not been unaware of the fact even back then. If anything, he'd reveled in that hatred born of a very real, desperate jealousy. It felt good back then to be the object of such envy, to feel himself the superior mage of the two, the favorite of their masters, the golden boy destined for great things. As they had worked together to unravel the mysteries of the Noswraiths, he'd made no secret of his delight as his understanding opened faster than Gaspard's did, as his experiments proved more and more satisfactory. Power that eluded Gaspard was just within his grasp.

Nevertheless, despite his hatred, Gaspard had tried to stop him that fateful night.

"Not tonight," he'd said, his eyes round and fearful in the candlelight. *"Wait a little, Silveri. Wait until tomorrow. We'll do it then."*

He'd sensed the madness in Soran's soul and hoped to buy

just enough time for the fit of insanity to pass.

All for nothing. The Nightmare was already too alive, vivid, and potent in Soran's mind. He'd felt that he *must* create, must write the spell, or he would simply burn from the inside, consumed by his own despair.

Gaspard had stood to one side, a candle in his hand. And he'd watched.

Poor Gaspard. Poor fool. He'd watched, and his jealousy had grown like a monstrous coiling snake, ready to crush him. And Soran had been too blind to all but his own desolation to realize it.

He shook his head as he pressed upward, his ears ringing with the Thorn Maiden's whispers, inarticulate but full of menace.

A faint glow of light fell from the top of the tower, serving only to deepen the surrounding shadows where *she* hid, clinging to the walls, her roses blooming and blazing, revealed to his magicked sight.

He reached for the spell inside his shirt. Without drawing it out, he broke the seal. The magic inside shimmered in response to his touch, ready for use. Gods, how he'd hoped it would never come to this! He'd known the Thorn Maiden would be his death in the end . . . just, not like this.

But there was no other choice.

He rounded the last turn and approached the open doorway, peering into the lighted chamber. The very chamber where all this horror began. Again, he was thrown back to those days long gone—for Gaspard sat at the little candlelit table even as he used to, holding a black swan-feather quill in his hand, with parchments scattered around him. He looked up as Soran entered the room.

Soran paused, shocked. This was not the youthful Dusaro Gaspard he had known. Here was a man aged not by time but by fear. His once black hair had turned completely white, and his eyes were huge, sunken into the hollows of his skull. Scars riddled his skin where the Thorn Maiden had torn into him.

"Ah. Silveri." Gaspard raised a hand in a welcoming gesture and indicated the chair opposite his at the table. "I thought you might come. Here, have a seat."

Soran hesitated briefly, then crossed the room, pulled out the chair, and sat. "Where is she, Gaspard?" he said.

"Oh, she's here." Gaspard tapped his forehead with one finger. Then he shifted his hand down to his side and pulled back a fold of his robes, revealing his bare torso. An ugly knot of darkened flesh bulged just below his ribcage. In that strange reddish light, it seemed as though something moved under the skin, something living, churning.

"And here," Gaspard said, resting his hand over the knot. He closed his eyes, and a shudder ran through him, as though he might soon fly apart at the seams. "I'm sure you guessed it already, Silveri. A *bialaer* spell. A containment. I thought if I drew her out of the spellbook and planted her inside of me, I could control her. But she's eating away at the spell. Getting her roots into more and more crevices of my brain. I can't get her out now. And . . . and I can't hold her off much longer."

He bowed over the table, hands clenched together, his fingers tightening as though trying to hold onto his very soul. "Mage Bifaren detected Noswraith magic. And Mage Orisys, you remember him? Good fellow, our master of calligraphy in the fifth year. They both came to me at different times, confronted me, wanted to know if I was delving into the forbidden arts. I put them off, but I knew they'd come sniffing around again soon enough. I was afraid. Afraid they would interrupt my work before I could gain true mastery of this . . . this . . . this beautiful creation of yours.

"So I let *her* kill them. I didn't even realize I was doing it, not consciously. But she'd been . . . *whispering* to me. At night. Those few short hours when I dared to sleep. She promised me things. And I listened to her, let her loose even though I knew I should fight and fight and fight. She was as good as her word. She killed Bifaren and Orisys. Others too, I think. I'm not sure anymore. And while she was out, she got her roots into other minds, always growing, always spreading.

"I realized too late what was happening—that my containment spell wasn't working, that she was gaining the upper hand. The only thing keeping her from totally overpowering me was the book—your book, the spellbook. Even when she passed from it to me, it kept a hold on her. That's powerful magic you wrote, Silveri. You always were a wonder . . ."

He rubbed a hand down his face, pulling at the skin under his eyes. "In a moment of self-control, I gave the spellbook to a snatcher and told him to hide it. Then I tried to have him killed so that I couldn't find it again. But always *she* was there, thwarting my every move. She didn't let them kill him. She tried to catch him, but he was clever and managed to stay one step ahead of her. Until tonight apparently." He cast Soran an exhausted look. "She got him tonight. And destroyed the book."

"I know," Soran said. "I was there."

"Then you know there's no stopping her now." Gaspard held up the quill, chuckling mirthlessly. "I had that snatcher girl steal this for me. Right out of the Evenspire. I couldn't take it myself or the Miphates would suspect what I was doing. So I arranged for it to . . . disappear. Do you recognize it?"

Soran nodded. "It was mine."

"Quill-bonded." Gaspard spun the quill between his fingers. "Some say the bonding ceremony traps some of the mage's power in the quill itself. Most agree this is nonsense, the practice a mere tradition, but I thought, why not give it a try? Why not use the very quill Silveri used to write the Noswraith into being? I thought if I had even a small piece of your power, I could make the *bialaer* spell work." He tilted his head, looking at Soran from under heavy brows. "Do you think I'm a fool?"

"No, Gaspard."

"Liar." Gaspard smiled painfully. "I *know* you do. But that's all right. If you do, it's only because you see me more clearly than I have seen myself all these years. Such a fool, such a fool!"

"You aren't the only one," Soran said quietly.

Gaspard chuckled again. Then he gasped and pressed a hand to the awful knot in his side. "She's coming. Soon. I'm trying to hold her back, but the containment spell is breaking. Your quill didn't help me at all, you know. And my powers just aren't a match for this . . . this thing you created."

"It's all right." Soran stood, rested his palms on the tabletop, and leaned toward Gaspard. "It's all right, my friend. I'm here now. I'll take her from you."

"You will?" Gaspard's eyes flitted to meet his, looking strangely young in his haggard features, like a frightened child's. "You'll save me?"

Soran pulled the spell out of his shirt. The seal was broken already, and he unfolded it, holding it up for Gaspard to see.

"A *bialaer*," Gaspard whispered. "You wrote one too?"

Soran nodded.

"And it will hold her?"

"Not for long. But maybe long enough."

Gaspard's face crumpled. Tears gleamed in his eyes. "I envied you," he said softly. "So much."

"There was nothing to envy."

A bitter laugh burst from Gaspard's pain-twisted lips. "Don't lie to me! Admit you wouldn't give up even one fraction of the magnificent power you carry inside. Admit it, Silveri!"

Soran bowed his head, dropping his gaze from Gaspard's face to the spell on the table before him. He leaned heavily into his hands, afraid suddenly that, despite the spell-strength flowing through his limbs, he would crumble and fall. He closed his eyes, twisting his face slightly to one side, his jaw tight.

"I would give it all up," he said, "for the chance to try again. For a chance to simply be a good man."

Silence hung in the air between them for a painful moment. Then Gaspard snorted. "Don't try to be—" He broke off with a cry, one hand clutching his side while the other caught the edge of the table, almost knocking the candle over. "She's coming! She's . . . she's coming . . ."

A terrible scream filled the small chamber, bouncing off each wall and out the open window into the night. Gaspard's skin began to prickle, and thorns pierced through, dripping blood.

Soran caught up his spell and stepped away from the table. This was it, the final moment between now and a tormented forever. And in that moment he saw everything. Everything! Helenia's face as he had first seen it, girlish and wild, full of mischief and haunting allure. His brother's face, its cold stoicism ripped through with fury and heartbreak, his cheeks spattered in bright red blood, his hand still gripping the hilt of a knife. Dornrise, overcome in thorny briars; the bodies of the slain torn apart in their sleep.

And Nelle.

He saw her again, dragging her boat up onto his shore. Then she'd turned and looked at him, her face like the sun breaking through clouds so dark he'd thought they could never disperse.

How he'd basked in her glow those two glorious stolen weeks!

It was more than he deserved.

He opened his eyes and raised the spell to the level of his face. "*Elanil hubisus mi. Tantril gorlendalil m'yathorne ta,*" he read. The old words rolled gently from his tongue, strangely incongruous amid the sound of Gaspard's screams.

The *quinsatra* opened at his summoning, first a sliver then gash. Magic poured through, drawn in long, shining strands, faster and faster. The tower creaked and groaned under the strain of so much energy entering this reality. The vines on the edges of his mind massed and coiled, creeping toward him.

He read on steadily, clearly. The words of the *bialaer* spell poured from his lips without pause.

"I thought I'd never see you again."

She was there. Speaking through Gaspard's mouth.

Soran didn't look up, continued reading the spell.

He felt her there across from him even as he refused to look. Shapely and beautiful, made of thorns and soft red roses, sitting

289

in Gaspard's seat. If he were to raise his gaze from the spell-page and look, he would see only Gaspard. But that was a limited version of reality. She was there, as real and present as though physically manifested.

"I thought you would forget me." She reached out to him. Petal-soft fingers brushed his cheeks. *"But you could not bear to be parted for long, could you, my love?"*

Her vines drew in around him, circling his chair, climbing his legs. She leaned closer, and he breathed in the perfume of crushed roses.

"It's too late. I have already chosen another. I have chosen one who wanted me, who did not fight me. He has given himself up to me as a lover should." Her fingers flexed, and thorns bit into his flesh. *"And now I should kill you."*

"Is that what you want?" Even as his physical mouth continued carefully reading the spell, his spirit spoke, gentle and low.

She hissed. Somewhere far away, he still heard Gaspard screaming, but most of his awareness had shifted to this reality.

"We are meant to be together," he said. In spirit form he reached out to her. *"You've known it all along. I've taken longer to realize the truth. But I'm here now. I'm here."*

She looked at him. And his vision split between this reality and a memory of Helenia looking at him in that same way. She stared into his eyes—and his vision was three-fold now, straining his sanity to the brink. He saw Helenia, beautiful Helenia in her delicate wedding veil and an off-shoulder gown that perfectly displayed her soft bosom, her elegant throat. He saw Gaspard, tormented and screaming, thorns tearing through his flesh, his eyes wide with frenzied pain.

And he saw the Thorn Maiden. His creation. Incredible in every detail. Her features formed of woven thorns, her lips of red rose petals, empty black holes for eyes. But through that emptiness, a spirit of intense power gazed out at him. She was beautiful, this being born of his mind. And he loved her. Loved her with a passion only ever felt by a creator for his work. But that love was also hatred, for he saw too clearly the flaws of his work, flaws reflecting his own frailty and futility. He loved and hated her as he loved and hated himself. She was his reflection, a glimpse into his soul . . .

"*Come to me, Helenia,*" he said again, his hand still extended. "*Let us be joined.*"

Suddenly, between them lay only a small empty space full of darkness that sparked as the threads of connection drew their spirits closer, closer.

"*Please, Helenia,*" he said.

In that moment she was perfect. She was the Helenia he remembered so vividly. No thorns. No darkness. Only beauty and spirit and passion and warmth.

"*Soran!*" she cried and threw herself into his arms.

As she came to him, the Thorn Maiden pulled out of Gaspard's mind and planted her roots deep inside her creator. He felt them plunge down, felt her grasp hold of him, joining her essence with his. Thorns tore through his body, and roses bloomed in his mind.

He completed the *bialaer* spell.

Nilarium claws dug into the stones, gouging out handhold after handhold as Nelle scaled the tower. Her bare feet picked out tiny crevices to aid her balance while a sharp wind blew in from the sea, whipping her shirt, thrashing her body, tugging her hair.

She felt the distance below her. This fall was too great. If she lost her grip, she would surely land on the stone wall below and break every bone in her body. She ought to look. Just as Mother had taught her, she should look and acknowledge the distance, accept the potential of certain death. It would steady her nerves.

But she refused to look. Her eyes, her very soul, fixed on the patch of light from the window high above, and she climbed for all she was worth. This climb was nothing compared to scaling the Evenspire, yet her fear then was nothing compared to the terror spiking up and down her spine tonight.

She had to reach Soran before . . . before . . . she didn't even know what.

A scream ripped through the night.

Nelle's head tipped back, her heart thudding in her throat. Was that Soran? She couldn't tell. Another scream followed, then another and another, each longer and more agonized than the last.

Movement. All around her. Nelle turned first to her right, then to her left. Clear moonlight bathed the tower, revealing nothing. But the sense of movement didn't cease. She could feel vines crawling up the tower all around her. They tore into the stones, little tendrils like grasping fingers. Roses bloomed, filling the air with their scent, strong enough to make Nelle gag.

She refocused her gaze on the window. The screaming overhead intensified, rolling across the night sky to the heedless stars above.

Soran.

Soran!

The screaming stopped.

Still several feet down from the window, Nelle froze in place, horrified. That silence was so much worse than any of the horrific sounds that had assaulted her ears. Her fingers tensed.

Then, all fears forgotten save the fear of what that silence might mean, she surged upward, reached the narrow windowsill, and hauled her torso through the opening. One sweeping glance revealed everything: Gaspard lying on the ground, his chair tipped over, his hands over his face; a candle burning bright in the center of a small square table; a spell page smoldering beneath the roiling power of its summoned and spent magic.

And Soran.

Standing upright, his back to the window. His hands hung at his sides; his head bent. His hair fell down his back, moving slightly in the breeze.

"Soran!" Nelle cried. She heaved herself through the window and scrambled to get her feet under her. "Soran, what—"

His body stiffened. He turned to her.

His eyes were black, like two pits in his face.

Deep in those pits, thorns churned.

Nelle drew back. "Soran, what have you done?"

His mouth dropped open. Roses bloomed from his tongue, spilled out over his jaw. Thorns erupted from under his skin, each one six inches long, dagger tips dripping with his blood.

He lunged toward her, hands outstretched. Nelle ducked under his grasping arms, hit the floor hard, and rolled. She came up again in a crouch, her nilarium claws flexed and ready for defense. Only there was no need.

Soran, driven by some unseen force, leaped for the window and climbed onto the open sill. Nelle just had time to throw out one hand, to shout a futile, "*No!*" before he cast himself out into empty space.

CHAPTER 22

ALL WAS STILL. SO STILL IT HARDLY FELT REAL.

This must be some alternate reality, separate from her life and existence. A reality where nothing mattered. Neither fears nor hopes. Neither nightmares nor dreams.

Somehow Nelle got upright. Somehow she staggered across the floor. Somehow she caught hold of the windowsill, leaned out, and stared into the darkness. Her *ibrildian* eyes searched below for some sign of a broken body, of pale white hair splayed out on stones.

All was still. So very, very still.

"Soran," she whispered. Her knees buckled, and she sagged

heavily, only just managing to keep herself upright. "Soran."

A groan sounded behind her.

Nelle turned. Gaspard, shuddering on the floor, rolled and slowly drew his hands from his face. He'd changed just since she last saw him, mere hours before. His dark hair, which had been streaked with white, was now entirely white. His face was haggard, aged far beyond his thirty-odd years. Many small cuts riddled his skin, beads of blood dripped to the floor and soaked into his garments, and a huge gash was visible through torn fabric just beneath his ribcage. He pressed his hands to it but, after a first grimace of pain, seemed to sigh with relief, as though some terrible pressure had been removed.

Still tentatively probing that wound, he lifted his gaze to Nelle, his eyes full of tentative hope. "Is . . . is she gone?"

Nelle nodded. Then she shook her head. "I don't know."

Gaspard closed his eyes. Still lying on the floor, he rubbed one hand down his face, smearing the blood in ugly streaks. His lips split in an agonized smile. "She *is* gone. She's out of my head. He did it." He chuckled ruefully. "Of course he did."

Nelle couldn't speak. She stood with one hand still gripping the window ledge, staring across the candlelit space at that broken excuse of a man. She ought to hate him but couldn't quite find the energy to do so.

She sank to the floor. Her sorrow was growing, but for the moment she could still swallow it back. She could still hold herself together, still keep from breaking into a thousand pieces, each fractured fragment as sharp as razor-edged glass. She planted her hands on the floor, the claws on her fingers digging into the stone, and simply watched Gaspard.

The mage pulled his arms under his body and pushed upright. Lifting his head, he saw Nelle and started as though he'd forgotten she was in the room. Then his eyes widened, and he pulled back. Was he afraid of her? Did he think she would attack? Well, maybe she would. Maybe she would use Mother's claws and tear his eyes out. Maybe she would imitate the Thorn Maiden and shred his limbs.

Maybe she'd just sit here.

Gaspard opened his mouth, shut it again, bowed his head. Then he spoke quietly, "I tried to use the *bialaer* spell. It was supposed to contain her, to bind her to one small part of me so I could maintain control over her. But she was too strong." He felt at the wound in his side again and shuddered as though repressing a gag. His face was gray when he lifted his head to look at her. "Silveri . . . he is more powerful than I'll ever be. His *bialaer* will work."

"It didn't work," Nelle said. "I saw him. The Thorn Maiden had him."

Gaspard shook his head. "If she truly had him, we would both be dead. She never would have let him leave. She would have stayed here in this world and continued spreading her roots throughout Wimborne. It's in her nature, you see. To spread, to overtake and overcome."

"Is she dead then?" The words came out dully, falling like stones from her lips. "Did he kill them both?"

"No. No, they aren't dead."

Nelle's head shot up. Her eyes widened. The jolt in her heart hurt more than she could bear, a painful hope. "How do you know?"

"Soran wouldn't be so foolish. If he were to die now, with the spellbook destroyed and nothing to restrain her, the Noswraith would simply climb into the next available mind. Nothing would be accomplished by his death. He's got to take her to a place she cannot escape."

Roseward.

A storm of thoughts burst in Nelle's mind. She struggled to catch them, to force them into comprehension. "He . . . he used this spell to bind her to him. So he can take her back to Roseward."

Once back on the isle, it wouldn't matter if or when she broke free. She could kill him, tear him to pieces. But with no other mind to climb into, to claim, she would be imprisoned. Floating through the Hinter Sea for all eternity.

Could it be true? Was it even possible? How could he have survived a fall like that? Had he used some other spell she hadn't seen, something to break his fall? Or maybe this was all vain wishing on her part. Maybe when she descended the tower, she would find his body broken to a bloody pulp.

Using the wall for support, Nelle got to her feet. When she staggered across the room, Gaspard cringed away from her. How strange to see him like this! This man, who had taken a stranglehold on her life and forced her to do his bidding. Now she saw that he was nothing more than a pathetic worm, hardly worth her notice.

She turned her face away and hurried to the door.

"Where are you going?" Gaspard called after her.

Nelle paused in the doorway. When she breathed in, the cloying scent of roses coated her nostrils, invaded her lungs. She closed her eyes, clicking the ends of the nilarium claws together. "I'm going to Roseward. I'm going to find him."

"Will you save him?"

She looked down at the trembling man kneeling on the floor in a pool of his own blood. Gaspard gazed up at her, pleading. "Please. Save him," he said, clutching the front of his robes over his heart. "And tell him . . . tell him I'm sorry. Tell him I never should have—"

"Actually," Nelle said, "I don't intend to ever speak your name again."

With those words, she exited the tower, leaving Gaspard behind. She listened to his whimpering as she descended until the turning stair took her beyond range of hearing.

Nelle searched the fortress for some sign of where Soran could have landed. He wouldn't have been able to jump into the ocean from the tower unless propelled by tremendous force. She found one spot on the ocean-facing wall that looked as if something heavy had struck there. Signs of scrabbling, gouges torn into the rocks. Was it possible Soran had survived the fall from that height, managed to climb over the parapets, and flung himself out into the water below? The Thorn Maiden didn't like water.

Nelle looked out from the wall, across the channel to where Roseward Isle lay, a mile from the shore. But in truth, it was much farther away than that. What was visible in this world was only a partial reality.

Could Soran swim the leagues of the Hinter Sea to return to Roseward?

Turning her back on the sea, Nelle made her way along the ruinous wall to the gate. There she used Mother's claws to climb down to the bridge, then slipped the claws from her fingers, stuffed them back in her pockets, and set out along the road. She would need a boat. No supplies though. If she couldn't make it to Roseward, she wouldn't survive long anyway.

Should she say goodbye to Papa?

She paused, tears gathering. Papa. Dear Papa. She felt the urge to turn back, to look up to the city, to let her gaze linger. To imagine the streets and alleys that would lead her back to him.

But no . . . no . . .

A breeze blew gently against her face like fingers brushing back strands of hair. And in that breeze she could almost swear she heard the whisper: *I release you from your promise.*

Papa was lost to her. He'd been lost to her long ago, though she'd been unwilling to realize it. He'd provided for himself as best he could, and her reentry into his life only complicated matters. He would miss her for a little while, perhaps. Just as he'd missed her the first time she disappeared. But then life would go on. Without her.

She couldn't use Papa as an excuse. Not anymore.

A boat waited on the shore, pulled up onto the sand as though the gods themselves had provided it for her. She made her way down to it, idly wondering if it might be the boat Soran had used to journey from Roseward to Wimborne.

Nelle pushed the boat out into the water, took up the oars, and, turning her back to the sea, pulled into the channel, stroke after stroke, until she'd broken through the surf out into open water. There she found a steady rhythm. As the lights of Wimborne faded into the distance, she knew she would never see them again.

She wasn't sorry at all.

Chapter 23

The blue wyvern perched on an outcropping of rock, its tail wound around its haunches, its good wing folded neatly across its back. The other wing, torn and useless, hung at an awkward angle, occasionally catching the sea breeze like a sail and nearly pulling the little creature from its perch. But it gripped the stone with its claws to maintain its position of watchful alertness, staring out across the endless expanse of water.

Several times it sniffed the air, chortled softly, then went still again. As the sky overhead lightened with coming sunrise, the wyvern acknowledged the dawn with a flap of its good wing. But it would never again rise into the air with its flock to greet the sun, singing a morning chorus.

Twisting its head around on its long neck, it peered at the cliffs above, seeking some sign of its brother wyverns. But the cliffs were empty, the little cave nests abandoned. As dawn progressed, the sky should be filled with wyvern song. Instead, a few lone seagulls wheeled through the air above.

Heaving a sigh, the wyvern gazed across the water again. The tip of its tail twitched, and it uttered a forlorn little *meep*.

Then its crest flared. Its blunt nose lifted, sniffing eagerly. Letting out a chortling bray, it scrambled down from its perch to scuttle across the sand as fast as its ungainly body could move.

A soggy, shapeless mound washed up on the shore. Water streamed through strands of white hair and a waterlogged shirt. A silvery hand reached out, gripped the rocky shore and pulled the exhausted body a little farther from the foam.

Meeping with joy, the wyvern rushed to its master, nuzzling his face and jabbing at his body with the claw ends of its batlike wings. Soran groaned and turned his head, blinking dully up at the wyvern. Then, despite himself, he smiled and held up one hand. The wyvern shoved its nose into his palm, chirruping and wriggling with irrepressible delight.

"I'm sorry, my friend," Soran said, breathing heavily. "Did you think you were abandoned?"

He turned his face again, pressing his forehead into the sand.

Waves lapped at his legs, threatening to drag him back into the sea. But he'd climbed far enough up the beach that he could safely lie still for a little while. If not for the strength spell he'd prepared in advance, he never would have survived the return journey.

But he had survived. And tonight, there would be an end. To everything.

Soran pushed his body up, resting first on his elbows, then his palms, then up into a kneeling position. The wyvern danced and chortled around him, climbing into his lap and onto his shoulders before sliding back to the ground again. Soran lifted his heavy gaze to the lighthouse. It looked so far away.

But he had to get up there.

The sun climbed in the morning sky, warming his limbs. He tipped his head back, closed his eyes, and drank in its rays. Knowing he couldn't put off the inevitable, he started to rise.

But a cry tore from his throat, and he sagged back onto his knees, nearly falling on his face. When he placed a hand on his side, his palm contacted a hard, tight knot.

Soran slowly looked down, pulled his wet shirt out of the way, and grimaced. A bulbous tumor the size of his fist jutted from beneath his ribcage. He prodded it with one finger and gasped with pain.

Something moved inside that knot. Something coiled tight.

A tangled nest of thorns.

So, the *bialaer* spell had worked. Better than he'd expected.

Getting to his feet was an agony, but he managed it and stood, swaying heavily, one hand pressed against his side. An urge to look back over his shoulder tugged at his heart. As though he might somehow send his gaze all the way back through the Veil to Wimborne's shore. As though he might somehow spy a pale, slim figure standing there, the morning sun bright on her fiery hair.

Such wishes were useless.

Not much longer now. One more day. One more sundown.

He made his way along the beach to the cliff path. The wyvern looped around him, sometimes scampering in front, sometimes trailing at his heels, never once letting up its chatter. The climb up the path was more difficult than Soran expected, and he was obliged to stop and breathe several times on his way. The thorns churning in his side felt like tiny teeth trying to chew their way out.

Hastily he suppressed that thought and pushed on up to the top of the cliff, staggering at last to the lighthouse door. It opened at his touch, the magic responding to his almost unconscious commands. He stood a moment in the doorway, gazing into the darkened room.

Strange . . . there was a time, not so long ago, when he would have given anything never to see this close, gloomy chamber again. There was a time when it had felt like a prison cell, its walls closing in to crush the life and spirit out of him.

Now, as he gazed into that room, he saw *her* everywhere. Nelle. Crouched by the fire, turning her flapcakes. Seated at the table, quill in hand, her brow puckered with concentration. Lying on the pile of furs in the alcove, her face relaxed in sleep, softly snoring. Standing at the armoire, turning to look back at him as he came down the tower stair.

He closed his eyes. And for a moment he could pretend that when he opened them, she would be standing there in truth. That she would approach him, with her eyes shining, her lips trembling, her heart in her hands.

I love you, Soran Silveri. I always will.

Was that a lie too?

A growl in his throat, Soran wrenched his eyes open and entered the room, crossed to the armoire, and flung open the doors. There lay the stack of wyvern spells, carefully dried and folded. He pulled them out and carried them to the doorway where there was light enough to read the carefully written words.

There on the doorstep, he opened each parchment and read each spell, calling the little daydreams back to life. They flitted free of the pages, shaking their wings, throwing back their heads, and chortling with joy at their liberation. The blue wyvern brayed from the ground, scampering in circles as his brethren took to the air. Several of them swooped down to touch noses with him before tilting their wings back and taking to the sky.

Soran watched the wyverns in their dance, and his heart swelled at the sight. He'd always loved them. Truly loved them with an untainted, joyous sort of love. These creatures of his mind, his fancy. Some were more beautiful than others, some more graceful, better formed. But he loved them all equally, from the most magnificent to the most ungainly. He had taken deep pleasure in the writing of them as he honed his craft.

Taking one of the spell pages, he bowed his head a moment, eyes closed. Then he blew sharp whistle. A bright yellow wyvern banked in the sky, wheeled about, and zipped down to him, alighting on his upraised wrist.

"There's a lot of sky out there." Soran stroked one finger down the wyvern's throat. It half closed its eyes, and he felt a purr vibrating beneath the scales. "I can't keep you here. It won't be safe for any of you after tonight."

He held the spell page just beneath the wyvern's nose.

It blinked, one eye shutting a moment before the other. It sniffed delicately at the parchment, then, with equal delicacy, put out its tongue and took the page into its mouth.

Soran felt the transference taking place—the thread of magic that bound the wyvern to him as its creator snapped. But the spell did not disintegrate. Instead, the magic simply coiled tight and nestled deep down in the core of the wyvern itself.

With a joyous bray, the wyvern spread its wings and launched into the air, its wings catching the sun as it climbed to the clouds above. Soran watched until it vanished, feeling as though a piece of his heart went with it.

But that was right. He must send away as much of his heart as possible before tonight. The Thorn Maiden would destroy whatever was left.

One by one, Soran called the wyverns to him. One by one, he held out his arm for a creature to perch, wings flapping awkwardly as it caught its balance. One by one, he offered a spell page. And each wyvern, instinctively knowing what to do, took the little spell into its mouth and swallowed it, claiming the magic for its own, claiming the right to its own existence.

They sang with joy as they took to the air again, flocking together overhead before setting out across the waves to leave Roseward behind forever.

Finally, Soran stood on the cliff's edge with only the blue wyvern at his feet. It sat quietly, its face forlorn, watching its brethren leave. As the last one vanished from sight, it blinked its goggly eyes up at Soran and uttered a pathetic little *meep*, its crest flattening.

"I know." Soran looked down at the wyvern, frowning sympathetically. "I'm sorry. I wish you could go with them."

Then, grimacing as pain shot through his gut, he knelt, took out the last spell page and offered it to the wyvern. It blinked again sadly, then accepted the offering. It swallowed, flared its crest, and burped, its tongue sticking out between its teeth. Then it lowered its crest, and its whole body sagged miserably. It may be free, but what did freedom mean without wings?

Soran rose, every movement painful. He pressed his hand into his side as though he could catch the pain and hold it at bay. Once more he felt the churning of thorns within the knot. The Thorn Maiden was furious. But while the sun was still high, she could do nothing.

The wyvern sat on the doorstep looking pathetic as Soran shut the lighthouse door. "You'd best not come with me," Soran said. "She'll be out hunting tonight. She likely won't take notice of you, but . . . you'd be wise to keep your head down, just in case." He smiled a little and stroked the wyvern one last time. "Wisdom never was your strong suit though, was it?"

The wyvern burbled unhappily and remained sitting on the doorstep as Soran set off along the cliff path. Just before he turned the bend out of sight, he heard the little creature utter a last sad bray.

He didn't look back. The poor creature didn't deserve its fate, living out the long years of its existence alone on Roseward without the companionship of its fellow wyverns. If he were kind, he would have torn the spell to pieces and ended the poor thing's life.

But he wasn't kind. He couldn't bear to destroy his creation. And maybe someday it would have opportunity to escape Roseward, to make a life of sorts for itself elsewhere. It was a simple being, after all. It didn't need much to keep it happy.

Shivering as the cold wind penetrated his damp shirt, Soran turned his gaze toward the distant chimneys of Dornrise. The island, which had for so long seemed small, now felt impossibly large. But he had all day to make it from here to there.

And then . . . and then . . .

CHAPTER 24

WITH EVERY STROKE OF THE OARS, NELLE EXPECTED TO feel the jolt as she passed through the Veil. Maybe this stroke. Maybe the next. The tension of expectation was almost enough to drive her mad.

But it didn't happen.

She kept going. A fearful thought whispered in the back of her brain: Maybe the bridge was already broken. Maybe she was too late. Maybe she would row all the way to the island, and it would just be a lump of rock covered in ruins, no sign of life anywhere. The Roseward she knew would have slipped away, untethered, deep into the Hinter Sea, never to be seen again.

No. She wouldn't believe it. She would not.

Nelle pulled harder at the oars, refusing to let herself look back over her shoulder. She would reach the Veil soon, and then she would be in a different world altogether, and then—

A chill like ice rippled across her soul. Her eyes blurred, filmed over with a flickering, rainbow-like shimmer. The sensation passed almost before she realized what had happened but left behind a pulsing aftershock that left her shivering on the rowing bench.

She gasped and nearly dropped an oar. Bent over on the bench, she waited for the aftershock to pass, waited for her bones to stop rattling beneath her skin. At last, she sat upright again, blinking hard.

Pale dawn light streaked the horizon, the black sky giving way to indigo, to violet, to pink. Nelle peered into empty space where Wimborne ought to be.

She'd made it. She was through the Veil. She was back on the Hinter Sea. With a stifled cry on her lips, Nelle turned in place, eager to see how close she'd come to Roseward. Her relief gave way to sudden, searing horror.

The island was gone.

"No," Nelle whispered. Her gaze shifted frantically to and fro, searching the horizon. Maybe Roseward had shifted somewhat, or maybe she was disoriented. It must still be there. Somewhere. "No, no, no, please!"

Nothing but empty ocean stretched around her as far as the eye could see.

The first surge of fear seeped out of her body, leaving her numb. Nelle felt the vastness of that great expanse like a weight on her soul. Eventually she picked up her oars and started rowing again, hardly aware she was doing it. There was simply nothing else to be done. She rowed and rowed as the sky brightened above.

After what felt like an endless interval, she lifted her head and shaded her eyes, peering toward the rising sun. Was that a ship she spied, its prow piercing the morning mist? Its masts looked tall enough to stab the sky, and full white sails billowed in the wind. It was coming her way, Nelle realized dully. Should she try to signal to it, try to wave it down?

Perhaps it was hours later. Perhaps mere moments. Time lost all meaning out here on the Hinter Sea. But suddenly the tall ship was upon her, looming large and surreal, the foaming waves parting to let it through. Its prow was a huge swan, brilliantly carved and crafted, each feather so distinct, one almost expected to see them stir in the wind. Its eyes had been painted so lifelike that Nelle wouldn't have been at all surprised had it turned to look down at her in her small, bobbing craft. Through the haze of golden morning, she could just discern figures on the deck, climbing the rigging. Some were small, ragged creatures, but those standing on the deck were tall and golden, almost godlike.

Armor flashed in the sunlight, so bright, so blinding, Nelle raised a hand to shield her face and turned away.

When she lowered her hand and looked again, the ship was gone. So suddenly, so completely, she wondered if she'd seen it at all.

Shaking her head, she set to work with the oars. Stroke after stroke, she made her way across the waves beneath the beaming sun and a flock of lazy clouds, feeling as though she would go on rowing forever.

A spurt of spray startled her. Shaking her head, Nelle realized just in time that one of her oars was sagging in its metal frame, ready to slip away. She caught it and pulled it back into the boat. Bullspit, she must have fallen into a daze! How long had she been out? And what had brought her back so suddenly?

Movement caught her eye. She lifted her head just in time to see something disappear under the waves. Something . . . she wasn't sure what. Frowning, she leaned her head over the gunwale to peer into the water.

Her heart caught in her throat.

Gagging with terror, Nelle sank into the bottom of the boat, only just having sense enough to haul the oars in with her. She crouched, her veins thrumming, her eyes squeezed shut. But she couldn't unsee that shadowy glimpse of something vast, dark, and many-tentacled gliding along the cool currents just beneath her.

Something bumped the wooden boards beneath her, a gentle knock that made the craft rock wildly. Nelle stuffed her fist into her mouth to stifle a scream. A small, thin, whimper vibrated through her tightened throat.

How long she lay there in abject dread she couldn't say. Her boat stopped its aggressive up-and-down motion, settling back into a gentle bob on the waves. No huge tentacles reached up from the water to catch the boat in a sucker-grip and drag it down to unknown depths of crushing darkness.

Nelle opened her eyes and stared up at the distant sky, at the little white clouds trailing across her range of vision. What a fool she was. What a bullspitting fool! She bit back curses, pressing the heel of one hand into her forehead. She should have known it would be useless even to try to return to Roseward. The bridge was broken. And that was that! Soran would face his end alone.

Why hadn't she tried harder to stop him back in the ruins? Why hadn't she been faster climbing the tower? Maybe she could have made a difference. How, exactly, she couldn't say, but . . . somehow.

She blinked. Tears burned on her face. With an angry growl she wiped them away, then frowned at her own hand, startled. A gleam of sunlight caught on something bright, something so thin and delicate she almost couldn't see it. She'd all but forgotten about it during her last eight months of life in Wimborne.

But there it was—her ring. The spell ring Soran had made for her, oh! So long ago now! Back when the harpens first came to Roseward. He'd told her a spell thread connected that ring back to him. If she were ever in any danger, she should tug on the thread, and he would feel it. And he would come to her.

It had worked in Ninthalor when she was held captive by Kyriakos. Soran had found her then.

She sat up in the bottom of the boat, gripping the sides for balance, and took in the hugeness of the Hinter Sea. There was no sign of Roseward anywhere, and it was ridiculous to even consider trying to summon Soran to her out here. But what if . . .?

She climbed back onto the rowing bench, taking care not to look into the water for fear of what she might see. Instead, she focused on the ring. Could there be some way to reverse the flow of that connection?

She held up her hand, turning it slightly. The ring was difficult to see. If she didn't know it was there, she would overlook it entirely. But the magic was still good. As she concentrated her *ibrildian* sight, the many-stranded spell thread began to brighten, to glow. Soran's work was strong, and the spell wasn't used up. Not yet.

She touched the ring with the index finger of her left hand, closed her eyes, and concentrated. She was part fae, after all— magic was in her blood. She didn't need the written word to channel it, for she was herself made partly from magic.

The ring shivered beneath her fingertip. She felt the power of the *quinsatra*, potent but condensed into that tiny band. And she felt the connection spell thread reach out from the ring. Reaching out to the source of its creation.

Nelle opened her eyes. The thread was still there, visible to her mortal eyes, shining from her ring, stretching across the water in almost exactly the opposite direction from where her boat was pointed. Biting her lip, Nelle gave the thread a gentle tug, once, twice . . .

Far away, at the end of the thread, she felt a slight pull of resistance.

Soran.

He was still alive then. Otherwise, surely the thread would have snapped. He was still alive, and she could still find him.

Uttering a wordless cry, Nelle scrambled to replace the oars in their locks, turned the boat around, and resumed rowing, pushing and pulling for all she was worth. She kept an eye on the spell thread, watching the gleaming ring on her thumb. Every so often she lifted her hand and tugged again, just to feel that resistance at the far end. On and on she rowed until her shoulders ached and her arms throbbed and her back threatened to break with exhaustion. The sun traveled overhead, burning down until she felt faint beneath its glare. Still, she pressed on.

How many hours remained until sundown? How many hours until the Thorn Maiden rampaged at will?

She lifted her hand and tugged once more. The ring glimmered, and the spell thread glinted in the sunlight.

Then it snapped.

Nelle stared at the little gossamer filament sparking with dying magic as it faded to nothing. At first she felt nothing. How could she? The hope she'd allowed to swell in her heart was still too great, too potent to be so suddenly undone. The spell couldn't be broken. It simply couldn't.

And Soran . . .

He couldn't be dead . . .

Fear and grief rose up, threatening to overwhelm her soul. And still she sat there, staring at the little ring, which faded swiftly now as the magic drifted away, back to the *quinsatra*.

Then a sound touched her ear. Distant, nearly obscured by the ocean wind in her ears, and yet unmistakable: the sound of surf crashing on stone.

She turned in her seat to look across the prow of her boat, across the water.

Roseward Isle loomed into view, floating free on the Hinter currents.

As Nelle crested the cliff path leading up from the beach, the blue wyvern brayed with joy. Springing from the doorstep where it had curled in a little ball, it flared its crest and flung itself at her knees with so much enthusiasm, it might have knocked her off her feet and falling to her doom.

But Nelle prepared for the impact. Dropping into a crouch, she caught the wyvern in her arms. "Hullo there, worm!" she said, shocked at the sudden tears clogging her throat. The creature scrabbled in her grasp, its hind claws inadvertently scraping her skin and leaving red marks. Its good wing slapped her face as its blunt nose nuzzled into her hair and neck. "Gods above, I never thought I'd be so happy to see you!"

Once the first wriggling spasms of joy passed, the wyvern calmed enough to let Nelle set it down and stand up. She was exhausted, her arms and shoulders throbbing, her back aching. But the need to find Soran drove her on. Was he still alive? Or had he died in the moment the spell thread broke? A good three hours remained before sunset, so the Thorn Maiden couldn't be out yet.

Maybe she still had time. She had to find him.

The lighthouse door was locked fast against her. She never had learned how to control the magic locks, which responded only to Soran's command. She knocked tentatively and called out, "Soran?"

How would he respond to her arrival? He'd be furious, of course. After everything she'd done, he would want nothing more to do with her.

He would just have to suffer her presence a little longer.

"Soran!" she called, and her tentative tapping turned into hard pounding with her fist. "Soran, are you there? Open up!"

No answer.

She looked around at the wyvern seated in the dirt behind her. It *meeped* and tilted its head. "You're no help," she muttered. Stepping back from the door, she scanned the tall tower. From this angle she could just see the windows high above. Was Soran up there now? Watching her? Refusing to acknowledge her?

Well, this time she hadn't come to Roseward unprepared.

Nelle fished the nilarium claws out of her pockets and slipped them onto her fingers. A quick flick of her wrist, and the claws unsheathed, glittering in the sunlight. She calculated the distance up the tower and couldn't quite repress a sigh. She was so bullspitting exhausted! But what did that matter? She'd rest plenty when she was dead.

"Wait here," she said, tossing the words over her shoulder to the wyvern. Then, taking a running start of ten paces, she leapt at the wall and dug her claws deep into the stones.

She climbed swiftly. The lighthouse was nowhere near as tall as the Evenspire—not even as tall as the Tyrane tower. The sea wind buffeted her, yet she continued upward, hand over hand, her feet braced against the stones for balance. Once she reached the open window and got her elbows hooked over the sill, it was the work of a few scrambling moments to haul herself up and get a leg swung over.

Before climbing inside, she paused to look around the tower chamber. There was the huge basin in the center, full of slick black oil. There was the mage's desk set against the one window-less wall, books and boxes piled all around it. There was the narrow cot bed.

No sign of Soran.

Nelle climbed in and circled the room slowly. She paused at the desk, idly picking up spellbooks, flipping them open, glancing at the spells, then setting them aside. She couldn't linger. Soran wasn't here, and she must find him.

But for a moment it was nice to simply be here. Here in this space that belonged to him. Here in this chamber where he'd lived for so long, where he'd fought countless nightly battles, giving his blood, giving his life to protect a people who had long ago forgotten his existence.

Stifling a sob, Nelle turned from the desk and gazed out the open window across the length of Roseward Isle. There stood Dornrise on its high outcropping, still magnificent and proud even after years of crumbling ruin.

He was there. She could feel it.

CHAPTER 25

STEPPING THROUGH THE MASSIVE FRONT DOORS OF
Dornrise was like stepping through a portal into the past.

Soran paused in the doorway, leaning heavily against the
frame. His face and body were slick with sweat, and his knees
trembled, ready to give out. He should have stopped long before
now. After all, what did it matter where he met his end? He had
made it back to Roseward. The Thorn Maiden could come and
kill him at any time. It made no difference.

But no. It had to be here. It couldn't be anywhere else.

He stepped through the door, walking in the patch of light
cast across the inlaid floor. He made his way slowly, wary of the

phantoms of memory floating on the edges of his vision. There was his father arrayed in lordly robes, prepared to head down to the harbor to meet an envoy from Luirlan or a merchant from Brygell. There was his mother, pausing in the doorway of her favorite morning room where she kept up with her copious correspondence, her pale hair neatly pinned at the nape of her neck.

And there was Ithan. His brother. A lad of some ten or eleven years, screaming as he slid down the banister, crashed into the wyvern newel, and collapsed in a heap of gangly limbs on the floor. Helenia was also there, of course. Standing at the top of the stair, laughing wildly, and pointing at the results of her dare.

How she had driven them both wild, prodding them on to greater and greater feats of foolishness for the sake of impressing her! How she had driven them both mad with their need to outdo one another.

Ultimately, she had driven them to their deaths.

No, that wasn't the truth. Soran shook his head with rueful acceptance. Helenia had merely lit the candle. They had touched the flame to the fuse on their own.

Soran paused before the set of portraits prominently displayed on the wall across from the stair. He gazed up into Ithan's face, captured brilliantly by a renowned artist Mother had sent for all the way from Luirlan. It was a good likeness, almost uncanny, capturing both his brother's spirit and—just there, in the corners of his eyes—his ever-simmering hunger. A hunger for power, for superiority, a driving, gnawing need to be master of all he surveyed.

That same hunger was reflected almost exactly in the eyes of the second portrait. In Soran's own likeness.

Turning his gaze from Ithan's face, Soran looked long and hard at his own image. This portrait had suffered more damage over the last fifteen years. A large slash across the throat of his painted self resembled a stroke from an assassin's blade. The Thorn Maiden's work, no doubt.

Had he ever truly been that young? He studied that handsome visage, those proud, eager eyes. Back then he'd believed the world was his for the asking. What he wasn't given freely, he would simply take, and who would stop him? Not even the Miphates could rein in the power they'd awakened inside him. No one could.

And so he had wrought his own undoing.

A spasm of pain shot through his body. Soran gasped and looked down at the ugly knot. Had it grown since the last time he'd looked at it? Was the Thorn Maiden swelling inside him, ready to burst free?

Turning his back on the portraits, he made his way to the stairwell. There he slumped down heavily on a step and leaned against one of the newels, breathing out a huge sigh. He was here. He'd made it. No need to walk farther. His eyes closed, and a small smile tugged at the corners of his mouth. After all these years, it was a relief to stop fighting.

Sitting there in a half doze, he allowed himself to think of Nelle. Despite everything, despite the ache of betrayal, they were pleasant thoughts. He recalled how, when he'd first seen her, she'd planted her small self squarely in front of him and demanded to know if he intended to eat the wyvern he carried in the sling. He pictured her seated beneath the alder tree in the center of the magic trap, singing her crude tavern song to lure the unicorn. He thought of her across from him at the table as they shared a plate of flapcakes.

He thought of her in his arms, her head resting on his chest. So warm, so close. So perfect a fit.

Too bad he hadn't met her sooner.

But no, that was a foolish thought! He'd met her at exactly the right time, at the time he would best appreciate the gift she brought into his life: true companionship, far deeper than the infatuated passion he'd once harbored for Helenia. Had he met her in his youth, he would have taken pleasure in her beauty but entirely overlooked the rare treasure that she was.

No, it was good that he'd known her only for a little while and only at the end. As he faced this, his final hour, he would keep thoughts of her close and say prayers of thanks to the gods for giving him those few precious images on which to dwell.

"Soran?"

He frowned and shifted uncomfortably on the stair, wincing at the pain shooting up his side. With a sharp shake of his head, he tucked his chin into his breast. He must be delirious. He could have sworn he heard her voice.

"Soran. It's me."

He turned away from the sound, pressing his head into the newel post. It was one thing to take comfort in memories, but this was too much. The last thing he wanted was for Nelle to be here now. Let him think of her safely back in Wimborne, far from the terrors of the night to come. Far from—

A hand rested on his shoulder. Another hand cupped his cheek, drew his face toward her.

"Soran, I'm here."

"No." Soran squeezed his eyes shut. But when he inhaled, he breathed in her scent—that bright, stubborn perfume of a wildflower struggling to grow between the cracks in a cobbled street, bruised underfoot yet still determinedly lifting its bright head again and again to the sun. He leaned his face into her hand, suddenly weak. Tears pricked his eyes, and he grimaced. "No, Nelle. Please."

She crouched before him, sliding her hand from his shoulder down his arm until her fingers gripped his. He couldn't feel anything but pressure through the nilarium, could not enjoy the touch of her skin. But she drew his hand to her lips even so and kissed his knuckles.

He opened his eyes, looking down at her. "Why are you here?" He didn't bother to ask how she'd crossed the Hinter Sea even with the bridge broken. She was Nelle. Of course she'd managed it. She could do anything she set her mind to. He shook his head sadly, and a tear escaped through his eyelashes and raced down his cheek. "Why, Nelle?"

She tipped her head to one side, still holding his hand close to her mouth, and smiled at him. His heart melted at the sight. "Why'd you think? I'm here to rescue you, of course."

"You can't rescue me. It's over."

"Yeah. Maybe." She kissed his hand one more time, then sat up on her knees, caught his face in both her hands, and pulled him toward her. "But I can still bullspitting try."

Her lips met his. Soft and tasting of salt, from the sea or tears, he couldn't tell which. At first he didn't respond. His whole body went still as stone.

Then he reached out and, ignoring the stab of the Thorn Maiden in his side, crushed her to his chest, kissing her again and again. She tangled her fingers in his hair, and when he tried to pull away, she wouldn't let him. He didn't resist. Why should he? Why should he think he could make Nelle do or not do anything against her will? So he let himself give in to the need he felt, to luxuriate in the touch of her lips, the warmth of her body, the taste and smell and feel of her.

When at last they both paused for air, he pulled her closer

still. She rested her head on his shoulder, her face tucked into his neck. Nothing mattered then. Monsters, betrayals, certain doom like the blade of an ax already in its downward stroke? None of that mattered. She was there in his arms.

After a time, she pulled against his hold and he reluctantly let her go. She sat back on the floor, holding his hands in both of hers, and gazed up at him. Her hair was loose and wild around her face, frizzy from the sea air and salt. She looked like a mad woman. He chuckled softly at the sight. How delightful to discover that even now she could make him laugh!

Then he bowed his head. Pulling his hands free of her grip, he squeezed his fingers into fists. "You shouldn't have come, Nelle."

With a noncommittal grunt, she shifted from the floor and sat beside him on the step. She leaned her head against his shoulder, and that simple gesture was enough to break his heart in two. For a few moments she was silent, but it was a thoughtful sort of silence, and he knew she would speak again soon.

"Who is that?" she asked at last. He gave her a sidelong glance as she nodded toward the two portraits on the opposite wall. "Is he your brother?"

"Yes."

"What happened to him?"

"He died."

She was silent for a little while again. He heard her draw a shuddering breath before she asked the question he knew was coming.

"Did the Thorn Maiden Kill him?"

"Yes."

"There's more to the story. More you ain't told me. About the Thorn Maiden."

"Yes."

She lifted her head from his shoulder. Her gaze burned into the side of his face, but he couldn't bring himself to look at her. "Well?"

He drew a long breath and let it out slowly. "When I was ten years old," he said, "my father's closest friend from the Carfina campaigns died of a fever, leaving his daughter bereft. In the weeks before his death, he sent a message to Dornrise, and my father journeyed to meet him. He was appalled to find his friend much reduced in status with nothing more than a pile of debts to leave his poor daughter. He promised his friend—one Captain Theran—that he would take his daughter under his wing and care for her as his own. This promise my father fulfilled to the best of his abilities, and no fault in what followed lies with him.

"Helenia Theran came into our lives like a hurricane from the sea. My brother, Ithan, and I had always been close. We were twins, you see, and had always been together, sharing a room, sharing games, toys, books, clothes, sharing thoughts and schemes. But I believe the moment we set eyes on her, a deep and irremovable wedge was driven between us.

"Helenia was the most beautiful creature. So full of dangerous spirit! She could drive us by turns to distraction and despair. For the first few years after her arrival at Dornrise, I thought I hated her. But it wasn't long before I realized the truth."

Nelle sat very still and quiet beside him. Her hand still gripped his, but she did not lean against his shoulder again. Instead, she maintained that silent contemplation of his face. He wished he could duck away from her gaze.

"I was, as you know, a student at the Miphates University," he said. "My brother was older and stood to inherit Dornrise, so Lord Silveri's second son must take up a suitable profession. When my talent was discovered, I was sent to Wimborne to study, but I came home as often as was permitted. It was perfectly natural that I should visit, after all. No one thought anything of it. But in truth, were it not for Helenia, I should not have been keen to see my family so frequently.

"By that time, my brother and I were at odds. There was always something, some dispute: a favorite horse of mine he ruined in my absence or some little piece of furniture appropriated from my room to his. At each of these slights, I would explode with anger, causing my poor mother to cry out that we should be the death of her, and my poor father to bodily separate us and threaten us with whips.

"In truth, I could not have cared less about those little things. It was the way he looked at Helenia that made me commit murder in my heart.

"At sixteen, she and I became lovers. It was a secret, of course, our comings and goings from each other's chambers. If my family were to discover our affair, she would be sent away to a convent on the other side of Seryth. But secrecy only strengthened our fervor. We believed ourselves in love.

"But what is love to a lad of sixteen? I was hardly faithful. Having discovered the joys of the flesh, I never thought to exercise restraint. The months between my visits to Dornrise were long, and Wimborne provided a limitless supply of warm and willing companions.

"However, I always told myself that my heart belonged to Helenia. I fully intended to take her as my mistress when I came of age, to set her up in some stylish house in Wimborne. Miphates, as you know, do not marry, but I saw no reason for that to impede my happiness. My family would never approve, but I had long since ceased to care for my parents' good opinion. I longed for the day when I would finally claim Helenia, anticipating with elation the look on my brother's face as he realized that she was mine, that she had always been mine, body and soul!

"Then one day . . . one terrible day . . ." He bowed his head and pulled his hand from Nelle's grasp to cover his face. Even now, even after all these long, terrible years, the pain remained. Dulled, perhaps. No longer the knife-like agony it had once been.

But present, nonetheless.

"A letter arrived from Dornrise. At that time, Gaspard and I were already deep into our illicit studies, consumed by the need to know and claim the power of the Noswraith spells. I had scarcely thought of Helenia in weeks, in months. It was nearly a year since last I'd been home. One would think, perhaps, that I would therefore be dulled to the blow. Nothing could be further from the truth.

"The letter was written in Helenia's hand—her elegant, curling script, every jot in place, every flourish gracefully drawn. It was an invitation. To her wedding."

He stopped speaking. He'd never told this story, never spoken the words out loud.

After a little while, Nelle whispered, "Your brother?"

Soran nodded. "It was . . . at the time, it felt like the ultimate betrayal." He huffed a derisive breath through his teeth. "I had considered her devotion to me unshakable, and hypocrite that I was, this proof otherwise shook me to the core.

"I sent no response. Perhaps if I had, or if I could have overcome my pride and gone to Dornrise at once to speak to Helenia . . . perhaps things may have been different. Instead, I festered in my heartbreak, my rage, my sickening hatred of both her and my brother. In my mind, I painted her as the slattern and him as the most libertine cad. Gaspard saw the effect of these thoughts on my work as we continued delving into the forbidden spells, and once or twice he tried to caution me. Each time I dismissed him with a glib word, a flippant gesture. For a little while, I even managed to convince myself that I didn't care, that our work mattered far more to me than Helenia ever could.

"I had made no plans to attend the wedding. I burned her invitation and wrote a careless few lines of regret, excusing myself from the event. But as the date approached, I became more and more distracted. Finally, when the day itself dawned, I stole from my chambers in the Evenspire, made my way down to the docks, hired a boat, and crossed to Roseward.

"Dornrise was packed with guests from all corners of Seryth and beyond. I was surprised at the expense lavished on the wedding, for I had assumed my parents would disapprove of the match. Helenia was penniless, after all. Hardly a fit match for Lord Silveri's eldest son. But no! Far from disapproving, they treated her as they would have treated their own daughter, sparing no expense.

"No one took notice of me. I did not wear my Miphates robes but dressed in humble garb and stayed on the fringes of the merriment. When the moment came for the bride to descend the front stair in the foyer, to meet my brother and walk with him through the crowds out into the rose gardens where the ceremony would take place, I stood along a back wall, out of sight.

"But Helenia saw me. She appeared at the top of the stair, resplendent in her bridal white, a cluster of roses in her hands.

She looked like some ethereal being, unreal in her beauty. I hated her in that moment as I had never hated anyone before. And my hatred must have flared like a beacon inside me, for her gaze turned to me directly, focusing on my face with such terrible intensity, I was transfixed. She descended the stair in all her glory, never once shifting her gaze, not even to look at Ithan, who waited for her with his hand outstretched. It was as though no one in that crowded space existed save the two of us.

"Perhaps I thought she would run to me. Perhaps I hoped she would break away from Ithan, gather her skirts, fly to my arms, and beg me to take her away from all this. A whole host of foolish fancies flitted through my mind. Instead, I found myself following the crowd out into the garden. There I watched the two of them, Helenia and Ithan, stand beneath an arbor of blooming red roses, and pledge their eternal love and devotion. It was a dream. A nightmare. But one from which I could not wake.

"I could not face the wedding feast. Following the ceremony, I intended to return to Wimborne, vowing that I should never return to Dornrise, that I should never see any of them again. How many times I have wondered why I did not follow through on that vow, why I did not run down to the harbor and away! Things may yet have turned out differently if I had.

"Instead, sick in mind and heart, almost craving more of the exquisite torture I already suffered, I stole away from the crowds and made my way up to Helenia's old room. I entered that chamber, which was so familiar to me, and stood for some while, eyes closed, smelling her perfume. Roses. She always smelled of roses.

"She found me there. While her guests toasted her and her newly pledged husband down below, she came to me, slipping into the room in a rustle of silk, bringing the scent of fresh roses with her.

"I turned to face her with rage in my heart. My hands reached out almost against my will, ready to close around her neck. But when I met her gaze and saw tears in her eyes, my hatred melted away.

"'Why?' I asked her. 'Why him? Why have you done this?'

"'Did you think I would wait around forever?' she answered even as she crossed the room, even as she threw herself into my arms. 'Did you think I would fold my hands, bow my head, and while away the years until you remembered I existed? Until you came and swept me away to become your mistress, your plaything, for as long as I pleased you? And then what? When my beauty faded and your love for me died, what would remain to me? A spoiled reputation and whatever brats you'd gotten off me. Is this how I should repay your father's kindness, your mother's care?'

I was shocked. Selfish bastard that I was, I had never stopped to consider that what I assumed our future would be wasn't the future Helenia desired. That my comfort would be her ruin.

"'But why him?' I demanded, selfish to the last. 'If you wanted a husband, you could have had anyone. Why Ithan?'

"She pressed her face into my neck, her fingers tangling in my hair. 'You think it so easy?' she said. 'You think a penniless girl like me entertains offers every day? Your brother is heir to Dornrise, Lord of Roseward. I shall be Lady Silveri. I shall move in the best circles, wear the finest gowns, boast the brightest jewels, be the envy of all I see!' Her voice was soft, but her words were bitter.

"Still, I could think of nothing but myself. I pushed her out to arms' length, my wrath only equaled by my lust. 'So you take him for his title?' I demanded. 'Are you so small, so selfish?'

"'Yes, Soran,' she answered me, taking my face in her hands. 'I am small. I am selfish. I am petty and grasping and desperate and frightened and furious. And I shall always hate you!'

"She kissed me then. And our hatred, our love, was like a fire engulfing us. We were lost to all reason, lost to everything but each other. Her wedding gown meant nothing to me, nor the vows she had just spoken. I cared for nothing but having her, holding her, making her mine once more. I cared for nothing but proving once and for all that it was me she loved and not my brother.

"I never heard him enter the room. I never saw him cross the space. I never heard him draw his blade. My first and only warning was the sudden terrible jolt that shot through Helenia's body, causing her to spasm in my arms. I pulled back, and it was like a nightmare—my vision darkened all around save for the view of her face. The pain in her eyes. The blood trickling from the corner of her mouth. She tried to speak, tried to say my name, I think.

"She crumpled against me, but I could not hold her. It was as though my spirit had fled from my body as well, leaving me senseless, useless. She fell to the floor in the mounds of her white skirts, lying between me and Ithan.

"He held the bloodied knife in his hand. Blood stained his cuff, his sleeve, his doublet. The eyes he lifted to meet my stupefied gaze were full of sorrow.

"I hardly know what happened from there. I think I attacked him. I think I got the knife from him, tried to stab him. We were found, parted. I seem to remember my father shouting, my mother screaming. Maybe they thought I had killed Helenia . . . I'll never know for sure, but I've wondered many times. I was the one discovered with the knife, after all. Maybe they thought I'd killed her in a jealous rage and then gone for my brother when he stepped in to defend her.

"However it was, I broke free of them and somehow escaped Dornrise back to the harbor and the hired boat I'd kept waiting. The haze of madness was so strong, I did not come to myself again until I was back in Wimborne, in my own chambers in the Evenspire. Then I wept, raged, hurled furniture at the walls, and smashed windows and mirrors, giving way to all the most futile paroxysms of despair a man can suffer.

"When the desolation passed, however, a sort of clarity came upon me. Or what seemed like clarity at the time. I know now that it was only a deeper, more dangerous madness.

"I gathered my tools—quills, inks, and a certain book I had stitched and bound myself. A red book adorned with a gold-leaf rose, a beautiful volume. I had made it to hold my first great creation spell. Now, looking at that rose, I smiled, thinking to myself how appropriate it was for the work I was about to do.

"Months earlier, Gaspard and I had set up a secret study in the Tyrane tower. He was there when I arrived, poring over some text. He started gabbling the moment he saw me, excited over some new discovery he'd made . . . but I couldn't hear him. I cleared the table with a sweep of my arm, heedless of his work, heedless of his protests, and arranged my own tools in place.

"He realized what I was doing. And he tried to stop me. He saw that I was quite mad and begged me to wait, to let the temporary insanity pass. But I could not wait. I saw everything so clearly, more clearly than I ever had before. The secrets that had always flitted just beyond our sight, the powers hovering just beyond my grasp . . . all were mine for the taking."

Soran bowed his head and breathed out a long sigh. The patch of light falling through the open doorway had shifted as he spoke. Shadows deepened as the sun began its descent toward the horizon.

Soon would come the night. The final night.

Nelle touched his arm softly. Gods, how he hated for her to hear all of this! But she deserved to know. She'd thrown in her lot with him, she'd given up her life, her future, for his sake. She deserved to know.

"I thought to resurrect her." Soran sighed. It was a relief to speak the words, to articulate the full extent of his hubris. "Or rather, not resurrect but . . . *recreate* her. I thought to use the forbidden magic to bring Helenia to life, not as the woman she was, but as the woman I wanted her to be. Beautiful. Sensual. Spirited. And wholly devoted to me.

"The words of the spell seemed almost to write themselves. The compulsion of true inspiration had seized me. Poor Gaspard stood by and watched, and his protests died away as the spell swelled in complexity and power. I pulled strand after strand of raw magic from the *quinsatra*, far more than I ever had before, far more than I'd ever seen any of my great masters or mistresses wield. I captured those strands in written form, and the very air of that tower glowed with a pulsing light that must have been visible across worlds.

"But there was a flaw. Of course, there was a flaw.

"I thought my love for Helenia was pure. I felt certain the vision I called into being would be equally pure. I did not stop to consider the warped nature of my passion. I did not stop to consider the wrath and the hatred I wove into those words of creation."

He stopped. Once again he lowered his head into his hands, closing his eyes tight. Trying not to see the blooming roses bursting into flame. Trying not to feel the twining thorns in his gut.

"This is why the power of creation is sacred to the gods," he said at last. "We only create from that which is already within us. Our creations are reflections of ourselves, nothing more, nothing less. I did not create a new Helenia—instead, I called to life a creature of my own mind."

As he'd written the spell, as he'd felt the being spring to life under each stroke of his pen, he'd known. Of course, he'd known. He could not have birthed such a monstrosity without realizing what he did. But by then the power flowed through him, and the flood was so profound, he let it carry him away, heedless of the consequences.

The Noswraith had manifested in Eledria. She had torn apart Vespre City, destroyed countless lives, wreaked destruction with the merciless mindlessness of a mighty storm.

"You know what came next," Soran said heavily. "King Lodírhal hunted me down, cursed me, and imprisoned me here for my crimes. He intended me to die, of course. He expected the horror I created to devour me long ago. He didn't expect me to hold out this long."

"What happened to your family?" Nelle asked quietly.

Soran shuddered. This was the part of the story he'd hoped not to tell. But now that she'd asked, he couldn't refuse to answer.

"I brought the Noswraith spell with me to Roseward," he said, "along with as many of my spellbooks as I could carry. I thought that would be the end of it. That I would hide away from the world till the end of my days. I thought so long as I did not open the spellbook, the Thorn Maiden would remain contained. I planned to warn my family, so they and all the folk of Roseward could flee before it floated out into the Hinter Sea.

"But that first night . . . I couldn't bear to let them see me. My hands were in agony from the newly cast curse, and more agonizing still was the shame of what I had done, what I had become. So, I crept back into Dornrise in secret, hid in my old rooms, and collapsed on my childhood bed, too exhausted by grief and terror to keep my eyes open.

"I dreamt it all. The most vivid nightmare, which will haunt me to my dying day. I saw the Thorn Maiden emerge from the spellbook. I saw her briars creep through Dornrise's halls and passages, tearing into wood, plaster, and stone. She found my brother first, and what she did to him . . ."

He couldn't speak it. Not out loud. The Thorn Maiden had fed off the murderous thoughts harbored in his heart, and she'd done such things to Ithan. Then she'd turned on his father, his mother,

344

both of whom he'd resented so viciously for permitting the marriage between Helenia and Ithan to take place. After that, she'd set upon the rest of the household.

"I didn't realize how easily she could escape. I didn't know then how to re-bind her or even realize there was need for such binding. She ran unchecked throughout Dornrise, and when I woke in the morning, exhausted by my dreams, when I stepped out into the passages and found the first body . . ."

A sob tore from his throat. Then another, and another. He was that same young man of so long ago. He was that arrogant fool, confronted suddenly, brutally, gruesomely, with the truth of his heart. The pain of this revelation was so much worse than the pain of his cursed hands, so much worse than the agony of the thorns that sliced into his flesh night after night, year after year, as he fought this monster of his mind.

Nelle's arms wrapped around him. He shuddered and tried to pull away, but she held on. Why? Why? Surely she must hate him now! Surely she must realize she'd thrown her life away for nothing. For a monster, a beast. He deserved no grace; he deserved no mercy. He deserved the death that came for him tonight.

Yet Nelle held him, her arms tightening against his resistance until he ceased to resist and allowed himself to lean into her, to sink his head on her shoulder, to let his tears fall freely. How long had it been since he'd wept? Not since that day, that hideous morning when he'd wandered the halls of Roseward and discovered the carnage his creation had left in its wake. The tears flowed now unchecked, enough to drown a bleeding heart.

At last, the torrent subsided. And Nelle was still there, still holding him. Her cheek rested against the top of his head and her hand stroked his cheek. He did not deserve this comfort, this gentleness. But he could not find the strength to pull away.

"Tonight, it ends," he said at last, the words rough in his throat. "Tonight, she will be free. And she will destroy everything . . . everything." He touched her hand, pressed her palm against his cheek. "She will kill you. And she will make me watch."

Nelle was silent for a little while. He felt her fingers tense against the puckered, scarred skin of his face. Then she sat up a little straighter, pushing him away from her. Did she finally understand? Did she finally realize the truth? Did she finally regret the choices that had led her to this place at his side?

She caught his chin in her hand, forcing him to look at her. Her eyes were bright with tears but gleamed with a fierce inner light.

"Well," she said, "we're just going to have to put a stop to her, ain't we?"

CHAPTER 26

NELLE STOOD IN DORNRISE'S FRONT DOORWAY, LOOKING OUT across the snarling brambles of dead roses. The sun was already starting its descent toward the far horizon. It would be dark soon.

The Nightmare Realm closed in around the edges of perception.

She turned and looked at Soran, still sitting on the step, waiting. He had one hand pressed to his side and grimaced with pain. The *bialaer* spell . . . Nelle shivered. He'd told her what he'd done, how he'd called the Thorn Maiden to uproot from Gaspard's mind and enter his. The *bialaer* spell had isolated her in a small part of his mind, containing her so that he could get back to Roseward. The growth was the physical manifestation of the spiritual condition.

It was a strong spell. Nelle felt the power of it pulse in the air around Soran. He could probably maintain it for weeks, months. It was much stronger than the version Gaspard had used in his attempt to control the Noswraith, and he had lasted eight months.

But could she bear to ask Soran to hold on? He had suffered so much . . . and that suffering was increased tenfold now. The Thorn Maiden sought to gnaw her way free, and her efforts would redouble after nightfall. And here in the Hinter air she was so much stronger. Was it fair to ask Soran to endure such pain just because she couldn't bear to live without him?

No. This had to be finished. Tonight.

One way or the other.

Nelle straightened her shoulders and returned to stand before Soran. His gaze seemed to fix on her bare feet, too heavy to rise to her face.

"Tell me how to bind the Noswraith," she said.

He closed his eyes. The white hair framing his face wafted as he shook his head.

"Come on then." Nelle crossed her arms. "I've got my quill and spellbook waiting for me back at the lighthouse. And I've picked up a few tricks, ain't I? Why don't I try it? Surely I can write a new binding spell. It's not like I'm trying to create a Noswraith of my own. All I got to do is catch her and hold her in a new spell. Should be doable, right?"

Slowly he lifted his chin, his head tilted to one side as he looked up at her from beneath his puckered brow. "If I had years to teach you, years to help you hone your skills, even then . . ." He shrugged. "The Thorn Maiden is more powerful than you realize."

Nelle narrowed her eyes at him. Gods, how arrogant could this man be? "She's *your* creation."

He raised an eyebrow.

"Which means she's only as powerful as *you* could make her. Right?"

"That is . . . one way of looking at it, yes." Soran sat up straighter, twisting his stiff neck, then laced his fingers together lightly, letting them dangle between his knees. "It would take a power equal or superior to mine to bind her."

Nelle quirked her lips in a little smile. "I can do it."

"No, you cannot."

"Well, we're doomed anyway, ain't we? I might as well try." She crouched in front of him, resting her hands on his. "Tell me the spell. Tell me how you held her all these years. I've got just enough time to make it back to the lighthouse, and if you can hold her at bay one more night, I can write it down."

He stared into her eyes. It was painful, almost oppressive to

349

be so close to him, feeling the full brunt of his despair. But Nelle wouldn't look away. She met his gaze without flinching, and she watched the despair falter as a little flicker of admiration lit his expression.

"You are a fool, Miss Beck," he said at last.

"Don't I know it, Mage Silveri," she replied with a grin. Then she touched his cheek, trailing her fingers along the ridge of one large, puckered scar. "Tell me how you do it. Let me try."

He nodded slowly. "Very well. Listen closely—it's an old spell, and it's written mostly in Old Araneli. You might have better success if you write it in your own tongue. It begins like this."

He began to speak words Nelle did not know. They poured out too quickly for her to follow, but she nodded and listened, concentrating, trying to soak in what he said. She felt the power in the words. In this spoken form they couldn't summon magic from the *quinsatra*, but the potential for the summoning was there.

And they were too much. Too complex, too strange. Too many. Her stubborn optimism crumbled away as she listened, as she realized how futile her idea truly was. No wonder he didn't want to tell her. It was simply a waste of time.

Then again, what other choice did they have?

Soran reached the end of the spoken spell and chuckled, a dark, mirthless sound. "That is the first part," he said.

Nelle swallowed. "How many parts are there?"

"Five."

"Oh."

Soran took her hand and squeezed it gently. "You see, my darling? It's impossible."

My darling? Nelle ducked her head as a warm flush flooded her face. How silly to take so much pleasure in such simple words! But she didn't care. She was going to die tonight, probably within the next hour or two. Maybe she deserved a little silliness.

She lifted her chin, faced Soran again, and set her jaw. "I've got to go now. I didn't bring my quill and book with me, so I've got to hurry if I'm going to reach the lighthouse before sunset. I . . . I think you ought to stay here."

He gave her a quizzical look. "Nelle—"

"No, hear me out! That containment spell of yours is strong. I can tell it is. You're planning to just let her go the minute she rises, but you don't have to. Fight her. Please. For a little while. Give me a chance to get back to the tower, give me a chance to try the binding spell. What have you got to lose?"

"You," Soran said. "I told you, the Thorn Maiden won't kill me first. She will find you and make me watch as she tortures you, as she rips you to pieces. And I will be powerless to stop her." His grip on her hand tightened. "You've got to leave Roseward. There are still boats down in the harbor. You'll have to take your chances on the Hinter Sea. You can get food from the larder for your journey, and your own innate magic will sustain you longer still. Your *ibrildian* blood will make you a target anywhere you go in Eledria, so you'll have to be—"

"Do you even hear yourself?" Nelle laughed outright. She couldn't help it. The sound simply burbled up and escaped, and she didn't try to hold it back. Then she stood up, bent over, and kissed him soundly on his parted, surprised lips. Backing away a step, she rapped the top of his head with her knuckles. "I've told you before, and I'll tell you again—*I* decide where I go, what I do. Not you. And I've decided I'm staying here on Roseward. You can choose to fight or not. You can choose to let the Thorn Maiden tear you to bits. But I'm going to write that bullspitting binding spell, gods help me. And if she gets me before I can finish, at least I'll know I died trying."

She shook her head, laughing again even as tears prickled in the corners of her eyes. "I'm not abandoning you, Soran Silveri. Never again."

He stood. He was so tall, so broad, almost frightening in his sheer physical presence. He looked down at her, his eyes searching her face. The air seemed to heat in the space between them as his eyes caught and held hers.

Then he took her face between his cold, cursed hands. She shuddered at the chill of the nilarium but closed her eyes as he tilted her head up to his. His lips pressed against hers, and it was like the sacred touch of souls. She shivered again in response to that touch. If only she could lose herself wholly within this moment, could let this kiss lead to another and another.

But he broke away too soon, his lips hovering just above hers. His eyes, so close she could see the little flecks of green in the gray, were full of light even as the shadows in the hall deepened.

"I love you," he said.

It was the first time he'd said it.

Despite everything—all the loss, the fear, the anticipation of horrors to come—a rush of happiness filled Nelle's heart. She kissed him again softly, lightly, and smiled one last time. "I'll see you in the morning, sir," she said.

Then she turned and raced across the foyer and out the door into the snarling tangle of dead roses. The sun was sinking fast now, and she didn't have much time.

Soran watched Nelle until she was out of sight.

How strange it was that he should have met her now. That after all these years, all these sins, the gods would see fit to send her into his life. It was a grace entirely undeserved. He'd never been a praying man, had always considered his intellect bastion enough against the vastness of unknown worlds and realities. And when his intellect betrayed him, when he discovered the true sordid depths of his own depravity, he'd assumed the gods would want nothing to do with the likes of him.

Now he wished he knew how to pray. Wished he knew how to

give thanks for those stolen moments, for the love that had bloomed in his scarred and battered heart, making him feel young again, giving him hope that somewhere in the world out there, goodness grew and life flourished. Not a world he could enter . . . no, it was much too late for him.

But it was a mercy just to know that it existed. Somewhere.

The shadows lengthened. Soran peered up at the orange-streaked sky. The sun had dropped beyond his line of sight, and already the first faint stars twinkled overhead.

He turned and strode back into the hall. Inside, it was already almost as dark as night, for the faint twilight could not penetrate the overgrown tangle of briars choking the windows. All around the edges of his vision, he sensed movement.

When he pressed his hand to his side, the Thorn Maiden was there.

She would kill Nelle tonight.

"No." Soran clenched his jaw, his spirit rising in his breast with a strength he hadn't realized he still possessed. He would save her. One last time. He would fight and keep the Thorn Maiden at bay. He wasn't fool enough to believe Nelle could actually write the binding. She couldn't. The fact was as simple as that. But he could keep her alive one more night.

And when day dawned and she found him torn to pieces, she would realize the futility of her sacrificial gesture. She would, of her own free will, take a boat and leave Roseward behind forever.

He must protect her this one more night.

Soran lifted his gaze from the floor to peer up the stairs. His old suite of rooms was up there. Once he'd kept a stash of spells hidden under his bed. Were any left? Nothing that would be much use against a Noswraith, but still . . .

Gasping at the pain in his side, he started up the stair, gripping the banister and pulling himself along, each step an agony. The Nightmare Realm closed in behind him, and thorns tore at the stones in his wake. He must hurry, hurry!

Just as he reached the top of the stair, a sudden burst in his gut made him double over, fall to his knees. His hand pressed harder into the knot, trying to physically hold back the pain. He cried out and fell to his face, his forehead pressed into the floor.

My darling, my love.

Helenia's voice whispered in his ear. He breathed in her heady perfume.

The night is here, and it is ours for the taking. Come, set me free. We shall be made one at last.

Chapter 27

Nelle raced against the setting sun back across Roseward.

Why had she been so bullspittingly short-sighted? She should have brought her quill and spellbook with her when she went searching for Soran at Dornrise.

Well, maybe it would turn out for the best. If Soran could distract the Thorn Maiden on the other side of the island, she would have a better chance at attempting this binding spell.

Oh, great gods above, what was she thinking? As if there were any chance she would be able to figure out a spell like that! But she had to try, otherwise what was the point of learning magic in the first place? Her *ibrildian* blood simmered in her veins, latent power just waiting to be tapped. Imagining she stood a chance was foolish, and yet, foolishly, she wanted to think it anyway.

Darkness closed in at her heels. She shouldn't have lingered so long at Soran's side. But leaving him was difficult, since she would probably never . . . since tonight they would both . . .

She ran faster still. All the scrapes and aches and pains she'd accumulated through the previous night, all the soreness in her muscles from rowing across the Hinter Sea faded away as she sucked in great gasps of Hinter air.

As the world darkened, her fae-sight sharpened, clarifying what the shadows tried to obscure. She tried not to peer into the deeper shadows, tried not to look for mounding, churning, crawling vines and blooming roses. The lighthouse loomed ahead of her, so close! She panted for breath, and a stitch in her side made her stagger, but she kept doggedly onward.

A little chortling bray erupted in the night, and the next moment, an awkward waddling shape hastened toward her, one wing flapping, tall crest flared. "Worm!" Nelle halted, bent over with hands on her knees, lungs heaving as she sucked in deeper breaths. The wind picked up from the sea and blew cold against her sweaty skin while the wyvern wound around her shins, burbling nervously. "Best not to stay here tonight," she said, stroking its crest down flat. "The Thorn Maiden is coming. I don't know if I can stop her. If you know what's good for you, you'll take your ugly hide away somewhere fast!"

With those words, she bent suddenly and planted a kiss on the wyvern's blunt nose. It squawked and leaped back, almost tripping over its own winding tail. Then, flaring its crest, it preened and cooed, altogether pleased with itself.

Nelle shook her head. "I mean it," she said while fishing the nilarium claws from her trouser pockets. "Get out of here while you still can." She slipped the claws onto her fingers and looked up to the open window high above, her goal. Taking another breath and letting it out in a whispered prayer to any gods who might care to hear, she leaped, sank her claws into the stone, and began to climb the lighthouse.

This ascent felt longer. The higher she climbed, the farther away the world below her felt, as though it had all dropped away into a void from which there could be no return. The wyvern's chortles echoed in her ear for a little while but soon vanished, drowned out by the voice of the wind and the more distant but persistent voice of the sea lapping the shore far below. She climbed higher still, and even those sounds faded to nothing, leaving her in a little cocoon of silence.

Hand over hand she ascended, her bare feet searching for little crevices for her toes. She thought of Mother—of her carefree laughter, of the smile she'd tossed Nelle's way just before beginning that last fateful climb that brought her doom. She thought of Papa—bruised and beaten down by life, so fearful of the world in which he never quite belonged.

She thought of Sam. His long hair falling in his face. His quick grin and teasing glances. She thought of that shocked stillness in his face when the knife drove into his side, when the pain rose up to claim him.

Oh, Sam. Sam. He would still be alive if not for her.

Nelle shook the tears from her eyes and pressed on. Why was the window so far away? Night had fallen hard now. Stars gleamed overhead, strange stars in a strange sky, distant worlds separated by the vast reaches of the Hinter.

Her every sense strained for some sign of the Thorn Maiden. None came. Was Soran holding her at bay? Was he still alive? Oh, gods above, let him still be alive!

This time, when she reached the windowsill and pulled herself into the room, she didn't stop to look around, not even to check Soran's desk for quills and ink. She didn't need ink. He'd magicked her quill when he performed the quill-bonding ceremony. It could write without ink.

She raced down the tower steps, round and round, her right hand trailing along the wall for support. She felt the protective spells implanted in the stones, Queen Dasyra's work. Those spells were awakening now, preparing for the Noswraith's assault. Did this mean the Thorn Maiden was already on her way? Had she so quickly broken through Soran's defenses? Had she already . . .

A thin cry in her throat, Nelle raced down the last few turns at a breakneck pace. She emerged through the hole in the ceiling, sprang over the unrailed side, and landed hard on the floor below. Her hands and ankles stung, but she rolled lightly, letting the rest of her body absorb the worst of the impact, and came upright in a crouch.

Her book. Her quill. Still there on the table where she'd left them. It was odd to see them there after all this time, in that familiar place. The sight was enough to warp her memories, making her almost believe that eight months hadn't passed since she last stood in this room, pulled out this chair, and sat at this table. It suddenly felt like yesterday. And, in a very real way, it was.

She drew the spellbook toward her. Its pages contained no spells; everything she'd written, she'd already used up. The rest of the book was empty, waiting for whatever spell she cared to add to it.

Nelle picked up her quill, tested the nib against the corner of the page. Ink flowed in a nice, neat stroke. Good. It was ready.

Now . . . what?

She bowed over the book, staring at that blank page. Her mind seemed to stutter and stop. In the back of her head she could still hear the echo of Soran's voice speaking the Old Araneli words of the spell in a long, fluid stream.

He was right. There was no way in all the nine hells she could write such a spell. She couldn't even remember where to begin.

She lacked the skill, the understanding. Gods above, she couldn't recall more than a bullspitting word or two! And that was only the first part of five.

So, what could she do?

Nelle's limbs began to shake. All too vividly she recalled the slithering touch of the Thorn Maiden's vines, the bite of her thorns. Inhaling, she believed she breathed in the poisonous sweetness of roses. She'd seen what that monster could do using the minds of mortals, and also in her physical manifestation. She was vast; she was terrible. She was unstoppable. Perhaps her creator could have formed a fresh binding, but Nelle? With her two weeks of training and her shaky hand?

But she had to do something.

Soran's voice echoed in her memory: *"He said he told the story. That is all."*

Nelle closed her eyes, bowed her head, and pictured the *ibrildian* boy. The long-lost prince. She saw him bent over the page she had given him, his hand flying as he made his strange marks, slashes, blots, and lines, which had looked so random and meaningless to her eye.

"He told the story . . . and it became true."

It made sense, didn't it? Or it *almost* made sense if she didn't try too hard to grasp the idea.

The magic she drew from the *quinsatra* was channeled via the words she wrote. And the words became reality. Like her flaming spell-sword. The mind connected with the physical characters on the page, and magic was born.

If it could work for individual items, could it not work for more as well?

How far could she take and develop the . . . the story?

She opened her eyes again and stared at the blank, intimidating page. It seemed to mock her. Well, time she showed it who was in charge here! She took her quill and drew a long, slashing line right through the center of the page from top right corner to the bottom left. She smiled grimly. Then, with a little shrug, she tilted the book and began to write along that diagonal line. With no regard whatsoever for either penmanship or spelling, she wrote:

Ons up on a tym, I stod befor the gaits of Dornris Hall.

Something shivered against her skin.

For an instant, the merest fraction of an instant, her vision seemed to double. She was here, bowed over the book, quill in hand . . .

But she also almost, *almost* saw the gates. Moonlight revealed them in all their ruin, half falling from their hinges, the wrought iron bent and warped, the posts strangled by aggressive briars. Beyond them, the drive led through the snarling thicket of thorns to the great house's open front door. It was a shadow image, not quite real, but . . .

Nelle wriggled her shoulders, rolled her neck, and bowed over the page:

I wus cold. Te wind wus sharp as it blu in from across the watr.

Again, her perspective doubled. She felt the close stillness of the room around her but simultaneously shivered as an icy wind penetrated her stolen shirt and raised gooseflesh on her skin. She firmed her jaw and narrowed her eyes.

Then she smiled.

I held an ax in mye hands.

Always before he had needed his vision spell to see the Nightmare Realm around him. Now, no spell was necessary.

She was in his body, in his mind.

Soran pushed up from the floor. The physical world around him was dark and still, but the overlying reality of the Nightmare was alive with movement. The Thorn Maiden's briar arms climbed the walls, crept across the floor, and swarmed the ceiling. Roses bloomed and burst into flame, silken petals crumbling, emitting a sweet stench.

He rose to his feet, panting hard. Sweat poured down his face as he staggered down the hall. He must get to his old set of rooms. Somewhere in there, he might find a spell. Something, anything he could use as a weapon. The nightmare briars reached up to snag his legs, but he was still in control for the moment. They couldn't hold him longer than a second or two before he broke free.

Why do you flee? My love, my darling! You called me into you. You want me, you need me!

She was all around him. Her voice whispered from the burning roses, shivered in the clinging briars, trembled in the fluttering leaves.

Forging on, Soran turned a corner into the long stretch of hall from which the private family rooms branched. The whole space was choked in vines.

But it wasn't real. Not yet. The *bialaer* spell still held, and the Noswraith could not physically manifest.

Forcing his vision to clarify, Soran concentrated on physical reality. He saw the same long dark hall, its walls deeply gouged but empty of thorny vines. He pushed forward, hands outstretched. Here and there, the reality of the Nightmare became too strong and the vines caught him, tore at him, constricting his movements. He kept going, heedless of the terrible cuts lacing his skin, and pushed through to a door near the end of the hall. He stumbled and fell forward, his hands catching hold of the door handle, which gave under pressure.

The door swung inward. Soran fell with it, landing heavily on the floor.

Come, my love. No more of these foolish games.

He lifted his face from the floor. She stood before him. Helenia. Clad in a thin, soft gown that clung to her dark skin, the ties across her bosom temptingly loose. She smiled her deadly, seductive smile that always set his blood to boil, one hand toying with her gown's ties, tugging until they loosened still more.

At last! At last! she whispered. *No one can stand between us now. That devilish little slut is far away.*

A shimmering gleam caught Soran's eye, a thread of magic with one end embedded in his side, in that ugly, writhing knot beneath his skin. The other end vanished within Helenia's breast, anchored fast.

She saw where he was looking, and her smile turned into a terrible grimace. *Enough of this!* she whispered. *Set me free, Soran. You know this spell cannot hold me for long.* She took hold of the spell thread and twisted until it strained as if wanting to snap. But it would not break. She twisted again, then yanked at it viciously, and with every harsh movement, the lovely image of Helenia melted away a little more, revealing the terrifying figure of thorns in its place.

Soran closed his eyes. He must focus. When he opened his eyes again, the world was dark, too dark to discern more than the vague outlines of furniture. But he knew this room's layout well enough.

Too weak to stand, he crawled on his belly across the floor, making for the bed, where he used to stash stray spells. Something useful might remain. Once close enough, he stretched out one hand and fumbled through dust balls and bits of random debris. Something rustled. A piece of paper.

His heart gave a bound.

Yanking the single sheet out, he pushed upright to sit leaning against one of the bedposts. He unfolded the paper, scanned the words and . . . and . . .

"Nine hells, what is *this?*" he cried.

Thorns swarmed in around him, poured over the edge of the bed, and crawled from beneath. With an inarticulate cry, Soran tried to scramble to his feet, but the vines bound his ankles together, twined up his calves, and tugged until he landed hard on one side.

The Thorn Maiden knelt before him, her rose-petal face close to his. Her long, branchlike fingers toyed with the connection thread of the *bialaer.*

If you set me free, I can manifest in your world, and you will never again be lonely.

"I won't have time to be lonely," he snarled. "*You'll rip me apart before I draw three breaths!*"

Never. I would never hurt you.

Even as the words spilled from her silken lips, her thorns dug into his flesh. Blood flowed, and he screamed with pain. The binding thread strained, pulled as taut as a harp string, and the knot in his side bulged, threatening to burst.

Soran, Soran, the Thorn Maiden crooned. She touched his face gently with the back of her hand. Then she gripped his jaw in her long fingers, driving thorns to the bone. *We both know how this must end. You cannot hold me much longer. I grow stronger with each passing moment. Let me go, my love. Let me go, and I—*

Movement in the doorway caught the corner of Soran's eye, and he swiveled his gaze. His eyes widened.

The Thorn Maiden, seeing the abrupt shift of his attention, twisted her long vine-corded neck, the sightless black holes of her eyes focusing.

You! she hissed.

Her arrival was so silent, he might easily have missed her. It was Nelle. Or . . . almost Nelle.

A flickering phantom-like image stood at the door, vanished, and reappeared, slightly more solid than before. The image possessed neither color nor a sense of flesh-and-blood dimension, but it was Nelle, nonetheless. She flickered out, came back in a more defined form, and fixed her gaze on Soran. With a shake of her head, she vanished and reappeared again.

This time she saw the Noswraith.

Her mouth opened, and the air around her seemed to vibrate

with a savage cry that couldn't quite stretch across realities to touch Soran's ears. Yet he felt it, just as he felt the magic rippling from the phantom image as she hurtled into the room, raising a shadowy, shapeless haze over her head.

But when she swung that haze in a downward stroke, it solidified for just long enough. He watched an ax blade rip through the Thorn Maiden, chopping off one arm just at the shoulder.

The Noswraith shrieked, dropping her hold on Soran, her vines quivering with shock at the violence of the blow. Soran pulled his head up, shook hair out of his eyes, and peered back into the Nightmare Realm.

Shadows shifted and writhed, long vines stretching like eager fingers to snatch at Nelle, to catch and crush her. Her image was harder for him to see. The magic sustaining her presence was strong, if uncertain. Was Nelle truly creating this spell? Every time she lashed out with the shadowy ax, her blows rang true. The razor edge sliced through branches and roses alike, and the Thorn Maiden screamed with rage and pain.

Then one of her vines caught Nelle's wrist. The girl's mouth formed an O of surprise, her eyes rounding a mere instant before the Thorn Maiden wrenched her off her feet and slammed her against the wall. The phantom image flickered out and back again, sustained by the stubborn magic but too weak to resist the Noswraith's grasp. Her teeth flashed in a gritted snarl. She raised her free hand to pull at the gripping vines. When thorns tore into her palms, she flickered out in response to the pain but was back again in a moment. That was one stubborn spell!

Soran got one leg up, ready to rise, to hurl himself at the monster. But what good would that do? He was a physical man, and these images were immaterial. He couldn't touch the Noswraith as she could touch him, not without a spell.

A spell . . .

He cast about, spied the lone paper lying a few feet away, and lunged for it. It was a foolish little piece of magic, but it was all he had. Wiping blood from his eyes, he swiftly read out the lines, felt the *quinsatra* open and the magic slip into his grasp.

The Thorn Maiden raised her hand, each finger tipped with a huge thorn aimed at Nelle's phantom face. The tips of her thumb and forefinger hovered a mere inch from her captive's eyes, which stared out from Nelle's face in a blaze of defiance.

"*Helenia!*" Soran shouted.

The Thorn Maiden turned. Black-void eyes fixed on him, she opened her mouth and hissed.

Soran flung the spell. It struck the Noswraith in the center of her face and exploded, spattering slime everywhere. It sizzled and burned everything it touched.

The Thorn Maiden shrieked in surprise and let go of Nelle, her thorny hands tearing at the sticky slime, which only caught her hands and fastened them to her head. Other hands formed from the tangle of her briars, ripping and tearing at her own head and body. But everything the slime touched became coated and sticky, and she broke her own limbs in her efforts to wrench free.

Nelle sank to the floor. Her phantom image almost vanished entirely, but she shook herself back into existence and stared up at the thrashing Noswraith. Scrambling upright, she raised both hands high. At the apex of the arch, the ax suddenly, brilliantly appeared in her hands, as clear as any physical truth.

Nelle swung.

The blade sliced through vines and thorns and arms, straight through the Thorn Maiden's neck, the force of momentum carrying Nelle along until it thunked hard into the wall.

The Thorn Maiden's black-void eyes peered out from between her many hands. For an instant she looked like Helenia again.

She blinked.

Her head rolled back from her shoulders and fell to the floor. As it rolled, it vanished in a puff of darkness like smoke.

The vines along the floor, walls, and ceiling retracted, Skittering and hissing, they rushed straight for Soran and plunged inside of him, into his gut, down into that place in his soul where the *bialaer* was affixed. He screamed and collapsed in overwhelming pain.

CHAPTER 28

"*SORAN!*"

Nelle tried to take a step toward the fallen mage, but the sudden spike of fear disrupted her concentration. As her foot fell, she lost solidity and jolted back into her physical body a mile away.

She jerked upright in her chair, nearly dropping the quill. The words on the spellbook page swam before her eyes.

"Bullspit!" she muttered, refocusing to send her awareness back to Dornrise. Her hand shook as she applied it to the paper, scrawling out another sentence, drawing magic from the *quinsatra* to sustain her.

The bedchamber in Dornrise came back into focus, its shadowy shapes overlaid with the shimmering haze of the Nightmare Realm. Nelle gave her projected form a little shake and shifted the handle of the ax in her hand. This split awareness was spittin' difficult to maintain!

Soran lay on the ground beside the bed. She saw thorny vines spilling out of the ugly knot in his side, eager to tear free.

Using more care than last time, she approached his body and knelt. He was still breathing, thank the gods! His chest heaved with each labored inhale and exhale, and his eyes were half-open, sightless, staring into nowhere. The *bialaer* spell rippled through his body, pulsing out from his bones in ugly waves of *quinsatra* light. The power required to maintain this spell was tremendous.

But as long as Soran kept the Thorn Maiden bound inside him, she could not be bound into a new spellbook.

Nelle sat back on her heels, studying Soran and the spell. Back in the lighthouse, she paused over the story she was telling with ink and magic. She could see what she needed to do to break the spell, to sever the Thorn Maiden from Soran. But if she did it, the Noswraith would physically manifest. Nelle shivered, recalling the horror of that unleashed monster tearing into the walls of Ninthalor, ripping through stone like it was nothing.

Could she do this? Did she honestly believe she could create a binding strong enough to hold a Noswraith? Because if she broke Soran's spell and failed to create that binding, they were done for.

While her physical body bowed over the spellbook a mile away, shoulders tensed, the nib of her quill poised and ready, Nelle's phantom body stood slowly, taking care not to lose her form, and hefted the ax.

"Nelle?" Soran's eyelids fluttered. His gaze sharpened as he peered into the shadows above him. Could he see her? "Nelle, are you there?"

"I'm here." Her voice echoed weirdly across distance and realities. She adjusted her stance and swallowed hard. *"Let her go, Soran. It's time."*

He frowned. She wasn't sure he heard her, but his hand moved to the bulge at his side, and the pain she saw in his face broke her heart. "I can't let her loose," he said. "I can't let her find you. She'll tear you apart."

Back in the lighthouse, Nelle set her jaw. "That's a risk I'm willing to take," she whispered.

Her hand moved. The quill darted across the page, words pouring from her soul. Her phantom self swung the ax two-handed up over her head and brought it slicing down into Soran's side. The phantom ax passed through his physical flesh, cutting straight to the spell inside him and into that knotted mass where a shimmering thread wound tight around a central coil.

The edge of the blade found the thread and cut clean through.

When the bursting power of the broken spell erupted in

SYLVIA MERCEDES

Nelle's face, she hurtled back out of Dornrise, out of that reality, and slammed into her physical body so hard that she crashed over backwards in her chair, her quill flying from her hand.

She lay for a moment, seeing nothing. Slowly her vision swam back into focus, and she gazed up at the rafters. She drew a breath, and it snagged in her throat.

Soran!

She hadn't planned to be thrown out of the room. She'd planned to be there with him, ready to catch and bind the Noswraith before it could physically manifest. Was the Thorn Maiden already in Dornrise? Had she already poured into physical reality and torn her former master apart?

"No, no, no!" Nelle scrambled upright, falling over herself in her haste. Every nerve of her body sharpened, and the magic she'd summoned from the *quinsatra* responded, blazing from her fingertips and the corners of her eyes in little trailing flames. She grabbed her overturned chair, set it back in place. Wait, where was her quill? There, across the room near the door.

With a curse on her lips, Nelle sprang from her seat, crossed the room in a few leaping strides, and snatched up the quill.

Boom!

The door rattled in its frame. All around it, little bursts of spell writing sparked in the walls. The protections Queen Dasyra had put in the lighthouse walls strained but held.

On the other side of the door, visible through cracks in the

376

slats, something moved. Something massive, something heavy.

A voice of sweetest softness whispered: *I know you're in there, pretty maid.*

For some while, Soran lay lost in pain that burst in a series of small explosions through his head, down his spine, across his soul. Spells were not meant to be broken like that, with such violence.

But when the agony faded, he returned to himself. The room clarified around him. He lay on the floor in a pool of blood, and when he started to move, physical pain stabbed his side. He grimaced, pressing a hand to the wound, and looked down. A gush of pus and blood flowed from where the *bialaer* spell had protruded. It smelled loathsome, but such a sweet relief! He closed his eyes, allowed himself to savor that relief despite the throbbing.

Then his eyes flared open. The Thorn Maiden! She was free. Free and corporeal somewhere on Roseward.

He grabbed the bedpost and used it to haul himself upright. Clamping his hand to his side, he breathed heavily. An overwhelming horror of helplessness threatened to undo him. He had no more spells. Nothing that could possibly work against a Noswraith unleashed. The Rose Book was gone, and Nelle . . . Nelle . . .

377

"Nelle!" he whispered.

The next moment he staggered to the door, then ran along the hall. The urgency of fear eclipsed his pain. He had to get to Nelle. He must stop the Thorn Maiden. Somehow.

Nelle stood before the shuddering door, her quill clutched to her heart, her eyes round with terror.

Boom.

The door rattled in its hinges, and her *ibrildian* sight sparked again as Queen Dasyra's spells flared and gyrated in the stones all around. The spells were some of the strongest magic Nelle had ever seen. Strong enough to withstand the manifest Thorn Maiden?

A slithering movement drew Nelle's eye. A thread of vine crept under the door, shooting out delicate tendrils across the floor. Nelle screamed and stamped her bare foot down on it. Tiny thorns tore into her callused heel, but the vine retracted.

It didn't matter. The spells couldn't hold her back. Not forever. Not for long.

Nelle whirled and, limping a little, returned to the table and her waiting spellbook. The pages glowed. It was a good spell—an odd spell, imprecise, messy, and wild, but good. Would it be enough?

"Write the story," Nelle muttered, brandishing her quill. The door rattled again under another crashing assault. The stones of the tower wall groaned, and Nelle could almost feel the climbing vines of the Thorn Maiden clutch at them, trying to tear them apart. The entire structure would tumble down, crushing her in the rubble.

Nelle concentrated on the lines of scrawled writing before her and, for a moment, panic froze her, body and mind. She couldn't think, couldn't find a single word.

Then, with a frustrated sniff, she wrote: *Bullspit.*

Magic flared on the page, warm against her face.

A grim smile tugged at the corner of Nelle's mouth as she forced her hand to keep going, to keep writing.

I tok mye ax in wone hand, a noose in ta other,
and I wakled to the dore.

Her mind began to split as the words flowed faster and faster. She kept writing, allowing the split to happen, allowing the division of reality. Her physical body remained bowed in place even as her phantom self manifested in the darkness behind her, ax and noose in hand. Obeying the spell, she approached the door.

The Noswraith waited just outside. It existed in the Nightmare Realm even while physically manifested. Nelle could feel the double reality of its being just outside, just beyond the barrier of Queen Dasyra's spells.

Her phantom self took another step. Then another.

And she walked right through the door into a world of snarled, tangled thorns.

There you are! the Thorn Maiden cried. *At last!*

Dozens of arms lashed toward Nelle at once. With a wild cry, she slashed with her ax, cutting through vines and thorns alike. They fell around her, littering the ground, writhing like snakes in death throes. But more arms came, and more, and more.

In the center of the tangled mass, the Thorn Maiden stood, a massive giantess, beautiful and terrible, with a face of blooming roses.

Soran raced along the cliff path above the sea. The Hinter air already worked on his wounds, and he felt stronger now that the Thorn Maiden was no longer inside him. He pushed his body faster and faster, his mind tormenting him with fear even as his heart throbbed with determination.

He came within sight of the lighthouse and skidded to a stop. "Seven gods!" he breathed.

The tower was covered in thorns. Writhing, living vines climbed from the foundations to the roof. They squeezed and pulsed, threatening to crush the lighthouse to dust.

Nelle . . .

A cry ripping from his throat, Soran surged forward, waving his arms over his head like a madman and shouting, *"Helenia! Helenia!"*

She didn't hear him. She couldn't. Her hatred for Nelle, her jealousy, was too great. It was his own hatred, his own jealousy. Those roiling, hideous, vile feelings he'd harbored for his brother, caught by magic and given life, were like a force of nature.

And here he stood—weaponless, wounded, exhausted. Helpless as a child before this massive evil of his own creation. For a moment, he could not speak, move, or even breathe.

Then he whispered:

> *"Red blooms the rose in my heart tonight,*
> *Fair as the dawn, new as the spring."*

A mound of thorny movement rolled out from the main mass around the tower, billowed upward, and took the shape of a woman's body made of thorns and leaves and roses.

Soran kept speaking, his voice too low to allow for any song. But the words carried through the darkness, caught on the ocean breeze.

> *"Dark flows the tide, but the stars they shine bright*
> *And summon my soul now to sing."*

She approached him, her movements roiling, fluid, and the perfume of roses filled the night. Soran watched her approach, his body quaking with dread at this thing he had made. She stopped a few feet from him, looming ten foot high at least. Her empty eyes fixed upon him. Eyelids of rose petals fell and rose.

As they rose, the shape of the face altered, the strangeness of the thorns melting into flesh, and he beheld the lovely face of the girl he had once believed he loved.

Gazing up at her, he sang:

> *"Come down to the water, my love, my love,*
> *Come down to the banks of the sea."*

Her full lips moved in response, her voice husky and sweet:

> *"Come down to the boat, set sail in the night*
> *And your true love forever I'll be."*

As she sang, the vines rippled around her. She sank down from that lofty height, shedding petals as she assumed human form. She was naked in the moonlight, her hips swaying, her perfectly formed limbs graceful as she approached him. Her long black hair floated around her like a cloud, framing her exquisite face.

"Soran!" she cried.

He held out his arms, and she ran to him, flung herself into his embrace. And this was the dream he had written, come at last to life. Helenia reborn. Alive, and fully his.

Her soft hands cupped his face as she gazed up at him from beneath her thick lashes. "Oh, Soran!" she said, her fingertips gently tracing the many hideous scars. "What has happened to you, my love?"

He didn't answer. He couldn't answer.

"Never mind." She drew his face down to hers, kissing the scar over his right eyebrow, her lips lingering. "Never mind. I'm here now at last. Oh, how I've missed you! I feel as though I've been lost for years in some terrible dream! I called for you, searched for you, but you always fled. But it was only a dream after all. You would never flee from me. Not you, not my Soran."

She kissed his cheek, kissed his jaw. Then her lips hovered just beneath his. Her breath was soft on his face, and he closed his eyes, inhaling the scent of roses.

"Kiss me," she whispered.

He held so still. His limbs were like marble, but his heart pounded wildly against his ribcage.

"Kiss me, Soran."

He shook his head slowly. "Helenia," he began but stopped, his voice thick with unshed tears.

"Kiss me, or I'll kill her."

He opened his eyes. Helenia was there, but the Thorn Maiden

was as well. And behind her in the darkness, thorns ripped at the lighthouse protections. Stone groaned, and one of the protection spells flashed as it broke apart, magic scattering in pieces, floating back to the *quinsatra*.

I'll shred the flesh from her bones.

Helenia's fingers turned to thorns, digging into his face.

Kiss me. Kiss me now.

Soran wrapped his arms around her, pressing her hard against him. His lips lowered to hers in a hard, violent kiss. Her hands slid from his face to the back of his neck, thorns tearing. He tried to pull back, but she held fast, kissing him again and again. Her thorns ripped through his clothing and sliced into his skin, not in spirit, but in true, physical reality. Yet a part of him still believed it was Helenia's soft, supple form he held, part of him still flamed with desire and carnal need.

Blood poured down his body in streams, soaking into the ground at his feet.

At last, the Thorn Maiden said in Helenia's voice. *We are as were always meant to be. One flesh. One life. One death.*

Blood oozed from a gash in Nelle's forehead, warm and sticky as it slid down her skin. She dashed it away with her free hand, determined not to let it drip and mar the spell taking shape beneath her pen. She reached the end of the page and paused to turn it, to keep going.

Her phantom self, out in the darkness, paused as well, ax poised in a backward arc. It was only a second, but even that was too long. A thorny vine wrapped around her arm, yanked at the ax, and nearly pulled her off balance.

Nelle cried out. Her pen moved again, hastily pouring out more words. The magic surged through her spirit, and her phantom self escaped the vine's hold, ignoring the scrape of thorns tearing long gashes down her forearm. She whirled and hacked with her ax, and the vine fell at her feet. Another vine reached for her waist, but she was just quick enough, her blade slicing true. She was getting faster, stronger.

But the Thorn Maiden was unrelenting. Always there were more vines, always there were more thorns. Roses bloomed and flamed before Nelle's dazzled eyes, and her vision blurred with exhaustion.

You're too late.

Nelle hacked at another reaching arm, determined to ignore that voice. But the Thorn Maiden would not be ignored. She parted her briars, and Nelle saw through the Nightmare Realm into the physical world.

She saw Soran standing on the edge of the cliff, bleeding from innumerable wounds. In his arms he held a woman. A beautiful naked woman crowned in blood-red roses. And he kissed her with a passion of desperation that seemed to pulse from his soul in a shockwave, powerful enough to knock Nelle back a step.

Nelle stared at the image, frozen. For a breath, a heartbeat, the hand holding her quill froze in place over the spell.

He may tell you he loves you. But he lies.

Her phantom self shivered, faded. The spell faltered, the magic threatening to break apart.

He can never love another. He gave his heart to me long ago.

Nelle swallowed.

Then, grinding her teeth, she set her quill to the page and brandished her ax. As her physical body resumed writing, furiously pouring words onto the page, her phantom self ran. Thorns lashed at her from all sides, but she was too quick, too nimble. She leaped, dodged, ducked, and never once did her gaze shift from her goal. From Soran, sagging in the arms of his lover.

He's mine.

The distance between them closed. The thorns writhed on all sides, ripping at her very existence. Blood spattered the table, the page, the plume of her pen.

Mine.

Another three paces. Another two.

Mine for eternity.

With a wordless cry, Nelle hauled her ax back over her shoulder and swung it as hard as she could, straight for that manifest body. The blade passed through without touching the Thorn Maiden's physical form, plunging to her core where a huge red rose bloomed with fire within a thicket of briars.

The ax blade severed its stem.

The Noswraith jolted.

Helenia choked, pulled back from Soran, her eyes rounding with shock. Her hands clutched his shoulders even as her head swiveled, turning to look at the phantom figure behind her.

Nelle dropped the ax. Then she reached out and caught the burning rose as it fell.

"No, Helenia," she said as her fingers closed around the blossom. In the lighthouse, seated at the table, she smiled grimly. "You are mine."

Her pen moved. She crushed the rose in her fist.

CHAPTER 29

THE EXPLOSION EXPANDED FROM ITS EPICENTER, RIPPLING across Roseward. It flattened trees, shattered the ward stones, and tore great fissures deep into the ground. It struck Dornrise, and the hall groaned, resisted . . . then crumbled in on itself, the foundation crumbling, the walls splintering, the windows shattering in showers of glass. Dust and debris buried the old dead roses.

But when the blast hit the lighthouse, it rebounded off Queen Dasyra's lingering protections. The tower swayed slightly as though battling a great gale, then settled back on its foundation, firm as ever. The protection spells sparked like embers, raining brilliant drops of magic to the ground below.

Nelle sat back in her chair. Her hand shook so hard, she could no longer hold the quill. It slipped from her fingers and floated to the floor, and she lacked the strength to pick it up. Neither did she have the strength to wipe away the blood running into her eyes from a gash in her forehead. She closed her eyes instead and simply sat there, slowly becoming aware of all the cuts and gashes on her body, all the places where the Thorn Maiden got through.

For a long while she sat, breathing in and out. Part of her still expected the door to crash inward and vines to rush in and overwhelm her. But after that initial thunderous burst of magic, all had gone terribly still.

Slowly, fearfully, Nelle opened her eyes.

The spellbook lay closed before her. She'd slammed it shut just after writing the last line. Power pulsed out from the compressed pages, the power of her binding spell and the fiercer, greater power of the barely contained Noswraith.

It wasn't enough. The spell held her for now, but it wouldn't hold her for long. One night, maybe two. Then Nelle's little binding would disintegrate, and her spellbook would fall apart, and the Thorn Maiden would be free again.

But for now . . . for now . . .

For now, it bullspitting *worked.*

Nelle smiled. It was foolish, idiotic even. But she couldn't help it. She smiled and sagged in her chair and whispered, "Boggarts and brags!"

The smile slowly faded, however, and she simply stared at the spellbook cover. Something was wrong. Her mind was so dull and exhausted that she couldn't quite put her finger on it. There was a definite wrongness to the world, something she ought to be concerned about. She blinked, tilted her head.

Then she sat bolt upright. "Soran!"

She was out of her chair and across the room the next instant. She fumbled with the door latch, her shaking fingers not wanting to obey her, but managed to turn it, to jerk the door open, and stepped out into the cold world. Dawn tinged the sky a dusty pink, and she didn't need her *ibrildian* sight to see the body lying a few yards away on the edge of the cliff.

Her heart in her throat, Nelle staggered across the threshold. Her body ached from many small wounds, but she ignored them, forcing her legs to obey her, to move faster. At Soran's side, she fell to her knees.

His shirt was shredded to blood-soaked ribbons, and terrible bleeding cuts, far deeper than any of Nelle's wounds, riddled his flesh. He lay with his back to her, his face turned toward the sea.

"Soran?" Nelle whispered. She hesitated, swallowed painfully, then took hold of his shoulder and rolled him onto his back. His body was horribly limp and lifeless, his pale skin a mass of cuts. She pressed her ear to his chest, then closed her eyes and

SYLVIA MERCEDES

breathed out a prayer of thanks. He lived!

Lifting her head, she leaned over him, pushing bloody hair out of his face. He looked strangely gentle. Despite the wounds, despite the old scars, despite the terrors he'd just endured, she believed the softness in his face offered a glimpse into what he must have looked like as a child.

"Soran," she whispered, stroking his cheek, "we did it. I ain't quite sure how, but we did it. The Thorn Maiden is bound. I finished the spell. It won't hold her for long, but . . . but . . ."

But they would have another day. Another day together before another night of battle and terror and probable death.

And what more could any two people ask for in this lifetime? Just one more day.

Forget about eternity. Just one more day.

She bowed her head, shivering with sobs, then wiped the tears away roughly with the back of her hand and pressed her lips gently against Soran's. His mouth remained still beneath hers, and she tasted blood on her tongue.

Pulling back a little, she smiled. "I love you, Soran Silveri," she whispered. Then she patted the side of his face smartly. "Do you hear me? I said I love you! Wake up and tell me you love me back, why don't you?"

His right eye twitched. His brow puckered. He turned his head slightly, groaned, and his eyelids fluttered open, struggling against the blood caking his lashes. His vision focused, blurred, and focused again as he looked up into her face.

"N-Nelle?" His voice was a raw croak. "Are we alive?"

She nodded. "Yeah. For now, at least."

With that, she kissed him again, and this time he responded. His hand lifted, trembling in the air before he rested it on the back of her head. And for the next few moments, the next few throbbing heartbeats, it didn't matter that the spell wouldn't hold, it didn't matter that the nightmare would soon escape. It didn't matter that they would have to face her while still exhausted from the previous fight, or that she would know what to expect, or that they couldn't possibly survive another night.

For the moment, they held each other close.

The sun rose to shine upon one more day.

"What's that out there?" Nelle asked.

Soran couldn't quite bring himself to lift his head from Nelle's shoulder. They sat together on the cliff's edge, the sea wind playing across their slowly healing bodies. All he wanted was to stay like this for as long as possible, breathing in the scent of her hair.

She was a wonder. Such a wonder! How she'd managed to contain the Noswraith, he couldn't begin to guess. Some trick of her wild, ridiculous, uncouth magic, no doubt. Professional curiosity told him to sit up and ask questions, to demand to see the spellbook. But professional curiosity be damned. His arm was around her waist, and her cheek rested against the top of his head, and nothing else mattered.

"It's getting closer. I think it's . . . a ship."

Soran's eyes were already closed, so he could only squeeze them a little tighter, wishing he could pull her closer to him, somehow hold onto this beautiful moment. But it was too late.

They would not die by the Thorn Maiden's hand.

"It *is* a ship. I think I saw it before. Yesterday, out on the Hinter Sea. Look at it, Soran! Do you see the prow with the swan's head?"

"It's Lodírhal."

He heard her gasp and felt her freeze in his arms. Then, though he tried to resist, she struggled out of his hold and got to her feet. Taking hold of his hand, she tugged, ordering, "Stand up. Come on. If we've got to face him, we'll do it together."

A few feeble protests rose to his lips. Nelle could hide, after all. Even now, she could race across the island, take refuge in Dornrise, and wait until the King of Aurelis had come and gone.

Soran smiled bleakly as he clambered to his feet and stood beside her, looking out across the water. He might be slow to learn, but even he did learn eventually. He knew better than to even try to tell Nelle what to do or where to go. He knew better than to try to protect her against her will. She would decide for herself, and he must honor her decision.

Besides, Lodírhal could hardly have missed the massive exertion of *ibrildian* magic she'd used throughout the night. He would be coming for her as well as for his recalcitrant prisoner.

They watched together as the beautiful tall ship approached Roseward. It anchored a quarter of a mile from the rocky shores and lowered a small boat to the water. Even from that distance, Soran could see Lodírhal as he climbed nimbly down a ladder into the boat and took a seat in the prow. The King of Aurelis would be hard to miss with his long golden hair and his powerful figure that seemed to emanate an unconscious aura of magic wherever he went.

Soran felt Nelle's fingers entwine with his and looked down into her face. The bloody gash across her forehead was mostly healed, leaving behind a puckered scar. Dried blood flecked her skin, spattered amid her many freckles. But he scarcely noticed, lost as he was in the depths of her vivid blue eyes. She was the most beautiful thing he had ever seen.

"Peronelle Beck," he said, "I . . . I wish you would save yourself."

"I know," she answered.

"But I'm glad you're here."

"I know that too." She smiled at him then, a smile that filled his heart to bursting. "Are you ready then?"

CHAPTER 30

Nelle stood beside Soran at the lighthouse door with the spellbook containing the Noswraith tucked under her arm. She could feel the Thorn Maiden writhing inside it, eager to burst free. Once the sun set, she would probably break her bonds and overtake all of Roseward.

But by then both Soran and Nelle would be dead, so it didn't matter.

Lodirhal and four tall fae—two women and two men—climbed the cliff path. Nelle's eyes widened as they appeared over the cliff's edge into her line of sight. First, the women, armed to the teeth, clad in elaborate golden armor so exquisitely worked that it appeared more decorative than practical. No doubt this impression was all part of a deadly illusion. After them followed the two men in long robes and bejeweled headdresses. Mages, Nelle guessed.

Lodírhal appeared last of all. And though he was less elaborately garbed than the other four, there could be no mistaking his mastery over all he surveyed. Tall, strong, and beautiful beyond reason, with features of exquisitely carved ivory and eyes like chips of living sky. To compare the likes of Kyriakos to him would be as ridiculous as comparing a strutting rooster to the incredible glory of a peacock in full display. He was breathtaking. And utterly terrifying.

A shiver ran down Nelle's spine. Funny how after everything, after all the terrors she'd faced these past two nights running, the prospect of certain death still had the power to frighten her.

And she saw death in the gaze Lodírhal fastened on Soran.

Soran stiffened, squeezing her hand, and she cast him a quick sidelong glance. He glanced back at her, and she offered a swift smile. His eyes softened slightly, though the line of his scarred mouth remained firm and hard.

Then he moved to stand partially in front of her. Even now he felt that ridiculous unconscious urge to shield her.

Flanked by his two guards, Lodírhal approached until he stood a mere two yards away. The rising sun gleamed on his hair, turning it to burnished gold. The right-hand guard thumped the butt of her spear in the dirt and spoke in a voice like a lioness's roar: "Kneel before the King of Aurelis!"

Soran obeyed at once, dropping heavily to his knees. Nelle, a little slower, found herself standing in full view of the fae king. Nearly choking on a breath, she dropped to the ground behind Soran, bowed her head, and shifted the spellbook to clutch it against her chest. A long silence followed, broken only by the wind's sighs as it wound around the tower. Nelle struggled with conflicting desires: to peer up at the mighty king or to keep her head down and somehow avoid his notice.

At last, a voice of liquid gold spoke.

"Word reached me of an attack on the shores of Noxaur. My servants tell me that Lord Kyriakos is dead and that Ninthalor was razed to the ground." A pause followed, as sharp and deadly as a knife. Then: "By a Noswraith."

Soran drew a long breath. "Yes, Your Majesty."

"I scarcely dared believe it," that golden voice continued, warm and rich as honey. "But more reports followed the first. I was told of massive thorns tearing through stone, of vines ripping limb from limb, of towers toppled and walls crumbled to dust. Last of all, an eyewitness reported seeing a mortal mage on the shores of Noxaur, a man with white hair, a scarred face, and hands cast in pure nilarium."

Another long, terrible pause followed. Nelle could resist no longer. She lifted her chin just a little, peering up from beneath her brows at the terrible figure of the king. Lodírhal took no notice of her. His attention remained fixed on Soran.

"I debated setting out on this voyage," he said slowly, "hunting for your lost little island. I thought to myself, 'Let the Noswraith kill him. It will be a just end to all his wicked deeds.' It is as well I did not listen to my own counsel, for you have inexplicably survived your monster. I shall have to execute you after all for breaking the terms of your imprisonment."

So saying, the king held out his right hand. The armored woman beside him drew her sword in a single fluid motion. She turned and presented it hilt-first to her master, who accepted the blade without a glance her way. He took a step forward. "Have you any final words, mortal mage?"

A frenzied drumming seemed to erupt inside Nelle's head. Was this it? Would the fae so easily, so simply, swing that sword and end Soran's life? Chop the head from his shoulders as he knelt there in the dirt? After everything, was this the end?

"No!"

The faces of the four silent fae turned, their strange bright eyes fixing on her like lance points. The king turned more slowly, as though unwilling to shift his attention from Soran. The sword in his hand now pointed at Nelle, its tip suspended in the air just before her nose.

"Ah!" he said, raising one eyebrow. "So those reports were true as well—an *ibrildian* has come to Roseward. And what do you hold there?" He dipped the sword to indicate the spellbook, which Nelle still pressed over her heart. She watched his face go suddenly white, the lines of easy beauty tensing into a momentary mask of fear. He swiftly controlled his expression, however, and lifted his chin slightly. "The Noswraith. So, you have bound it anew, have you?"

Nelle nodded. "If you kill us now, there won't be no one to bind her again." The words sounded strangled and weak, but she met the fae king's eye without flinching. "She'll get out, and she'll tear your whole world to pieces."

Lodírhal's perfect mouth tilted in a cruel smile. "It won't matter, little Hybrid. I shall be long gone from this place by then. The Noswraith will remain trapped on Roseward for all eternity. As far as I'm concerned, she is welcome to this gods-forsaken island. And as for you . . ."

He raised his hand, beckoned slightly. Moving swifter than thought, the two armored women caught Nelle by her arms and dragged her away from Soran, out into the open space before the lighthouse.

"Please!" Soran barked. "Please, great king, do what you like to me, but she doesn't deserve to die!"

"Deserve? Perhaps not. But she is *ibrildian*." Lodírhal paced slowly around to stand before Nelle, but it was Soran he studied with some interest. "And she is of some importance to you, I see. Interesting. Which would please you more? To die first so you need not watch her die? Or to let her die first so that her fear is not prolonged?"

He swung his blade without looking, and the edge stopped just under Nelle's chin, poised and perfectly still. Terrified, she swallowed and strained away but then swiveled her eyes toward Soran, determined that he would be the last thing she saw before the killing blow fell. When his gaze met hers, she saw the desperate helplessness there, the near-frantic sorrow. He blamed himself. Of course he did. He couldn't protect her because she bullspitting refused to be protected.

Even as tears slid down her cheeks, even as her chin trembled with the dread of certain death so near, she looked into his eyes and tried to make him see her love. Tried to make him see that, while she regretted many things, she did not regret the choice that brought her to this end with him.

"What? No answer?" Lodírhal laughed, a bright, brilliant sound, incongruous with the deadly intent in his eye. "In that case, I shall choose for you."

He drew back his sword. Nelle fixed her gaze on Soran as hard as she could while the final few beats of her heart pulsed in her throat.

A shadow passed overhead.

From the corner of her eyes, Nelle saw Lodírhal pause and look up into the sky, shading his eyes with one hand. The other four fae murmured in their strange language, and the guards relaxed their grip on Nelle's arms. Sagging in place, Nelle tore her gaze from Soran to look up.

At first, she could make no sense of the shape she saw. Was it a cloud drifting down too close to the ground? Or a wild swan, perhaps? No, much too huge. She'd never seen a swan before, but she knew they weren't as big as horses with wingspans of twenty feet or more.

Then a little yelp of surprise burst from her throat, and she exclaimed, "Bullspitting boggarts, it's the wyvern!"

The beautiful white feather-winged wyvern the young *ibrildian* boy had written to life in the lighthouse was even bigger now than when she'd last seen it, when the boy climbed on its back and flew away into the *ruvyn-satra*; but it was still just as graceful, just as ethereal.

But who was the figure sitting astride the winged being? Nelle squinted, shook her head, and looked again. It couldn't be the boy! This was a man fully grown. His skin was a rich golden brown, and his hair black as darkest midnight, flowing long in the air behind him.

Three times the wyvern circled the assembled figures on the cliff's edge before landing in a clear space off to the right. The mounted figure slid easily from its back and stood to his full height. He was not as tall as Lodírhal but still an impressive, towering figure clad in robes of rich, multi-colored hues that shimmered with iridescence in the sunlight with each stride he took. As he approached, he cast a glance down at Nelle.

It really was the boy. Those strange, purple, tilted eyes of his were unmistakable set in that fine-boned face.

He raised an eyebrow and gave her a smile so disarming and so incongruous, given the situation, that Nelle hardly knew how to react. Then he faced the king and tossed another of those smiles his way.

Lodírhal met the smile with a grim, hard stare.

"Well met, Father!" said the boy who was now a man. "I see you're having yourself a nice little murder before breakfast. Couldn't even wait for a cup of tea? How very proactive of you. A fine quality in a king, I'm sure."

"Castien." Lodírhal spoke the name coldly and planted a fist on his hip. "What brings you to this remote stretch of the Hinter, I wonder." His tone implied that he would not deign to ask the question outright and hardly cared for an answer. Yet the gleam in his eye demanded a response.

The newcomer shrugged carelessly. "I come a-hunting." He indicated Nelle with a sweep of one hand. "That mortal there— whom you seem to be in the act of relieving of her head—is in possession of a particularly powerful Noswraith. Since you have seen fit, in your great and glorious wisdom, to make the keeping of Noswraiths my solemn princely duty . . ." He let the sentence trail off into silence.

Lodírhal's lip curled in the slightest of sneers. "Your mother sent you."

"Perhaps."

Nelle gaped, her gaze swiveling between the king and his son, but landing and resting on the son. How was this possible? The last time she'd seen him, he was but a child, frail, emaciated, hollow-eyed, and ragged. How could he have changed in so short a span of time?

Then again . . . what was time in this world? In the eight months since she'd fled Roseward and returned to Wimborne, only a day had passed for Soran. Now, since her return to the island, she would be willing to bet many more months or even years had passed in her own world. Who could say where the young prince had been since vanishing into the *ruvyn-satra*, what worlds he'd visited, and what times he'd experienced?

King Lodírhal turned his sword slightly in his hand, like a cat poised and still except for the twitch at the end of his tail. "What I do with my own prisoners is none of your concern," he said. "Nor is it your mother's, for that matter."

"Ah, but Noswraiths are my concern, according to your sovereign will. And that Noswraith is on the verge of breaking free, I fear."

"It will be contained well enough on this island," the king said.

"*Well enough,* you say." The prince sniffed and shook his head. "And what will you do when this lonely little island

405

eventually bumps up against other shores? How will you stop the Noswraith from slipping free then? No, no, best you let me take the spellbook back with me to Vespre. It will be safer in my library."

When the prince motioned to the guards holding Nelle's arms, they tightened their grips and looked to their king. He gave a slight nod, however, so they released her and stepped back a pace. Nelle caught herself with one hand, the spellbook pressed against her chest.

Lifting her head, she looked across to Soran, who met her gaze intently. Was he trying to tell her something?

The prince stepped between them, cutting off her view with brilliant folds of embroidered robes, and crouched, bringing his face down to her level. "Good morrow, sweet Nelle," he said, holding out his hand. "You haven't aged a day."

She looked up into his strange purple gaze, feeling like a mouse caught in a snake's hypnotic stare. Slowly she shifted the spellbook into his waiting hand. His fingers closed around the binding, but when he started to pull away, she held on a little tighter. "Help us!" she hissed.

His beautiful mouth tipped in a knowing smile. Then he tugged the book out of her grasp and rose smoothly, turning away from her as he laid the book across his forearm and flipped it open.

For a terrible flashing instant, darkness flooded the worlds and thorn-covered vines stretched up out of the pages to shred his face.

The prince slammed the book shut and blinked several times, his expression mildly taken aback. "Well now. That is quite the impressive bit of spell work. An impressive binding as well, if somewhat haphazard." He tucked the book under his arm and turned to his father again, that enigmatic smile still teasing the corner of his mouth.

"If you are quite satisfied," Lodírhal demanded with a sweep of one arm toward the waiting wyvern, "I have business yet to complete."

"Yes, yes, I know. So many murders, so little time."

"*Execution,* my son." There was a dangerous edge to the king's voice. "These are my prisoners. They have broken the law, and in so doing have brought death and destruction on our people."

"Our people, yes." The prince thoughtfully rubbed a finger along his upper lip. "You are speaking, I suppose, of the attack on Ninthalor."

Lodírhal's eyes narrowed slightly. "Two hundred Noxaurians lost their lives. I cannot treat such wanton destruction lightly."

"All servants of Kyriakos," the prince replied. "And Kyriakos himself met his end in that attack . . . thus breaking the curse that bound me, setting me free. For that, I should think you owe his killers at least some small favor."

"Favor?" Lodírhal tossed his head and barked a mirthless

laugh. "Perhaps it was Kyriakos I owed a favor! Two hundred years of peace is no small gift!"

"Mother might think otherwise."

These words, spoken very softly, struck home. Nelle watched the king's face freeze, not even the faintest tick revealing a trace of emotion, which was in its way telling.

"Very well," the king said after an extended silence. "No more of your games, my son. Tell me what you want."

The prince swept one arm, indicating first Nelle and then Soran. "I want these two mages. Two exceptionally powerful mortal-magic users to serve me in Vespre, guarding my library. As you know, fae magic is of little use against Noswraiths. And mortals are so very . . . well, *mortal*. I tend to lose mages faster than I can replace them." He cast his father a sharp glance. "It would be a shame to waste two such creatures when I have much better use for them."

"And should they not be held accountable for the deaths they have wrought on our kind?" Lodírhal growled.

"Indeed, they should," the prince answered swiftly. "By being made to serve out their days protecting Eledria by imprisoning Noswraiths, containing them as they can, and battling them when they must." He took one step toward his father, a subtly aggressive gesture, although he softened it by placing a hand on his heart and bowing his head ever so slightly. "This is my request, Father: that you will enable me to better accomplish the great task which you have set me. Nothing more, nothing less."

He returned and held his father's stare. Nelle felt the tension of power in the air between them like the roiling of the *ruvyn-satra* itself. She watched Lodírhal's face, desperate to see which way he would be swayed—by his desire for blood and revenge or by the logic presented to him by his son.

And which would she prefer? She longed for life, of course, for herself and for Soran. But what would such a life be? Swept away to some strange fae city, serving in a . . . in a library? A library of spellbooks, of Noswraiths? Could there be a more dreadful fate?

She shifted her gaze from the king back to Soran, who still knelt, his shoulders back, his head up. He was watching her, his eyes bright with things he longed to say. At the sight of him, her fearful heart calmed its frantic beating. Whatever their fate may be—whether death now by the sword or a future of battling nightmares in the service of a fae prince—they would be together.

At last, Lodírhal shook his head and uttered a derisive snort. "You are too like your mother. Too able to persuade me against my will. You make me weak in the same breath that you promise to make me strong."

"Does this mean you will grant my request?" the prince asked.

The king waved a hand and turned away. "Yes, yes! Take the Noswraith and take the mages as well and let me never set eyes on them again!"

Nelle let out a breath, sagging back onto her heels. They wouldn't die! Not yet, anyway. She was so lightheaded with relief, she feared she might faint.

Lodírhal barked a command to his four companions and started for the path down the cliff. "And what of the curse?" the prince called after him, stopping his father in his tracks.

The king turned a narrow-eyed stare back at his son.

"This mage is hardly of use to me with his hands like that," the prince said, nodding at Soran and giving his father a significant look. "I need him able to hold a quill at the least."

Murder sparked in Lodírhal's eyes. But he said nothing, only strode over to Soran, reached down, and caught him by the wrists. Holding both hands up between them, he uttered a string of words, and Nelle saw the *quinsatra* open and the magic pour through into this world, surrounding Soran's hands in a glow.

The nilarium coating his fingers began to move, to shift, to melt away in long, rolling droplets. She saw Soran clench his jaw against the pain while sweat beaded his forehead.

But the melting nilarium rolled away and vanished into thin air, leaving behind two pale hands. Hands of flesh and blood.

When Lodírhal let go and backed away with a snarl, Soran brought his hands closer to his face. He stared at them wonderingly, his pain forgotten as he moved each finger, testing its strength and dexterity.

Then he looked across at Nelle, and for the first time she

could remember, she saw joy in his face. Pure, unadulterated joy.

.

CHAPTER 31

THE PRINCE CONTINUED TO WORK HIS PERSUASIVE influence on his father, convincing Lodírhal to take the two mortal mages on his ship and bear them personally to Vespre. Lodírhal protested, but when the prince pointed out that he couldn't very well bundle them both onto his wyvern and fly them all the way to the Umbria Isles, the king at last relented. He barked a command to his guards, and the two stern fae women took Soran and Nelle by the arms and led them forcibly to the path.

"My quill!" Nelle cried, straining to look back over her shoulder. She met the prince's eye. "My quill! It's inside!"

The prince nodded his understanding. She saw him enter the lighthouse just before her stumbling footsteps carried her down the path out of sight. Queen Dasyra's protection spells did not hold him back for an instant. Perhaps they recognized the son of their maker.

It was foolish, Nelle knew, to care so much about a quill. Yet she disliked the idea of going on into whatever strange life lay ahead of her without it.

Soran turned on the path several times to look back at her, and she took comfort in his gaze. The worst of the Thorn Maiden's cuts had already healed over into scars, adding to the terrible pattern on his face.

But they're the last scars, Nelle thought, her heart giving a little flutter of hope. *The Thorn Maiden won't hurt him ever again.*

When they reached the beach below the cliff, the guards hurried them along toward the boat.

A sad little chortle sounded from among the rocks. Nelle turned in time to see the blue wyvern scuttle toward them, its good wing flapping like a sail in the breeze. The guards stopped to confront the beast, brandishing their spears. An incongruous sight, given their ferocity and the wyvern's gracelessness. It stopped short and flared its crest at them, showing its teeth and tongue in a hiss. The guard holding Nelle's arm let go and took an aggressive step forward, drawing her spear back.

"Don't hurt it!" Soran's tone was commanding enough to

make the two guards hesitate. "It's my own creation. It's coming with me."

The guard holding his arm tightened her grip, her eyes narrowing, and looked to Lodírhal, who was already climbing into the shore boat. He merely took his seat in the prow and folded his arms with great dignity. It wasn't a refusal.

She glanced at Soran and shrugged slightly. "Go on, then," she said, and released him.

Soran hastened to the wyvern, crouched, and gathered it in his arms. The little creature draped across his broad shoulders, tail twitching, its crest rising and falling by turns. As they passed Nelle, it gave her a smug look. She resisted the urge to stick her tongue out at it.

Following orders, they climbed into the boat and sat quietly in the bow, as far from the king as possible. The fae mages sat in the middle, dignified and silent, while the two guards pushed the boat out into deeper water, their long legs splashing in the foam. They sprang nimbly inside, took up the oars, and turned the boat toward the swan-prowed ship.

While Nelle huddled close to Soran on the narrow seat, the wyvern's wing flapped against the top of her head. She turned and looked back at Roseward, to that familiar strip of beach, and the path she'd walked so many times. To the lighthouse still standing tall and proud, now abandoned. As they pulled farther out into the water, she turned her gaze toward the outcropping across the isle where Dornrise had stood. It was gone now. After all it had faced, after everything it had endured, the blast of the Thorn Maiden's binding had been too much for it. The Great House of the Silveri family was mere rubble.

"Are you sorry to go?"

At the low murmur of Soran's voice, Nelle turned her back on Roseward and looked up at him instead. His eyes, though still bright with the joy of his newly lifted curse, were somewhat shadowed, his brow puckered with concern.

"I ain't sorry," Nelle answered. She took his hand—his warm, living, unscarred hand, and threaded her fingers with his. "I ain't sorry," she repeated firmly.

Soran smiled softly, lifted his other hand, and gently touched her cheek, savoring the sensation. "We're being taken to the Umbrian Isles," he said. "A dark part of the worlds, located in the Twilit Realm between the Day and Night courts of the fae. Vespre is known as the Doomed City. It . . . it won't be an easy life, serving the Prince of the Doomed City."

Nelle shrugged and leaned her head against his shoulder. "I ain't ever had an easy life. Not sure I'd know what to do with one if I had it."

She closed her eyes. And just for a moment, she saw them all again: Cloven and Gaspard, Papa and Sam. And Mother. Beautiful, dangerous, madcap Mother. She smiled softly and, with a whispered prayer, let them go. Them, and the rest of her former life.

She opened her eyes again and met Soran's gaze. His hideous scars remained. No lifted curse could possibly restore him to beauty.

Nelle placed her hand on his cheek and drew his lips down to hers, kissing him softly. He kissed her back, and for a moment they forgot themselves.

Then the wyvern squawked and shoved his blunt nose between them, forcing them apart. It burbled and hissed in Nelle's face, its tongue flicking her nose.

"Bullspitting worm," Nelle growled.

Soran tipped back his head and laughed, the sound ringing bright across the waves. Overhead, a graceful white wyvern swooped low, casting its shadow across them, then set off flying for the far horizon.

ABOUT THE AUTHOR

Sylvia Mercedes makes her home in the idyllic North Carolina countryside with her Handsome Husband, sweet Young Lady, the Tiny Gentleman, and a pair of cats affectionately known as the Fluffy Brothers. When she's not writing she's . . . okay, let's be honest. When she's not writing, she's running around after her little girl, cleaning up glitter, trying to plan healthy-ish meals, and wondering where she left her phone. In between, she reads a steady diet of fantasy novels.

But mostly she's writing.

After a short career in Traditional Publishing (under a different name), Sylvia decided to take the plunge into the Indie Publishing World and is enjoying every minute of it.

Don't miss Sylvia Mercedes's new romantic fantasy

ENTRANCED
PRINCE OF THE DOOMED CITY
BOOK 1

Meanwhile be sure to read The Rose of Dornrise *and learn the secrets of Soran Silveri's dark past.*

Visit www.SylviaMercedesBooks.com/free-book2 *to get your free copy.*

Made in the USA
Coppell, TX
10 January 2024

27522348R00245